PROTECT THE PRINCE

Also by Jennifer Estep

THE CROWN OF SHARDS SERIES

Kill the Queen
Protect the Prince

THE ELEMENTAL ASSASSIN SERIES

Spider's Bite
Web of Lies
Venom
Tangled Threads
Spider's Revenge
By a Thread
Widow's Web
Deadly Sting
Heart of Venom
The Spider
Poison Promise
Black Widow
Spider's Trap
Bitter Bite
Unraveled
Snared
Venom in the Veins

THE MYTHOS ACADEMY SERIES

Touch of Frost
Kiss of Frost
Dark Frost
Crimson Frost
Midnight Frost
Killer Frost

PROTECT THE PRINCE

A CROWN OF SHARDS NOVEL

JENNIFER ESTEP

HARPER Voyager
An Imprint of HarperCollins*Publishers*

PROTECT THE PRINCE. Copyright © 2019 by Jennifer Estep. Excerpt from CRUSH THE KING copyright © 2020 by Jennifer Estep. All rights reserved. Printed in the United States of America. No part of this book may be used or reproduced in any manner whatsoever without written permission except in the case of brief quotations embodied in critical articles and reviews. For information, address Harper-Collins Publishers, 195 Broadway, New York, NY 10007.

HarperCollins books may be purchased for educational, business, or sales promotional use. For information, please email the Special Markets Department at SPsales@harpercollins.com.

Harper Voyager and design are trademarks of HarperCollins Publishers LLC.

FIRST EDITION

Designed by Paula Russell Szafranski
Map designed by Virginia Norey
Title page and chapter opener art © Kaissa/Shutterstock (sword);
© ksanask.art/Shutterstock (rays around sword)

Library of Congress Cataloging-in-Publication Data has been applied for.

ISBN 978-0-06-279764-3

19 20 21 22 23   LSC   10 9 8 7 6 5 4 3 2 1

To my mom, my grandma, and Andre—for your love, patience,

and everything else that you've given to me over the years.

And to my teenage self, who devoured every single epic fantasy book

that she could get her hands on—for finally writing your very own

epic fantasy books.

Pretty, pretty princes,
All in a row.
Who will they marry?
Where will they go?

This girl, that girl,
Maid, lady, queen.
Who snares the princes' hearts
Remains to be seen.

—ANDVARIAN COURT SONG

ACKNOWLEDGMENTS

M y heartfelt thanks go out to all the folks who help turn my words into a book.

Thanks go to my agent, Annelise Robey, and to my editor, Erika Tsang, for all their helpful advice, support, and encouragement. Thanks also to Nicole Fischer, Pamela Jaffee, Angela Craft, and everyone else at Harper Voyager and HarperCollins.

And finally, a big thanks to all the readers. Knowing that folks read and enjoy my books is truly humbling, and I hope that you all enjoy reading about Evie and her adventures.

I appreciate you all more than you will ever know.

Happy reading! ☺

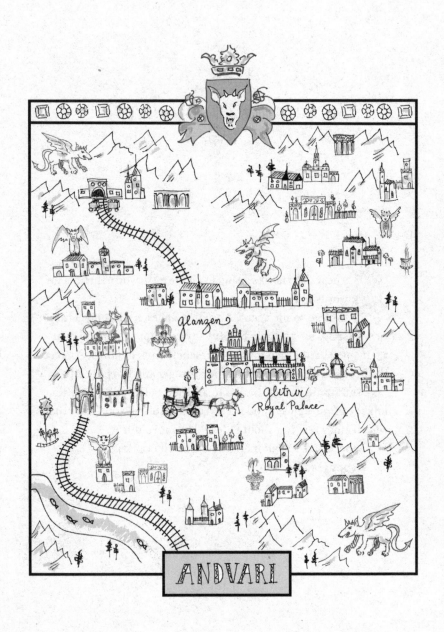

glanzen

glitzir
Royal Palace

ANDVARI

PART ONE

The First Assassination Attempt

CHAPTER ONE

The day of the first assassination attempt started out like any other.

With me girding myself for battle.

I perched stiffly in a chair in front of a vanity table that took up the corner of my bedroom. The long, rectangular table was made of the blackest ebony and adorned with all sorts of drawers and cubbyholes, along with crystal knobs that glinted at me like mocking eyes.

The morning sun slipped past the white lace curtains and highlighted the tabletop, which featured carvings of gladiators clutching swords, daggers, and shields. I looked down at the figures, which were embossed with bits of metal, along with tiny jewels. They too seemed to stare up at and mock me, as if they knew that I shouldn't be here.

I leaned forward and traced my fingers over the carvings, wincing as the metal tips of the weapons and the sharp facets of the jeweled eyes dug into my skin. I wondered how many other women had sat here and done this same thing. Dozens, if not more. I also wondered if they'd all been as uncomfortable as I was.

Probably not.

After all, this table and the other fine furnishings had been their birthright, passed down from mother to daughter through the generations. The women who'd come before hadn't stumbled into this position by accident like I had.

Someone cleared her throat, and I resumed my previous stiff perch. Fingers fluttered around me, adjusting my sleeves, smoothing down my hair, and even slicking berry balm onto my lips. A minute later, the fingers retreated, and I raised my gaze to the domed mirror that rose up from the table like gladiator arenas did from the Svalin city landscape.

More figures were carved into the wide band of wood that encased the mirror. Gargoyles with sapphire eyes and curved, silver horns that were pointed at the strixes, hawklike birds with feathers that glinted with a metallic, amethyst sheen. The creatures looked like they were about to leap out of the wood, take flight, and tear into one another, just like the gladiators on the tabletop did. A single pearl-white caladrius with dark blue tearstone eyes adorned the very top of the mirror, as though the tiny, owlish bird was peering down at all the other creatures below, including me.

Someone cleared her throat again. I sighed and finally focused on my reflection.

Black hair, gray-blue eyes, pale, tight face. I looked the same as always, except for one notable thing.

The crown on my head.

My gaze locked onto the thin silver band, which was surprisingly plain, except for the small midnight-blue pieces of tearstone that jutted up from the center. The seven tearstone shards fitted together to form a crown, as if the silver band itself wasn't enough indication of who and what I was now.

But it wasn't the only crown of shards I was wearing.

I reached over with my left hand and touched the bracelet that circled my right wrist. It was made of curls of silver that had been twisted together to resemble sharp thorns, all of which wrapped around and protected the crown in the middle of the design. The crown embedded in the bracelet was also made of seven tearstone shards, but it contained one thing that the actual crown on my head did not.

Magic.

Like other jewels, tearstone could absorb, store, and reflect back magic, but it also had the unique property of offering protection from magic—deflecting it like a gladiator's shield would stop a sword in an arena fight. Each midnight-blue shard in my bracelet contained a cold, hard power that was similar to my own magical immunity. The cool touch of the jewelry comforted me, as did the magic flowing through it.

I needed all the help I could get today.

Someone cleared her throat for a third time, and I dropped my hand from my bracelet and focused on my reflection again.

I slowly tilted my head to the side, and the silver crown swayed dangerously to the right. I straightened up and tilted my head to the other side, and it swayed in that direction.

"I still feel like this stupid thing is going to fall off," I muttered.

"It will *not* fall off, my queen," a low, soothing voice murmured. "We've put plenty of pins in your hair to make sure that doesn't happen."

A woman moved forward and stood beside me. She was on the short side, and the top of her head wasn't all that much higher than mine, even though I was seated. She was about my age—twenty-seven or so—and quite lovely, with blue eyes, rosy skin, and dark, honey-blond hair that was pulled back into a pretty fishtail braid that trailed over her shoulder. She had a thick, strong body, but her fingers were long and lean and freckled with small, white scars from all the pins and needles that had accidentally poked into her skin over the years.

Lady Calandre had been Queen Cordelia's personal thread master for the last few months of the queen's life. And now, she was mine. As were her two teenage sisters, Camille and Cerana, who were hovering behind her.

"Are you pleased with your appearance, my queen?" Calandre asked.

I studied my blue tunic in the mirror. A crown of shards was stitched in silver thread over my heart, while still more silver thread scrolled across my neckline and flowed down my sleeves, as though I had wrapped myself in thorns. Standard black leggings and boots completed my outfit.

"Of course. Your work is exquisite, as always."

Calandre nodded, and pride gleamed in her eyes at the compliment. She adjusted the long bell sleeves of her blue gown, even though they were already perfectly draped in place. They too were trimmed with silver thread, in keeping with the colors of the Winter line of the Blair royal family.

My colors now.

"I still wish that you had let me make you something grander," Calandre murmured. "I could have easily done it with my magic."

She was a master, which meant that her magic let her work with a specific object or element to create amazing things. In Calandre's case, she had complete control over thread, fabric, and the like. My nose twitched. I could smell her power on my tunic, a faint, vinegary odor that was the same as the dyes that she used to give her garments their glorious colors.

Calandre had tried to get me to don a ball gown for today's formal court session, since all the attending nobles would be decked out in their own finery, but I'd refused. I wasn't the queen everyone had expected, and I certainly wasn't the one they wanted, so draping myself in layers of silk and cascades of jewels seemed silly and pointless. Besides, you couldn't fight very well in a ball gown. Although in that regard, it didn't really matter what I wore, since every day at Seven Spire was a battle.

"Forget the clothes," another voice chimed in. "I still can't believe that people sent you all this *stuff*."

I looked over at a tall woman with braided blond hair and beautiful bronze skin who was lounging on a blue velvet settee. She was wearing a forest-green tunic that brought out her golden amber eyes, along with the usual black leggings and boots. A large silver mace was lying next to her on the settee, with the spikes slowly stabbing the plump cushions to death.

Paloma waved her hand at the low table in front of her. "C'mon. How much stuff does one queen need?"

Every inch of the table was covered with baskets, bowls, and platters brimming with everything from fresh produce to smelly cheeses to bottles of champagne. Other tables throughout the room boasted similar items, as did the writing desk, the nightstand beside the four-poster bed, and the top of the armoire. Not to mention the cloaks, gloves, and other garments piled up in the corners or the paintings, statues, and other knickknacks propped up against the walls. I'd gotten so many welcome gifts that I'd resorted to perching them on the windowsills, just so I would be able to walk through my chambers.

Paloma grabbed a white card out of a basket on the table. "Who is Lady Diante, and why did she send you a basket of pears?"

"Diante is an extremely wealthy noble who owns fruit orchards in one of the southern districts," I said. "And it's a Bellonan tradition to send the new queen a gift wishing her a long and prosperous reign."

Paloma snorted. "Funny tradition, sending a gift to someone you're plotting against."

Calandre's lips puckered, and her two sisters gasped. Calandre was a Bellonan courtier who was traditional and polite to a fault. She didn't much care for Paloma's bluntness, but she didn't say anything. She might be a master, but Paloma was a much stronger morph.

Calandre stared at the morph mark on Paloma's neck. All morphs had some sort of tattoo-like mark on their bodies that indicated what creature they could shift into. Paloma's mark was a fearsome ogre face with amber eyes, a lock of blond hair, and plenty of sharp teeth.

The ogre must have sensed Calandre's disapproving gaze, because its blinking, liquid eyes shifted in her direction. The ogre looked at her a moment, then opened its mouth wide in a silent laugh. Calandre's lips puckered again, and she let out an indignant sniff, which made the ogre laugh even more.

"Well, then, perhaps you should taste test the pears," I sniped. "Just to make sure that Lady Diante isn't trying to poison me."

"That's an excellent idea," Paloma drawled. "Especially since I know that mutt nose of yours would never be able to stand having poisoned fruit in here."

Calandre winced, and her two sisters gasped again at Paloma so casually calling me a *mutt*. The common, if somewhat condescending, term referred to those with relatively simple, straightforward powers like enhanced strength or speed, as well as people like me who seemed to have very little magic. But I didn't mind. I had been called far worse things. Besides, Paloma was my best friend, and I found her honesty refreshing, especially after so many years of people smiling to my face, then spewing venom behind my back.

Paloma plucked a pear from the basket and sank her teeth into it. She grinned, as did the ogre on her neck. "See? Not poisoned."

I rolled my eyes, but I couldn't help grinning back at her.

"Well, eat fast. Because now that I'm properly attired, it's time for our first battle of the day."

I thanked Calandre and her sisters for their services. The thread master curtsied to me, gave Paloma another disapproving sniff, and left. While Paloma ate another pear, I cinched a black leather belt around my waist, then hooked a sword and a dagger to it.

A queen shouldn't have to carry weapons, at least not inside her own palace, but then again, I was no ordinary queen.

And these were far from ordinary weapons.

The sword and the dagger both gleamed a dull silver, and both of their hilts featured seven midnight-blue jewels that formed my crown-of-shards crest. But what made the weapons truly special was that they were made entirely of tearstone. The sword and the dagger were far lighter than normal blades, and they would also absorb and deflect magic, just like the blue tearstone shards in their hilts and in my bracelet would.

A matching tearstone shield was propped up beside my bed, but I decided not to strap it to my forearm. Carrying a sword and a dagger was noteworthy enough, but taking the shield as well would make me seem weak, something that I could ill afford.

I traced my fingers over the symbol in the sword's hilt. Despite their dark blue hue, the tearstone shards glittered brightly. Over the past several months, the crown of shards had become my personal crest. At first, because it had kept showing up on objects that other people gave me, like my bracelet and weapons. But now, everyone associated the symbol with me, whether I liked it or not.

Part of me hated the crown of shards and everything it stood for. The crest was yet another reminder that I was a pretender who had attained the throne only through a series of unexpected and extraordinary events.

More often than not, the crown of shards reminded me of all the swords—all the *enemies*—that wanted to cut me down. And perhaps worst of all, the symbol was traditionally associated with only the strongest Winter queens, something that was particularly troubling since I still had no idea what being a Winter queen really meant, especially when it came to my magic.

But in a strange way, the symbol comforted me as well. Other Blairs, other Winter queens, had survived life at Seven Spire. Perhaps I could too.

Time to find out.

Paloma finished her second pear. Then she got to her feet, grabbed her spiked mace, and hoisted it up onto her shoulder. The weapon made her look even more intimidating. "You ready for this?"

I blew out a breath. "I suppose I have to be."

She shrugged. "It's not too late. We could still sneak out of here, run off, and join a gladiator troupe."

I snorted. "Please. I wouldn't get across the river before Serilda and Auster hunted me down and dragged me back."

Paloma grinned, as did the ogre on her neck. "Well, then, you should give Serilda, Auster, and everyone else what they've been waiting for."

I snorted again. "The only thing they've been waiting for is to see who makes the first move against me. But you're right. I might as well get on with it."

I touched my sword and dagger again, letting the feel of the weapons steady me, then walked over to the double doors. Just like on the vanity table, gladiators and other figures were carved into the wood. I stared at them a moment, then let out a long, tense breath, schooled my face into a blank, pleasant mask, and opened the doors.

As soon as I stepped into the hallway, the two guards posted by the doors snapped to attention. They were both wearing the standard uniform of a plain silver breastplate over a short-sleeved, dark blue tunic, and each one had a sword buckled to his belt.

I smiled at them. "Alonzo, Bowen, you're both looking well this morning."

The guards dipped their heads, but that was their only response. Several months ago, back when I'd just been Lady Everleigh, the guards would have talked, laughed, and joked with me. Now they stared at me with wariness in their eyes, wondering if I would do or say something to hurt them.

I tried not to grimace at their watchful, distrustful silence and set off down the hallway. Paloma fell in step beside me, her mace still propped up on her shoulder. In addition to being my best friend, Paloma was also my personal guard, and the former gladiator took great pride in casually threatening anyone who came near me.

The queen's chambers were on the third floor, and we quickly wound our way downstairs to the first level.

Seven Spire palace was the heart of Svalin, the capital city of Bellona, and just about everything in the wide hallways and spacious common areas was a tribute to the kingdom's gladiator history and tradition, from the tapestries that covered the dark gray granite walls, to the statues tucked away in various nooks, to the display cases bristling with swords, spears, daggers, and shields that famous queens and gladiators had used long ago.

But the most obvious signs of Bellona's past were the columns that adorned practically every room and hallway. Seven Spire had once been a mine, and the columns were the supports for the old tunnels where my Blair ancestors had dug fluorestone and more out of the mountain. Over the years, the columns had been transformed into works of art, and they too were covered with gladiators, weapons, gargoyles, strixes, and caladriuses, just like the furnishings in the queen's chambers.

But what made the columns truly impressive was that they were all made of tearstone, which could change color, going from bright, starry gray to dark, deep midnight-blue, and back again, depending on the sunlight and other factors. The tearstone's shifting hues brought the gladiators and creatures to life, making it seem as though they were circling around the columns and constantly battling one another.

I pulled my gaze away from the columns and focused on the people here. After all, they were the ones who could truly hurt me.

Even though it was early on a Monday morning, people filled the hallways. Servants carrying trays of food and drinks. Palace stewards heading to their posts to oversee their workers. Guards making sure that everything proceeded in an orderly fashion.

Everyone went about their business as usual—until they saw me.

Then eyes widened, mouths gaped, and heads bobbed. Some people even dropped down into low, formal bows and curtsies, only rising to their feet after I'd moved past them. I gritted my teeth and returned the acknowledgments with polite smiles and nods, but the bowing and scraping were nothing compared to the whispers.

"Why isn't she wearing a gown?"

"Doesn't she know how important today is?"

"She won't last another month."

The whispers started the second I walked by, and the hushed comments chased me from one hallway to the next, like a tidal wave that was surging up and about to crash down on me. If only. Drowning would be a far more merciful death than what I'd gotten myself into here.

From the rumors I'd heard, the servants and guards had

started a pool, placing bets on how long my tenuous reign would last. I was wondering that myself. I'd been queen for only about three months, and I was already thoroughly sick of the politics, infighting, and backstabbing that were the palace's equivalent of the gladiator fights that were so popular in Bellona.

Even Paloma with her spiked mace and the glaring ogre face on her neck couldn't quiet the chatter. I gritted my teeth again and hurried on, trying to ignore the whispers. Easier said than done.

Paloma and I rounded a corner and stepped into a long hallway, which was empty, except for the usual guards stationed in the corners. I focused on the double doors that stretched from the floor all the way up to the ceiling at the far end. The doors were standing wide open, and I could see people moving around in the area beyond.

The throne room.

Even though I had been here countless times before, my stomach dropped, and my heart squeezed tight, but I kept trudging forward, one slow step at a time. There was no turning back, and there was no running away. Not from this.

A lean, muscled, forty-something man wearing a red jacket over a white ruffled shirt was standing by the windows off to one side of the doors. The sun streaming inside made his black hair and eyes seem as glossy as ink against his golden skin, and it also highlighted the morph mark on his neck—a dragon's face made of ruby-red scales.

The man was giving his full and undivided attention to a silver platter filled with bite-size fruit cakes perched on the windowsill. He studied the cakes carefully, as if he were making a most important decision, then selected a raspberry one, popped it into his mouth, and sighed with happiness.

He must have spotted Paloma and me out of the corner of his eye because he glanced in our direction. He quickly popped another cake into his mouth while we walked over to him.

"Ah, there you are, Evie," he said. "I was just enjoying some treats before the main event."

In addition to being a former queen's guard and ringmaster, Cho Yamato also had a serious sweet tooth, as did his inner dragon, since its black eyes were still locked on the tray of cakes.

"I'm glad to see that Theroux is making himself at home as the new kitchen steward," I drawled. "And doing his best to ply you with desserts. Or did you steal those from some poor, unsuspecting servant?"

Cho grinned at my teasing. "I stole them, of course. Theroux's desserts aren't nearly as good as yours, but some treats are better than no treats at all, right?" He didn't wait for an answer before he downed a kiwi cake.

Joking around with Cho loosened some of the tension in my chest. I might not like being queen, but at least I had friends like him and Paloma to help me with the dangerous undertaking.

He finished his cake, then eyed me. "Are you ready for this?" he asked in a more serious voice.

"As ready as I'll ever be."

He gave me a sympathetic look, as did the dragon on his neck. "Well, then, let's start the show."

Cho dusted the crumbs off his fingers and smoothed down his red jacket. Then he strode over to the open space between the doors.

"Announcing Her Royal Majesty, Queen Everleigh Saffira Winter Blair!" Cho used his ringmaster's voice to full effect, and the words boomed like thunder, drowning out the conversations in the throne room.

He moved to the side, and everyone fell silent and peered at me. I gritted my teeth yet again, fixed a smile on my face, and stepped inside.

The throne room was the largest one in Seven Spire. The first floor was an empty, cavernous space, except for the massive tearstone columns that stretched up to support the ceiling high, high above. Shorter, thinner columns also rose up to support the second-floor balcony that wrapped around three sides of the room.

More gladiators, weapons, and creatures were carved into the columns, and the ceiling was one enormous battle scene made of gleaming stone, metal, and jewels. In the center of the ceiling, Bryn Bellona Winter Blair, my ancestor, was about to bring her sword down on top of the Mortan king, whom she had defeated in combat so long ago in order to create her kingdom.

My kingdom now.

As much as I would have liked to stare at the ceiling and pretend like everything else didn't exist, I dropped my gaze and focused on what was in front of me.

A wide blue carpet with silver scrollwork running along the edges led from the doors all the way across the room before stopping at the bottom of the raised stone dais at the far end. Bellonan lords, ladies, senators, guilders, and other wealthy, influential citizens lined both sides of the carpet.

A brutal gauntlet if ever there was one.

I squared my shoulders, lifted my chin, and strode forward, as though this had been my birthright all along, and not something that I had blundered into after the rest of the Blair royal family had been assassinated.

People stepped up to both sides of the carpet, nodding, smiling, and calling out inane pleasantries. I returned the words and gestures in kind, not letting my worry or apprehension show. I might not know how to be queen, but I excelled at keeping my true feelings bottled up inside where no one could see them. Sometimes, I thought that was half the battle.

Back behind the line of well-wishers, Paloma walked along, matching my pace. Her suspicious gaze scanned everyone, and she still had her mace on her shoulder. She was taking her duties as my personal guard seriously, even though I'd repeatedly told her that I wasn't in any physical danger from the nobles.

They would be quite happy to eviscerate me with their cruel words and sly schemes instead.

Finally, I reached the steps that led up to the dais. Three people were standing off to the side.

One was a forty-something woman and obviously a warrior, given the sword and the dagger holstered to her black leather belt. Her short blond hair was slicked back from her face, revealing the sunburst-shaped scar at the corner of one of her dark blue eyes. She was wearing a white tunic that featured a swan swimming on a pond, surrounded by flowers and vines, all done in black thread.

Serilda Swanson, the leader of the Black Swan gladiator troupe and one of my senior advisors, executed the perfect Bellonan curtsy. I clenched my teeth a little tighter to hide another grimace. I would never get used to people curtsying to me, especially not someone as strong, lethal, and legendary as Serilda.

The second person was also a woman, although she was older, somewhere in her sixties, with short red hair, golden amber eyes, and bronze skin. She was clad in a forest-green tunic and was leaning on a cane topped with a silver ogre head. The figure matched the morph mark on her neck.

Lady Xenia, an Ungerian noble, tilted her head at me.

The third person was a fifty-something, stern-looking man with short gray hair, dark bronze skin, brown eyes, and a lumpy, crooked nose that had obviously been broken many, many times. Like the other guards, he was wearing a short-sleeved blue tunic, but my gaze locked onto his silver breastplate, which featured a feathered texture and my crown of shards emblazoned over his heart. Even though he had been sporting the breastplate for weeks, I would never quite get used to seeing him wearing my crest instead of Queen Cordelia's rising sun.

Auster, the captain of the palace guards. My captain now.

Captain Auster's fingers flexed over the sword strapped to his belt, and he gave me a traditional Bellonan bow, holding it far longer than necessary, as if each extra second showed his devotion—and his determination not to let me be assassinated like Cordelia had been.

Auster finally straightened. I gave him a genuine smile, and his stern features softened a bit, if not his readiness to grab his sword and defend me until his dying breath.

Even though they weren't standing anywhere close to the carpet, Serilda, Xenia, and Auster all stepped back, as if further clearing my path.

I stared up at the queen's throne sitting on top of the dais. The chair was crafted of jagged pieces of tearstone that had been dug out of Seven Spire and fitted together centuries ago. The throne gleamed with a soft, muted light, shifting from starry gray to midnight-blue and back again, just like the columns did. The changing colors represented the Summer and Winter lines of the Blair royal family, as well as the everlasting strength of the Bellonan people.

I had seen the throne many, many times before, but now that it was mine, I found it far more intimidating, especially since the top featured the same crown-of-shards crest that adorned my tunic, bracelet, sword, and dagger. I had never paid any attention to that symbol before the royal massacre, but now, it was everywhere I went. Sometimes, I thought I would have been far happier if I had never seen it at all. I certainly would have been much safer.

Summer queens are fine and fair, with pretty ribbons and flowers in their hair. Winter queens are cold and hard, with frosted crowns made of icy shards.

The words to the old Bellonan fairy-tale rhyme echoed in my mind, as though all the queens who had come before were whispering them to me over and over again. I listened to the phantom voices a moment longer, then exhaled, slowly climbed up the dais steps, turned around, and sat down on the throne.

That was the signal everyone had been waiting for, and all the lords, ladies, senators, guilders, and others strode forward, stopping a few feet away from the bottom of the dais. They split into their usual cliques and began gossiping, while servants handed out sweet cakes, fresh fruits and cheeses, and glasses of blackberry sangria.

I looked up at the second-floor balcony. More nobles milled around there, eating, drinking, talking, and watching me, although they were all poorer and thus far less important than the ones on the first floor.

I started to drop my gaze when I noticed a man sitting by himself in the top corner of the balcony. He was wearing a long gray coat over a black tunic, and his dark brown hair gleamed under the lights, although a bit of stubble darkened his strong jaw. His handsome features were as blank as mine were, and I couldn't tell what he was thinking, although his blue eyes burned into mine with fierce intensity.

My nostrils flared. Even though he was as far away from me as possible, I could still pick out his scent—cold, clean vanilla with just a hint of spice—above all the others in the room. I drew in another breath, letting his scent sink deep down into my lungs, and trying to ignore the hot spark of desire it ignited inside me.

Lucas Sullivan was the magier enforcer of the Black Swan troupe, a bastard prince of Andvari, and my . . . Well, I didn't know exactly *what* he was to me. Much more than a friend, but not a lover, despite my pointed advances on that front. But I cared about him more than I wanted to contemplate, especially now, when I was facing another battle inside my own palace.

So I dropped my gaze from his and studied the nobles again.

Even though I had been queen for about three months, ever since I had killed Vasilia, the crown princess and my treacherous cousin, this was my first formal court session. Practically every noble from across the kingdom had journeyed here to discuss business and other matters, and it was important that things went well. I doubted they would, though. The nobles weren't going to like some of the things I had to say.

While the nobles chattered and downed their food and drinks, I discreetly drew in a breath, letting the air roll in over my tongue and tasting all the scents in it. The people's floral perfumes and spicy colognes. The fruity tang of the sangria. The pungent aroma of the blue cheeses that the servants were slicing on the buffet tables along the walls.

I opened my mouth to start the session when one final scent assaulted my senses—hot, jalapeño rage so strong that it made my nose burn with its sudden, sharp intensity.

Most people scoffed at my mutt magic, but my enhanced sense of smell was quite useful in one regard—it let me sense people's emotions, and very often their intentions. Garlic guilt, ashy heartbreak, minty regret. I could tell what someone was feeling—and often what they were plotting—just by tasting the scents that swirled around them.

I'd had years to hone my mutt magic, so I knew that jalapeño rage meant only one thing.

Someone here wanted to kill me.

CHapter TWO

I glanced from one side of the throne room to the other and back again, searching for an immediate, obvious threat.

Lightning sizzling in a magier's palm. A morph shifting into their other, stronger form. A stone master cracking the ceiling above my head. A mutt yanking their sword free and speeding toward the dais.

But I didn't see anything like that. I didn't see anything unusual, so I drew in another breath, tasting all the scents in the air again. The jalapeño rage was as strong as ever, although so many people were milling around that I couldn't tell who it was coming from.

I was going to find out, though.

Determination filled me, along with more than a little cold rage. Too many people had already died, and I hadn't survived the royal massacre just to be assassinated in my own throne room three months into my reign.

I kept my pleasant smile fixed on my face, not giving any hint about the danger, and watched the nobles talk and eat. When their first wave of gossip and hunger had been satiated,

I lifted my hand, calling for silence. Everyone on the first floor turned toward me, while the nobles on the balcony took their seats.

"Welcome, my esteemed countrymen and -women," I called out in a loud voice. "You honor me with your presence and most especially with your loyalty."

"As you honor us," they said, echoing the traditional response with far less enthusiasm.

Before I could begin the session, one of the nobles broke free of the crowd and strode forward, stopping at the bottom of the dais. Lord Fullman was a short man with thinning blond hair and a round belly that showed just how much he enjoyed his food and drink. As the owner of several fluorestone mines, he also controlled a lot of land, men, and money, and he was someone that I could ill afford to piss off.

Fullman made a gallant bow, sweeping his hand out to the side, then straightened up. "My queen," he crowed in a booming, confident voice. "Let me be the first to offer my formal congratulations on your reign."

"Thank you," I replied, although I was inwardly bracing myself.

Fullman had been at court for years, and he preferred to put his boot on people's throats and grind them down until they did his bidding, the same way that his miners chipped fluorestone boulders into smaller, more manageable sizes.

He smiled, although his expression took on a sharp edge. "Although I do have a question. What's this nonsense I hear about you visiting Andvari?"

Annoyance shot through me at Fullman speaking to me as if I were a child rather than his queen, but I kept my face fixed in its pleasant mask. Losing my temper and sniping back at him wouldn't help matters, although I couldn't help but sigh on the inside. I hadn't thought word would spread so quickly about my upcoming trip, but I should have known better. All it took was the softest whisper, and within hours, everyone at court knew about my plans.

Surprised murmurs rippled through the crowd. Not everyone had heard about my upcoming trip, and Fullman smirked at his friends and enemies alike, proud that he had broken the news.

"Yes," I called out. "King Heinrich has invited me to Glitnir for several days of hospitality and trade talks."

"And why should you journey so far?" Fullman asked, a sneer creeping into his voice. "Especially so early in your reign? We wouldn't want you to be seen as bowing down to the Andvarians. That wouldn't be good for Bellona. Outside influences never are."

He pointedly looked up at Sullivan, who was still sitting in the top corner of the second-floor balcony. Sullivan stared back at the noble. To anyone else, the magier would seem perfectly calm, but I could smell his peppery anger all the way down here on the dais. It was almost as strong as the jalapeño rage of whomever wanted to kill me.

Sullivan was the bastard son of the Andvarian king, something that no one at this court—or any other—would ever let him forget. From the rumors I'd heard, everyone was gossiping and speculating about why Sullivan was here and especially what his relationship to me really was.

Most people thought that he was my lover, even though we rarely touched in public and had never so much as kissed in private. But I was a queen, and he was a handsome prince who had spent the last few months in my court, so of course there would be rumors about us, even if we did nothing to encourage them.

For once, I wished the gossip were true. At least that way I would have gotten a little bit of pleasure out of the situation. My gaze traced over Sullivan's broad, muscled shoulders. Quite a lot of pleasure.

So far, I'd managed to ignore the whispers and innuendos, but no longer. I didn't know what Sullivan was to me, but at the very least, he was my friend, and I wasn't going to let some pompous lord look down his nose at him just because Sullivan was a bastard.

"I'm visiting Andvari because it wouldn't be proper to ask King Heinrich to come to Seven Spire," I said, a hard tone seeping into my voice, "considering the fact that his son, Prince Frederich, was murdered here, along with Ambassador Hans and several other Andvarians. Or have you forgotten about that?"

Fullman swung back around to me, surprise flickering in his pale blue eyes. He hadn't expected me to push back so forcefully. His lips puckered, and I could almost see the wheels spinning in his mind as he rethought his strategy to get whatever it was he really wanted.

"Of course not. That terrible tragedy will never, ever be forgotten." He drew in a breath to deliver the *but* I knew was coming next. "But traveling to Andvari sends the wrong message. That Bellona can't stand on her own. That she can't take care of herself."

He phrased it in terms of the *kingdom,* but everyone knew that he really meant *me.* Agreeing whispers surged through the crowd, although no one stepped forward to join forces with Fullman against me. They were waiting to see how this game would play out.

"Other, more important matters need your attention," Fullman said, another sneer creeping into his voice. "I'm sure there are plenty of things at the palace to keep you busy."

I had been *busy* ever since I'd become queen. Most of my time had been spent weeding the turncoat guards out of Seven

Spire and undoing the many cruel policies that Vasilia had enacted while on the throne. I'd barely had a minute to myself, which was why this formal court session was happening today, three long months into my reign, instead of three days after I'd taken the crown, as was tradition.

And now, here it was. The moment I had been dreading ever since I'd first sat down on the queen's throne the night that I'd killed Vasilia. The first true challenge to my rule, less than ten minutes into the court session. I had to give Fullman credit for his restraint. I'd expected him to attack me at the five-minute mark, at the very latest.

On the surface, it seemed like a perfectly reasonable request. But if I gave in to Fullman now, and especially if I stayed at Seven Spire, then everyone would see me as weak. Even more troublesome, I would be seen as ceding to the wishes of a lord— one who was wealthy and powerful enough to raise his own army to try to take the throne from me.

I couldn't afford to do that, but I also wasn't going to bow down to him or anyone else. I had done that for all the years I'd been the royal stand-in, the royal puppet, when I'd had to smile and nod and hold my tongue no matter how badly someone used, abused, insulted, or mistreated me. I was never doing that again.

Never.

Besides, I had other reasons for going to Andvari, reasons that were just as important to my survival as this verbal sparring match.

So I lifted my chin and stared down my nose at Fullman. Easy enough to do, since I was sitting on the throne a good six feet above his balding head.

"And I can't think of anything more important than repairing relations with Andvari and brokering a new peace treaty between our kingdoms," I said. "Especially given the recent actions of the Mortan king against Bellona, against *my family*. The Andvarians weren't the only ones who died. Or perhaps you've forgotten about the assassinations of Queen Cordelia, Princess Madelena, and several noble members of this court, some of whom were purported to be your friends?"

My voice was pleasant, but my words were anything but. More murmurs surged through the crowd, this time agreeing with me, and even Fullman had the decency to wince.

Serilda, Xenia, and Auster all nodded their approval. Behind the nobles, Paloma was grinning, as was Cho, who was standing beside her and nibbling on another tray of cakes. I didn't look up at Sullivan.

But Fullman recovered quickly. He wasn't giving up his agenda without a fight. "Well, if you are so determined to travel to Andvari, then let me assist you."

I arched an eyebrow. "And how do you propose to do that?"

A wide, satisfied smirk stretched across his face, and the scent of sour, sweaty eagerness surged off his body. I'd made a mistake asking him such an open-ended question, and I'd just walked straight into whatever trap he truly had in mind.

"The ranks of your personal servants are a bit thin and are comprised of people with limited resources and shockingly small amounts of magic." He glanced over at Serilda, Xenia, and Auster, then pointedly looked up at the balcony again. This time, Fullman fixed his harsh, accusing gaze on Calandre.

The thread master stiffened in her seat, and her fingers fisted in her blue skirt. Calandre might have worked for Queen Cordelia, but she didn't have nearly as much money, power, and influence as other thread masters, and Vasilia had tossed her aside for one of Fullman's richer, stronger cousins. At Seven Spire, being poor and weak in your magic was even worse than being a bastard.

Fullman sneered at Calandre a moment longer, then faced me again. "I would be happy to give you some of my servants to help fill your staff."

I barely managed to hold back a derisive snort. Servants? More like *spies*. Oh, Fullman's people might cook my food and wash my clothes, but they would also report my every move back to him.

"How generous," I murmured. "I'm quite happy with my current staff, but I'll take your offer under advisement."

His lips puckered again at my deflection, but his sour expression quickly melted into another smug smirk.

"Actually, that's only part of my offer." He paused for dramatic effect. "I think the best way to protect both you and Bellona is for my eldest son, Tolliver, to be your official consort."

Loud gasps surged through the crowd, followed by furious whispers, and several nobles shot Fullman dirty looks, obviously wishing they had been as quick-thinking, brazen, and devious enough to offer up their own sons to wed and bed me.

I silently cursed my own foolishness. I still wasn't used to being the center of attention, much less the target of everyone's schemes, and I had miscalculated how aggressive Fullman would be. And now I had to deal with his ridiculous proposal, along with the fallout from it. With a few simple words, the pompous lord had just launched a dozen new plots against me. Now, every single noble would start calculating how they—or one of their relatives—could win my hand in marriage.

Fullman snapped his fingers, and a taller, thinner version of himself stepped out of the crowd. Tolliver tried to smile at me, but it came off as more of a leer, and his gaze was firmly fixed on my crown rather than on my face.

Several of the nobles frowned at Fullman, but no one objected to his proposal, given how rich and powerful he was and how easily he could turn his wrath on them. Even the nobles who were Fullman's equals in power, land, men, and money kept quiet. They probably wanted to see what I would say to his offer before they made their own gambits.

I gritted my teeth and tamped down my anger. I hadn't thought that things would deteriorate so quickly, but I should have known better. To everyone here, I was still just Everleigh, an orphan girl with no real magic, money, or power who had been a distant seventeenth in line for the throne. Despite the fact that I had survived the royal massacre and had killed Vasilia in front of them, the nobles still thought that I was weak. At Seven Spire, weakness bred treachery, and treachery bred death.

The only good thing about Fullman's preposterous proposal was that it told me that he wasn't the one who wanted me dead right here and now. No, he wanted me to marry his son and get his hands on the throne that way. And then he would probably have me assassinated.

Auster glared at Fullman, and the captain's hand curled around his sword, as though he wanted to cut down the smug lord. I knew the feeling.

Serilda and Xenia were still standing next to Auster, and they both looked at me, wondering how I would handle this. Out of all the scenarios we had prepared for, this wasn't one of them. I'd thought the nobles would wait at least another month before trying to secure my hand in marriage, but I should have known better about that too. These were turbulent times in Bellona, and everyone was scrambling to cement what wealth, magic, and power they already had, as well as claw for even more.

Fullman used my silence as an opportunity to keep talking. "It would be far better for you to marry a Bellonan, rather than an outsider. After all, Princess Vasilia consorted with Nox, that wretched Mortan lord, and look how badly he led her astray."

Loud, mocking laughter erupted out of my lips. "Oh, please. No one ever led Vasilia *astray*. She decided to murder her mother all on her own. Nox and the Mortans were just a means to an end for her."

Fullman winced for a second time, and he actually waited a few moments before trying again. "Yes, well, my point remains the same. We wouldn't want any outsiders to unduly influence *our* court."

Once again, he pointedly looked up at Sullivan. It seemed as though Fullman had heard the rumors that Sullivan and I were . . . whatever we were, and he wanted to cut off the other man from the throne. I could have told him that Sullivan had no interest in being my consort, but Fullman wouldn't have believed me. To him, money and power were the most important things, instead of the principles that Sullivan believed in, principles that I found both admirable and frustrating.

The other nobles also stared at Sullivan. Once again, I could smell his peppery anger, but his face remained a perfect, blank mask. Sullivan understood how these courtly games worked, and he knew that you *never* let anyone see how much they hurt you.

Fullman jabbed his elbow into Tolliver's side, forcing the younger man to smile at me again. Tolliver even batted his eyelashes, as though the mere sight of his supposed adoring gaze would be enough to make me swoon, stumble down off the dais, and throw myself into his thin arms.

Fullman must have sensed my disgust because he elbowed Tolliver again, and the younger man stopped his ridiculous attempt at flirting. They both stared at me, clearly expecting an answer, as did everyone else. The other nobles, my friends, the guards. Even the servants stopped passing out food and drinks to see how I would handle this.

"You're moving rather quickly, Fullman," I drawled. "I've only been on the throne three months, and you're already planning my wedding. Tell me, do you have my children's names picked out as well?"

Loud, mocking snickers rang out at my scornful words. I could trade barbs with the best of the nobles, something that everyone was going to realize soon enough.

An angry flush stained Fullman's cheeks, but he wet his lips and kept going. "Of course not. But Tolliver has long admired you. The two of you grew up together. Don't you remember?"

"Oh, yes, I remember Tolliver," I said, my voice sharpening. "I remember how I once asked him to dance at a royal ball in this very room. I also remember how he laughed and told me that he would rather dance with a gargoyle than ever put his arms around me. I believe that was when we were sixteen, maybe seventeen. I'm not sure of the exact date. The parties and insults tend to blur together as the years pass."

Fullman's eyes widened, while Tolliver's face turned an interesting shade of purple. This time, shocked gasps rang out instead of mocking laughter. The nobles hadn't thought that I would be so bold as to insult someone as powerful as Fullman. They didn't realize that I was just getting started.

I glanced at my friends. Auster was grinning, as were Paloma and Cho. Serilda nodded her approval, while Xenia gave me a sly wink, as did the ogre on her neck. I still didn't look at Sullivan, though. I didn't want to add to the rumors about us.

So far, Fullman had been doing all the talking, plotting, and manipulating. It wasn't enough for me to merely block his attacks. I needed to show the nobles that I was a force to be reckoned with, just like Cordelia and Vasilia had been.

I might secretly think that I was a fraud, a pretend Winter queen, but I could never let anyone see my insecurity. I had tried to be nice, polite, and reasonable with Fullman, but no more. Fighting back was the only way I was going to survive for any length of time.

So I stood up, walked down the dais, and stopped at the bottom of the steps. The nobles retreated a few feet, and I paced back and forth in front of them, choosing my next target carefully. I also scanned the crowd again, searching for the source of that jalapeño rage, but I still couldn't pinpoint it to figure out who wanted me dead.

"Although I suppose that Lord Fullman has a point. I should pick out someone to marry. After all, it's not like any of you would say no, is it?"

No one responded, and not so much as a whisper broke the tense, heavy silence.

Finally, I stopped in front of Lady Diante, who had sent me that basket of pears. Diante was in her seventies, with golden eyes, ebony skin, and short, iron-gray hair that was twisted into tight curls. She was one of the most powerful nobles and Fullman's equal in terms of land, men, and money. Even better, she and Fullman were bitter rivals.

"What about you, Diante?" I asked. "Which one of your grandsons would make a good consort?"

Her eyes narrowed. She didn't know what I was doing, but she wasn't going to pass up this opportunity. "I have several grandsons who would suit you quite nicely, my queen," she said in a deep, throaty voice. "Pick out any one you like."

She waved her hand, and three men scurried forward to stand beside her, all with the same golden eyes and sharp cheekbones that she had. I looked at each one of them, as though I was considering picking out a husband as casually as Paloma had plucked a pear out of that fruit basket.

"Funny you should say that. Because I remember a time several years ago when Queen Cordelia suggested matching me to one of your grandsons. What was it you said to her?"

Diante frowned, and her eyes narrowed again, as if she was trying to recall that particular insult and how much it was going to damage her now.

I tapped my fingers on my lips, as though I was searching for the answer, then snapped them together. "Oh, yes! You laughed and said that you would never marry any of your grandsons to me, a lowly mutt. And then you added that any baby I had wouldn't have enough magic to make it worth the milk it took to feed the child."

More shocked gasps rang out. Diante grimaced and opened her mouth, probably to apologize, but I stared her down, and she had the common sense to keep quiet.

When I was sure that she was going to hold her tongue, I stared out at the nobles in front of me, as well as those up on the balcony, who were leaning forward in their seats, totally invested in the drama.

"Let me be clear," I said, my voice booming out almost as loudly as Cho's had. "I will choose a consort when *I* am ready, and not one moment before. And if you think to sway me with gifts or pretty words, remember this: I didn't just stumble into Seven Spire the night I killed Vasilia. I was here for fifteen long years before that, so I know every single one of you. I know your strengths, your weaknesses, and especially the petty little schemes you like to inflict on one another."

The nobles shifted on their feet and in their seats. They hadn't expected me to be so blunt, but I didn't care about bruising their egos. Not anymore. I was already sick and tired of their fucking games, and if I didn't take control of the court—of *them*—right now, then I never would.

"I remember every single insult any of you ever hurled my way, from the time when I was a child right up until the royal massacre. I haven't forgotten your cruelties, and I'm certainly not going to reward you for them now."

"Then what are you going to do?" Diante asked, although her voice was low, and I almost thought I saw a bit of grudging respect glinting in her eyes.

"There is an old saying, one that we are all quite proud of: Bellonans are very good at playing the long game."

Everyone nodded, and several folks stood up taller with pride. Bellonans were good at playing the long game, at being patient and lying in wait for their enemies to make a mistake so they could move in and finally, fully decimate them. No one played that game better than the Seven Spire nobles, and they'd taught me how to play it too.

"For years, you've all been playing a long game, trying to curry favor with Cordelia, Vasilia, and even Madelena. Well, I'm here to tell you that you've all lost."

A collective sound of uneasy agreement rippled through the room.

"Cordelia is dead, Vasilia is dead, and whatever deals they struck with you are dead as well." I looked from one noble to another. "*I* am queen now, and I will not be bullied, cowed, or otherwise intimidated or insulted by any of you."

"So what *will* you do?" Fullman asked, a sneer still in his voice.

I stared him down. "I will be fair, and I will be just, and I will do what is best for Bellona. To make us strong and ready against the growing threat of the Mortans and anyone else who is stupid enough to fuck with us. And if any of you have a problem with that, then you can leave Seven Spire right now and never come back."

I phrased it in terms of the *kingdom,* but everyone knew that I really meant *me.*

Once again, silence descended over the room, and no one moved or spoke. The harsh echoes of my words were still reverberating through the air, but cold calculation was already seeping back into the nobles' faces as they thought about the best strategy to get what they wanted. Bellonans recovered very quickly that way.

I had been brutally honest, but I also had to be reasonable. I had to give the nobles *something,* some excuse to at least pretend to go along with me today, or I wouldn't have a throne to come back to after my trip to Andvari. I glanced over at Serilda and Xenia, who both nodded. We'd discussed this at length.

So I tipped my head to Fullman and Diante. "But you're both right about one thing. I need help to make Bellona strong again. And that's why we are here today. So I can make sure that your concerns are being addressed, and we can all work together to do what is best for Bellona and guide our people and our kingdom to even greater prosperity."

I looked over at a tall man with short, curly black hair, dark brown eyes, and ebony skin who was standing next to the buffet tables. He was wearing a long-sleeved blue tunic like the other workers, but the crown-of-shards crest stitched in silver thread over his heart marked him as the kitchen steward. Theroux, another member of the Black Swan troupe.

"But no law says that we have to do what's best for our kingdom on empty stomachs," I said.

A few people laughed politely at my attempted joke, which was more than I expected, given how I'd lashed out at them. A small victory, but I'd take what I could get.

I gestured at the kitchen steward. "Theroux and his staff have prepared some delicious refreshments. So please, enjoy their hard work while I meet with everyone."

I nodded at Theroux, who whispered to the servants around him. They grabbed their trays of food and drinks and started circulating through the crowd again.

I did the same, moving from one noble to the next, and making inane chitchat just as I had done at hundreds of other events. Only this time, people moved toward instead of away from me, which was a bit overwhelming and claustrophobic, but I gritted my teeth and carried on.

Out of the corner of my eye, I spotted Paloma frowning at me. We had agreed that I would talk with the nobles, but she'd expected me to do it sitting on the dais, not down in the crowd. But there were too many people and too many scents, and I couldn't tell where the jalapeño rage was coming from unless I mingled with everyone.

If I did only one thing right today, then I was going to find the person who wanted me dead.

An hour later, I had made one lap around the room and had spoken to the most important nobles, although I still wasn't any closer to identifying who wanted to murder me.

But most of the nobles had been appeased, and I was about to head up to the second-floor balcony to see if my would-be killer might be lurking there when Diante plucked a glass of sangria off a servant's tray. She held the glass up high, and everyone quieted and faced her.

"It's long past time we toasted to Queen Everleigh's reign," Diante called out. "Shall we?"

I looked at Diante, who gave me a bland smile in return. She hadn't forgotten how I'd humiliated her, and she was making it clear that she was still in the game. The other nobles followed her example, even Fullman, and soon everyone was holding a glass of sangria.

A young, pretty blond servant hurried over to me. Unlike the plain crystal glasses that everyone else was drinking out of, a silver goblet inlaid with dark amethysts perched on her tray.

"Here you go, Your Majesty," the woman said in a high, sing-song voice. She must have had to fetch the goblet from wherever it was stored because she was a bit out of breath.

I smiled. "Thank you."

She smiled back and dipped into an awkward curtsy. She must be new. Or perhaps she was nervous at serving the queen. Part of me still couldn't believe that I was actually that person now.

The young woman straightened up, smiled again, and held out the tray. Everyone stared at me, wanting me to grab the goblet so they could get on with the act of toasting and supposedly celebrating my reign. I held back a sigh. Perhaps the blackberry sangria would at least make the rest of the court session bearable.

I had just touched the goblet when the scent of jalapeño rage filled my nose again.

To hide my surprise, I curled my fingers around the silver stem and pretended to admire the jeweled goblet. I'd lost the scent among all the perfumes and colognes, and I'd almost given up hope of finding it again.

My nostrils flared, and I drew in a breath, letting the air roll in over my tongue and tasting all the scents in it. And I finally realized that the jalapeño rage wasn't emanating from one of the nobles—it was coming from the servant standing next to me.

I studied her. Blond hair, pretty face, polite smile, blue tunic. She was dressed and acting like the other servants, but two things set her apart. One was the jalapeño rage blasting off her in hot, caustic waves. The second was her eyes, which were a deep, dark purple, like the amethysts in the goblet. I knew another person with eyes like that, and she had tried to kill me more than once.

Maeven, the bastard sister to the Mortan king.

Maeven had worked as the kitchen steward at Seven Spire for months, all so she could eventually poison and assassinate Queen Cordelia and the rest of the Blair royal family. And now here was another woman with amethyst eyes offering me a drink, just like Maeven had once upon a time.

This couldn't be a coincidence.

I wondered if this girl had worked for Maeven in the kitchen all along and had stayed behind after Maeven and Nox had fled from Seven Spire. I also wondered if she was one of the Mortan royal bastards, consigned to a life of carrying out assassinations and other foul deeds for her legitimate relatives. Either way, she wasn't getting away with it.

No one was murdering me today, especially not in my own fucking throne room.

Diante must have gotten tired of holding up her glass because she cleared her throat, obviously wanting me to get on with things. I wondered if she knew about the plot to kill me, but there was no time to find out. Not if I wanted to turn the tables on my would-be assassin.

So I plucked the goblet off the tray. But instead of raising it high, I signaled for another servant and grabbed a regular glass of sangria off his tray. The blond woman frowned and retreated a few steps, but I wasn't going to let her slip away so easily.

I turned toward her. "Tell me, girl, what's your name?"

She wet her lips. "Libby, Your Majesty."

"Well, Libby, it seems silly for me to drink from such a fine goblet when everyone else is using regular glasses. Although I do hate to let good sangria go to waste. Why don't you take the goblet? After all, you were the one who so thoughtfully fetched it."

Before she could protest, I shoved the goblet into her hand.

By this point, Paloma, Cho, Serilda, Xenia, and Auster had realized that something was wrong, and they were discreetly worming their way through the crowd toward me. On the second-floor balcony, Sullivan was doing the same.

Libby, if that was even her real name, might have been surprised by my handing her the goblet, but she sidled forward and offered it to me again.

"Oh, no! I couldn't possibly drink out of the queen's goblet!" she said in that high, breathy, innocent voice.

I curled my fingers even tighter around the plain glass still in my hand. "Funny. I've been at court for years, and I don't remember there *ever* being a special goblet for the queen. It must be a new tradition. Perhaps Vasilia started it."

Libby blinked, not sure what to say.

I shrugged. "Anyway, I'm giving it to you as a reward for your excellent service. So go on. Drink up."

I lifted my glass, as did everyone else, although Diante, Fullman, and the other nobles were frowning, wondering why I was paying so much attention to a servant.

Libby clutched the goblet, but she didn't drink the contents. And I knew that she wouldn't, especially since I could now smell the soft, floral poison in the goblet, only partially masked by the fruity sangria.

I lifted my own glass even higher. Everyone around me did the same, except for Libby.

"What's wrong, Libby? Is the sangria not to your liking?" I arched my eyebrow. "Or perhaps you simply don't want to drink the poison you slipped into the goblet?"

Shocked gasps rippled through the crowd. Somewhere behind me, Auster let out a vicious curse, but I didn't need him to protect me.

Surprise flashed in Libby's eyes, but she didn't bother denying it. Her lips twisted into an evil sneer, and she tossed her serving tray onto the floor. The tray clattered across the stone, making several nobles gasp again and back away, which created an open ring of space around the two of us.

Libby hadn't killed me with her poison, but she wasn't giving up. She lifted her hand, and purple lightning exploded on her fingertips.

"Die, you Bellonan bitch!" she snarled.

Then she reared back her hand and threw her magic at me.

chapter three

Well, Libby tried to throw her magic at me, but I was quicker, and I hurled my glass at her.

My aim was true, and I beaned her in the nose. The glass didn't break, but the sangria splattered against her face like blackberry rain.

Libby yelped in surprise and staggered back. She lost her grip on her magic, and her lightning dissolved in a shower of purple sparks. She also lost her grip on the silver goblet, which clattered to the floor. The sangria spilled out and started smoking on the blue carpet.

People screamed and scrambled back. Paloma, Cho, Serilda, and Xenia had been hurrying toward me, but the stampeding nobles pushed them back.

"Guards!" Captain Auster yelled above the commotion. "Protect the queen! Protect the queen!"

The last time I'd heard him scream those words had been during the royal massacre, and hearing them again took me back to that awful day. The throne room, the nobles, even Libby standing in front of me. In an instant, they all vanished, replaced by overturned tables, splintered chairs, and bodies littering the grass like bloody, broken dolls.

So much blood. So many bodies.

"Guards!" Auster yelled again. "Protect the queen! Protect Everleigh!"

The sound of my name broke the spell, and I snapped back to the here and now. Determination surged through me. I had survived that assassination attempt. I would survive this one too.

I yanked my sword free of its scabbard. The tearstone blade felt as light as a swan feather in my hand, but the slight weight steadied me. I had killed Vasilia with this sword, and I would do the same to this new enemy.

Libby swiped the sangria out of her eyes and lifted her hand again. More purple lightning exploded on her fingertips, and I could smell the hot, caustic stench of it even above the fruity tang of the sangria. She wasn't as strong as Maeven, but she was still a powerful magier.

"Maeven sends her regards!" Libby hissed.

Then she reared back and threw her magic at me.

I lifted my sword so that I was holding it upright, with the blade in front of my body, as though I were trying to use the weapon to protect myself from her power. In a way, that was exactly what I was doing, since the tearstone sword was designed to deflect magic.

But the sword's ability to deflect magic was nothing compared to *mine*.

Magiers, morphs, and masters might look down their noses at mutts, but us mutts had all sorts of skills—strength, speed, enhanced senses. But I had a far more unusual and valuable skill than most.

I was immune to magic.

I felt the burning, sizzling power of Libby's lightning the second it popped into her hand. A cold, hard power rose up inside me in response, eager to lash out and completely throttle her hot, crackling magic.

So I let it.

Libby's lightning slammed into my body with brutal, breathtaking force. My tearstone sword deflected some of her magic, as did the tearstone shards in my bracelet, but the electric heat of her power danced across my skin, trying to burn me alive. So I reached for my own magic, for my own immunity, and used it to push back against the lightning. I'd left my gladiator shield in my chambers, but in a way, my immunity was an even stronger, better shield, this invisible barrier that I could twist, bend, and shape however I wanted.

And right now, I wanted to use it to throttle all that damned lightning.

I pictured my immunity like a fist punching back against Libby's magic. She might be powerful, but my magic was stronger than hers, and my immunity shattered her power. The lightning blasted against my body, but it snuffed out an instant later, dissolving into a shower of purple sparks that dropped down and started smoking on the carpet, just like the poisonous sangria was still doing.

Libby's mouth dropped open in surprise. She obviously thought that one bolt of lightning should have been more than enough to kill me, but she reared her hand back and tossed another bolt at me. This time, I used my tearstone sword and the force of my immunity to slap the magic down onto the floor like it was a ball I was hitting in some child's game.

The lightning exploded against the flagstones, sending more purple sparks shooting everywhere and causing the nobles to scream again and retreat even farther away.

Libby must have realized that her lightning wasn't going to get the job done because she reached under her tunic and drew out a silver dagger from the small of her back.

"Death to the Winter queen!" she hissed.

My nose twitched. A soft, lavender scent wafted off the dagger. At first smell, it was pleasant enough, but I drew in another breath, and I sensed the foul rot lurking in the deceptively light, sweet aroma. The blade was poisoned, even more so than the sangria had been. I might be immune to magic, but I had no idea what kind of poison was on that dagger, and I couldn't let her so much as scratch me with it.

Libby lashed out with the dagger, trying to bury the blade in my heart. Music started playing in my mind, and I let the quick, steady beat carry me away.

As a child, I had never been much good at fighting, despite Captain Auster's repeated attempts to teach me. But I had always loved music and dancing, and Serilda had realized that the key to turning me into a gladiator was to treat fighting for my life as though it were just an elaborate dance that I needed to learn for some ball. She had spent the last several months training me, and now, I could hold my own against the best, most skilled warriors.

My feet, legs, arms, and hands moved through the familiar patterns of this deadly dance, and I ducked out of the way of Libby's vicious attack, then swiped out with my own sword in a brutal counterstrike.

Libby lunged back, whirled around, and faced me again. She moved to her left, and I twirled my sword around in my hand and followed her, matching her step for step. The two of us danced in a slow circle, analyzing and cataloguing the other's strengths and weaknesses.

A tense, heavy silence dropped over the throne room. No one said a word, and the only sound was the faint *thud-thud-thud-thud* of our footsteps. This time, instead of stampeding away, the nobles tiptoed forward, forming a ring around Libby and me and watching our every move.

It reminded me of fighting in a black-ring match at the Black Swan arena. Bellonans loved their gladiator blood sport, and the nobles more so than most. They wouldn't pass up this chance to see me in action again, despite the danger to themselves.

This had morphed from an assassination attempt into a test.

As I circled around, I spotted Captain Auster, who had shoved his way to the front of the crowd, along with my friends. He started to put himself in between the assassin and me, but Xenia latched onto his arm. He started to pull loose, but she shook her head.

"It's all right, Auster," I called out. "It shouldn't take me much longer to kill this assassin."

Libby let out a low, mocking laugh. "The only one who's dying is you."

"We'll see."

We kept circling each other. No one spoke, and no one moved except for Libby and me. The throne room was eerily quiet, but I could still hear that phantom music playing in my mind, guiding me through the steps I needed to complete in order to finish this dance and kill my enemy.

Libby grew tired of our circling, and she lunged forward and lashed out with her dagger again. But she wasn't trying to kill me with it. Not really. Now she was just aiming at my arms and trying to get close enough to cut me, to let the poisoned blade do its foul work.

I dodged her blow and spun away again. Then, before she could retreat, I moved forward and swung my sword out in a series of quick, vicious moves. I needed to knock that dagger out of her hand first, and then I could bury my sword in her heart.

But Libby realized what I was doing, and she avoided my attacks.

Around and around we went, each one of us moving in for a strike that the other either ducked or blocked. This went on for the better part of three minutes. Libby had obviously trained with her dagger, but I had been taught by Serilda Swanson, one of the finest warriors in all the kingdoms, and I slowly started to wear down the younger woman.

I opened a slice along Libby's left forearm. Then one along her right thigh. And finally a deeper gash across her stomach that had her screaming and stumbling back.

Libby stared at me, pain, fury, and magic shimmering in her amethyst eyes. I expected her to throw her lightning at me again, but she clamped one hand over her stomach, trying to stop the bleeding, and tightened her grip on the dagger still in her other hand.

"Finish her off!" Diante called out.

"Kill her!" Fullman agreed.

"Gut her where she stands!"

More shouts of encouragement rang out from the nobles, both here on the first floor and up in the balcony. They were all eager for this blood sport to reach its inevitable conclusion.

Libby's gaze flicked over the people gathered around us, as if she was just now realizing that if I didn't kill her, someone else would.

In addition to Auster and the guards, Paloma had her mace clenched in her hands and a murderous look on her face, as did the ogre on her neck. Serilda and Cho were both clutching their swords, Xenia was holding her cane, and Sullivan was standing by the balcony railing, blue lightning crackling in his palm, ready to rain down his own power on her.

The magic leaked out of Libby's eyes, replaced by growing dread. She looked down at the blood gushing out from between her fingertips, and she blanched, her face suddenly pale. She would bleed out if she didn't get help soon.

"It's over," I said. "You've failed. Put down the dagger. Now."

Libby glanced at the blade in her hand, then looked at me again. Something surprising filled her eyes.

Fear—complete, utter, paralyzing *fear*.

More fear than I had ever seen anyone show before. More fear than I had ever smelled from anyone before. The sharp, coppery tang of it rolled off her in waves, even stronger than her jalapeño rage had been earlier.

"I can't go back," she whispered. "Not to *him*."

Tears filled her eyes, and I got the sense that they were tears of fear, instead of pain. She kept staring at me, debating her options. She had only two—surrender or death.

"Put down the dagger," I repeated. "Just put it down."

Libby shook her head and staggered back another step. "You don't know what he does to people who fail. I can't go back," she whispered again. Then her jaw clenched, and her face hardened. "I *won't* go back."

She wrapped both hands around the dagger and lifted it overhead. I tensed, expecting her to try to attack me again, but Libby had something far worse in mind.

She whipped the dagger down and plunged it into her own stomach.

"No!" I yelled, surging toward her.

But I was too late. Screaming all the while, Libby twisted the dagger even deeper into her own stomach, then ripped it out. The blade slipped from her hand and clattered to the floor. Her legs buckled, and she landed next to it.

The nobles gasped, while my friends cursed. I hurried forward and dropped to my knees beside Libby. Blood had already pooled under her body, staining the stone a slick, glossy red. The warm, coppery stench punched me in the gut. It matched the smell of her fear.

Libby looked up at me. Pain glazed her amethyst eyes, but

her lips drew back into a grim smile. "I'm just the first. There are . . . more of . . . us . . ."

"How many more?" I demanded. "Who are they? Where are they? Are they already inside Seven Spire?"

"We're . . . everywhere . . ." she rasped.

Libby laughed, as though her cryptic words were highly amusing, although her chuckles morphed into a racking cough that sent blood bubbling out of her lips and trickling down her chin. I started to grab her shoulders to try to shake some answers out of her when I realized that the blood sliding down her face wasn't red—it was as black as black could be.

I drew in a breath. I could still smell the coppery scent of her blood, but another, stronger aroma drowned it out—the deceptively sweet, light, lavender aroma of the poison on her dagger. It was spreading through her veins and quickly killing her, even more so than the gruesome wound she'd inflicted on herself.

Libby blinked a few times, and tears leaked out of her eyes. "It's not . . . so bad . . ." she mumbled. "Doesn't hurt . . . as much . . . as other things . . ."

She was talking to herself instead of to me, although after a few seconds, her gaze locked with mine again. Another grim smile curved her lips.

"Don't worry . . . I won't . . . die alone . . ." she rasped. "He's coming . . . for you too . . ."

I started to ask who *he* was, but once again, I was too late.

Libby exhaled, her eyes became fixed and frozen, and her body relaxed, even as more blood gushed out of her stomach wound.

My would-be assassin was dead—and she had left me with far more questions than answers.

chapter four

No one moved or spoke, although everyone watched to see what I would do next. I was wondering that myself.

I shifted on my knees, causing my shadow to move on the floor. My gaze locked onto the dark outline, specifically the crown on my head, and I gingerly reached up and touched the thin silver band. Calandre had been right. The crown hadn't fallen off, hadn't really moved at all, despite my vigorous fight with the assassin. I shuddered and dropped my hand down to my side.

Footsteps sounded, and a shadow fell over me, blotting out my own grotesque one. Captain Auster crouched down on the other side of Libby. He looked at me, making sure that I was okay, then down at her, making sure that she was dead.

The silver dagger was lying on the floor where she had dropped it. Auster started to reach for it, but I held out my arm, stopping him.

"Don't touch that. It's poisoned."

Auster bowed his head. "Yes, my queen."

Yes, my queen.

Those three soft, simple words stabbed into my heart

like the sharpest sword, reminding me yet again that I was the cause of this gruesome situation. Disgust filled me. Not because Maeven had sent someone to assassinate me. I'd been expecting that for weeks. No, what truly disgusted me was that someone—*he*—had scared this woman, this girl, enough to make her kill herself rather than surrender. What a fucking waste of a life.

But Libby had made her choice, and there was no bringing her back. I let out a long, weary sigh and slowly got to my feet. I turned away from the dead woman and realized that I still had a problem.

The nobles.

Now that the fight was finished, everyone was staring at me—or, rather, at the sword in my hand.

Fullman, in particular, was eyeing the tearstone weapon with obvious, hungry interest. Everyone had seen me use the blade to slap away Libby's lightning, and it seemed as though they all thought that it was the source of my power.

People still didn't know how I'd managed to survive Vasilia's lightning during the royal challenge. Oh, rumors had flown fast and furious, and everyone had speculated about what kind of magic I might have. Herbs, protection charms, glamour-filled jewelry, ancient runes. I'd heard all those theories and a dozen others that were even more ridiculous.

But no one seemed to know about my immunity, and the nobles still thought that I was a mutt with an enhanced sense of smell and nothing more. Now they would probably assume that my sword had saved me from Libby's lightning, and Vasilia's as well. That my weapon had some special power or property that set it apart from normal tearstone.

That was better than them trying to use my magic for their own ends, but I'd have to be careful of thieves from now on. Not only would they lust after my sword, but they'd also want the dagger on my belt, the bracelet on my wrist, and the shield in my chambers.

I tightened my grip on my sword, as though I didn't want to let it go, even though the danger had passed. Even more hunger sparked in Fullman's gaze, as well as in those of some of the other nobles. Good. Every lie they believed gave me an advantage over them.

The longer I stared at the nobles, especially Fullman's smug face, the angrier I became. I fully expected Maeven to keep trying to kill me, either by proxy or in person, until one of us was dead. Someone *always* wanted to kill the queen. That was my burden to bear, whether I liked it or not.

But what made me truly *livid* was that none of the nobles would have cared whether I lived or died. If the assassin had killed me, they wouldn't have even waited until my body was cold before they started scheming to see which one of them could take the throne.

I would always have to fight Maeven and the Mortans, but I wasn't going to fight my own people too. Not anymore.

"Did you enjoy the show?" I called out. "Did you enjoy watching that girl kill herself after she failed to kill me?"

No one answered, but I didn't want them to.

Cold rage surged through me, and I didn't try to hide it. Not this time. Instead, I stabbed my sword at the girl's body. A few drops of blood flew off the end of the blade and spattered onto the floor at the feet of Fullman and the other nobles, but I didn't care about that either.

Let them get drenched in the blood of all the people they'd had to kill the same way that I was. Let them hear the screams of their dead loved ones ringing in their ears. Let them have nightmares about all the innocent people they'd seen slaughtered. Maybe then they would understand who our true enemy was.

"This is what I'm facing," I snarled. "This is what we are

all facing. Do you think the Mortans will stop with just me? They want *all* of us dead. Anyone in Bellona who could possibly be a threat to them is at risk. That includes the sorry lot of you, whether you realize it or not, along with your children and spouses and everyone else you care about."

I turned around in a circle, glaring at first one noble, then another. "I *am* going to Andvari. And I am going to secure a new peace treaty with King Heinrich. While I'm gone, you all have a decision to make. You can set aside your petty differences and power struggles and stop your fucking games. You can stand with me and help me protect Bellona against the Mortans. Or you can sit back, do nothing, and wait to be slaughtered, just like the Blairs were slaughtered. The choice is yours."

I gave the nobles one more disgusted look, then whirled around and stormed out of the throne room.

I expected someone to come running after me. Paloma, maybe, or Captain Auster. But my friends must have realized that I needed a few minutes alone because I didn't hear any footsteps.

I didn't really think about where I was going, only that I wanted to get away from the blood, death, and poisonous politics. I marched down a couple of hallways, rounded a corner, and shoved through some glass doors.

I wound up on the royal lawn.

I jerked to a stop, my body tensed, and my gaze cut left and right. For a moment, I felt as though I had stepped back in time to the massacre nine months ago, and I half expected to see a group of turncoat guards rushing to cut me down, just as they had that awful day.

It took me several seconds to realize that there were no guards, turncoat or otherwise, and that I was the only person here. I drew in several slow, deep breaths, trying to get my rage and memories under control.

It was mid-September, the last, waning days of summer, although the morning sun had already baked the air. Perfectly manicured grass rolled out for thousands of feet, while stone paths wound past towering trees and enormous flower beds filled with bright, colorful blossoms. Bees buzzed through the heavy, sticky air, moving from one blossom to the next, and the scent of pollen mixed with the flowers' heady perfumes and tickled my nose.

Everyone had flocked to the court session, so the lawn was deserted. No guards roamed along the paths, and no one lounged on the black, wrought-iron benches. Good. I wanted to be alone right now.

I strode forward, not quite sure where I was going, other than away from everyone inside the palace. But my respite would be brief, at best. The queen was *never* left to her own devices. And since someone had just tried to kill me, Paloma and Captain Auster would probably show up any second, along with several guards. But I was determined to enjoy this moment of relative peace and quiet for as long as possible, so I walked on, putting even more distance between myself and the palace.

Eventually, I stepped off the path and stopped in a spot in the grass. This was where the royal massacre had taken place and where so many people had died, including Isobel, the cook master who'd been like a second mother to me.

Evie! Evie!

Isobel's screams sounded in my mind, and I almost thought that I could smell her scent—powdered sugar mixed with cinnamon. At least, that had been her scent before a turncoat guard had shoved his sword through her chest, drenching Isobel in her own blood.

Suddenly, the sun wasn't so bright, and the day wasn't so

unbearably hot. Instead, a chill swept over me, and I had to wrap my arms around myself to hold back a shiver. I hurried on.

I wound up at the low stone wall that cordoned off the lawn from the two-hundred-foot drop below. Seven Spire palace jutted out of the mountain of the same name, and the lawn offered sweeping views of the Summanus River as it tumbled down from the surrounding Spire Mountains and flowed toward the southern sea.

Down below, seven cobblestone bridges arched over the river and led into Svalin. Buildings of all shapes and sizes stretched out for miles, including the hulking dome of the Black Swan arena near the edge of the city. But no matter how large or small, well-kept or run-down, the buildings all boasted metal spires at the corners of their roofs. The sharp, slender points represented swords and Bellona's gladiator tradition, and they also emulated the seven towering tearstone spires that topped the palace and gave Seven Spire its name.

Normally, I loved the views of the river and the city, but right now, the pointed spires glinting in the sunlight reminded me of Libby's poisoned dagger. Once again, I couldn't help but feel disgusted that the young woman had wasted her life trying to end mine.

But my thoughts quickly turned from Libby to Maeven, since I knew that she was the true architect of this assassination plot, just as she had been of the Seven Spire massacre. I wondered where Maeven was, and especially what she was doing.

Was she in Svalin? Hiding in some fine home and waiting for word of my murder to reach her ears? Or was she farther away? Maybe even back in Morta? I didn't know, and I supposed that it didn't really matter where Maeven was, only what she would do when she realized that her plot to kill me had failed.

But I unfortunately knew the answer to that question—she would once again try to murder me as soon as possible.

"A crown for your thoughts?" a low voice murmured.

My heart stuttered at the sound of his voice. I drew in a breath, letting his cold, clean vanilla scent fill my lungs. Suddenly, my heart was beating so hard and fast that I thought it might pop right out of my chest and tumble down over the rocks, but I didn't care. Instead, I drew in breath after breath, letting his scent seep deep down into my lungs and using it to drive away the lingering stench of the assassin's blood and poison.

Lucas Sullivan stepped up to the wall next to me and looked out over the city. While he admired the view, I admired him, greedily drinking in his dark brown hair, piercing blue eyes, and the stubble that clung to his jaw. I had been so busy dealing with various crises and trying to secure the throne that I hadn't seen much of him over the last several weeks. And never like this, when it was just the two of us, alone.

"Hello, Sully," I drawled. "Did Serilda send you to check on me? To make sure that I wasn't tempted to do another swan dive over the cliffs and put myself out of my own misery?"

A crooked grin lifted his lips. "No, Serilda didn't send me. I wanted to check on you myself."

My heart stuttered again at the obvious concern in his voice, but I forced myself to rein in my attraction and especially my feelings. Sullivan had made it absolutely clear that we could never be together, a bastard prince and a queen, and I was going to respect his wishes, no matter how much they hurt us both.

He turned toward me. "You did well today."

I arched an eyebrow. "You mean because I survived being poisoned and assassinated for the second time this year at Seven Spire?"

He shook his head. "No. I meant that you did well during court. Dealing with the nobles. You're good at it."

"You sound surprised."

He shook his head again. "I shouldn't be. I know that you

lived at the palace after your parents were killed when you were younger. But the way you handled Fullman and Diante . . . It was very skillful. I couldn't have done that."

"You're the magier enforcer for the Black Swan troupe. Surely wrangling some scheming nobles isn't any harder than keeping gladiators and their enormous egos in check."

Another faint smile lifted his lips. "You know as well as I do that things were far simpler at the Black Swan and that the gladiators could take out their anger and frustrations on each other in the arena. I would much rather deal with an angry gladiator with a sword in their hand and fury in their heart than I would a noble with sly words on their tongue and schemes galore in their mind."

I couldn't argue with that.

"Besides, I was never very good at being at court, at . . . dealing with people." A dark, distant look filled his eyes, as though he was thinking back to his own experiences in the Andvarian royal court.

"What happened? Was it your father? Did he treat you . . . poorly?"

"No. He was actually very good to me, and to my mother as well. We had our own chambers in the palace, and we were always included with the queen and her children, my half brothers. Everything was always equal—except for how other people treated us."

His jaw clenched. I could well imagine how the Andvarian nobles had tried to use him, and his mother too, to further their own agendas.

Sullivan shrugged, as though he was trying to slough off his anger, along with his bad memories. "The palace games never seemed to bother my mother, but they infuriated me. I always wondered why people couldn't just say what they meant and do what they promised."

"Is that why you left?"

"Partly. There were also some . . . extenuating circum-stances."

Those circumstances must have been quite extreme, given the tension in his voice and the scent of ashy heartbreak that swirled around him. I waited, hoping he would elaborate, but he didn't.

"And now you're going back to Andvari, back to the Glitnir royal court," I said. "All because of me."

He nodded. "You were correct before. Securing an alliance between Andvari and Bellona is the most important thing right now. If we aren't united, then we'll both fall to the Mortans."

"Is that why you set up the trip?"

As soon as I had killed Vasilia, I had started thinking about the best way to repair relations between our kingdoms. To my surprise, Sullivan had volunteered to contact his father, and he had brokered the deal for me to travel to Andvari.

He shrugged again. "More or less. But I also want to see my mother, and Gemma too. I want to make sure that she's really okay."

Gemma was Sullivan's niece and the king's granddaughter. The girl had been part of the Andvarian contingent that had been at Seven Spire during the massacre, and she was the only one of them who'd survived the slaughter. I wondered if she had nightmares about it like I did. Probably.

Sympathy filled me, and I laid my hand on top of his, which was resting on the stone wall. Sullivan jerked, as though my soft touch burned, but he didn't pull his hand out from under mine and step away like he had in the past. Instead, he swayed toward me, a hungry look in his eyes. It matched the aching, breathless hunger pounding through my own body.

A gust of wind whistled down from the mountains, whipping my black hair around my face. Sullivan lifted his hand, as though he was going to brush my hair back, but then his gaze drifted up and locked onto my crown. The slight weight suddenly seemed as heavy as a boulder crushing my head, and my heart along with it.

Sullivan's lips twisted, and he dropped his hand to his side and slid his other one out from under mine. I stretched out my hand to grab his again, but I thought better of it and curled my fingers into a tight fist instead. For a moment, I could still feel the warmth of his skin against my own, but another gust of wind swept over us both and ripped that away as well.

Sullivan cleared his throat, pretending like he hadn't noticed my reaching for him, and lowered his gaze from mine.

"What's that?" he asked. "There, on top of the wall?"

I looked down. Two large hearts had been crudely carved into one of the stones, along with the initials *J + K* running down the center where the hearts overlapped. I grimaced. I hadn't realized where I was standing, but I should have. I had always gravitated toward this spot.

"Oh," I said in a light voice, trying to brush off his questions. "It's just a carving. Nothing important."

Sullivan raised his eyebrows. "People only say that when something is actually very important."

He wasn't going to let it go, so I sighed, then tapped my finger on the hearts. "Have you ever heard the story of Queen Johanna Blair and her lover, Killian?"

Sullivan shook his head.

"It's a famous Bellonan love story. Johanna was the younger sister of Jocelyn, the crown princess, and Killian was a palace blacksmith. They used to play together as children, and they eventually fell in love. Johanna's mother, Queen Deborah, didn't approve of her daughter's relationship with a lowly blacksmith, but it was tolerated because Johanna wasn't inheriting the throne."

Sullivan asked the obvious question. "But?"

"But Jocelyn was killed in a boating accident, and Johanna became the crown princess. You know as well as I do that every noble is expected to marry well and secure bigger and better fortunes, lands, titles, and alliances for their family. That's especially true when it comes to royals."

This time, Sullivan grimaced. He'd said something similar the night he'd told me that we could never be together. Even though he had been right back then, and was still right now, it hadn't made his words hurt any less, and it didn't ease my heartache, frustration, or longing.

And he was right about something else. Things had been far simpler at the Black Swan, when he was just a magier enforcer and I was just a gladiator, than they would ever be here, especially when it came to our feelings and our damned duty to ignore them.

"Let me guess," Sullivan said in a low, strained voice. "The queen picked out someone else for Johanna to marry, and Killian was heartbroken."

"Of course. Killian couldn't stand to see Johanna marry someone else, so he left the palace and got a job in the city. But that's not the end of their story." I pointed to a spot in the distance. "See that bridge? It's called Pureheart. All the bridges have names, but I particularly like that one."

Sullivan squinted in that direction. The seven bridges that arched over the Summanus River were all more or less the same, but the bridge I was pointing at had one extra, notable feature—the enormous bell sitting at the far end. At one time, the bell had been a bright, polished silver, but the weather had slowly tarnished it to a dull, unremarkable gray.

"Killian wasn't a mere blacksmith," I continued. "He was a metalstone master who made all sorts of amazing things, but his specialty was musical instruments—flutes, whistles, harps.

Once Johanna's engagement was announced, Killian was commissioned to make Heartsong—a beautiful bell to ring in the couple's marriage. But he had other ideas."

"Heroes always do," Sullivan drawled.

"Killian made Heartsong as instructed, right down to all the swords, flowers, vines, and hearts that the queen wanted carved into the silver, and then he loaded it onto a wagon. But instead of delivering it to the palace, some friends helped him set up the bell on the far side of the bridge, where it sits to this day."

"Then what happened?"

I smiled. "Then he started ringing it."

Sullivan frowned. "What? Why?"

"Killian rang and rang and rang that bell. Heartsong lived up to its name, and the chimes echoed throughout the city. Everyone came to the river to see what was going on. Queen Deborah and Princess Johanna also heard the commotion and walked out to this very spot." I gestured down at the bridge again. "As soon as the queen and Johanna appeared, Killian stopped ringing the bell. With everyone watching, he strode out to the middle of the bridge, declared his love for Johanna, and begged the queen to let him marry her. Killian said that he would do whatever the queen wanted, if only he could be with Johanna."

"And what did the queen say?" Sullivan asked.

I grinned. "She did one of your favorite things. She gave him a test."

He snorted.

"The queen told Killian that if he truly loved Johanna, then he should come and get her."

"That doesn't sound like much of a test."

I pointed down. "She told Killian to come get Johanna *that* way."

Sullivan leaned forward, and we both stared down. Balconies, terraces, and columns adorned much of the outside of

Seven Spire, but this section of the royal lawn overlooked the steep, jagged cliffs that plummeted down to the river two hundred feet below.

"The queen told Killian that if he was brave enough, strong enough, to climb up the cliffs and reach Johanna, then they could marry."

"And did he?"

"Of course." I tapped my finger on the two hearts and the initials. "Johanna and Killian carved this on their wedding day. From all accounts, the two of them were happily married until they died, and Johanna's reign was long and prosperous."

Sullivan shook his head. "You Bellonans certainly do love your spectator sports."

I grinned. Johanna and Killian's tale was one of my favorites, especially because theirs wasn't the end of the story—it was just the beginning.

"We do love our spectator sports, and we also love our traditions." I pointed at another stone a few feet away that also featured two overlapping hearts, along with initials. "Thanks to Johanna and Killian, several people have scaled Seven Spire in order to be with their loves. And not just those in the Blair family. Other royals, nobles, servants, and guards have all done it. We call it the Pureheart trial."

Sullivan's gaze flicked from one stone to another, staring at the linked hearts and initials. His mouth twisted a bit, as though he wished he'd never asked about the carving. Part of me wished he hadn't asked either, since it only highlighted the differences between us. Andvarian, Bellonan, bastard, queen. Things that no fairy-tale climb up some cliffs would ever truly change.

I cleared my throat. "But of course, it doesn't always end happily."

"No?"

I gestured at another stone that featured one heart that had been broken in two, along with two initials. "That one is for a nobleman named Elric. He fell to his death during the climb."

Sullivan grimaced.

"Elric is the only one who ever actually died," I continued. "Although lots of people have broken their arms and legs."

He eyed the jagged cliffs again. "I can't imagine why."

"The climb has ended in other ways too." I gestured at another stone that featured a single heart with a large S carved in the middle. "That one is for Sabrina, one of my Blair cousins. She was an orphan like me, with no real family or money. She climbed up to the top."

"What happened?"

I shrugged. "Sabrina's lover was waiting up here, but she decided not to marry him after all. She said that if he was more concerned about being disinherited than losing her, then he could keep his bloody money, and she would marry someone who truly loved her, someone who would fight for her, someone who would climb the cliffs for *her*, instead of the other way around. She's the most famous person to complete the Pureheart trial, other than Killian."

That story finally put a smile back on Sullivan's face, and some of the tension eased from his shoulders. "Do people still climb the cliffs to declare their love?"

"Not really. The last time anyone tried was about thirty years ago. A man started to climb up, but he chickened out. His lover was so angry that she told him to slink away like the coward he was, and that man was never seen nor heard from again."

Sullivan laughed. I concentrated on the low, husky sound, trying to imprint it on my mind the same way I had his scent and the icy color of his eyes and the curve of his face whenever he smiled.

"Well, one thing is for sure," he murmured, staring down at the cliffs again.

"What?"

"You'd have to be desperately in love to do something that stupid and dangerous."

He kept his gaze fixed on the cliffs, but my heart still squeezed tight. The stories might be grand and romantic, but we both knew that love didn't always fix things. Sometimes, it just made them worse.

"You should go back inside, highness." Sullivan jerked his head to the right. "Your storytelling has drawn an audience."

I glanced over my shoulder. Several nobles were now milling around the lawn, pretending to admire the flowers while not-so-secretly spying on me.

Fullman and Diante were among the watchers, and neither seemed pleased to see me with Sullivan. Fullman was glaring at the magier, while Diante's arms were crossed over her chest. The two nobles still had aspirations of marrying me off to one of their broods.

To my surprise, Serilda was here as well, lounging on a bench with a glass of blackberry sangria, while Cho was standing next to her, eating cakes from a small tray. Both of them were watching me with amused expressions. No doubt they had seen this kind of drama play out dozens of times during their years as Queen Cordelia's guards. Unfortunately, doomed love was a rather universal story, no matter what station or kingdom you were born into.

Including their own. Serilda and Cho obviously cared deeply about each other. I even thought that they loved each other, and I had no idea what was stopping them from being together. Perhaps the same mix of duty, honor, and pride that had come between Sully and me.

Despite her smile, Serilda's eyes narrowed in thought, and

I could sense the faintest bit of magic wafting off her. In addition to being a fierce warrior, Serilda was also a sort of time magier, although she didn't get visions of the past or future like other magiers did. Instead, she saw possibilities, different ways that people might act and react, and different things that might come to pass based on the choices that people made.

I wondered what she saw when she looked at Sullivan and me. Heartbreak, most likely. That's all I could see when I looked at him.

Serilda drained her sangria, set her glass on the bench, and got to her feet. Cho popped the last of the cakes into his mouth and put down his empty tray.

I sighed, knowing that my brief respite was over and that it was once again time for Queen Everleigh to do her duty. "I should go."

"Thank you for telling me those stories," Sullivan said in a soft voice.

Our gazes locked, and I drew in a breath, tasting his scent again. Full of minty regret, just like mine was.

Sullivan stretched out his fingers, as though he was going to cover my hand with his, but at the last moment, he curled his hand into a fist, just as I had done earlier. He wouldn't touch me like that, not with so many people watching, no matter how much he might want to.

I looked down at our hands, his on one side of the carved hearts and mine on the other. So close, yet so far apart. That's the way it would always be between us.

And that hurt my own heart more than I'd ever thought possible.

CHAPTER FIVE

I left Sullivan standing at the wall and headed over to Serilda and Cho, who met me in the middle of the lawn.

"Sorry to disturb you," Cho said in a cheery tone, "but we thought it best to come fetch you before your loyal subjects decided to swarm you again."

I eyed the nobles. Fullman kept glaring at Sullivan, while Diante was talking to her grandsons and gesturing at me, as if she was trying to get one or all of them to come over and try to woo me.

"I suppose I should be grateful that Fullman and Diante didn't demand that I marry someone right then and there in the throne room."

"Too bad they didn't," Serilda drawled. "It would have been amusing watching you dance your way out of that."

I gave her a sour look. "You're enjoying my misery far too much. You're the one who put me in this position, remember? You're the one who made me queen."

"You made yourself queen," she corrected. "And I'm not enjoying your misery."

"Much," I accused.

She grinned. "Much," she agreed. "But misery or not, our job is to keep you alive. Dealing with the nobles and their petty schemes is up to you, Evie."

I sighed. Sometimes I thought that being queen was like trying to wrangle a pond full of baby ducks that were constantly squawking at, swimming circles around, and trying to drown me, all at the same time. *Quack, quack, quack.*

"But you handled the nobles well," Cho chimed in, trying to put a positive spin on things.

I resisted the urge to throw up my hands in exasperation. "Why does everyone seem so surprised by that?"

Serilda shrugged. "Because no one remembers that you've been here all along, watching the nobles, learning their games, and surviving their schemes. But after today, none of them will forget it again. I heard several of them inside, whispering and frantically trying to remember every mean and nasty thing they ever said about or did to you."

I snorted. "Well, that should keep them busy for a good long while."

Cho chuckled. "Yes, it should."

I scanned the lawn, searching for the rest of our friends. "Where are the others? Have you learned anything about the assassin yet?"

"Theroux is questioning the kitchen staff, trying to find out how long that girl had been working here," Serilda said. "Auster is doing the same with the guards, trying to track her movements through the palace and determine if she ever went into the city. Xenia is searching the girl's room, and I asked Paloma to get Sullivan to examine the goblet and the dagger, to see if he can figure out what kind of poison she used."

In the distance, one of the glass doors opened. Paloma strode outside and headed toward Sullivan.

I turned back to Serilda and Cho. "And what are we going to do?"

"We're going to get some answers about your would-be assassin, Maeven, and everything else," Serilda replied.

"How are we going to do that? The girl is dead."

"Yes, but there is someone else at Seven Spire who is still very much alive." She grinned again, but this time her expression was cold and predatory instead of warm and friendly. "And I am very much looking forward to getting answers out of him— one way or another."

I followed Serilda and Cho back inside the palace. We walked to the end of a hallway, pushed through a door, and went down a set of stairs. Then another set of stairs, then another. It didn't take me long to realize where we were going.

The palace dungeon.

Located on the very bottom level of Seven Spire, deep within the belly of the mountain, these hallways were dim and empty. The only sound was the faint rasp of our boots against the flagstones, but the murky shadows and eerie quiet soothed me. At least no one was plotting against me down here.

Our twisting, turning route took us past a large, gaping hole in one of the walls. Serilda, Cho, and I stopped and peered through the opening.

A beautiful stained-glass door used to stand here, fronting the workshop of Alvis, the royal jeweler I had been apprenticed to for years. Xenia had told me that she and Gemma had fled down here during the massacre and that Alvis had used his metalstone magic to collapse the wall and ceiling to stop the turncoat guards from reaching them. Then the three of them had escaped using a secret passageway in Alvis's workshop.

Sometime during Vasilia's brief reign, the crushed stones had been removed, as had the jewels, tools, and tables that had filled Alvis's workshop, leaving it an empty, hollow shell. I drew in a breath, but I couldn't even sense the metallic tang of his magic anymore.

Sadness rippled through me, along with anger that Vasilia had taken something else away from me, even though she was dead, but I pushed the emotions aside. The most important things were that Alvis was alive and well and that I would see him and Gemma during my trip to Andvari.

Serilda didn't say anything, but the scent of her salty grief filled the air. She didn't enjoy seeing Alvis's workshop like this either. Cho reached over and squeezed her shoulder. She nodded at him, then walked on, and Cho and I followed her.

A few minutes later, we arrived at a door at the end of a long hallway. Instead of a regular door, this one was an enormous round dome, as if half of a silver shield had been set into the wall. A single figure was inlaid in the center of the metal—a woman with a braid trailing over her shoulder and a sword in her hand who seemed to be glaring at anyone who dared to approach. Another image of Bryn Blair, my ancestor and the first queen of Bellona.

Two guards I recognized as gladiators from the Black Swan troupe were posted outside the door, and they snapped to attention as Serilda strode toward them.

"Any change?" she asked.

"No," one of the gladiators said. "He's been quiet so far."

The two guards took hold of the large ring set into the metal and used their combined mutt strength to wrench open the door. The loud *screech-screech-screech* of it sliding across the floor made me wince, and the harsh sound echoed off the walls and rattled down the hallway.

Serilda stepped through the opening. I followed her, but Cho stayed outside with the guards.

We walked along a wide corridor with regular-size metal doors embedded in the walls. The cells in the front part of the dungeon were empty, and we stepped into another corridor. More cells lined the walls here, but they were empty as well, and we strode past them to the very back of the dungeon, which opened up into a single, large room.

Tearstone bars cordoned off the back third of the area. Three separate cells were set into the wall, but only the center one was occupied. Straw covered the floor there, softening the stone, although it had molded weeks ago, given the drops of water that continually trickled down the back wall like tears dripping off someone's face.

The only pieces of furniture, if you could call them that, were a small metal-frame cot with dirty, threadbare blankets that didn't quite cover the equally dirty mattress, and two wooden buckets tucked into opposite corners. One of the buckets held water, while the other was being used as a chamber pot. My nose twitched, and my stomach roiled at the sour, pungent stench.

A man was curled up on the cot, using his arm as a pillow for his head. He was turned toward the back wall, away from us, although his feet were dangling off the side of the cot, as though he didn't want his ridiculously high-heeled boots to soil the mattress. Or perhaps he didn't want the mattress to soil his boots. Hard to tell.

"Hello, Felton," Serilda called out.

The prisoner slowly lifted his head and sat up so that he was facing us. He was a short, thin man who had grown even thinner during the months he'd spent here. His black hair still gleamed under the fluorestones, although it had lost its shiny luster, and an unkempt beard had grown out around his once perfectly groomed and styled mustache.

He was wearing the same clothes he'd had on the night I'd

killed Vasilia, although the gold thread on his black tunic and pants was frayed and had lost its elegant sheen, just like the rest of him had. The only part of him that wasn't a grimy mess was his black boots, which were still surprisingly clean and shiny, given the moldy filth that coated the cell.

Felton had been Queen Cordelia's personal secretary, and he had helped Vasilia, Nox, and Maeven murder her and the rest of the Blairs.

"Serilda," he rasped. "Finally ready to start torturing me?"

She shrugged. "That depends on how forthcoming you are. And, of course, on the wishes of my queen."

Felton focused on me, and his black gaze sharpened. "Queen?" he snarled. "She's no bloody *queen*."

"I think that crown on her head says otherwise, but who am I to make such judgments?" Serilda replied. "You always said that I was nothing but a stupid, lowly miner's daughter whose ambitions were higher than her birthright."

Felton's face twisted into a smug sneer at that long-ago insult. I didn't know everything that had gone on between them during the years they'd both served Cordelia, but Serilda and Felton despised each other. She had taken great glee in marching him to the dungeon after Cho had captured him during the royal challenge, and Felton had been rotting in this cell ever since.

"But insults aside, we came here for information," Serilda said. "Information I'm certain you have, Felton."

His eyes narrowed. "And what information would that be?"

She gestured at me. "Who tried to poison the queen today."

"Tried to?" He glared at me again. "It's too bad they didn't succeed, Everleigh, and put an end to your wretched farce of a reign."

Even though he was the one behind bars, his words still hit me like a slap across the face. They echoed my own fears that I was a weak, miserable fraud, instead of a strong, true Winter queen.

Felton had always excelled at dishing out insults, especially to me. I might be good at hiding my emotions, but Felton had known me for a long time, and he realized exactly how much his words hurt me. Another smug sneer twisted his face, and a hot, embarrassed blush scalded my cheeks, despite the cool, damp air.

"Face it, Everleigh," he said in a snide tone. "You'll never be half the queen Vasilia was."

"You mean that I won't arrange to have my mother, sister, and royal cousins assassinated?" My voice was as cold as the stone walls. "If that's the case, then I will be quite happy *not* to follow in Vasilia's footsteps."

Felton rolled his eyes at my rather pitiful attempt to mock him with his own words, but he got to his feet and walked over to the bars. "Why did you two come here? In case you can't tell, I'm busy counting the cracks in the walls."

"You were in league with Maeven," Serilda said. "I want to know everything she ever said to you, especially about the Mortan royal bastards."

He arched an eyebrow. "Ah, so that's who tried to kill sweet little Everleigh. One of Maeven's many relatives. Let me repeat my earlier sentiment—it's too bad they didn't succeed."

I ground my teeth to keep from sniping back at him. I would never win a war of words with Felton, despite his current situation.

"You should be nicer to your queen," Serilda snapped, her voice taking on a hard edge. "She's the only reason you are enjoying your current accommodations, instead of bleeding from every orifice."

She waved her hand at a table in the corner covered with swords, daggers, and tools. I could smell the stench of old, dried blood on them all the way across the room. Curiously enough, more blood coated the tools than the weapons. Or maybe that wasn't curious at all, considering where we were.

Serilda wandered over and picked up a small hammer. Then she started flipping it end over end in her hand, as though she was getting a feel for the tool the same way she would a sword. The motions made a small pendant glitter in the hollow of her throat—a swan made of shards of black jet with a blue tearstone eye and beak. Another one of Alvis's designs, just like the bracelet on my wrist and the sword and the dagger belted to my waist.

"Surely you haven't forgotten how quickly I can make someone talk," Serilda purred. "After all, you stood here many times and watched me work on those who would have done Cordelia and Bellona great harm."

Felton's gaze locked onto the hammer. He swallowed and scuttled away from the cell bars, as if remembering just how ruthless she had been in defending her queen and kingdom.

I knew that the palace guards had nicknamed Serilda the Black Swan years ago because of all the death she'd brought to Cordelia's enemies, but I hadn't realized that she had tortured those enemies for information too. I wasn't surprised, though. Once Serilda gave you her loyalty, it was yours for life. Even though Cordelia had thrown her out of Seven Spire for daring to suggest that Vasilia would one day kill the queen, Serilda had kept on helping Cordelia as best she could from afar.

"There's no need for threats," I said. "I know how to loosen Felton's lips."

"*You*?" He sneered at me again. "Break *me*? Please. You're even more delusional than I thought, Everleigh."

I walked over so that I was standing on the opposite side of the bars from him. "You seem to forget that I spent the last fifteen years being tortured by you every single day. Don't you recall all those boring teas, recitals, and charity luncheons you took such obvious, gleeful delight in ordering me to attend? Because I certainly do. I also remember all the nasty things you said to me. All the times you mocked my appearance or lack of magic or whatever else you found fault with."

The sneer slipped from his face, and he gave me a far warier look. "What does that have to do with anything?"

"I spent a lot of time at those events daydreaming about how I would get my revenge on you, if the chance ever presented itself." I held my hands out wide. "And that fortuitous day has finally arrived."

Felton shook his head, as if pushing away his fear. "And what are you going to do, Everleigh? Unlike Serilda, you don't have the stomach or the spine for torture."

I slammed my hand up against the bars. Felton jumped back at the sharp *bang,* ruining his attempt to remain cool and unconcerned.

"And that's where you're wrong, you vicious little weasel," I hissed. "I would happily cut you to ribbons for what you did to Isobel. Not to mention all the other people who died during the massacre. Part of me wants to do it anyway. Not for any sort of information, but just to make you *hurt,* just to watch you *bleed,* just to hear you *scream.*"

Felton swallowed again. He saw the cold rage on my face and heard the icy fury in my voice. Good. I might be a pretender queen, but I wasn't pretending when it came to this, and these weren't empty threats.

"But luckily for me, I don't have to bathe in your blood to make you talk. I don't have to cut you with a sword or dagger. I have to do only one simple thing."

"And what's that?" he whispered.

I smiled. "Take away your boots."

Felton's black eyes widened, and his gaze dropped to his precious boots, the last remaining vestige of who and what he had been.

"Vanity is a weakness, Felton," I said in a soft voice. "And

I have never, ever seen you without those boots. When I was younger, I used to think there was something wrong with your feet. In my kinder, more fanciful moments, I imagined that you were a merman, or some other fairy-tale creature, and that those boots were your way of hiding your webbed toes. But as I got older, I realized that you simply didn't like being the shortest person in the room. After all, that makes it *so* much harder to look down your nose at other people. Either way, I think it's finally time to satisfy my curiosity, don't you?"

"You wouldn't dare," he protested.

I leaned forward so that he could see exactly how serious I was. "I don't have to *dare* anything. I am the *queen,* and I will slice you to shreds for *fun.*"

He stared back at me, and I saw something in his eyes that I had never seen before—fear.

"Your choice, Felton. You can either tell me everything you know about Maeven, or you can lose your boots. And if that doesn't make you talk, well, we can always try Serilda's bloodier methods. I'm quite eager to give them a go."

He wet his lips and opened his mouth, but no words came out. I gave him another moment, but he still didn't speak, so I turned around, as though I was going to leave, and winked at Serilda. Her lips twitched, but she held back her smile.

"Okay, okay!" he called out. "I'll tell you what I know. Just leave my boots alone."

I turned back around to him and crossed my arms over my chest. "Talk fast, Felton. I have a kingdom to run."

His lips puckered like he wasn't going to answer me, so I pointedly dropped my gaze to his boots. Felton sighed and gave in.

"Whoever attacked you was probably a member of the Bastard Brigade," he said. "That's what the bastard offspring of the Mortan royals call themselves, according to Maeven."

"How many of them are there?" I asked.

He shrugged. "I don't know. But I would guess at least a few dozen, maybe more. All of varying ages, from children to elderly adults. Most of them have some sort of power, but the majority are magiers, able to summon lightning, snow, wind, fire, and the like. There are even a few mind magiers. Maeven is their leader, since she's the strongest in her magic."

I frowned. "Wait a second. There aren't that many Mortan royals. The king and his children, and only a few others. But you're telling me that there are dozens and dozens of royal bastards?"

Felton shrugged again. "According to Maeven, the Mortan royals purposefully have only one or two legitimate children, so that the line of succession is always crystal clear."

Serilda snorted. "And then they have as many bastard children as they can to do their dirty work."

From what I'd learned over the past few months, the Mortan royal bastards worked in kingdoms all across this continent and the ones beyond, spying, thieving, and carrying out assassinations and other deadly plots. That way, if the bastards were ever caught, then the Mortan king could deny knowing what they had been up to. A clever if cruel scheme.

"The Mortan royals think that there is strength in numbers," Felton said. "At least among the bastards."

"But not among the legitimate children," Serilda said, continuing his train of thought. "Legitimate offspring are just more competition for the throne."

He nodded. "Yes, that's how the Mortans see it."

"And the bastards aren't equal to the legitimate royals," I murmured, thinking of my earlier conversation with Sullivan. "Not in the ways that truly matter. Still, Maeven doesn't strike me as the type to bow and scrape to anyone, not even her own king."

"The king is her older brother," Felton said. "Apparently, the two of them were raised together and get along well enough. Or are at least united enough in their greed, ambition, and hatred of Bellona to work together to destroy it, to destroy *you*. Make no mistake, Everleigh. Today's assassin is just one of dozens in the Bastard Brigade dedicated to conquering this continent for Morta. They don't care who they have to work with, or what they have to promise that person, or how long it takes to turn someone to their side. And they especially don't care who they have to hurt and kill in order to achieve their goal."

"I wonder how Maeven feels about doing her brother's bidding," I murmured. "How she feels about being so far from home for months at a time and risking her life while the king sits safe and secure on his throne in Morta."

"Who the fuck cares about Maeven's *feelings*?" Felton sneered. "She's just another bastard, and the king will use her until she's dead, just like the Mortans have been doing for generations."

My mind churned, thinking about everything I knew about Maeven. Despite my hatred of her, I had to admit that she was smart, cunning, sly, patient, and exceptionally strong in her magic. I had never met the Mortan king, but he couldn't be *that* much more powerful than she was with her lightning. Maeven could have easily been queen of Morta herself.

Perhaps she would be one day.

Maybe it was my earlier talk with Sullivan, but a thought occurred to me about bastards and royals and this whole situation. The more I turned over the idea in my mind, the more threads I could see to it—threads that just might grow strong enough someday to strangle the Mortan king.

"What are you smiling about?" Felton muttered.

"Just a game I might be able to play," I murmured.

He frowned, as did Serilda, but I didn't explain my cryptic words. The thought was still too new and fragile to give voice to it yet. Besides, I had no way to actually implement my idea.

"What about Nox?" Serilda asked. "Is he a bastard too?"

Felton shook his head. "No, Nox is a legitimate Mortan royal. One of the king's nephews. Apparently, he wanted to prove himself to the king and to Maeven, so that's why he came to Seven Spire and spent all those months fucking Vasilia and pretending to be her guard."

"That's it?" Serilda snapped when he fell silent. "That's all you know about Maeven and the Mortans?"

Felton crossed his arms over his chest. "Unlike Vasilia, Maeven was never loose with her words, and she certainly wasn't forthcoming with her grand plans. Even after Cordelia was dead, Maeven was very careful to keep up appearances, and she continued working as the kitchen steward right up until the day of Vasilia's coronation."

That sounded exactly like the Maeven I knew, always plotting, always scheming, and never, ever revealing what she was really up to until after you had blundered into her trap. It was a strength of hers, but I was starting to wonder if it could be a weakness too.

Or perhaps I could *make* it into a weakness without her even realizing it—until it was too late.

"Thank you, Felton. You've been most helpful." I looked at Serilda. "Make sure the guards come and take away his boots."

She grinned. "Happily."

Felton surged forward and wrapped his hands around the bars. "What? No! You said that you would let me keep my boots if I helped you!"

I gave him the same cold, thin smile he had always given me right before he had ordered me to do something particularly unpleasant. "I lied. You don't deserve to keep your precious boots, Felton. You don't deserve anything at all. Not when you orchestrated the murders of so many innocent people, including Isobel. You're lucky that I don't let Serilda hack you to bits, and you're even luckier that I don't do it myself."

He opened his mouth, but I held up my finger, and he actually swallowed his protests.

"If you say one more *word,* then I will cut those boots off you myself, and your toes along with them," I hissed.

Felton's eyes narrowed, and fury sparked in his black gaze. Then he took another look at my face. Whatever he saw there must have convinced him how serious I was, because he slowly backed away from the bars, as if he didn't want to be anywhere near me. Smart man.

"Goodbye, Felton. I hope you enjoy your time in that cell. You're going to be in there for the rest of your miserable life."

I gave him another cold glare, then left him to rot.

erilda and I went back to Cho and the guards stationed at the dungeon entrance. I told them to remove Felton's boots and to not be gentle about it. The guards grinned and headed toward his cell.

Felton started screaming less than a minute later. I let the sweet sounds of his suffering soak into my heart, then left.

I spent the rest of the day dealing with the aftermath of the assassination attempt. Meeting with the nobles and soothing their concerns, reviewing the kitchen staff and procedures with Theroux, and doing the same with Captain Auster and the guards.

My friends investigated as well, but they didn't find out much. Libby had been working in the kitchen for about three months, which meant that Maeven had probably sent her to the palace as soon as I had become queen. Then the girl had just waited to get close enough to try to kill me.

Xenia thought that more Mortans might already be inside Seven Spire, waiting for their own opportunities to murder me, but I doubted it. Like Felton had said, Maeven was careful. She might have snuck Libby onto the kitchen staff, but she wouldn't try the same trick twice. Besides, she had to realize that if the assassination attempt failed, we would question every single person at the palace. So I doubted there were any other Mortans here. No, Maeven would do something else the next time she tried to murder me.

Something worse.

But there was nothing I could do about that, so I moved on to something that I could control—my trip to Andvari.

Over dinner with my friends, I told them that I wanted to leave as soon as possible. I didn't want to give Maeven another chance to try to kill me before I negotiated a new treaty with King Heinrich. Sullivan agreed to tell his father about the change in plans.

By the time we finished dinner, I was exhausted, so I retired to my chambers, where Calandre and her sisters were waiting.

The two girls plucked the pins out of my hair, and then Calandre mercifully lifted the crown off my head and set it on the vanity table. I resisted the urge to massage the heavy, lingering weight of it out of my scalp.

The silver band gleamed under the lights, while the tearstone shards looked like tiny blue swords jutting up from the metal. I touched one of the shards. The sharp point pricked my finger like a needle, drawing a drop of blood. I winced and pulled my hand away from the crown. I should have known better.

I should have known better about even taking the throne in the first place, but I pushed away those treacherous thoughts. It was far too late for regrets.

Calandre and her sisters pulled off my boots, along with my clothes, then wrapped me in a soft blue robe.

Paloma stood next to the vanity table with her mace propped up on her shoulder and watched the thread master and the two teenage girls to make sure they didn't stab me with a dagger hidden up their sleeve or run a poisoned brush through my hair.

I thought the two girls were going to faint at the suspicious looks that Paloma and her inner ogre kept giving them, but they ran a warm bath for me and left, along with Calandre.

Once they were gone, Paloma prowled around my chambers, making sure that no assassins were lurking behind the curtains or hiding under the bed, even though she had already done that the moment we'd first entered. Once she was certain the room was secure, she left, although she told Alonzo and Bowen, the two guards posted outside, to be vigilant and not to let me go anywhere without summoning her.

I took a bath, changed into my nightclothes, and crawled into bed. I tucked my sword under one pillow and my dagger under the other one. The matching shield was propped up against my nightstand within easy reach.

Only when I was surrounded by weapons did I finally lay back against the pillows. To my surprise, I fell asleep quickly, although my dreams were just as dangerous as my day had been . . .

Isn't it lovely?" I asked in a high, excited voice.

Ansel, my tutor, looked out over the room. "Mmm. Yes, I suppose it is."

We were in the main dining hall of Winterwind, my family's estate in the Spire Mountains in northern Bellona. Normally, at the dinner hour, the hall would have been empty, except for me, my parents, and Ansel, but this evening, dozens of people had crowded in to celebrate my parents' fifteenth wedding anniversary.

Flames crackled in the fireplace, while candles flickered on the mantel, bathing the hall in a soft, golden glow. Yuletide was only a few weeks away, and red, green, and silver fluorestones had already been strung up on the mantel and all around the fireplace, adding more light and plenty of holiday cheer to the festivities. Pine trees had also been set up in metal stands in the hall's four corners, although no glass decorations adorned their branches yet.

A large table ran down the center of the room, and a feast had been laid out for everyone to enjoy. Roasted lemon-pepper chicken, garlic mashed potatoes, apricot-glazed carrots, kiwi cakes, cranberry-apple pies. All my favorites. I breathed in the delicious scents.

My father's laughter rang out, and I focused on my parents, who were standing next to the fireplace, greeting their guests.

Lady Leighton Larimar Winter Blair, my mother, had the same black hair and gray-blue eyes that I did, while Jarl Sancus, my father, was a tall man with brown hair and blue eyes. They made a handsome couple, and they clearly loved each other, given the way their eyes warmed and their faces softened every time they snuck an adoring glance at each other.

Peppery anger filled my nose, overpowering the feast's aromas, and I realized that the scent and the emotion were coming from Ansel. I glanced up at my tutor, who was staring at my parents. My father slid his arm around my mother's waist, and Ansel's lips puckered. He probably didn't like them being so openly affectionate, since he was always so cold, remote, and distant.

Ansel had come to Winterwind three months ago, after my old tutor had retired. Unlike the rest of the staff, who laughed and joked with each other, Ansel kept to himself. He spent most of his time in the library, either preparing or teaching me my lessons or reading by the fireplace long into the night. My mother was the only one whose company he enjoyed, and she was the only one who could ever coax a smile out of him.

But Ansel was not without his admirers. Giselle, one of the kitchen workers a few years older than me, walked over and planted herself in front of him. He tried to look past her at my parents again, but she sidled in that direction, cutting off his view of them.

"Do you want something, Giselle?" Ansel asked in an annoyed tone.

"I thought you could use a drink." She offered him the glass of cranberry wine in her hand.

"No, thank you," he replied.

"Are you sure you don't want some?" Giselle murmured, taking a sip of wine, then licking her lips. "Or perhaps I could interest you in something else. Something more . . . robust?"

She toyed with the peekaboo lace on the front of her blue gown, as if her meaning wasn't already clear enough.

I crinkled my nose. Ewww. Sure, Ansel was handsome with his blond hair, violet eyes, and tall, muscled figure, but he was also in his forties, just like my parents were. He was easily twice Giselle's age.

Ansel gave her an annoyed frown. "No," he repeated in a much sterner voice. "Now, why don't you run along and play with the other little girls?"

Giselle's cheeks flamed. She gulped down the rest of her wine, as if to prove that she wasn't a little girl, then stormed off.

Ansel watched Giselle a moment longer, then grabbed the bronze pocket watch hooked to a short chain clipped to his vest. Ansel always carried the watch, which he constantly checked. I wasn't quite sure why. It wasn't like the hours moved any faster the more often he looked at it.

But I'd grown curious about the watch, and I'd snuck a glance at it one day when he'd laid it on the table during my lesson. To my disappointment, it was a plain bronze watch, with no magic or glamours. Ansel must have bought it at some secondhand shop, since a large, fancy cursive M was engraved on the cover, instead of his own A.

Ansel nodded, as though something about the time pleased him, then let the watch drop back down against his vest. "Come along, Everleigh. Let's greet your parents."

Despite the fact that everyone had been getting ready for the dinner all day long, Ansel had still made me finish my lessons like usual. We were among the last to arrive, and we had to hug the wall to make our way over to the fireplace.

Several people called out greetings to Ansel, but he nodded and moved on, never taking his gaze off my parents. We were almost to them when he snapped his fingers at one of the servants and grabbed a glass of cranberry wine off the man's tray. I thought he might take a sip, but he only clutched it in his hand.

Finally, we reached my parents. We had to wait until they finished speaking with a noblewoman before my parents turned toward us.

My father reached out and hugged me tight against his side. "There's my Evie."

I grinned and hugged him back.

"What do you say that we sneak away early in the morning and go down into the mine? We've opened up a new chamber of tearstone I want to show you."

My father's mine was located on the edge of Winterwind, and I loved exploring the cool, dark caverns and chiseling bits of tearstone, fluorestone, and more out of the rough, jagged walls.

I hugged him again. "Yes!"

"Jarl," my mother said in a soft, chiding voice. "You know that Evie has to finish her lessons before she goes gallivanting off with you."

Ansel stepped up beside my mother. "Oh, I think that Evie can skip tomorrow's lesson."

I blinked at his unexpected generosity. Sometimes, I thought that Ansel would have lectured me around the clock, if he could have.

My mother smiled, then laid her hand on his arm. "Thank you, Ansel. That's very kind."

He stared down at her hand, then cleared his throat and shifted away from her. "You're welcome, my lady."

Before I could chime in and thank him, Ansel stepped forward and held out the glass of wine in his hand to my father. "Here, Sir Jarl. You look like you could use a drink."

"Indeed, I do." My father winked at the other man, then grabbed the glass and took a large gulp of wine.

To my surprise, a thin smile creased Ansel's face, and he seemed almost . . . happy. Strange. Nothing ever seemed to make my serious, stoic tutor happy.

"Good," my father said. "It's settled. Evie and I will leave for the mine first thing in the morning—"

He turned his head and let out a loud cough. My father cleared his throat and opened his mouth, but all that came out was another cough.

My nose twitched. I hadn't noticed it before, but a foul, sulphuric stench was floating through the air, growing stronger and stronger, despite the fresh tang of the pine trees in the room. I drew in a breath, trying to figure out where the stench was coming from.

My father kept coughing, each sound louder, longer, and harsher than the last.

Concern creased my mother's face. "Jarl? Are you okay?"

My father tried to smile, but he started coughing again. And this time, he didn't stop.

He coughed so violently that the glass slipped from his hand and shattered on the floor. That foul, sulphuric stench rose up again, even stronger than before. It took me a moment to realize that the harsh aroma was coming from the spilled wine and exactly what it was, but sick understanding quickly filled me.

Poison—my father had been poisoned.

I sucked in a breath to scream out the words, but my father collapsed.

"Jarl!" my mother yelled, and fell to her knees beside him. "Jarl!"

He looked up at her. He coughed again, and blood bubbled out of his lips and trickled down his face. And that was just the beginning. More blood streamed out of the corners of his eyes, his nose, even his fingernails. The coppery stench of it drowned out the poison. All around us, people yelled and rushed forward, trying to figure out what was wrong.

"Get the bone master!" my mother screamed.

But it was too late. My father coughed a final time, and then his head lolled to the side. He stared up at me and tried to smile, but his lips turned down instead of up, and even more blood oozed out of his nose and trickled down his face. His blue eyes were still fixed on me, but they were wide and glassy now, and he wasn't seeing me anymore.

My father was dead.

My stomach roiled, and I clapped my hands over my mouth to keep from vomiting.

*"Jarl!" my mother screamed again, shaking his shoulder.
"Jarl!"*

She opened her mouth to scream again when a loud boom rang out, along with a violent tremor that shook the manor house and sent me stumbling against the side of the fireplace.

The noise and the tremor vanished an instant later, and a tense, heavy silence dropped over the dining hall.

"What was that?" someone whispered.

As if in answer, footsteps pounded in the hallway outside, growing louder and closer. Screams rang out as well, along with the clash-clash-clash of swords banging together.

"Mortans," my mother whispered, fear crackling through her voice. "The Mortan bastards have come for us."

Men and women carrying swords and shields rushed into the dining hall. They let out wild screams and yells and charged forward, swinging their weapons at every single person they could reach.

Behind them, a woman wearing a midnight-purple cloak and clutching a ball of swirling purple lightning in her hand glided forward. Instead of having a hot, electric burn, her lightning seemed bitterly cold, like it would freeze you on the spot.

The woman waved her hand, and what looked like purple hailstones shot out from her fingertips, growing in size, even as their rough edges sharpened into thick, daggerlike points. The hailstones punch-punch-punched into the chest of the closest guard like frozen throwing stars, killing him.

I staggered back as though I were the one who'd been hit, and the horrible reality of what was happening slammed into my mind.

Winterwind was under attack . . .

My eyes snapped open, and I sucked in a breath. For a moment, I could still feel the weather magier's frigid power, and I could still smell the sharp, coppery tang of my father's blood. But then the warm, summery air washed over me, while the softer, more pleasant aroma of the vanilla candles crowded together on the nightstand filled my nose. Another welcome gift from one of the nobles.

I scrubbed my hands over my face. This wasn't the first time I'd woken up from a nightmare. Ever since the massacre, my sleep had been more restless and troubled than not, with all sorts of dark, shapeless things trying to murder me as well as my friends. Just last night I'd dreamed that Maeven had burned Sullivan to ash right in front of me.

I supposed that today's assassination attempt had sent my mind spinning back to the night my parents had died. Sadly, watching my father choke to death on his own blood and the Mortans storm into the dining hall hadn't been the worst things that had happened at Winterwind.

Not even close.

I scrubbed my hands over my face again, wishing I could shove the awful memories out of my mind. I felt like I couldn't get a single moment of bloody *peace* anymore, not even in sleep.

I lay in bed until my breathing was even again, my heart had quit racing, and the sweat had cooled on my body. All the while, I stared up at the ceiling over the queen's bed, my bed now, although it was several minutes before I actually focused on it, instead of my horrible memories.

Unlike the throne room with its metal and jeweled accents, this ceiling was plain, with only a single symbol carved into the stone—a woman's hand wielding a sword.

I grimaced. The symbol was yet another reminder of all the queens who had come before me, all of whom seemed to be stronger, smarter, and more powerful than I could ever dream of being, especially considering the fact that I'd almost been murdered in my own throne room today.

Still, the symbol also reminded me of my duty. For better or worse, I was the queen of Bellona until I either died of old age or someone murdered me. Right now, I was betting on the second option, but that didn't mean I had to make it easy for my would-be killers.

If I couldn't sleep, I might as well get up and fight.

I sighed and then threw back the covers and got out of bed.

chapter seven

I put on black leggings and boots, along with a plain blue tunic, one without any of Calandre's silver-thread embroidery. I also waded into the pile of clothes in the closest corner, fished out a midnight-blue cloak, and slipped into it as well, making sure to pull up the hood over my head to cover my hair and shadow my face. Then I grabbed my sword and my dagger from underneath my pillows and strapped them to my belt.

By this point, it was almost midnight, which meant that everyone in the palace should be asleep, except for the guards. No one should knock on my doors until morning, much less enter my chambers, but I still shoved my pillows underneath the covers to make it look as though I was sleeping, just in case Paloma, Serilda, or someone else checked on me. I also left the fluorestone lamps on their current dim settings to further sell the illusion.

Oh, I doubted the old pillow trick would fool anyone for more than a few seconds, but I didn't want someone to stick their head into my room and panic when they didn't see me.

And I especially didn't want anyone to know that I could leave my chambers without going past the guards outside.

I pulled the covers a little higher on my pillows, then crept over and put my ear close to the doors, listening. Every few seconds, a faint *creak* of leather would sound, along with the soft *scuff-scuff* of boots on the flagstones, indicating that the guards were still awake. Good. They would hopefully keep anyone from entering before I returned.

Once I was sure that the guards hadn't heard me moving around, I went over to the ebony bookcase that took up most of one wall. Given my hectic schedule, I hadn't had time yet to clear all of Vasilia's things out of my chambers, and painted portraits of my cousin still lined the shelves. Of course the servants had offered to remove the items, but I'd decided to do it myself, just in case Vasilia had left behind any notes or other sensitive information.

I picked up a gold frame and stared at Vasilia's blond hair, beautiful features, and gray-blue eyes. Blair eyes, just like mine. Tearstone eyes, some people called them, because of all the tearstone my ancestors had dug out of Seven Spire and the surrounding mountains.

In the portrait, Vasilia was wearing a gold crown studded with pink diamonds shaped like laurel flowers. I traced my fingers over the crown, then down her face. Vasilia was smiling, and satisfaction filled her eyes, but the longer I studied her image, the more it seemed as though her lips twisted into a sneer and her eyes narrowed, as though she were mocking me about what a terrible queen I was—and just how short-lived my reign would be.

She was probably right about that.

I sighed and set the photo back on the shelf. Despite my hatred of her, I had to admit that Vasilia would have been a much better queen than me, especially when it came to palace politics. She would have masterfully played the nobles against one another during the court session until she had gotten exactly what she wanted from them, instead of floundering around and losing her temper like I had.

I sighed again, but there was still work to be done, so I grabbed hold of a midnight-blue book with a silver-foil title running down its spine—*A History of Bellona and Her Gladiator Queens*. I tilted the top of the book back, then let go and watched it snap forward. A faint *click* sounded, and the bookcase swung back from the wall, revealing a secret passageway.

Many of the old mining tunnels still remained in the palace. This one had been walled off to create a way for the queen to secretly escape from her chambers, should the need ever arise. I'd learned about the tunnels years ago, during one of my history classes. The royal tutor had given me, Vasilia, and our Blair cousins a map of the palace and had challenged us to find as many of the secret passageways as possible. I'd spent days exploring every nook and cranny, and I'd eventually stumbled upon this passageway, although no one else had.

When I was younger and Vasilia and the other children were being particularly cruel, I would often hide in some of the lesser-known passageways until my tears had dried, my hurt and embarrassment had faded, and I felt strong enough to creep back out and face them again. Sometimes, Isobel would coax me out of the dark corridors around the kitchen with mugs of hot chocolate and plates of cherry-almond cookies.

But Isobel was dead, and I was all alone tonight.

Serilda, Cho, and Captain Auster probably knew about this secret passageway, since they had spent so much time guarding Cordelia. Xenia probably knew about it too, given how well-informed she always was. But I doubted that any of my friends realized that *I* knew about the passageway. So I dropped my hand to my sword and stepped into the tunnel.

The door slid shut behind me, plunging me into total, unrelenting darkness. I carefully took a step forward. As soon as my foot touched the next flagstone, a fluorestone shaped like a sword flared to life in the ceiling above my head, providing some much-needed light.

I glanced around, but the passageway looked the same as I remembered—a narrow corridor with a low ceiling and rough walls covered with thick, gray cobwebs. I studied the ground, but no footsteps marred the dust on the flagstones, and the air smelled old, musty, and still. Only the spiders roamed here now.

I took another few steps forward, and that first fluorestone winked out, although a second one shaped like a shield flared to life in the ceiling up ahead. One by one, the alternating sword- and shield-shaped fluorestones lit up, and then cut off as I walked along.

I went about a hundred feet down the passageway before another corridor opened up to my right. Fifty feet later, another corridor curved off to the left. But instead of taking one of the branches, I stayed in the main corridor until it ended in a set of narrow, steep steps. I wound my way up the steps to the fifth floor, then went down another corridor.

This passageway ended in a stone door. Once again, I crept up to the door and put my ear close to it, but I didn't hear any whispers of movement on the other side, so I turned the metal handle. Another faint *click* sounded, and the door swung outward.

I peered around the door, but the hallway beyond was empty. So I stepped around the stone slab and pushed it shut behind me, waiting for the faint *click* of the lock. The door blended in seamlessly with the rest of the wall.

Unlike the first-floor common areas with their wide corridors, high ceilings, and display cases filled with dazzling treasures, this passageway was much smaller and shorter, with only a few wall tapestries. I listened again, but everything remained quiet, and I didn't smell any perfumes or colognes that would indicate that someone was nearby. Once I was sure that I was alone, I hurried down the corridor, eager to get on with my mission, even if it would most likely end up being a fool's errand.

A few twists and turns later, I reached a wooden door at the end of the hallway. No figures, weapons, or symbols were carved into the wood, but this door was perhaps the most important one in the palace, given what lay beyond it.

No guards were posted here, although I could smell Sullivan's magic, indicating that he had used his magier power to lock the door. Of course he had. I sighed. This was going to hurt. But there was no other way to get past his magic, so I stepped forward and reached out.

Blue lightning flared to life the second my fingers wrapped around the doorknob.

The lightning exploded with furious intensity, shocking me over and over again and trying to scorch my hand to ashes, along with the rest of me. I gritted my teeth against the searing, burning pain, reached for my immunity, and sent it shooting out at Sullivan's magic.

Sweat dripped down my face, my hand shook from the strain, and I had to grind my teeth even tighter to keep from screaming, but my immunity finally throttled Sullivan's power, and his blue lightning disappeared in a cloud of bright sparks.

It took me a few seconds to unclench my jaw and peel my fingers off the knob. I shook the lingering sting of his power out of my hand and wiped the sweat off my forehead. Then I twisted the knob, opened the door, and stepped through to the other side.

Just like in the secret passageway, fluorestones flared to life the second I entered the room and shut the door behind me. One by one, all four corners lit up, along with a row of fluorestones running down the center of the ceiling, clearly illuminating everything.

The front part of the room featured a purple velvet settee

flanked by two chairs, along with a table, all arranged around the fireplace. A writing desk covered with pens, papers, and books stood next to the fireplace, with a tall, freestanding mirror nestled in the corner. A four-poster bed, along with a nightstand and an armoire, dominated the back of the room. A vanity table was wedged in between the armoire and a door that opened up into a bathroom done in white tile.

By Seven Spire standards, it was a fairly modest room, even for a palace steward, and the furnishings were perfectly ordinary. But this was no modest space, and these were no ordinary things.

This was Maeven's room.

This was where Maeven had lived while she'd been masquerading as the kitchen steward, and this was where she had plotted against Queen Cordelia and the rest of the Blairs. Maeven had used her magic to escape, along with Nox, the night that I had killed Vasilia, but she had left her room behind, along with all her things.

Of course Serilda, Cho, and Captain Auster had searched the area, but they hadn't found anything noteworthy. Sullivan had also examined it, looking for any booby traps or obvious signs of magic, but he hadn't discovered anything either. Even Theroux had visited to see what papers or notes Maeven might have scribbled down about her duties as the kitchen steward, but he hadn't found anything out of the ordinary either.

I hadn't had a chance to come here yet, but after the assassination attempt, this seemed like the right time. Besides, it was the last chance I would get before we left for Andvari. Maybe I would see something the others had missed, or maybe I would leave as disappointed and frustrated as they had. Either way, searching Maeven's room seemed like a better use of my time than tossing and turning in bed and worrying about what fresh plot she was probably already hatching against me.

I made a slow circuit of the room, looking for anything that would tell me more about Maeven. I examined every piece of furniture, tapping on all the tables and chairs, along with the writing desk, the nightstand, the armoire, and even the bedframe, searching for secret compartments, but I didn't find anything. Furniture, pillows, blankets, pens, books. Everything was what it appeared to be and nothing more. Felton was right. Maeven had been very careful, even here in her own room, where no one had been watching her.

To my surprise, Maeven had taken her position as the kitchen steward quite seriously, and I found several recipe cards on the desk, along with proposed menus and notes about which wines paired best with certain dishes. Of course she had taken her position seriously. Maeven had put a lot of time and effort into killing Cordelia, and she wouldn't have wanted to get dismissed for not doing her job before she could strike.

But Maeven seemed to have a whimsical side as well, since several storybooks were mixed in with everything else, along with maps of places I had never heard of before. I couldn't tell if the maps went with the storybooks or if they were distant kingdoms that the Mortans wanted to eventually conquer.

The only other thing remotely interesting was a jewelry box on the vanity table. The wooden box itself was nothing special, but the jewelry inside was *magnificent*. Chandelier earrings, polished cuffs, necklaces that looked more like delicate strands of lace than hard metal.

I'd been apprenticed to Alvis for fifteen years, so I could tell that the pieces had been exquisitely designed and painstakingly handcrafted by a metalstone master. Each item, from the tiniest earring to the widest cuff, was worth a small fortune. Maeven apparently loved jewelry even more than she did maps and storybooks.

I ran my finger over some amethysts embedded in a silver

choker. Magiers often wore amethysts to augment their own power, and I could feel and smell the stench of her lightning flowing through the stones. No beauty glamours or other soft, subtle magics for Maeven. Every gem in her jewelry box practically dripped with raw, brutal power. I half expected the amethysts to shock my fingers, but of course they didn't.

I checked the box just like I had everything else. I took all the jewelry out of the various spaces and felt around the purple velvet inside, once again searching for secret compartments.

I didn't really expect to find anything, but then my fingers brushed up against a small button hidden inside the velvet, and a drawer popped out from the bottom of the box. I pulled it open and stared at the item inside.

A signet ring.

I grabbed the ring and held it up to the light. Tiny feathers were etched into the silver band, while a small, flat circle of jet was inlaid in the center. A fancy cursive *M* was embossed in silver in the jet and ringed by midnight-purple amethysts. My nose twitched. The amethysts reeked of Maeven's magic just like the rest of her jewelry did. I wondered what the *M* stood for, though. Maeven? Morta? Both?

Either way, Maeven had hidden this ring for a reason. Oh, I doubted there was any real clue in it, but I slid it into my pocket anyway. Perhaps it was petty, but I wanted to take something away from her for a change.

That was the only secret compartment in the jewelry box, so I searched through the rest of the vanity table, but nothing in it told me anything more about Maeven.

Besides her kitchen steward tunics, she had a few more personal items in the armoire, including a beautiful lilac ball gown, while berry balms, shimmering eye shadows, and scented lotions were lined up on the bathroom counter. But they were just clothes and makeup. Silk and thread stitched together, and colored oils and powders pressed into metal tubes, and there was nothing noteworthy or sinister about them.

I was almost ready to admit defeat and return to my own chambers when the scent of magic gusted through the room.

At first, I thought that I was imagining the hot, caustic stench or had just wandered too close to the jewelry box again. But I drew in a breath, and the aroma intensified, strong enough to burn my nose.

I clutched my sword, whirled around, and scanned everything again. Sullivan had checked for magical traps, but my nose told me that he'd missed something.

And that's when I realized that the mirror in the corner was glowing.

I'd already checked the freestanding mirror, a long, oval glass housed in a plain ebony frame. But now the surface was glowing and rippling as though it was made of liquid silver. My eyes narrowed.

It was a Cardea mirror.

The mirrors were named after Cardea, the glass master who had supposedly created them. The mirrors let people communicate with each other over great distances, or sometimes even physically move themselves and objects from one mirror—and place—to another.

I must have done something to trigger its magic. My gaze cut to the clock on the wall. Or perhaps this midnight hour was the scheduled meeting time between someone in the palace and whoever was on the other side of the glass.

Either way, I wanted to know who had a window into Seven Spire, so I drew my sword and pressed myself up against the wall, so that I could look into the mirror, but whoever was on the other side couldn't see me. And then I waited.

The silver glow grew brighter and brighter, and the surface began to ripple even more violently, as though it were a lake being assaulted by gale-force winds. The hot, caustic stench of magic filled the room, and I had to twitch my nose to hold back a sneeze. A few seconds later, the silver glow dimmed, the ripples smoothed out, and a woman appeared in the glass.

Maeven.

Her blond hair was swept up into a simple, elegant bun, and her eyes glittered like two dark amethysts against her flawless skin. Her features were quite lovely, although the perpetual, displeased pucker of her lips made her seem much older than her forty-something years.

A silver choker studded with amethysts and moonstones glittered around her throat, although it was so wide and tight that it seemed more like a collar than a piece of jewelry. A matching amethyst-and-moonstone ring glinted on her finger.

I studied the silver-thread embroidery on her lilac gown, but I didn't see any symbols in the loops and swirls. Bastards probably didn't get to wear the royal Mortan crest.

Maeven leaned forward. I held my breath, wondering if this might be a Cardea mirror that you could actually step through from one side to the other, but she stayed where she was.

"Libby?" Maeven's low, silky voice echoed out of the mirror. "Are you there? Is it done?"

Of course. I should have realized what this was about the moment she appeared.

Still clutching my sword, I stepped forward so that I was standing in front of the mirror where she could see me. "So sorry to disappoint, but I survived your assassination attempt."

Maeven's face hardened. "And Libby?"

"She killed herself with a poisoned dagger after she failed to kill me."

Maeven shrugged, as if the girl's death didn't bother her,

but her lips puckered again, and her nostrils flared with anger. Perhaps the Mortan bastards weren't as disposable as I'd thought. At least not to one another. I filed the information away for future use.

While Maeven digested my news, I studied everything I could see in the mirror around her. The magier looked to be in her private chambers, although all I could make out of the furnishings was a writing desk covered with papers and potted plants sitting on a nearby shelf. The plants didn't look like much, green sprigs with a few flowers, but the pots were painted rich jewel-toned shades and arranged in a row from lightest opal to darkest jet, and all the colors of the rainbow in between.

"I'm surprised it took you this long to try to kill me again," I said, breaking the silence. "I suppose that you wanted me to lower my guard and think that I was safe here at Seven Spire. You should have known better than that."

"Perhaps," Maeven murmured. "I'll keep that in mind for next time."

"I am curious about one thing, though."

"And what's that?"

"What kind of poison did Libby use?"

"Why does it matter?" she muttered. "Especially since she failed?"

I shrugged. "I was just curious what kind of poison caused her so much agony. Libby's was not an easy death. But I'm sure you've realized that, since you're probably the one who gave her the poison. Tell me, were you also the one who told her to kill herself instead of surrendering?"

Maeven actually jerked back, as though my words had wounded her, and it took her a moment to blink away her surprise.

"Where's your crown, Queen Everleigh?" she asked, a mocking note creeping into her voice. "Or have your countrymen taken it away from you already?"

"Not yet," I replied. "But at least I have the chance to wear it. Sadly, I can't say the same for you."

Her eyes narrowed. "What do you mean?"

"I've been down in the dungeon, talking to Felton. You remember Felton, don't you? The accomplice you so unceremoniously left behind the night that you and Nox fled from Seven Spire?" I waited for her to respond, but she didn't say anything, so I continued. "He's been quite a fount of information about you and your Bastard Brigade."

A muscle ticked in Maeven's jaw, and her nostrils flared with anger again, but she didn't respond. I paused a moment, carefully planning my next verbal attack. This was the beginning of my long game with the magier, and I couldn't afford to get anything wrong, not so much as a single word, and reveal my true intentions.

I started pacing back and forth in front of the mirror. "Before the massacre, I was actually planning to leave Seven Spire for good. I was going to ask Cordelia for permission during the luncheon. But then you and Vasilia put your assassination plot into motion, and everything changed for me."

"Why were you going to leave?" Maeven asked, not even bothering to keep the curiosity out of her voice.

"I hated my life here. I hated being the royal puppet, the royal stand-in. My Blair cousins were always off doing so much more noble things, so much more *important* things, instead of sitting through boring social events like I had to. It was like I was some poor servant girl trapped in a fairy tale, only my fairy godmother never showed up to give me a way out of my own miserable life." I stopped pacing and looked at her. "Although given my current circumstances, one could argue that *you* were my fairy godmother, murderous bitch that you are."

Maeven snorted and crossed her arms over her chest.

"Still, for as much as my cousins looked down their noses at me, it was even worse for you, wasn't it?" I paused. "It always is, when you're bastard born."

Her lips puckered yet again, but she didn't respond to my taunt, so I resumed my pacing, thinking about what to say next and how to best plunge another verbal knife deep into her heart.

"Felton didn't know exactly how many people are in your Bastard Brigade, but it doesn't really matter."

"And why is that?" Maeven snapped, finally rising to my bait.

I stopped and looked at her again. "Because none of you will ever sit on the Mortan throne. So who cares if your king's orders get you and your cousins slaughtered like sheep?"

She blinked, as though she had never thought of it that way. Her brow furrowed, and her arms slowly dropped to her sides.

"For as miserable as my life was here, Cordelia never ordered me to do anything more strenuous than make polite chitchat. But you? I can't even *imagine* the horrible things you've done for your king. What's it like? Going hither and yon on your brother's orders and doing his dirty work while he sits in his palace in Morta?" I shook my head and clucked my tongue in false sympathy. "It doesn't seem like much of a life to me. Then again, I don't suppose that many in the Bastard Brigade make it to ripe old ages. Face it, Maeven. Your life doesn't matter, and neither do the lives of your bastard relatives. Not to your king."

But my insults certainly mattered a great deal to Maeven. Rage sparked in her eyes and stained her cheeks a dark, ugly red. Her hands curled into fists, and purple lightning crackled along her knuckles, as though she was thinking about blasting me with her magic.

I didn't know if her lightning would actually come through the mirror, but I tightened my grip on my sword and reached for my own immunity, ready to defend myself.

"It matters, we matter, *I* matter because I am *proud* to serve!" Maeven hissed. "Morta is stronger than Bellona will ever be, and soon we will crush you and swallow up your pathetic kingdom!"

I gave her a thin, razor-sharp smile. "We'll see about that. Although I've always wondered exactly *why* it was so important to Morta to conquer all the other kingdoms. And why specifically target Bellona and the Blair family? You have plenty of land, magic, and resources. Why not be happy with all that you have?"

Maeven tilted her head to the side, studying me as if I were some exotic creature in a menagerie that she'd never seen before. She let out a soft, sinister laugh. "You still don't know, do you? What being a Winter queen really means?"

"Then tell me." This time, I was the one who couldn't keep the anger, questions, and frustration out of her voice.

The nobles might not realize that I was a pretender, but Maeven certainly did. She knew that I was only queen because of Vasilia's arrogance and failure to kill me during the massacre.

She laughed again, and the mocking sound scraped against my skin like sandpaper. "Oh, no, Everleigh. You'll have to figure that out on your own. Although you'll be dead long before you know what it really means to be a Winter queen, much less actually become one."

Become one? How could I become something I already was? Every word she said only confused me more.

Maeven opened her mouth, as if she was going to taunt me again, but then she looked off to the right at something I couldn't see through the mirror. She nodded, almost as if she was signaling to someone, then focused on me again.

"As much as I've enjoyed our little chat, I have other things to attend to," she purred. "But I'll leave you with a piece of advice—you should wear your crown as often as possible."

I couldn't help but ask the obvious question. "And why is that?"

She leaned forward so that her face was close to the mirror. Magic crackled in her amethyst eyes, and a mocking smile curved her lips. "Because you won't be alive to wear it much longer, Queen Everleigh."

I stepped up to the mirror, but before I could deliver some clever, cutting remark, Maeven waved her hand. A silver light exploded in the center of the mirror, so bright that I had to turn away from it. By the time I looked back at the glass, the light had vanished, taking Maeven along with it, and the mirror was just a mirror again.

My nemesis was gone, but I knew that it wouldn't be long before Maeven and her Bastard Brigade tried to kill me again.

THE SECOND ASSASSINATION ATTEMPT

CHAPTER EIGHT

We left for Andvari three days later.

I stood in the main palace courtyard, watching trunks being loaded onto wagons. Calandre and her sisters flitted from one trunk and wagon to the next, making sure they contained the necessary clothing, fabrics, and other supplies. I'd told Calandre that she and her sisters didn't have to go to Andvari, but she had said she would never forgive herself if she let me go to another royal court without the proper servants and attire.

My friends were here too. Sullivan and Xenia were talking and sipping mugs of mochana, while Serilda, Cho, and Paloma were speaking with some of the gladiators-turned-guards who were staying at Seven Spire.

"You should let me come with you," Auster said. "It's my duty to protect you."

I looked at the captain, who had been pleading his case for the last five minutes. "I need you to stay here, Auster. The nobles respect you. Even better, they fear you, along with your guards. I need you to keep the peace between Fullman, Diante, and everyone else and make sure that the palace stays secure. It won't do me any good to broker a treaty with the Andvarians if I don't have a throne to come back to."

Auster opened his mouth to protest, but I cut him off.

"Besides, it's not like I'm going alone. Serilda, Cho, and the rest of my friends will take good care of me. They have so far. I trust them to protect me, and you should too."

Auster stared at Serilda and Cho, who were still talking to the gladiators-turned-guards. Pride filled his face, softening his stern features. "Serilda and Cho are two of the finest guards to ever serve Bellona. If anyone can protect you from this Bastard Brigade, it's them. But that doesn't mean that I still won't worry." He paused, as if he was having trouble voicing his thoughts. "I already lost one queen. I don't want to lose you too, Everleigh."

Auster had never been verbose, and the months of torture he had endured at Vasilia's hands had made him even quieter. So I knew what an effort it was for him to share his worry.

I squeezed his arm. "You won't lose me. I survived my first session with the nobles. Dealing with King Heinrich will be as easy as baking a pie in comparison."

He smiled at my joke, but his eyes remained dark and troubled. I smiled back at him, but my expression was as forced as his was.

"I will do my duty and hold the palace until you return," Auster said. "Be safe, my queen."

He bowed low in the traditional Bellonan style, and I returned the gesture with a formal curtsy. Auster straightened up and gave me another tight, forced smile, then headed over to talk to the gladiators-turned-guards, along with Serilda and Cho.

Footsteps scraped on the stone, and Paloma strode over to

me, with her mace propped up on her shoulder. "You ready for this?"

I sighed. "I feel like you ask me that every single day."

"Because there's some new challenge or crisis or devious plot that you have to deal with every single day." She shook her head. "Being the queen's personal guard isn't *nearly* as much fun as I thought it would be. All I do is stand around and watch while you try not to lose your temper with people."

"So sorry to bore you," I sniped.

"I haven't gotten to fight anyone in *weeks*. Not like the other gladiators have," she grumbled, and the ogre on her neck actually pouted a bit.

Many members of the Black Swan troupe were now working at Seven Spire. Theroux had taken over as the kitchen steward, Aisha was the head of the bone masters, and several gladiators moonlighted as guards. Serilda hadn't disbanded her troupe—it made her and everyone else far too much money to do that—so the gladiators and others took turns working at the palace and putting on the usual weekend shows at the Black Swan arena. Paloma was clearly longing to return to the action. Couldn't blame her for that. She had been a gladiator long before we'd become friends.

"You should forget about being nice and let me crack a few skulls." Paloma hoisted her mace off her shoulder and swung it back and forth like a clock pendulum, making the spikes whistle through the air. "A couple of whacks upside the head would make the nobles fall in line."

Calandre and her sisters chose that moment to walk by, so of course they heard Paloma's words. Calandre sniffed, while her sisters let out their usual shocked gasps. I gave them a reassuring smile, but Calandre arched her eyebrow in response and shepherded her sisters into one of the wagons.

My fake smile twisted into a very real grimace. "We're not in the arena anymore, which means that you can't whack people with your mace, and I can't run them through with my sword, no matter how much I might want to," I said, muttering the last few words.

"Oh, we're still in the arena. You just have to fight with words now, instead of weapons." Paloma thought about it. "But that doesn't change the fact that I'm right and that it's terribly boring. However do you stand it?"

I gave her a sour look, but she grinned, as did the ogre on her neck.

We watched while a few final things were loaded onto the wagons, and then it was time for me to be loaded up as well.

Auster had suggested that I ride in a plain enclosed wagon like everyone else, in order to make it more difficult for any would-be assassins to target me, but I'd refused. It would have made me seem weak and cowardly, especially since I'd been holed up in Seven Spire since the night I'd killed Vasilia.

The people needed to see their new queen looking well and strong, so I climbed into an open-air carriage at the front of our procession. Cho was in the driver's seat, with Paloma riding beside him. Serilda, Sullivan, and Xenia were following in the wagon behind my carriage.

Cho looked over his shoulder at me. I nodded, telling him that I was ready. He slapped the horses' reins, and the carriage jerked forward. Even though I'd been expecting the violent, rocking motion, I still almost slid off the slick leather seat. At the last second, I managed to latch onto a metal bar embedded in the side of the carriage and hold my position.

I couldn't help but think it was the perfect example of how I was barely holding on to everything right now, including the throne.

But this trip had been my idea, and there was no turning back. The palace gates opened, and we left Seven Spire, crossed the bridge, and entered the city.

The trip to Andvari hadn't been formally announced, also

to help cut down on would-be assassins, but so many wagons leaving the palace at once made people curious, and they trickled out of their shops and homes to line the streets and watch the convoy roll by.

I sat as straight and tall in the bouncing carriage as possible, silently hoping that Calandre had put enough pins in my hair to keep the silver crown from falling off, clattering to the cobblestones, and rolling away down the street. Not exactly the message I wanted to send.

We entered one of the many plazas spread throughout the city. Water rose and fell in sweeping waves in a gray stone fountain shaped like two embracing lovers that stood in the center of the wide, open area. A few folks were throwing coins into the fountain, making wishes, but most people were gathered around the wooden stalls that lined the plaza, selling freshly baked bread and cuts of meat.

As soon as the carriage clattered into view, everyone turned to stare at our procession.

"The queen!" someone shouted over the steady *clomp-clomp-clomp-clomp* of the horses' hooves. "It's the new queen!"

In an instant, everyone left the stalls behind and hurried forward. People hopped up onto the rim of the fountain, and one particularly quick, industrious girl waded through the water and climbed up into the crook of the lovers' arms so that she had the best view possible.

Cho looked over his shoulder at me again. "I'm going to go around a few times! Let them really see you!"

I grimaced, but I nodded back. Cho steered the horses around the fountain, but instead of exiting through the street on the far side of the plaza, he tugged on the reins and circled around the fountain again.

I plastered a smile on my face, lifted my hand, and waved. The people realized what Cho was doing, and they clapped in appreciation. A few folks also yelled and cheered and whistled, but the carriage was going slow and was close enough to the edge of the crowd that snatches of conversation drifted over to me.

"She's not much to look at, is she? Not like Vasilia was. Now she looked like a *proper* queen."

"She's not even wearing the queen's crown. Why, you can hardly see that tiny band on her head."

"Don't insult the poor woman. She'll probably be dead in another month."

I had to grind my teeth to keep the smile from slipping off my face. The Bellonan people didn't have any more confidence in me than Maeven did. I wondered if they were placing bets on how long I would be queen, like the palace servants and guards were. Probably.

Cho made two more laps around the fountain, then steered the carriage out of the plaza.

The second the crowd was behind us, my hand plummeted to my side, the smile dropped from my face, and I sagged back against the cushions. At that moment, I wanted nothing more than to lie down on the floorboard, curl up into a ball, and hide for the rest of the ride, but I couldn't do that.

The queen of Bellona never, ever cowered.

So as Cho swung into the next plaza, I straightened up, plastered another smile on my face, and waved to everyone. All the while, though, I tried to ignore the harsh comments speculating about my impending demise, along with my own fear that my people were right and that my death would come sooner rather than later.

Given all the laps around the various plazas, it took us almost an hour to reach the rail station on the edge of the city. Normally, given the warm, late-summer weather, we would have driven the wagons to Andvari, especially given my sizable entourage of friends, servants, and gladiators-turned-guards. But Serilda and Cho had pointed out that the last time we had taken wagons into the mountains, a weather magier had unleashed a blizzard that had almost killed the entire Black Swan troupe. We weren't going to risk being trapped like that again, so we were taking the train to Andvari.

A rail line ran from Svalin all the way to Glanzen, the capital of Andvari, although from the reports I'd heard, few people had been journeying there since Vasilia had falsely blamed the Andvarians for the massacre. So I was also hoping that my taking the train would convince others to start doing the same and help to restore a more normal level of travel and trade between the two kingdoms.

Workers were lined up outside the train, along with the leader of the rail guild, all as curious to set eyes on me as the people in the plazas had been. I went down the row of them, shaking hands, asking about their jobs and families, and cracking jokes. The workers were polite, but they didn't seem overly pleased to see me, and the guilder brushed off my attempt to set up a meeting when I returned to Bellona. They all probably thought that I would be dead soon, like everyone else did.

Finally, all the luggage and people were loaded on board, and I stepped into the queen's private car at the very back. The only other time I had ridden the train was when I'd first come to Svalin after my parents had been murdered, and I was pleasantly surprised by the cushioned settees, chairs, and other comfortable furnishings.

But the biggest surprise was that everything was still swathed in Cordelia's red-and-gold colors, and her rising-sun crest still adorned the furniture. Vasilia must have had more important things to do than redecorate the train in her garish fuchsia-and-gold colors and sword-and-laurels crest. Still, my heart ached as I trailed my fingers over the rising sun carved into one of the tabletops. Cordelia should have been here, and she should have been taking this trip. Once again, I felt like I had just stumbled into being queen, and I had to resist the urge to snatch the crown off my head and toss it out the window.

Fifteen minutes later, the steam engine screamed, and the train slowly pulled out of the station. I sat in a seat next to the windows and peered out at the passing scenery. My friends moved around the car and up into the ones beyond, checking on things. I should have been working too, going over strategies for dealing with King Heinrich with Xenia, talking about security with Serilda and Cho, or even just trying to laugh and relax with Paloma, but I needed some time to myself, so I stayed in my seat.

The others must have sensed my mood because they left me alone—except for Calandre. Her sisters were riding in another car, but she'd boarded this one, although she had been huddled in the corner so far, drawing in a sketchbook. Finally, she worked up the nerve to come over to me.

Looking ill at ease, Calandre cleared her throat. "My queen? May I sit?"

I waved my hand toward the opposite seat, and she dropped into it. We silently scrutinized each other for the better part of a minute before she cleared her throat again.

"I wanted to ask you something that has been on my mind for several weeks now."

I waved my hand again, telling her to continue.

"Don't take this the wrong way," she said. "I was quite honored to be chosen to be your personal thread master . . ."

"But you're wondering why I picked you?"

Calandre nodded. "Yes. I only became Queen Cordelia's thread master because the man serving her took ill and no one else was readily available. But Cordelia was never very particular about what she wore or how she looked, and she kept me on out of routine and convenience."

She grimaced, as though what she was about to say next pained her. "And Cordelia didn't care that my father was a common tailor who married a minor noblewoman and that neither one of them had much money. She also didn't care that I don't have nearly as much magic as others at court."

Her cheeks flushed, and I knew she was thinking about Fullman's insult. "After Cordelia's death, Vasilia chose someone else as her thread master, and I was banished to a little workshop on the seventh floor. Even though I was expecting such a thing, it was still . . . humiliating to be dismissed so abruptly. But as you know, I have never been particularly powerful or popular at court."

"Neither was I—and look at me now."

Calandre's blue gaze lifted to the crown on my head. "You certainly have . . . prospered in recent months."

I arched an eyebrow. "That's a nice way of saying that I killed my cousin."

She grimaced again. "Perhaps you should tell me if there is anything special that you require of me or my sisters while we're in Andvari." She gestured at her sketchbook on a table in the corner. "I've already started designing a gown for the royal ball the king is holding in your honor. I would be happy to show it to you."

"There's no need. I know you'll make something lovely."

Calandre frowned. "Lovely is not good enough for the queen of Bellona. You need something *spectacular,* and I'm not sure that I can give it to you."

"*Lovely* is more than good enough for me," I said in a firm voice. "I'll leave *spectacular* to the preening peacocks at court."

She smiled a little at that, but her features remained troubled, as if she was worried about my suddenly dismissing her from my service. Her fortunes must have fallen even further than I'd realized when Vasilia had chosen someone else as her thread master.

I studied the other woman, wondering how much I could trust her. But I had to start trusting other people, even if just a little bit. My friends were already spread too thin trying to help me hang on to the throne, and I needed more allies.

"Do you remember that royal ball I spoke of during the court session?"

She nodded. "The one where Tolliver insulted you."

"Tolliver didn't just insult me," I replied. "He stepped on the hem of my gown and made me trip. Everyone saw me fall, and I ripped my gown and scraped my hands, which only made Tolliver and his friends laugh more. I got to my feet and ran into the closest bathroom. I was going to stay there until the ball was over and I could sneak back to my room, but another girl came inside. And the strangest thing happened—she actually used her magic to fix my dress and help me clean up."

Understanding dawned in Calandre's gaze.

"I told everyone at court that I remember every insult, every cruel and petty thing they ever did to me."

She frowned, not seeing my point. "So?"

I shrugged. "So I remember the small kindnesses too."

Calandre's brows furrowed together, and she gave me an incredulous look, as if she couldn't believe that I had chosen her now because of how she had taken pity on me all those years ago. She didn't speak for several seconds.

"Thank you for answering my question," she said. "Let me know if you need anything else, my queen."

I waved my hand, dismissing her. Calandre nodded at me again, then retreated back to her corner seat, opened her sketchbook, and returned to her design.

And so I was alone again—until Sullivan sat down across from me.

Even though I had seen him in the courtyard earlier, I still drank in the sight of him. The way the sunlight made his dark brown hair gleam like polished mahogany. How his eyes could seem as cold as ice or as hot as stars, depending on his mood. The dark stubble that always made me want to smooth my hand over his jaw. The way his long gray coat perfectly draped over his broad, muscled shoulders. Sometimes, I wondered if I would ever get tired of looking at him. I doubted it.

Sullivan glanced at me, then stared out the windows, still giving me some space, but I didn't have time to brood. Not anymore. Besides, this trip was just as important to him as it was to me.

"How does it feel?" I asked. "To be going home?"

He shrugged. "No different than all the other times I've returned over the years. I would always visit my mother whenever the Black Swan troupe was close to Glanzen. She still lives in the palace."

"And your father? Did you always visit him as well?"

A humorless smile lifted Sullivan's lips. "Sometimes."

All sorts of dark feelings and hidden meanings oozed out of that one word. I waited for him to elaborate, but Sullivan kept his thoughts to himself. Perhaps he didn't want his relationship with his father to color mine.

So I tried a different tactic to get him to open up. "And what about Dominic, your older brother?"

"You mean the beloved crown prince? The one nicknamed Prince Charming?" His smile twisted into a grimace. "Sometimes."

Once again, all sorts of feelings and meanings were packed into that one word, and once again, he didn't elaborate.

"But I always spend time with Gemma, Dominic's daughter." Sullivan's tight expression eased into one of genuine happiness. "She's my favorite niece."

"She's your only niece," I pointed out. "I'm looking forward to seeing her. And Alvis."

"And they're looking forward to seeing you too, highness. You're all that Gemma talks about every time I speak to her through my Cardea mirror."

Sullivan had a mirror in his room at Seven Spire that was similar to the one I'd discovered in Maeven's chambers, although I hadn't told him or anyone else about my conversation with her. After she had disappeared, I had tried to get the mirror to work again, but with no success. Maeven must have been the only one capable of sensing and triggering its magic.

I had wanted to use Sullivan's mirror to speak to Gemma, and especially Alvis, and make sure that they were okay. But Sullivan had had a difficult time getting his father to host me, and I hadn't wanted to add to the tension by talking to anyone behind the king's back. Besides, I would see Gemma and Alvis soon enough.

But I forced myself to put my feelings aside and think like a queen, which meant picking Sullivan's brain about King Heinrich.

"Do you think your father will agree to a new peace treaty?" I asked the question that had been weighing on my mind for weeks.

I had done everything I could think of to smooth things over with Heinrich, including immediately restoring trade agreements with Andvari and vehemently denouncing the Mortans as the ones responsible for the Seven Spire massacre. I had also sent Heinrich a letter apologizing for Vasilia's actions and expressing my deepest sympathies and condolences for the loss of his son, his ambassador, and his countrymen.

I had heard nothing in return.

Heinrich hadn't sent me a letter, and he hadn't made any public comment about the Mortans. His silence worried me.

If the king didn't agree to a new treaty, then I would have traveled all this way for nothing, and returning to Seven Spire empty-handed would only further weaken my position with my own people. I had to go back with *something,* some new treaty or trade agreement that would convince the nobles to work with me instead of against me. If I didn't, then it was just a matter of time before Fullman, Diante, or someone else challenged me for the throne, or Maeven tried to assassinate me again, or both.

Not only that, but failing in my first diplomatic mission would reinforce my own belief that I wasn't worthy of being queen, much less a Winter queen, whatever that really meant.

The uncertainty on Sullivan's face filled me with even more concern. "I don't know, highness. I just don't know. My father has always been . . . difficult. Then again, I didn't stay at the palace and marry a nice Andvarian girl like he wanted, so perhaps that's why our relationship has been strained in recent years. But now that Frederich is dead . . ."

His voice trailed off, but he didn't have to finish his thought. We both knew how delicate the situation was between Bellona and Andvari.

I waited, hoping that Sullivan might offer some more insights into his father, but he turned back to the window, lost in his own thoughts.

In that moment, I wished that I could have protected him from this. That I could have spared him from returning home and facing all the pain clearly waiting for him there. But I couldn't protect Sullivan from his emotions or his past any more than I could protect myself from my own.

So I stared out the window too, watching the miles churn by and wondering what fresh new misery awaited us both in Andvari.

CHAPTER NINE

expected Maeven to set another trap somewhere along the way, perhaps even try to derail the train, but our journey proceeded without incident. Three days later, our train pulled into the main station in Glanzen.

Serilda, Cho, Sullivan, and Xenia had already gotten off to secure our route to the palace, but I was still in the queen's car with Paloma. She opened her mouth, but I stabbed my finger at her.

"If you ask me if I'm ready for this, I'm going to scream," I muttered.

Paloma grinned, as did the ogre on her neck.

I glared at her a moment longer, but then I rolled my eyes, and a begrudging smile crept across my face. This was the last moment I would have with my friend for hours to come, and I wasn't going to waste it being annoyed, especially since I didn't know what would greet me at the palace.

Outside the train, the Blair royal march began to play. Paloma squeezed my arm, silently wishing me good luck, then slipped out the side door, leaving me alone. The march kept playing, and I used the time to check my reflection in the mirror in the corner.

Calandre and her sisters had spent most of the morning fussing over me, since I was scheduled to go straight from the train station to the Glitnir throne room to meet with King Heinrich. Calandre had tried to get me to don a gown, but I'd insisted on wearing my regular blue tunic, black leggings, and boots, and I'd strapped my tearstone sword and dagger to my black leather belt like usual.

The thread master had sighed at my lack of fashion sense, but I'd told her that my outfit was a necessary evil and that I at least wanted to be able to fight if I was attacked. My pragmatism about another assassination attempt finally made her give in, but she'd won a small battle by making me wear a new tunic that featured silver thread on the sleeves, along with a crown-of-shards crest that stretched across my chest. The symbol might as well have been a bull's-eye, telling assassins where to aim, but I hadn't wanted to hurt her feelings, so I'd told her that it was lovely.

Calandre had also tried to get me to don one of the more elaborate crowns she'd packed, but I'd refused in favor of wearing the same thin silver crown with small blue tearstone shards that I'd sported at Seven Spire.

Glitnir was Heinrich's court, and I didn't want to outshine him in any way. Things were already tense and difficult enough between our kingdoms, and I needed his help too badly to offend him, especially by doing something as silly as wearing a crown larger than his.

Camille, Calandre's youngest sister, was a paint master, and she'd worked her magic on my face, using silver shadow to make my eyes seem more gray than blue and adding berry balm to my lips. My shoulder-length black hair lay in loose waves, and my only jewelry was the crown-and-thorn bracelet that Alvis had given me the day of the massacre.

Outside, the royal march finally trailed off, and the last boisterous notes faded away. Then Cho's booming voice sounded.

"Presenting Her Royal Majesty, Queen Everleigh Saffira Winter Blair, of Bellona!" His voice rang out like thunder, and the car door slowly slid back.

I drew in a breath, then let it out and strode outside.

The platform looked like the one we had departed from in Svalin—a stone slab dotted with iron benches with the main rail station building in the distance. I took a few steps forward and stopped, and that's when I realized that the people here weren't rail workers and guilders.

They were Andvarian royal guards.

More than three dozen men and women formed a semicircle around the platform. They were all dressed in long-sleeved gray tunics trimmed with black thread, along with black leggings and boots, in keeping with the colors of the Ripley royal family. Normally, during an official visit, the guards would have been wearing ceremonial swords with jeweled hilts and leather scabbards studded with metal scrollwork.

Not today, not for me.

Each guard had a regular sword clutched in their hand and a dagger hooked to their belt. They were also wearing breastplates made of dull silver that was probably much stronger than it looked. But perhaps the most telling things were the way that the guards glared at me and the hot, peppery anger that blasted off them in strong, continuous waves.

I shouldn't have been surprised. After all, I was the embodiment of Bellona, the place, the people, and especially the family who had murdered their beloved prince and ambassador and had almost killed the king's granddaughter. I hadn't expected a warm welcome, but I had been hoping for a bit less hate and hostility.

My friends weren't any happier about the situation. Sullivan was deep in discussion with an Andvarian woman, while Serilda, Cho, and Xenia were standing off to the side. Calandre and her sisters were behind my friends, nervously studying everyone around them.

Paloma was stationed a few feet away with the Bellonan gladiators-turned-guards. Her hand was curled around the mace on her belt, and her amber eyes were narrowed, along with the ones of the ogre on her neck, as if she was silently daring the Andvarians to attack me. Tension hung in the air like a cold, wet blanket, smothering any pretense of warmth or friendliness.

But there was no turning back, so I plastered a smile on my face and headed toward Sullivan. At my approach, he murmured a few final words to the woman, then moved back. But instead of rejoining our friends, he stood in a little bubble of space all by himself, clearly caught between two worlds. He was definitely not a Bellonan, but he wasn't quite an Andvarian either.

I focused on the woman. She was about my age, late twenties, with topaz eyes, beautiful ebony skin, and shoulder-length black curls held back from her face by gray crystal pins. She was wearing a gray tunic, and a sword and a dagger dangled from her belt, the same as the other guards. But the Ripley royal crest—a snarling gargoyle face—was stitched in black thread over her heart, indicating her importance.

The woman didn't smile. I hadn't really expected her to, given the situation, but the raw, naked hate that filled her eyes surprised me, as did the strong scent of ashy heartbreak that wafted off her. This woman utterly despised me. Not a great omen of things to come.

She pressed her fist to her heart and bowed in the traditional Andvarian style. "Queen Everleigh, welcome to Glanzen.

I am Rhea, captain of the royal guards." She recited the usual platitudes in a cold, flat voice, not meaning a single word.

"Hello, Captain Rhea. I want to thank you and your guards for your generous hospitality." I made my voice warm and pleasant, following the standard protocol script.

Rhea's jaw clenched, but she dipped her head, acknowledging my politeness. "I will escort you to the palace. King Heinrich is eager to meet you."

I just bet he is. I kept my sarcastic thought to myself, though.

With Rhea leading the way, and the Andvarian guards surrounding us, my entourage and I left the platform, walked through the rail station, and exited on the street. From there, I climbed into an enclosed carriage. Paloma got inside with me, while a couple of Bellonan guards perched on top of the vehicle. And then away we went, rolling through the streets of Glanzen.

I had been to Glanzen once with my parents, but my memories of that childhood trip were faint and dim, so I peered out the window, trying to see everything at once.

Glanzen was similar to Svalin with its cobblestone streets, wide plazas, and bubbling fountains, but everything here was older and much more refined, polished, and elegant. The Andvarians' tall, slender homes and shops made Bellona's shorter, squatter buildings seem like pale imitations and crude, brittle shells in comparison.

And it wasn't just the shapes and sizes that were different. Every single structure featured exquisite, intricate stonework, from the vines that flowed through the curved steps to the flowers that adorned the smooth arches to the fluted columns that supported many of the buildings. It was like the entire city had been crafted with the utmost care by a legion of masters, and some new wonder of stone, metal, wood, and glass was waiting around every corner.

Like Bellona, mining was one of Andvari's main indus-
tries, thanks to the Spire Mountains that ran through much
of the kingdom. But whereas Bellona was known for its fluorestone, tearstone, and coal, the Andvarian mines were filled
with precious metals and jewels. That glitz decorated many of
the structures, whether it was gold leaf lining the windows,
hammered bronze curling up a column, or garnets, moonstones, and other gems encased in a fountain rim.

But perhaps the most striking difference between the two
kingdoms was what adorned the buildings. In Bellona, metal
spires decorated all four corners of any home or business. Even
the massive domed arenas like the Black Swan featured spires,
as a tribute to the swords, spears, and other weapons used in the
current gladiator matches and those throughout Bellonan history. There were no such spires in Glanzen, and something else
lurked on the rooftops here.

Gargoyles.

The moving, breathing, living stone creatures crouched on
many of the roofs, ranging from tiny rocks no larger than owlish caladriuses to hulking, boulder-size brutes bigger than the
Floresian horses pulling the carriage. No matter their shape and
size, almost all the gargoyles had curved horns on their heads,
wings on their backs, and sharp talons on their paws, along with
mouthfuls of long, jagged teeth that were perfect for tearing into
and then crushing anything—or anyone—unfortunate enough
to get in their way.

I spotted a couple of gargoyles flying back and forth across
the street. The creatures were soaring through the air as fre-
quently and casually as the eagles that cruised over the Summanus River outside Seven Spire, looking for fish to pluck out
of the water.

Andvarian legends claimed that the gargoyles served as
protectors, not just of the buildings they nested on top of, and

the mines they burrowed into, but of the entire kingdom. Of course there were gargoyles in other kingdoms, but they were found naturally only in Andvari, and there was some magic, some quirk of nature that made the gargoyles here much more powerful than those that lived elsewhere.

The creatures were one of the main reasons why Morta hadn't been able to conquer the other, smaller kingdom yet. The gargoyles were the fierce, natural enemies of the strixes, the enormous hawklike birds with purple feathers that Mortan soldiers often rode into battle. Still, the gargoyles and the magic they possessed were probably another reason why the Mortan king lusted after Andvari, along with the kingdom's mines.

The carriage stopped to let other traffic cross the street, and a shadow fell over the vehicle, blocking the sunlight. I looked up again and realized that a gargoyle was sitting on a nearby rooftop, staring down at me.

The creature was roughly the size of a large dog, with two sharp horns that jutted up like curved swords from its dark gray forehead and a long tail tipped with what looked like a stone arrow. The gargoyle's eyes burned a bright sapphire-blue, and its gaze slowly sharpened as it studied me, as if it was thinking about how I might taste for dinner. Gargoyles mostly ate gravel and other small stones, along with mice, rats, birds, and the like, but this one looked like he wanted to branch out and snack on my blood and bones. I shivered and leaned back against the cushions.

Thirty minutes later, the carriage slowed, and I peered out the window again. We had arrived at Glitnir, the glittering, gleaming heart of Andvari.

The palace was made of a pale marble that was somewhere between white and gray, and it glowed like an enormous opal in the noon sun. Balconies, terraces, and crenellations adorned the palace's wings and towers, along with large, diamond-shaped windows. Ribbons of hammered gold, silver, and bronze flowed across the stone and curled up many of the steps, walls, and archways, while precious gems added little pops of color here and there, as though they were flowers blooming in the marble and opening up their jeweled petals to the blue sky.

The centerpiece of the palace was a tall, wide wing topped with an enormous dome that rose above all the other levels. Several spiked towers jutted up out of the dome, making it look like a crown of swords.

Gargoyles were flying from one tower to the next and back again, although not nearly as many as I'd expected. Perhaps the creatures preferred to explore the city or the rolling, wooded hills of the surrounding countryside during the day before coming back to the palace to roost at night.

My carriage rattled to a stop in the main courtyard. I climbed out, with Paloma trailing along behind me, her hand on her mace again. Serilda, Cho, Sullivan, and Xenia got out of their carriage, while the rest of the Bellonan servants and guards climbed down from their vehicles. We all milled around the courtyard, studying everything around us.

Especially the Andvarian royal guards.

Guards lined the courtyard walls three deep in places, all armed with swords and angry glares that were aimed at me. Maeven didn't have to send another Bastard Brigade assassin after me. Not here. Any one of these guards would probably be more than happy to shove a blade in my back to avenge their murdered prince and ambassador. I would have to be even more careful here than at Seven Spire.

But I wasn't the only one the guards were glaring at. They were also eyeing Sullivan with . . . well, I wasn't quite sure what to call it. Some of the guards smiled and nodded, seeming happy to see him, while others gave him stares that were almost as dark and murderous as the ones they were directing at me.

Sullivan politely returned the nods, although his face remained a blank mask. I could smell the emotions blasting off him, though. Lots of hot, peppery anger and vinegary tension, mixed with a surprising amount of minty regret and ashy heartbreak. The first two made sense, but I wondered at the others. Why would Sullivan regret coming home? And what—or who—here had broken his heart?

Captain Rhea walked over to me. "King Heinrich is waiting in the throne room."

Instead of giving me a chance to respond, Rhea whirled around and strode away. Oh, yes. She definitely hated me. Still, all I could do was follow her.

My friends fell in step with me. Paloma, Serilda, and Cho surrounded me on three sides, their hands on their weapons. Sullivan was on the far side of Cho, once again not quite with us, but not with the Andvarians either. Xenia was a few feet behind us, stabbing her cane into the ground over and over again. The sharp, steady beat was oddly comforting.

I glanced over my shoulder. Calandre and her sisters were walking behind Xenia, along with the rest of the Bellonan entourage. The Andvarians brought up the rear, their hands also on their weapons, steadily shepherding us into the palace.

No escape now.

We left the courtyard, stepped through a wide archway, and entered the palace. The inside of Glitnir was even more ornate than the outside, and gold, silver, and bronze gleamed everywhere, from the threads in the fine rugs underfoot to the framed paintings that covered the walls to the crown molding that lined the ceilings. Gold, silver, and bronze leaf also ringed the windows, while chandeliers made of precious gemstones dripped down like rainbow icicles clinging to the ceilings.

I had known that Andvari was a wealthy kingdom, much wealthier than Bellona, and even Morta, but something sparkled and flashed in every hallway and around every corner. The sheer, dazzling, luxe opulence was overwhelming, and I felt like a drab little girl walking through some rich queen's life-size jewelry box and gaping at all the beautiful facets.

Finally, we reached the end of a long hallway and stopped in front of a set of enormous double doors that stretched from the floor all the way up to the ceiling. The Ripley royal crest—a snarling gargoyle face—was carved into the stone and stretched across both doors. This crest was studded with sapphires and diamonds bigger than my fists, indicating that we had arrived at the throne room.

Captain Rhea looked at me. "Your friends, servants, and guards will enter through another entrance and will be seated on the second-floor balcony with the lesser nobles. You will walk straight down the length of the room to where King Heinrich is waiting on the dais at the far end. Do you understand?"

I bristled at her cold commands, but I swallowed my annoyance. Now was not the time to remind everyone that I was a queen—not when I was surrounded by so many hostile guards. Besides, the captain's order was the same thing I had done at Seven Spire during the court session and a common practice during visits by foreign royals, so there was little reason to object to it.

But I heard the underlying threat in Rhea's voice. Any deviation from her orders could result in some very unpleasant consequences for me.

Rhea gave me another hard warning stare. "Good. Let's proceed."

She gestured at my friends. Serilda, Cho, Paloma, and Xenia all gave me encouraging nods, then followed Rhea through another door in the wall a short distance away. That left me standing alone in the corridor with Sullivan, with the Andvarian guards flanking us.

Under the guards' sharp, watchful, suspicious stares, Sullivan finally closed the distance between us.

"My father respects strength above all else," he murmured in a low voice. "And Dominic will follow my father's lead. So just be yourself, highness, and everything should be fine."

He gave me a small, crooked grin that made my heart squeeze tight with longing and other things I couldn't afford to think about right now.

"Thank you for the advice," I whispered.

His grin dropped away, and he shook his head. "Don't thank me until it's over."

I ached to thread my fingers through his, to feel the warm, reassuring strength of his hand pressing into mine. The urge was so strong that I had to curl my own hand into a fist to keep from reaching for him. Instead, I limited myself to a single, polite nod. Sullivan stared at me a moment longer, his blue gaze burning into mine, then turned and disappeared through the same door the others had gone through.

Now I was truly alone, except of course for my escort of royal guards. I glanced from one Andvarian face to the next, but they all glared back at me, the same as before. Tough crowd.

I stood in the hallway, staring at the closed doors, for the better part of ten minutes. The guards shifted on their feet and whispered among themselves, but I stood perfectly still and quiet. Maybe I should have been angry, but the delay didn't bother me. I had spent the last fifteen years at Seven Spire waiting for some boring tea, recital, or other event to begin. Besides, the lag gave me a few extra minutes to convince myself that I could somehow win the king's favor and earn his trust, along with a new treaty—or at least try to convince myself that I could do it.

I might not think that I deserved to be queen, or that I had the skills, strength, or magic to truly be a Winter queen, but it was my duty to do what was best for Bellona. Performing well in Heinrich's court would be an important step forward, not just for my kingdom but for me personally. It would be a sign that perhaps my pretender status could slowly morph into one of true confidence and power. That was my hope, anyway.

The opening strains of the Blair royal march sounded, although the thick doors muffled the loud, cheery music. The march played and played, but the doors still didn't open. While I waited, I touched my sword on my belt, then my dagger beside it, and finally the silver bracelet on my wrist. Perhaps it was silly, but feeling the tearstone shards and their distinctive crown crests under my fingertips soothed me.

Over the past several months, I had done so many things that had once seemed utterly impossible. I had survived a massacre, won a black-ring gladiator match, and triumphed in a royal challenge to the death. What was one angry, grieving king and a court full of hostile nobles compared to all that?

The Blair royal march ended. In the distance, a faint *creak* sounded, slowly growing louder and louder, as the double doors were drawn back, revealing the throne room beyond.

I fixed my face into a benign, pleasant mask, then strode forward for my most important performance as queen so far.

Showtime.

I stepped through the open doors, my gaze flicking left and right, taking in everything around me.

In many ways, the Glitnir throne room was like the one at Seven Spire. An enormous, cavernous space with columns here and there, a second-floor balcony that wrapped around three sides of the area, and a throne perched on a raised dais.

But that's where the similarities ended.

A wide black carpet led from the doors all the way to the dais at the opposite end of the room. The Ripley gargoyle crest done in glittering silver thread marched down the center of the carpet, repeating itself over and over again, while black banners bearing the same silver-thread crest hung from many of the columns.

But those weren't the only gargoyles in the throne room.

The creatures' faces were carved, embossed, or emblazoned on practically everything, from the floor to the walls to the columns. Most of the gargoyles were made of silver, with flashing jewels for eyes, and the bright, winking facets made it seem as though the creatures were glaring at me, the treacherous Bellonan in their midst.

I glanced up, half expecting to see real gargoyles circling overhead, ready to swoop down and tear me to pieces, but the ceiling only featured chandeliers made of jet, along with alternating patterns of white and gray diamonds. It took me a few seconds to peer past the dazzling gems and realize that the chandeliers were also shaped like enormous gargoyle faces, all of which seemed to be glaring down at me. I grimaced and dropped my gaze.

I had always thought that the Seven Spire throne room was grand, but I was once again reminded just how much wealthier Andvari was than my own kingdom. And the wealth wasn't limited to the furnishings. It was also on full display on the people.

Nobles lined both sides of the carpet, all of them dressed in fine silks and velvets and practically dripping with gold and gems. The stench of beauty glamours and other soft, subtle magics clung to their jewelry, and I had to twitch my nose to hold back a sneeze. Still more finely dressed nobles were seated on the second-floor balcony.

Guards clutching silver spears were spaced along both sides of the carpet. I wondered who the guards were supposed to protect—me or the nobles. Hard to say, since the nobles were giving me the same murderous stares as the guards.

I kept my shoulders up and my head held high as I walked along, trying to seem regal, confident, and queenly. My gaze focused on the people on the raised dais at the opposite end of the room. I'd seen paintings of the royal family, so I knew who they were.

King Heinrich Aldric Magnus Ripley was sitting front and center on a large throne made of polished jet. White and gray diamonds were embedded in the top of the chair, fitting together to form the gargoyle crest.

Heinrich looked to be in his fifties and had the same dark brown hair, strong jaw, and piercing blue eyes as Sullivan. The king was wearing a black tunic, along with leggings and boots, and a short, formal gray jacket covered with medals and ribbons stretched across his shoulders. He was a handsome man, although his face seemed pale, and wide streaks of gray glinted in his hair. A silver crown set with pieces of jet, along with white and gray diamonds, rested on his head. It was easily three times the size of my own crown.

I drew in a breath, tasting the air. Despite the distance between us, I could still easily pick out the king's scent—cold vanilla mixed with a hint of caustic magic. Not surprising, since Heinrich was a magier, just like Sullivan.

My gaze shifted to the man standing beside Heinrich. He was in his mid-thirties, a few years older than Sullivan, and he too had his father's dark brown hair, strong jaw, and blue eyes. Crown Prince Dominic was also wearing a gray jacket, along with a sword and a dagger, and he too smelled of vanilla and magic. Another magier, just like Heinrich and Sullivan.

To my surprise, a woman was standing to the right of the king, although she was much farther back on the dais. She had to be in her fifties, the same as Heinrich, although her beautiful bone structure and lovely tan skin made her look much younger. Her black hair was piled into a high bun, and her dark green eyes were the same color as her gown. A gold, heart-shaped locket dangled from a chain around her neck. I had never seen a portrait of her, but I still knew who she was: Dahlia Sullivan, the king's mistress.

A fourth and final person was standing on the dais next to Dominic. The girl was about thirteen, with blue eyes and dark brown hair that was pulled back into a pretty braid. Crown Princess Gemma, Dominic's daughter and the girl I had helped save during the Seven Spire massacre. She had grown up so much since the last time I'd seen her on that horrible day, and she looked far more mature than I remembered. Taller, stronger, and more confident too.

Unlike everyone else, Gemma was smiling, and she kept bouncing up and down on her toes, as though she could barely contain her excitement. The quick movements made her dark blue skirt swish back and forth.

The smile on my face grew far easier to hold and much more genuine the longer I stared at Gemma. I winked at her, and she beamed back at me.

One of the noblewomen sidled forward, stepping up to the carpet a few feet away from the bottom of the dais. She looked to be about my age and was one of the most beautiful women I had ever seen. Her auburn hair hung in loose waves that cascaded past her shoulders, while smoky shadow accentuated her bright jade-green eyes. Her flawless skin was a lovely topaz, and her lips formed a perfect red heart in her face.

She wore a stunning gown made of green silk trimmed with gold thread shaped like vines and flowers, and square emeralds gleamed in the gold choker that ringed her neck. Even among all the other finery, her clothes and jewels were outstanding, and I could tell that she was among the wealthiest nobles. Her choker alone would have easily bought a small island in the Blue Glass Sea. She kept glancing around, as if she was searching for someone.

I walked past the woman. I was almost to the bottom of the dais when a man stepped out of the crowd and stopped at the edge of the carpet, even beyond where the guards were stationed. Several people frowned, wondering what he was doing, but he only had eyes for me, and I for him.

He was an older man, in his late sixties, with ebony skin, hazel eyes, and wavy black hair peppered with a generous amount of gray. He was wearing a dark gray tunic, and a black cloak was draped over his shoulders. His features were as familiar to me as my own, and even more precious, since I'd thought him lost to me forever.

"Alvis," I whispered.

I had expected the former Seven Spire jeweler to be here, but that knowledge didn't lessen the impact of finally seeing him again. My heart lurched, my breath caught in my throat, and my feet stopped. I stood there, frozen in the middle of the carpet, staring at him.

Alvis stared back at me with his usual stern, inscrutable expression. Then his eyes crinkled, his face softened, and he opened his arms.

Somehow, I managed to choke down the sob rising in my throat. Suddenly, I wasn't thinking about proper protocols or the guards with their spears. My feet moved of their own accord, and I ran toward him.

Gasps rang out, and several guards stepped forward and lowered their spears, but I kept going. Let them attack me. Let them stab me. Nothing mattered but getting to Alvis.

I threw myself forward, wrapping him up in a tight, bone-crushing hug. I drew in a breath, and his scent—that sharp, metallic tang of magic that was uniquely his—filled my lungs. That's when I knew that it was truly him and that I wasn't just imagining this as I had so many times before.

Alvis hugged me back just as tightly. More shocked gasps and sharp whispers rang out, as the nobles gossiped about our impromptu reunion, but I didn't care. I'd lost Isobel, and I'd thought that Alvis was gone too, so I was going to cherish this moment for as long as possible, no matter the consequences. Let the nobles think me weak, let the king deem me an overwrought fool. I didn't care about any of that—not one damn bit.

"All right, all right. That's enough," Alvis grumbled in a low voice that only I could hear. "Winter queens aren't supposed to be so openly emotional. Especially not in a place as dangerous as this."

I hugged him again, still not caring how emotional I was being, then dropped my arms and stepped back. "I need to ask you about being a Winter queen," I murmured. "I need to ask you about a great many things."

I discreetly reached over and tapped the silver bracelet on my wrist—the one he had made. His gaze focused on the bracelet, then flicked to the sword and the dagger belted to my waist.

A shadow darkened Alvis's face. "I know. But right now, you have a king to greet."

He bowed to me, then stepped back. I turned and faced the king again. Then I drew in a breath and strode forward until I was standing in the center of the carpet at the bottom of the dais.

A couple of guards shifted on their feet, as though they were afraid that I was going to charge up the steps and try to murder their king, but Dominic waved his hand, and the guards held their positions. Interesting that he would signal the guards instead of the king. The crown prince must have more power and influence than I'd realized.

King Heinrich stared at me for several long seconds. Finally, he tipped his head the smallest bit, and I dropped into the perfect Bellonan curtsy, as protocol dictated. I held the curtsy far longer than necessary, silently apologizing for Vasilia's cruel, wicked actions. Then I rose to my feet and looked up at the king again.

Heinrich studied me from head to toe, taking in everything from my modest tunic to my tearstone weapons to my black boots. Eventually, his gaze locked onto the thin crown on my head. A frown creased his face, as if he wasn't quite sure what to make of me, although his features quickly melted into a more neutral expression. Not friendly, but not hostile either. The best I could expect, given the circumstances.

"Queen Everleigh, welcome to Glitnir," Heinrich said in a loud, booming voice.

"Thank you for hosting me, King Heinrich. You and your people honor me with your hospitality."

Several nobles let out loud, derisive snorts.

"Perhaps we should show her the same hospitality that her cousin showed Frederich," a low, angry voice muttered.

I looked to my right. To my surprise, it wasn't one of the nobles who had spoken—it was Captain Rhea.

I hadn't seen her enter, but she was now standing at the bottom of the dais, close to Dominic.

She realized that I'd heard her, that everyone had heard her, but instead of ducking her head in embarrassment, she lifted her chin and shot me a venomous glare. She obviously held a grudge for what had happened to the Andvarians. I'd expected that, but she seemed to be taking their deaths very personally.

I stared at Rhea, letting her know that I wasn't intimidated by the hate burning in her eyes, then faced the king again. I didn't say anything, and neither did he. The seconds ticked by, and the tension grew and grew.

I glanced up at the second-floor balcony. Serilda, Cho, Xenia, and Paloma were clustered together, along with the rest of the

Bellonan entourage, all of them surrounded by Andvarian guards. Sullivan was standing by himself in the corner, once again not a part of either group.

For the first time, I realized just how precarious my position was. My friends couldn't help me, given the distance between us, and I was completely exposed and vulnerable in front of the dais. With one word, one flick of his finger, King Heinrich could order his guards to surge forward and punch their spears through my heart.

I opened my mouth to break the silence and try to ease the tension when the scent of sour, sweaty eagerness filled my nose. Not an unusual scent, given all the schemes that were probably hatched in the palace on a daily basis, but the aroma was far stronger than it should have been.

So I drew in another breath, and a second scent joined that first one—hot, jalapeño rage. The sharp, fiery scent cut through all the others, indicating a deep well of emotion that belonged to a single person. And just like at Seven Spire, I knew exactly what it meant.

Someone here wanted me dead.

drew in another breath, tasting the air again, but the scents remained the same—sour, sweaty eagerness and hot, jalapeño rage. The longer I concentrated on the aromas, the more I realized that the strongest one was the rage.

My gaze cut left and right, wondering who bore me such ill will. But there were simply too many people for me to pick out exactly who the scent belonged to, unless I went around and started sniffing people like a bloodhound. Now that would really give the Andvarians something to gossip about.

Captain Rhea glared at me again, then looked up at the king. "I still don't know why you let her come here." She spat out the words. "You should have let me kill her the moment she stepped off the train. Not let her waltz into the throne room like nothing happened to your son. Like my father and the others weren't murdered."

My stomach clenched. Her father had been slaughtered at Seven Spire? No wonder she hated me.

"Your father was a dear friend and a great ambassador for

our people," Heinrich said. "I have not forgotten what happened to him."

I grimaced. He was talking about Lord Hans. So that's who Rhea's father was. It made sense that the ambassador's daughter would hold such a high position at Glitnir.

"But your insults and theatrics won't do the dead any good." Heinrich leaned forward and speared her with a cold gaze. "*I* am the king, and *I* make the decisions. Not you, Rhea. You would be wise to remember that."

She flushed at the sharp, stinging rebuke, but that didn't solve my problem. I had to do something to show everyone that I wasn't afraid of Heinrich or Rhea or the guards. Otherwise, Maeven wouldn't be the only one trying to kill me, and my mission would be doomed before it ever really started.

"Perhaps there is a way we can settle this unpleasantness," I said. "Once and for all."

"And what would you suggest?" Dominic spoke up, his blue gaze locking with mine. "Tell me, Queen Everleigh, what could possibly make my brother's murder and the attempted murder of my daughter any less *unpleasant*?"

His voice was cold and authoritative as he mocked me with my own words. He might be nicknamed *Prince Charming,* but he certainly wasn't being that to me. As much as I wanted to snap back at him, I focused on the king again. Heinrich was the one who was important right now, not Dominic.

"I came here to formally, publicly apologize for Vasilia's actions, which lead to the deaths of your son, Prince Frederich, and your ambassador, Lord Hans, as well as the rest of the Andvarian entourage."

Heinrich stared at me with an unreadable expression, then waved his hand, telling me to continue. How gracious of him.

"But Vasilia's actions were not *my* actions," I said in an even louder, stronger voice. "I had no part in the massacre, and I never wanted to see any harm come to the Andvarians."

I turned and looked around, focusing on first one noble, then another one. "But while you were all here, safe in Andvari, *I* was at the massacre. I was fighting for my life, and I know the horrors of that day far better than any of you."

At my harsh, accusing words, some of the nobles actually winced.

"You weren't the only people who lost loved ones. Nobles, guards, servants. They were all senselessly slaughtered. My queen, my cousins, my family died that day, including a woman named Isobel, who was like a second mother to me."

I glanced over at Alvis. Tears gleamed in his eyes, and a muscle ticked in his jaw. He too was thinking about Isobel.

I looked back over the crowd again. "But what did any of you do about the massacre? Nothing—absolutely nothing. *I* was the one who avenged your prince, and your ambassador, and all the other people—Andvarian and Bellonan alike—who were murdered. *I* was the one who challenged Vasilia, and *I* was the one who shoved my sword through her black, treacherous heart. So perhaps you should all think about *that,* instead of condemning me for a crime I didn't commit."

Cho had been teaching me how to project my voice, and my words boomed out like thunder. But they quickly faded to nothingness, and that tense silence descended over the room again.

"We know of your heroics during the massacre," Heinrich said. "Gemma has told me how you, Lady Xenia, and Sir Alvis helped get her to safety. The fact that you saved my granddaughter is the only reason you're still breathing."

His voice was even colder than before, and his face was as hard as the throne he was sitting on. But then his eyes narrowed, and the scent of his sharp, orange interest drifted down to me.

After a few seconds, the barest hint of a smile curved his lips, and satisfaction glimmered in his blue eyes, as though I'd passed some sort of test I didn't even know he was giving me. I'd seen that same look on Queen Cordelia's face many times, whenever she had outmaneuvered a noble before the other person had even realized that they'd fallen into her trap.

A sinking feeling filled my stomach. Heinrich hadn't let me come to Glitnir just to apologize. No, the king wanted something from me, and I could almost see the calculations going on in his mind as he thought about the best way to get it.

Rhea stepped forward again, her hands clenched into tight fists. "You can spout pretty words all you want," she snapped. "The fact remains that you're alive and Prince Frederich is dead. That my father is *dead*."

Her voice almost broke on that last word, and the scent of her ashy heartbreak punched me in the gut. She was angry, but she was also grieving. Both were emotions I knew all too well. And I realized how cruel and thoughtless my words had been. At least I had gotten the chance to avenge Isobel and everyone else—a chance that Rhea would never have.

Unless I gave it to her.

And I realized exactly how I could show Heinrich, Dominic, and everyone else that I was strong, that Bellona was still strong. Words weren't going to help this situation, but I knew something that would, something that almost always did.

At the very least, everyone would enjoy the show.

"You're right," I said. "I can't change what happened or the fact that your loved ones are dead. But we can still settle our differences—the Bellonan way."

Rhea regarded me with open suspicion. "And how is that?"

"With a black-ring match." I spread my arms out wide. "Right here, right now."

Shocked gasps rippled through the crowd, and everyone

started whispering. No one had expected me to do something so bold. No, they had expected me to bow and scrape and apologize until I was blue in the face. Maybe I should have. But that wouldn't win me anyone's respect, much less their cooperation. Besides, Sullivan had said that his father valued strength, and nothing showed how powerful you were more than winning a fight to the death.

"You're the captain of the royal guard," I said. "Surely, you've been to a gladiator bout or two. And I'm assuming you know how to fight. Or are those pretty weapons just for decoration?"

Rhea sucked in a breath as though I'd just slapped her across the face. She glared at me a second longer, then faced the throne.

"My king," she said through clenched teeth. "With your permission, I would like to take Queen Everleigh up on her generous offer to separate her head from the rest of her body."

Heinrich looked at Rhea, then back at me. More cold calculation filled his eyes, although he kept his face blank, as though it didn't matter to him who won.

"Very well," he said. "The Bellonans have always loved their barbaric gladiator tradition. So if it's a fight you want, Queen Everleigh, then a fight you shall have."

Heinrich called for a brief recess to let Rhea and me prepare for our impromptu battle.

I moved off to one side of the dais, and the nobles there scattered like rats, leaving me standing alone. None of the Andvarians wanted anything to do with me. No surprise there.

What *was* surprising was that Dominic stepped down from the dais, drew Rhea aside, and started talking to her. At first, I thought that he was speaking to her as any prince would to a captain about to go into battle—until he gently touched her arm.

Princes definitely didn't do *that* to their captains, and his lemony worry tickled my nose. Dominic was far more concerned about her than he should have been.

Rhea winced, as though his touch pained her, but she still leaned into it and stared up at the crown prince as if he was the most beautiful thing she had ever seen. I drew in another breath, and the soft, sweet aroma of her rosy love drifted over to me.

The captain of the royal guards in love with the crown prince? Now *that* was interesting.

I wasn't the only one who noticed their little tête-à-tête. Heinrich watched them a moment, then started speaking to Dahlia, who stepped up beside him.

Gemma drifted over to the corner of the dais that was the closest to me. She chewed on her lip and gave me a worried look, then gestured at Alvis, who went over to her. The two of them started whispering to each other.

Calandre and the rest of the Bellonan servants and guards remained upstairs, but Serilda, Cho, Xenia, and Paloma came down from the balcony and gathered around me. Sullivan also left the balcony.

"What do you think you're doing?" Xenia stabbed her cane against the floor in obvious displeasure. "Picking a fight with the Andvarians is *not* the best way to start this trip."

"Especially with the captain of the royal guard." Paloma eyed the other woman. "Rhea looks like she knows how to fight."

"That's because she does know how to fight," Cho said. "Something that Serilda spent a fair amount of time teaching her how to do."

My head snapped around to her. "*You* taught Rhea? Like you taught me?"

"Not exactly." Serilda shifted on her feet. "Rhea was already an excellent fighter. I just helped her improve her techniques the last time the Black Swan troupe toured through Glanzen."

"So you made her even deadlier than she already was. Terrific," I muttered. "Just terrific."

Rhea looked over and gave me a smug smile, as if she knew exactly what Serilda was telling me.

Cho laid his hand on my shoulder. "You're just as good as she is. You can beat her."

"Don't worry, Evie," Paloma chimed in, dropping her hand to her mace. "If she kills you, then I will be more than happy to avenge you. We might not be at the Black Swan anymore, but we'll always be gladiators."

Somehow, I held back a groan. My dying would be bad enough, but Paloma trying to kill Rhea afterward would only make things that much worse. I opened my mouth to tell my friend that under no circumstances was she to try to avenge me, but Paloma gave me a hot glare, as did the ogre on her neck, and I bit back my words.

I glanced around, expecting Sullivan to walk over to us, to me, but I didn't see him. Xenia realized that I was searching for him and discreetly pointed her finger to the right. I looked in that direction.

Sullivan was on the throne room floor, heading toward the dais, as though he was going to talk to his father. But someone stepped in front of him—the beautiful, auburn-haired woman I'd noticed earlier.

The woman smiled at Sullivan, and I could see the interest in her face as easily as I could the massive gargoyles carved into the columns. Sullivan gave her a curt nod in return. My heart clenched tight.

"Who's that talking to Sully?" I asked.

Cho cleared his throat before answering. "That's Helene Blume. She's from an old, prestigious noble family. Lots of money, lots of land, lots of power and influence at court."

Xenia studied the other woman, as did the ogre on her neck, and both of their faces scrunched up in thought, as if they were trying to remember something. Then Xenia's face relaxed, as did the one of her inner ogre. "Helene Blume. Oh, yes. Prince Frederich's fiancée."

I blinked in surprise. "What?"

"She was Prince Frederich's fiancée. The two of them were supposed to have been married . . . well, now. Sometime in the early autumn." Xenia paused. "At least until Heinrich broke off their engagement and offered Frederich up to Cordelia and Vasilia instead."

"How awful for her," I said.

Xenia shrugged. "You know how these things work. A match is only a match until someone better comes along."

"I wouldn't worry about Helene," Cho chimed in. "She always seems to land on her feet."

Serilda jabbed her elbow into his side, like he'd said something he shouldn't have.

"What do you mean?" I asked.

The two of them exchanged a glance. Then Cho gave me a bright smile, although the dragon on his neck grimaced.

"Oh, nothing really. Just that she's a noble with a lot of money, power, and opportunities." He hesitated. "If you really want to know more about Helene, then you should talk to Lucas. After all, he's . . . familiar with everyone here. Right, Serilda?"

Cho's words made perfect sense, but Serilda glowered at him as if he'd once again said something he shouldn't have. The two of them obviously weren't revealing everything they knew about Helene. What was so special about the other woman?

"Helene doesn't matter right now," Serilda said. "You need to focus on beating Rhea."

Before I could question them any more, Xenia started *tap-tap-tap*ping her silver cane on the floor, as though she was using the motion to further jog her memory.

"Heinrich breaking off Frederich's engagement to Helene

caused quite the scandal," Xenia said. "Her father, Marcus Blume, was absolutely furious, and he was pressuring Heinrich to marry Dominic to Helene to smooth things over. At least, until Marcus was killed in a riding accident several months ago. But rumor has it that Helene still might end up with Dominic. His wife died more than two years ago, and there's been a lot of pressure from the nobles for him to pick a new wife, especially now that Frederich is dead."

I glanced over at the crown prince, who was still talking to Rhea. With his dark brown hair, blue eyes, and tall, muscled figure, Dominic was quite handsome, and more than one noblewoman shot him an admiring glance, although he seemed oblivious to their looks. No doubt the women at court constantly vied for his attention. Sure, Gemma would one day be queen, but marrying the crown prince and being his official consort would be the next closest thing.

Dominic touched Rhea's arm again, then strode back up onto the dais. She watched him go with a sad, longing expression. I wondered what she thought of the rumors that Dominic might marry Helene.

Rhea must have sensed my gaze because she turned in my direction. She realized that I had witnessed her yearning after Dominic, and her face hardened. She didn't like anyone seeing her desire for him. Couldn't blame her for that. Crown princes didn't marry captains of the guard, no matter how skilled and pretty they were.

The captain marched over to the center of the black carpet, clearly wanting to get on with the business of killing me. Couldn't blame her for that either.

Paloma opened her mouth, but I stabbed my finger at her.

"Do *not* ask me if I'm ready for this," I muttered.

She grinned, as did the ogre on her neck. Apparently, they thought our little inside joke was hilarious.

I looked over at Sullivan. He was still standing next to Helene, although he was staring at me. He flashed me a brief, encouraging smile, but worry quickly filled his face. I wondered if it was for Rhea or for me. Or maybe it was for both of us. Either way, I forced myself to smile back at him, then walked over to the captain.

Rhea drew her sword from its scabbard and held it out by the blade, as per the Andvarian tradition of letting her enemy—me—see exactly what kind of weapons and magic they were up against.

Several pieces of jet were embedded in the silver hilt, along with three large, round rubies. Jet deflected magic, while rubies increased someone's strength. I drew in a breath, tasting the air. Those rubies were filled to the brim with magic, which would make the captain much, much stronger than me. A sharp tang of magic also emanated off Rhea herself, indicating that she was most likely a mutt with enhanced strength.

Terrific. Just terrific. But all I could do now was see this through to the end—and hope that I didn't die.

So I drew my own sword and held it out to her by the blade. Her topaz gaze locked onto the midnight-blue shards embedded in the hilt. "Those little pieces of tearstone might have let you outlast Vasilia and her lightning, but they won't protect you from me."

She grabbed her sword by the hilt and started twirling it around in her hand. I did the same with my own weapon, mirroring her move for move.

"If you know so much about how I killed Vasilia, then you should know that I don't need protecting, especially not from you."

"We'll see about that," Rhea hissed.

The nobles fell silent and tiptoed forward, forming a semicircle around us. Heinrich was still sitting on his throne, with

Dominic standing to one side of him, and Dahlia to the other. Gemma remained on the edge of the dais, with Alvis standing at the bottom of the steps.

In many ways, this was just like the black-ring match I had fought at the Black Swan arena and my more recent bout with Libby at Seven Spire. I wondered if the nobles here would bet on the outcome like the people had in the arena. Probably not. They seemed much too stuffy for that. We Bellonans might be barbarians, but at least we were honest in our greed, avarice, and bloodlust. I much preferred that to the Andvarians with their scheming eyes, sly smiles, and silent judgments.

Rhea started circling me and swinging her sword. Not attacking me, not yet, but getting a feel for how I moved, reacted, and held my own sword. All the while, she studied me, likely debating the best and quickest way to kill me.

I did the same thing, drawing in breath after breath and tasting all the scents in the air. She was definitely a mutt with impressive strength, given the stench of magic that burned my nose. She didn't need those pretty rubies in her sword to kill me. They were probably just for show and to keep people from realizing how truly powerful she was, which meant that she was smart as well as strong.

But perhaps the most curious thing was that Rhea's scent didn't contain the sour, sweaty eagerness and hot, jalapeño rage that I'd sensed earlier. She hated me, to be sure, but she wasn't the one who so vehemently wanted me dead, which troubled me far more than if she had been screaming curses and vowing to kill me.

A secret enemy was always much more dangerous than one right in front of you.

Finally, Rhea grew tired of circling me. With a shout, she lifted her sword, lunged forward, and attacked.

The music and moves that Serilda had spent so much time drilling into me filled my mind, and I snapped my sword up. Our two weapons banged together, throwing off a few red-hot sparks that dropped to the black carpet and quickly winked out.

Rhea bore down with her sword, using her superior strength to try to wrest my weapon out of my hand. I grimaced, as though I was already having trouble with her power, and started to fall to one knee.

Rhea pressed her advantage, just like I'd expected, and I quickly pivoted, spun to the side, and surged back up onto my feet all in one smooth motion. She wasn't expecting me to spin away, and she stumbled forward, almost doing a face-plant onto the floor.

"I told you before," I called out. "I don't need protecting."

Rhea whipped around, let out an angry snarl, and charged at me again.

Back and forth we fought in our semicircle of space, hacking and slashing at each other with our swords. Serilda was right. Rhea was an excellent fighter who matched me move for move. I didn't know how good the captain had been before Serilda's training, but now she was almost as good as Serilda herself.

Every blow that Rhea landed threatened to knock my own weapon out of my hand. My tearstone blade and the shards in the hilt absorbed some of the hard, bruising impacts, along with her strength magic, but not nearly enough of it.

Up to me to do the rest.

Rhea's biggest advantage was her strength, and she relied on it to win battles, even more so than she did the rubies in her sword. She wouldn't know what to do if I took her magic away. She would hesitate, and then I would have the advantage, at least for a moment. All I had to do was get close enough to touch her.

All I needed was one brief brush of my skin against hers, and I could snuff out her power with my immunity.

But try as I might, I couldn't force Rhea to lower her sword or break through her defenses long enough to lunge forward and actually *touch* her. I didn't want to give away the secret of my immunity, but I also didn't want to die. So I kept listening to that phantom music playing in my mind, biding my time and waiting for an opening. I didn't want to think about what I was going to do if I didn't get one.

The fight dragged on another minute, then two, then three. Rhea couldn't get a clear advantage over me, but I couldn't get one over her either. Finally, after a particularly furious exchange, she retreated, trying to get her breath back.

"Winded already?" I asked in a loud, mocking voice. "Looks like I work harder at being queen than you do at being captain."

I wanted to make her angry enough to do something reckless, and I definitely succeeded. Murderous rage glinted in Rhea's eyes, and she lifted her sword and charged at me again.

And this time, she didn't stop.

She lashed out with blow after hard, heavy blow, and it was all I could do to keep her from knocking my sword away. Still, I managed to block her strikes.

Until I tripped.

I wasn't quite sure what happened. I was moving forward for another attack when a sudden, sharp tang filled my nose, as if someone was using magic. An instant later, my boot snagged on the black carpet, even though it was lying perfectly flat. I stumbled forward, although I managed to catch myself and only go down on one knee instead of hitting the floor face-first.

Rhea screamed in delight, lifted her sword high, and rushed in for the kill.

That phantom music roared in my mind, the frantic, pounding beat telling me to *move, move, move,* but I knew that

I wouldn't be able to get to my feet in time to avoid her deadly, whistling strike.

With my right hand, I snapped up my sword to block hers. Without even really thinking about what I was doing, I lifted my left hand, desperately wishing that I could push my immunity out of my body the same way a magier could their fire, ice, or lightning—

Rhea's sword crashed into mine, but the blow wasn't nearly as hard as I'd expected it to be, and her weapon didn't cut through my defenses and plunge into my chest like I'd anticipated. She frowned, wondering what I'd done to derail her strike. I was wondering that myself, but I recovered much more quickly than she did. I leaned back on my knee, then kicked out with my other foot, catching the captain in the side of her own knee.

She shrieked, her leg buckled, and she tumbled to the floor, landing on her hands and knees. Before she could recover, much less lift her sword again, I lunged forward and snapped my blade up against her throat.

Rhea froze, as did everyone else. Silence descended over the throne room, and the only sounds were our harsh, raspy breaths.

"Do you yield?" I asked in a soft voice.

Fury shimmered in the captain's eyes. She couldn't believe that I'd beaten her, but she wasn't ready to give up. Her hand tightened around her sword, and hot, peppery anger blasted off her.

I pressed my blade a little deeper into her neck, not breaking her skin but letting her know that I could easily cut her throat before she even lifted her weapon off the floor.

Rhea froze again. This time, surprise filled her face. She couldn't believe that I hadn't already killed her. Maybe I should have. It was certainly within my right, since Rhea had been trying to kill me. If nothing else, it would have proved that I was just as strong and vicious as Vasilia and that the Andvarians should think twice before fucking with me.

But there had already been more than enough bloodshed between our kingdoms, and I was tired of people dying just to prove a point. Even people like Rhea who hated me.

"Do you yield?" I repeated in a louder voice.

"I suppose you'll kill me if I don't," Rhea muttered.

"Well, I would prefer not to dirty up my tunic with your blood and ruin my thread master's hard work." I leaned forward, letting her see how cold my eyes were. "But that is entirely up to you."

We stayed frozen in place, both of us on our knees, with my sword still against her throat. Out of the corner of my eye, I noticed a couple of guards creeping up on me with their spears.

Paloma let out a low, angry growl, dropped her hand to her mace, and stepped forward, putting herself in between me and the guards. The two men stopped short. They didn't want to fight an ogre morph, not even here, in their own king's throne room.

I turned my attention back to Rhea. "I'll ask you one more time: *Do you yield?*"

For a moment, I thought that she was going to spit curses and that I was going to have to kill her anyway. But the tension slowly drained out of her body, and she loosened her grip on her sword, which was still on the floor.

"Yes, I yield," she muttered.

I stared at her a second longer, making sure that she wasn't trying to trick me, then dropped my sword from her throat and got to my feet. I leaned down and offered my hand to her, but she ignored it and scrambled to her feet on her own.

Her hand tightened around her sword, as if she was going to attack me again, but instead, she turned and looked up at her king.

Heinrich had a thoughtful expression on his face, and he seemed more intrigued than angry that his captain hadn't defeated me. Dominic and Gemma both looked relieved, while Dahlia's face was a blank, pleasant mask, as though nothing noteworthy had happened.

Rhea squared her shoulders, strode over, and dropped to a knee at the bottom of the dais. Then she laid her sword on the floor. "I'm sorry, my king," she said in a low, strained voice. "If you wish to strip me of my rank, I will surrender my sword and leave the palace immediately."

Heinrich stared at her, then looked at me and raised his eyebrows. I was surprised that he was asking my opinion, but I shrugged, telling him that I didn't care what he did. After a moment, he waved his hand.

"There's no need for that, Captain Rhea," he said. "You fought well, and you did your father and Andvari proud. You may resume your duties as normal."

"Thank you, Your Majesty," she said in a relieved voice.

Rhea grabbed her sword, rose to her feet, and faced me. Once again, her hand tightened around the weapon, as if she wanted to swing it at my head again. No doubt she did, but I was tired—tired from the long journey, tired of everyone staring at me, and especially tired of fighting on what was supposed to be a goodwill trip.

"I am not your enemy," I said.

She snorted, despite the fact that I had just spared her life. So I looked up at Heinrich.

"I want us to work together to fight the Mortan king. *He* is the one who is ultimately responsible for your son's death, he is the one who is trying to pit us against each other, and he is the one that we must battle—not each other."

My words echoed through the room, but the tense silence quickly swallowed them up. I kept staring at the king. After several long seconds, Heinrich tipped his head, ceding my point, but I wasn't finished.

"We can stand united and defeat the Mortans together, or we can stand separately and watch our people be slaughtered and our kingdoms fall. The choice is yours, King Heinrich. I hope you make the right one."

My message delivered, I sheathed my sword, turned around, and strode out of the throne room.

CHAPTER ELEVEN

The double doors at the far end of the room were still open, and I marched straight toward them.

I kept my hand on my sword, glancing around for trouble. I might have defeated Rhea, but no doubt I had angered the guards who served her, along with the nobles. I'd thought that defeating the captain would prove my strength and make things better, but now I was wondering if I'd just made the situation worse.

Then again, that seemed to be my specialty.

I was almost to the doors when the two guards posted there stepped forward and crossed their spears together, barring me from leaving. I stared at first one, then the other, giving them my best queenly glare, the one I'd seen Cordelia deliver a thousand times.

The guards swallowed, but they held their positions.

"Let her go." Heinrich's voice boomed out behind me.

The guards lowered their spears. I glared at them again, then strode forward. Angry shouts rose up behind me.

"Where is she going?"

"How dare she walk out of here!"

"No one disrespects our king like that!"

I grimaced. Oh, yes. I had definitely made things worse. Not to mention the fact that I hadn't figured out exactly who in the throne room wanted to kill me.

But even if I'd wanted to, I couldn't go back and apologize. Not without appearing weak, which was something I could ill afford in this hostile palace so far from home. So I kept walking, peering into the corridors and rooms that I passed.

I hadn't gone more than a hundred feet when footsteps sounded, and Paloma ran up beside me, along with some of the Bellonan guards. Xenia was with them too, although she was walking at her natural pace and stabbing her cane into the floor every few steps.

"What are you doing?" Paloma asked. "Where are you going?"

"I have no bloody idea," I growled, stopping in the middle of the hallway. "All these bejeweled corridors look the same."

She grinned, as did the ogre on her neck. Seeing their smiles eased some of my disgust and anger, and I gave her a sheepish shrug in return.

"I'll say this for you, Evie," Xenia said. "You certainly know how to make a dramatic exit."

She stepped up beside Paloma, and she too had an amused look on her face, as did her inner ogre.

Perhaps it was the fact they were standing together and both smiling, but for the first time, I noticed just how much Paloma and Xenia looked alike. Sure, Paloma's hair was blond, while Xenia's was coppery red, and Paloma was decades younger than the older woman, but they both had the same golden amber eyes and bronze skin, and the ogre faces on their necks were eerily similar.

For a moment, I wondered if I was just imagining the similarities, but the ogre on Paloma's neck was almost exactly the same as the one on Xenia's, right down to the way the creatures' eyes studied me and the locks of hair that curled around their faces. Strange. Very strange.

I shifted on my feet, trying to figure out what to do next. Paloma and Xenia stared at me, as did the guards, waiting for me to give them some order, to lead them onward.

But I didn't know what to say, much less what to do. I didn't want the trip to be over, but I didn't see how it could continue.

And perhaps the worst part was that I hadn't even gotten a chance to speak to Heinrich privately, to truly offer my condolences on his son's death and attempt to arrange a new peace treaty between Bellona and Andvari. This was my first diplomatic mission as queen, and so far, it was a miserable failure instead of the rousing success I had secretly hoped for, that I desperately needed to help with my own problems at Seven Spire.

More footsteps sounded, and Serilda and Cho appeared, with Sullivan trailing along behind them. The magier stopped a few feet away, once again keeping his distance.

"The king wishes to invite you to dine with the royal family this evening," Sullivan said in a stiff, formal voice.

I blinked in surprise. "He isn't sending Rhea and the guards to kick me out of the palace?"

He shrugged, which really wasn't an answer. "My father asked me to convey his sincerest wishes that you join him for dinner and that you accept his hospitality and stay at Glitnir as planned."

He drew in a breath like there was more he wanted to say, but he grimaced instead, clearly miserable at being put in this awkward position.

I forced myself to ignore Sullivan's feelings and think about his words. Even though I had beaten his captain, Heinrich still wanted me to stay at Glitnir. Why? Then I remembered the cold calculation in the king's eyes. I wanted a new treaty with Andvari, but Heinrich wanted something from me too—something important enough to overlook how I had defeated Rhea.

But what could that be? I had no idea, which worried me. I couldn't play the game if I didn't know the rules or especially the stakes. Still, I'd come all this way, and I wasn't leaving without doing everything possible to get what I wanted and do what was best for Bellona.

So instead of storming away again, I reined in my anger and worry. "Tell the king that I will be delighted to dine with him."

Sullivan nodded. "As you wish."

He stared at me, his blue gaze searching mine, and I once again got the impression that he wanted to tell me something. Instead, he turned and walked away, his long gray coat swirling around him.

Still, as I watched him head back into the throne room, I couldn't help but think that I'd just gotten myself into even more trouble by accepting the king's invitation.

Sullivan moved out of my line of sight, but someone else stepped out of the throne room to take his place—Rhea.

Despite the fact that she was still clearly pissed, the captain marched over to me, along with several Andvarian guards. Paloma's hand drifted down to her mace again, and Rhea gave her a flat stare before looking at me.

"If you will follow me, Queen Everleigh," Rhea said through gritted teeth, "I will show you to your chambers. Your servants and guards are also being taken to the appropriate quarters."

She whipped around on her heel and strode off. I glanced at

my friends, but they shrugged, and I had no real choice but to follow the captain. At least she knew where she was going.

Rhea led us through hallway after hallway, each one more ornate and lavishly furnished than the last. I wondered if she had picked this particular route to remind me yet again of Andvari's staggering wealth. Probably.

But the dazzling, bejeweled palace wasn't nearly as fascinating as the gargoyles that inhabited it.

As we moved from one corridor to the next, I realized that several oddly shaped shadows kept sliding along on the floor beside me. At first, I couldn't figure out what the shadows were or where they were coming from. Then we entered a hallway with a domed, glass ceiling, and I caught sight of the gargoyles hovering outside.

They were all shapes and sizes, and they all seemed to be glaring down at me with their bright, jewel-toned eyes, just like the creature had earlier during my ride through the city. I shivered and hurried on, not wanting to give the gargoyles any excuse to crash through the ceiling and attack me.

Eventually, we climbed a set of stairs that spiraled up into one of the palace's towers and stopped at some double doors at the end of a long hallway. Rhea produced a skeleton key from her pocket and snapped the lock open. She signaled a couple of guards, who took hold of the metal rings and opened the heavy doors.

The captain hadn't said a word during our entire march, and she strode into the room without breaking her angry silence. Once again, I had no choice but to follow her.

Like everything else at Glitnir, the chambers were pristine and spectacular. The left side of the room featured gray velvet settees and chairs arranged around a fireplace, while the right side boasted a writing desk, along with other smaller tables and chairs. An enormous four-poster bed covered with a gray duvet and mounds of black pillows dominated the back half of the room, along with an armoire, a nightstand, and a vanity table that was even larger than the one in the queen's chambers at Seven Spire.

A set of double doors off to the left opened up onto a large stone balcony, while a door off to the right led into a bathroom done in gray and black tile. A gray porcelain tub mounted on silver gargoyle heads took up most of the bathroom, along with a long counter, a sink, and a toilet, all trimmed with silver.

Jewels glittered and gleamed everywhere I looked, from the sapphire knobs on the writing desk drawers to the diamond handles on the armoire to the rubies embedded in the wooden frame that circled the vanity table mirror. The area was even more opulent than the hallways and certainly richer than anything at Seven Spire, including the queen's chambers. Why, those sapphire knobs alone were easily worth more than the crown on my head.

"Several guards will be posted outside, in case you need anything, Your Majesty." Rhea spat out the words. "You should rest and prepare for dinner."

Her meaning was clear—I was not to leave the chambers until Heinrich summoned me.

Rhea didn't wait for a response before she stormed out of the room. The Andvarian guards followed her, although several of them stayed behind in the hallway outside and eyed the Bellonan guards with clear hostility.

"All things considered, that went pretty well," I murmured. "At least she didn't try to take my head off with her sword again."

"Oh, yes," Xenia drawled. "What amazing diplomatic progress you've made."

A knock sounded on one of the open doors, and Calandre bustled inside, along with her sisters and several servants carrying my luggage. Under Calandre's watchful eyes, the servants quickly unpacked my things. I told the thread master about Heinrich's dinner invitation, and she promised to return to help me get ready. Calandre left the chambers, with her sisters and the servants trailing behind her. Two Bellonan guards stepped forward and pulled the doors shut behind them.

Now that we were alone, Serilda, Cho, Xenia, and Paloma relaxed in chairs in front of the fireplace, but I started pacing from one side of the room to the other and back again, staring at the closed doors every time I passed them.

"Will Calandre and the rest of the servants and guards be safe out there?" I asked in a worried voice.

"Safe enough," Serilda said. "Our people will be given their own rooms next to the other servants and guards. There might be some skirmishes between our people and the Andvarians, but Heinrich will honor his offer of hospitality. Rhea will follow his orders, and she'll tell her people to do the same. Heinrich won't harm you or anyone in the Bellonan entourage while we're at Glitnir."

"But that doesn't mean someone else won't take matters into their own hands," Cho pointed out. "Everyone is still quite angry about Frederich's murder. I'll tell the servants and guards to be careful, and we will all do the same."

Serilda, Paloma, and Xenia nodded.

"I thought that when I killed Vasilia that I had killed her cruelty too. But that's not the case. She's still fucking me over, even from beyond the grave." I sighed and looked at Xenia. "What can I do to convince Heinrich that I had nothing to do with the massacre?"

Xenia shrugged. "I don't think you can. At least, not until you show him what happened. Even then, he still might not believe you. All you can do is see how Heinrich acts at dinner. Then maybe you can tell whether he'll agree to a new treaty."

"And if he doesn't?"

She shrugged again. "Then we will pack up, return to Bellona, and think of another way to deal with the Mortans."

Not what I wanted to hear, but telling hard truths was Xenia's job as my advisor. Still, I kept pacing in frustration.

"Well, I'm concerned about something else," Serilda said. "I've spent a lot of time at Glitnir over the years, and I've never seen Heinrich like this before."

Cho nodded, agreeing with her. "Me neither."

"Like what?" I asked.

Serilda tapped her fingers on her chair arm. "I don't know, exactly. Heinrich isn't the same as I remember. He almost looks . . . ill." Her eyebrows drew together, and her blue gaze grew dark and distant, as if she was trying to use her magic to sort through all the possibilities that might explain her unease.

"His son was murdered, along with his ambassador and his countrymen," Paloma pointed out. "We're all a harsh reminder of that, especially Evie. That's enough to make anyone ill."

"Yes, it is," Xenia murmured. "Yes, it is."

Her low, strained voice made it sound like she was speaking from personal experience, as did the scent of ashy heartbreak that wafted off her. But how could that be? As far as I knew, Xenia didn't have any children. Then again, I hadn't realized she was a spy either, much less a cousin to the Ungerian queen. I wondered if I would ever get to see the real Xenia, whomever she might be.

She shook her head, as if she was pushing away the memories, as well as whatever pain they brought along with them. "Anyway, we need to be out and about in the palace, gathering information, not sitting here." Xenia got to her feet. "I'll report back when I know more, Evie."

Serilda also surged to her feet and shot Xenia a pointed look. "As will I."

Xenia and Serilda had some long, complicated history that I didn't understand, but everything was always a competition between them. Sometimes, I felt like a tiny gladiator figurine trapped in an arena diorama, relegated to standing around and watching while the two of them played a perpetual tug-of-war with me.

Xenia and Serilda both promised to report back when they'd learned more, then left. Cho went with them to make sure that Calandre and the other servants were being treated well.

Paloma also headed toward the open doors. I started to follow her into the hallway, but she held out her hand, stopping me.

"I'm going to check on the guards," she said. "You need to stay here."

"What? Why?"

"Because Captain Rhea tried to kill you less than an hour ago, and she told you to stay put until dinner—or else," Paloma said in her annoying, matter-of-fact tone. "You might have beaten Rhea, but it's better not to tempt fate by giving her another crack at you. Don't worry. I'll help Cho make sure that everyone is taken care of, and I'll tell our people not to start any stupid fights with the Andvarians."

I threw up my hands in frustration. "But I'm the bloody queen! That's *my* job. Not yours."

Paloma shrugged. "And it's *my* job as your personal guard to keep you safe. And you will be much safer staying in here than you will be roaming the hallways where an angry guard could shove his sword into your back or one of the nobles could cut your throat. I'll come get you when it's time for dinner. Until then, try to relax, Evie. You've already fought for your life once today. Isn't that enough?"

Before I could protest, she stepped outside and signaled the guards to shut the doors behind her. Not only that, but as soon as the doors swung shut, I heard a loud, telltale *click*.

"Oh, no, you didn't!"

I rattled one of the rings, but the doors had been locked from the outside, confirming my suspicion.

I stared at the closed doors in disbelief. My friends had actually locked me in my room like I was an unruly child they didn't have the patience to deal with. Frustration surged through me, although I resisted the urge to scream and beat my fists against the stone. That would have been pointless. Besides, I didn't know who might be standing on the other side of the door, and I didn't want them to hear my petulant fit.

Sighing, I plodded over to the vanity table and sat down. Calandre had once again done an excellent job securing my crown to my head, and it took me a few minutes to remove all the tiny pins from my hair, set them aside, and pluck the band off my head.

I rubbed my thumb over the crown-of-shards crest in the center of the silver, wondering how things had gone so wrong so quickly. The midnight-blue shards glittered at me like seven tiny, narrow eyes, silently accusing me of being the reason for all these problems. I sighed, knowing it was the truth.

Once again, I was tempted to hurl the crown onto the floor and then stomp on it for good measure. But that would have been as childish and pointless as pounding on the locked doors, so I set it down on the table instead.

I didn't have anything to do until Calandre and her sisters returned to help me get ready for dinner, so I prowled around, studying the furniture and checking to make sure that Rhea—or someone else—hadn't left me any nasty surprises.

A decanter of poisoned wine sitting with the other bottles on a table along the wall. A trip wire strung along the bathroom floor that would send a crossbow bolt flying out of the shadows. A coral viper tucked in my bed, waiting for me to slip under the sheets so it could strike. I checked for all those things and a dozen others, but I didn't find any poisons, trip wires, or traps.

I also searched for hidden compartments in the furniture and secret passageways in the walls, hoping that I could slip out of my chambers undetected, but I didn't find so much as the smallest cubbyhole in the writing desk or a hidden closet in the bathroom. Of course these chambers wouldn't have a secret passageway. Heinrich would want his guests—especially the royal ones—to stay put and not roam around unsupervised.

My search had taken all of thirty minutes, and there were still hours to go before dinner. Frustrated and desperate, I went over to the glass doors that led to the balcony, wondering if I could get out of my chambers that way. I expected them to be locked from the outside, but the knobs twisted easily. I drew back the doors and strode outside.

The doors opened up onto a large stone balcony that curved outward like a crown. Sadly, there were no steps, and I didn't see a way to actually get off the balcony, unless I wanted to strip the sheets off my bed and make a crude rope with them. Even then, I was on the third floor, and I doubted I had enough sheets to reach the ground. So I was stuck here.

The balcony might not have any steps, but it did feature two cushioned lounge chairs arranged around a table that boasted a frosted pitcher of blackberry lemonade and several glasses. Bite-size kiwi cakes, strawberry tarts, and chocolate mousse cups were laid out on a silver tray, while another one held grapes, crackers, and cheeses.

A small white card was also propped up on the table. *Welcome* was written on the card in thick black ink, while a large, fancy cursive *D* was embossed in gold foil in the top right corner. I traced my fingers over the foiled letter, wondering who I had to thank for this. Prince Dominic? Dahlia Sullivan? Someone else?

Whoever it was had done their homework, since the table

featured some of my favorite foods. I didn't know whether to be flattered or concerned. Both, most likely.

My stomach grumbled, reminding me that I hadn't eaten all day, so I poured a glass of lemonade and carefully sniffed it. I also reached out with my immunity, but I didn't sense any magic. The drink was clean, so I took a sip.

The cold lemonade burst onto my tongue, the perfect blend of sweet and tart from the blackberries, lemons, and sugar, along with a faint, refreshing hint of mint. I also downed several cakes, grapes, crackers, and cheeses. The food was excellent, and it was the perfect light, refreshing snack to tide me over until dinner. I would have to thank the mysterious *D* for their thoughtfulness—and ask exactly how they knew what I liked to eat and drink.

I poured myself another glass of lemonade, then wandered around the balcony, examining the exquisite stonework, as well as the colorful clay pots filled with herbs and flowers lined up on the railing, basking in the afternoon sun. I'd never been much for plants, so the only thing I recognized was the mint, since the same type of sprigs were floating in the lemonade pitcher.

Still, I frowned as I fingered the mint leaves. Something about the pots and plants made me uneasy, even though they were just innocent bits of clay and color. Maybe it was because the leaves reminded me of the wormroot that Vasilia had used during the royal massacre, or how my father, Jarl, had been murdered with the same foul plant. I shuddered, dropped my hand, and turned away from the pots.

I went over to the center of the balcony, which curved outward and formed the top of the crown shape. I hadn't noticed it before, but the balcony overlooked the famed Edelstein Gardens.

Autumn had already taken hold here in Andvari. Trees

resplendent with red, orange, and yellow leaves towered over flower beds bursting with blue, purple, and pink blooms, while paths lined with black, wrought-iron benches curled past the beautiful blossoms.

And like everything else at Glitnir, the gardens were much more impressive than the royal lawn at Seven Spire. The trees were taller, the flowers brighter, the paths wider. Not to mention all the other features. One area boasted ponds covered with water lilies, while the space next to it was filled with striped sand and sunbaked rocks. In another section, black netting was strung up like spiderwebs in the treetops to contain the butterflies flitting around below.

Even more precious jewels and metals were woven in with the greenery. Trees made of hammered gold, silver, and bronze gleamed here and there, while roses with emerald stems, onyx thorns, and ruby leaves were set into the ground next to the actual, living flowers. Round moonstones lined the paths, while bits of silver frosted the black benches. The mix of metals and trees, gems and flowers, soft petals and hard stones made the area even more stunning.

And then there was the gardens' centerpiece—an enormous evergreen hedge maze. I squinted into the sun, trying to see the pattern the paths formed. The top part curved up in two separate places, almost like horns. Two more empty spaces looked like giant eyes, and the space below it seemed to be full of jagged teeth . . .

I grimaced. The maze was shaped like a gargoyle face. Of course it was.

A large, round dome jutted up where the gargoyle's nose would be. It looked like a gazebo was standing there, in the center of the gardens, isolated from everything else. No doubt it was a marvel of architecture and crusted with metals and jewels, and seeing it was your reward for navigating through the complicated maze.

A path ran past my balcony, so I leaned against the railing and watched the people below. Servants mostly, carrying crates, platters, and more. A few guards wandered by as well, making sure that everything was proceeding as normal. But Glitnir seemed to run as smoothly as a Ryusaman clock, just like Seven Spire did, and I soon grew tired of my spying.

I was just about to go back inside and take a nap before dinner when Sullivan appeared on the path below.

He strode over to the hedge maze entrance, which was directly across from my balcony, then stopped and started pacing back and forth. He was still wearing his long gray coat, and the tails snapped around his legs as if the fabric were mirroring the obvious frustration on his face.

I started to call out and jokingly ask him to rescue me from my high, jewel-encrusted prison, but a woman stepped out from underneath my balcony and walked over to him.

Helene Blume.

The afternoon sun brought out the flawless perfection of her topaz skin, along with the warm strands of red in her glorious auburn hair. She looked even more beautiful now than she had in the throne room.

Helene watched Sullivan pace for a few seconds, then stepped in front of him. "I know you're still upset with me." Even her voice was beautiful: soft, light, and feminine, with a hint of the Andvarian accent. "And I know I said this earlier in the throne room, but I want to apologize again. For everything."

Sullivan let out a harsh, bitter laugh, moved around her, and resumed his pacing. But Helene was not to be denied, and once again she stepped in front of him, stopping him.

"I truly am sorry, Lucas," she murmured. "For everything. I never meant to hurt you. That was the last thing I wanted to do."

He stared down at her. "So you've said. But you broke off our engagement anyway."

His words knifed me in the chest like a dagger, and all the air left my lungs in a sickening rush. *Engaged?* The two of them had been *engaged?* When? For how long? And why hadn't they gotten married?

Then another realization hit me—this *had* to be what Serilda and Cho had been hiding when I'd asked them about Helene earlier. Why hadn't they mentioned that she'd been engaged to Sullivan? Instead, Serilda had wanted me to focus on the fight with Rhea, while Cho had suggested that I ask Sullivan about the other woman. Maybe my friends had thought that the information would have been less surprising coming from him. Well, I was getting it from him now, and it was still plenty shocking.

Helene sighed, and a weary expression filled her face, as though this was an argument they'd had many, many times before. "You know that was my father's doing. Not mine. I wanted to marry you."

Sullivan let out another harsh, bitter laugh. "Your father never liked me. But even more than that, he wanted you to marry a real prince, a *legitimate* prince, instead of a bastard pretender like me."

He started to turn away, but Helene grabbed his arm, holding him in place.

"I never cared about any of that," she said. "I cared about you. I loved *you*, Lucas. No one else."

He stared down at her, his face hard, but the charred scent of his ashy heartbreak swirled through the air, overpowering the trees and flowers. Sullivan had loved her too, and quite deeply, given the strong, sharp aroma.

Helene glanced around, as if making sure they were alone. The servants and guards had vanished back inside the palace, and it was just the two of them—along with me.

They hadn't noticed me lurking on the balcony above, and I certainly wasn't going to call out to them. Maybe it was petty, but I wanted to know more about their relationship—and especially how Sullivan felt about Helene now.

When she was satisfied that they were alone, Helene tilted her head to the side, making her hair fall prettily over her shoulder. Her red lips curved into a smile. "Do you remember how much fun we used to have sneaking out of the royal balls?"

Her light, teasing tone cut through some of the tension, and Sullivan's face softened.

"I would do my duty. I would smile and laugh and dance and flirt with all the suitors my father wanted me to charm," Helene said. "And then, as soon as I could, I would slip away and sneak out here."

"And I would follow you," Sullivan replied in a low, strained voice.

"Yes, you would." She stepped closer to him, reached out, and toyed with one of the silver buttons on his gray coat. "And then you would find me and kiss me."

He didn't respond, but his gaze dropped to her perfect, heart-shaped lips.

"And I would kiss you back," Helene murmured, moving even closer to him. "And then we would go deeper into the gardens and spend the rest of the night together."

Sullivan still didn't respond, but a muscle ticked in his jaw, and his eyes narrowed, as if he was silently remembering all those same things.

Helene gave him another soft, teasing smile. "And then there were those times when I didn't want to find a dark, secluded spot in the gardens. All the times when I couldn't wait to be with you." She slid her hand past his coat and trailed her fingers up and down his chest. "If memory serves, one of those times was right here, in this very spot. When we got engaged. That was one of my favorite nights with you."

Her silky, throaty words stabbed me in the gut like a sword. Lucas Sullivan was a handsome man, a powerful magier, and a bastard prince. Of course he'd had lovers. But it still hurt to listen to one of those lovers talk about the passion they'd shared. And not just any lover, but someone who'd had his heart as well.

Someone who might have it still, judging from the anguished look on Sullivan's face.

Helene cupped his jaw with her hand. "Do you remember that night, Lucas? Because I certainly do."

"Of course I remember." His voice was as hoarse as hers. "I remember everything about that night. The color of your dress, how you did your hair, how you felt against me, how happy I was when you agreed to marry me."

His words slammed into my chest like a gladiator's shield, each soft syllable pummeling my heart into smaller and smaller pieces. He swayed forward, as though he was going to lean down and kiss her, and I had to resist the childish urge to squeeze my eyes shut to keep from seeing that. Or worse, him leading her into the hedge maze as he'd apparently done so many times before.

But at the last second, right before his lips would have met hers, Sullivan shook his head, forcing Helene to drop her hand from his jaw. He stepped away from her.

"Oh, yes. I remember everything about that night." His face hardened. "I also remember the next morning, when you returned my ring and broke off our engagement."

Helene's lips pressed together into a tight line. "I've told you a dozen times. My father forced me to do that. He threatened to disinherit me, along with my younger sisters, if I didn't do what he wanted, if I didn't marry who he wanted. I didn't care about the money, but I couldn't let my family suffer because of me."

"Yes, I know how powerful your father was, and how petty and vindictive. Although I have to admit that I was surprised when I heard about your engagement to Frederich." More hurt rippled through Sullivan's voice, and the scent of his ashy heart-break filled the air again. "Although knowing your father's ambition, I shouldn't have been surprised at all."

For the first time, a bit of anger flickered in Helene's eyes. "You're blaming me for *that*? *You're* the one who ran off and joined a gladiator troupe. I had no idea when—or if—you were coming back. So, yes, Frederich took pity on me, and we started spending time together. Of course my father saw that as an opportunity to convince Heinrich that I should marry Frederich."

"Until my father decided to break your engagement and marry Frederich to Vasilia to secure a treaty with the Bellonans," Sullivan said. "That must have been a bitter pill for you and especially your father to swallow."

She shook her head. "My father was furious, of course, but I was relieved. Frederich was a dear friend, but I never wanted to marry him. There's only one prince at Glitnir that I have ever truly wanted."

Helene stared at him, making it clear he was that chosen prince. She stretched out her hand toward him again, but Sullivan shook his head and stepped even farther away from her.

"I have work to do."

She arched an eyebrow. "For the Bellonan queen? I saw you speaking with her outside the throne room. She seems quite fond of you."

His eyes narrowed. "Are you jealous?"

She shrugged. "Of course. She is a queen, after all."

I grimaced. If she only knew that I'd been locked in my room and was witnessing her trying to seduce the one man I couldn't have. I doubted she would be so jealous then.

"I don't care what kind of relationship you have with Queen Everleigh," Helene declared. "I don't care if you are just her advisor, or if you're cooing sweet nothings in her ear, or if you're fucking her every single night. None of that matters to me. It's just the business of being a noble."

"Maybe I don't like that kind of business," he growled.

She let out an amused laugh. "Like it or not, it's the business you were born into, and it's the one you'll be in until the day you die. Just like me. So we might as well make the best of it—together."

Helene stepped forward. Sullivan started to move away from her again, but she reached out and grabbed his gray coat, holding him in place.

She stared up at him, her face serious. "The only thing I care about is what kind of relationship you and I can have moving forward. I've never stopped loving you, Lucas. And now that my father is dead, *I* am the head of my family, and I can marry whomever I like. So think about that, and especially that night you remember fucking me so well while you're serving—and servicing—your new queen."

She stood on her tiptoes and pressed a soft kiss to his cheek, leaving a red, heart-shaped stain behind on his skin. Sullivan stood rock-still, although his hands were clenched into fists, as though he was trying to keep himself from yanking her into his arms.

More hurt flooded my heart, but I couldn't blame Sullivan for his reaction. He'd made no promises to me. Quite the opposite. And he had loved Helene, perhaps even loved her still.

Helene stepped back. She waited a moment, clearly hoping that Sullivan would reach for her. But when it became apparent that he wasn't going to, she headed back inside the palace.

Sullivan watched her go with a desperate, hungry look on his face that wounded me far more than Helene's words and innuendos had.

After several seconds, he let out a long, tense breath, scrubbed his hand through his hair, and strode away in the opposite direction. He stepped back inside the palace and disappeared from sight, but I remained frozen in place on the balcony, wishing that I had stayed inside my chambers. Wishing that I had never heard what had happened between Sullivan and Helene, especially how much he had loved her.

But I wasn't the only one who'd been watching them.

A glimmer of glass caught my eye, and I looked to my left. Another balcony curved out from the third floor about a hundred feet away from mine. A woman was standing there, sipping a drink.

Dahlia, Sullivan's mother.

Well, now I knew who the mysterious *D* was. Dahlia must have ordered the refreshments to be set up on my balcony. As the king's mistress, she could easily do that. I appreciated her small kindness, although I was mortified that she had caught me spying on her son and Helene.

But Dahlia seemed amused by the awkward situation, and she smiled and gave me a friendly wave before disappearing back inside her chambers. I wondered at her benign reaction, but I had no way to interpret what it meant. I would have to ask Serilda, Cho, and Xenia what they knew about Sullivan's mother.

Either way, my appetite had vanished, and I set my lemonade glass on the table with the remaining treats. I started to head back inside my chambers when a shadow fell over me. A second later, a loud *thump* sounded on the balcony behind me, along with the sharp, distinctive *scrape-scrape-scrape* of claws against stone.

My breath caught in my throat, but I dropped my hand to my sword and forced myself to turn around slowly and not to make any sudden movements.

A gargoyle stood on the balcony.

Paloma had been wrong. I wasn't safe in my chambers.

I'd already had my heart broken, and now I was in danger of being eaten alive.

CHAPTER TWELVE

The gargoyle was about the size of a large dog, although much thicker and more compact, and far more dangerous.

It was made of solid gray stone and had a rough, weathered texture, although its skin seemed strangely flexible. Two horns sprouted up from its forehead, while jagged teeth curved up and out of its mouth. The sharp, daggerlike points on its horns and teeth matched the ones on the black talons that protruded from its paws, and its long tail ended in a single, deadly arrow-shaped stone.

The gargoyle cocked its head to the side, studying me with bright, blazing sapphire eyes, and I realized it was the same creature that had been watching me from the city rooftops earlier. Was this Maeven's doing? Had she somehow enchanted the gargoyle and ordered it to kill me?

My hand tightened around my sword, and I reached for my immunity. I didn't know how much magic gargoyles had, but I wasn't going to be eaten alive without a fight.

The creature's eyes narrowed, and it let out a low, angry growl, as if it knew exactly what I was thinking—

A girl's face popped out from behind the gargoyle's right wing, and I had to hold back a surprised shriek.

"That's enough growling, Grimley. I think you're scaring her."

The girl moved around the gargoyle's wing and stepped out where I could see her. Dark brown hair, blue eyes, pretty features.

"Gemma?" I asked. "What are you doing here?"

She stared at me, blinking and blinking as though she couldn't believe that I was really here. Then she let out a long, ragged sigh, rushed over, and wrapped her arms around me.

Her tight, enthusiastic hug surprised me and knocked me back against the railing. Grimley narrowed his eyes and let out another low, warning growl, telling me what he wanted me to do. I quickly put my arms around Gemma and hugged her back.

"I'm so glad you're okay!" She hugged me again. "I was so worried about you!"

Tears filled my eyes, and this time, my hug was entirely unprompted and completely genuine. "I was worried about you too."

I'd thought she was dead, and Alvis and Xenia along with her, but there was no need to tell her that.

Gemma and I stood there for the better part of a minute, hugging each other. A shudder rippled through Gemma's body, as if she was remembering everything that had happened that awful day at Seven Spire. Yeah, me too.

She held on to me a moment longer, then dropped her arms and stepped back. "I wanted to meet you at the rail station, but my father and grandfather wouldn't allow it." She rolled her eyes. "Stupid protocol."

I grinned. Gemma seemed to have as little use for protocol as I did. "I understand."

"I did make you a pie, though. Cranberry-apple, just like the ones you made at Seven Spire. I was going to bring it to you"—she winced—"but Grimley ate it."

The gargoyle opened his mouth and let out a short, sharp growl that sounded suspiciously like a burp, as if confirming her words. I wondered if he'd eaten just the pie or if he'd gobbled down the tin with it. I eyed his razor-sharp teeth. Probably both.

"That's okay." I looked at the gargoyle, then over the balcony at the steep drop below. "So you . . . flew up here on the gargoyle?"

"Of course, silly. How else would I get up here?" Gemma rolled her eyes again, then went over and started rubbing Grimley's head right behind one of his triangular ears.

The gargoyle grumbled with pleasure, then flopped down, rolled over onto his back, and stuck his short, stubby legs up into the air so that Gemma could lean down and scratch his tummy like he was an oversize puppy. Made of stone. With razor-sharp horns. And talons. And teeth that could either rip into or completely crush just about anything to bits.

"Is Grimley your . . . pet?" I asked.

The gargoyle fixed his bright blue eyes on me again and let out another low, angry growl.

"Hush, Grimley," Gemma said, still rubbing his tummy like he wasn't seconds away from jumping to his feet and eating me. "She didn't mean that. Grimley doesn't like the word *pet*. He's my friend. All the palace gargoyles are my friends, but Grimley is my favorite, and I'm his favorite human. That's why he came with me from the Spire Mountains when we fled from Bellona after the massacre."

The gargoyle had followed her from the mountains all the way back to Glitnir? Gemma truly must have been his favorite human for him to travel such a great distance.

Xenia hadn't told me about the gargoyle. Then again, she hadn't said much of anything about her journey with Gemma and Alvis. But I was getting the impression that the three of them had had more adventures—and had been in much more danger—than I'd realized.

Grimley let out a happy little grumble, and Gemma grinned and scratched his tummy again. I'd heard of people having special connections to gargoyles, along with strixes and caladriuses, and I had seen some of those connections with the trainers who worked with the creatures at the Black Swan troupe. But even with the trainers, there was always the slight worry that the gargoyles and strixes would turn on them someday, since the creatures would always be wild animals at heart, no matter how much time they spent around humans.

However, I didn't get any sense of that from Gemma and Grimley. She was totally unafraid of the gargoyle, and he seemed completely devoted to her. Perhaps she had some magic that let her have a deeper bond with the creature, or perhaps it was part of her royal blood. Legends said that the Ripleys were the first ones to ever befriend gargoyles.

Either way, I didn't want to get on Grimley's bad side, so I walked over, crouched down, and slowly held out my hand. The gargoyle stuck out his nose and sniffed my fingers.

"Magic . . . killer," he rumbled in a low voice that reminded me of gravel crunching underfoot.

I blinked in surprise. "He can talk?"

Gemma laughed. "Of course he can talk. All gargoyles can talk. Strixes too. Just not everyone can hear them."

"But you can."

She nodded, then beamed at me. "And you can too. That makes you really lucky."

I didn't know about that, but I kept my hand where it was, since Grimley was still sniffing my fingers.

"Magic killer," he rumbled again, his nostrils quivering. "Magic master."

Then he looked up at me, wagged his tail, and licked my hand as though we were old friends. His rough stone tongue scraped across my skin like sandpaper, but not unpleasantly so.

I wondered at his words, though. Magic killer? Magic master? Was he talking about my immunity? Or something else?

I didn't know, but he seemed to be warming up to me, so I cautiously reached out and scratched the spot in the middle of his forehead, right between his horns.

Gemma beamed at me again. "See? He likes that. I knew the two of you would be friends, just like Grimley and I are."

She threw her arms around the gargoyle's neck and hugged him, while Grimley wagged his tail again. It was perhaps the strangest friendship I had ever seen, but I knew how important it was to have a friend you trusted completely, even if that friend was made of stone.

Gemma hugged Grimley's neck again, then drew back. By this point, we were both sitting on the floor with the gargoyle. Another shadow fell over me, and I looked up and realized that Grimley wasn't the only gargoyle here. Others were sailing through the air above the gardens, just like they had flown over the glass ceiling inside the palace earlier.

Gemma waved at them, and the creatures grumbled back to her.

"You really are friends with all the gargoyles," I said.

"Of course," she replied. "And some of the ones in the city too. But Grimley will always be my favorite. And he's their leader now, even though he was born in the mountains instead of here at the palace."

"Just like you'll be the leader of Andvari someday."

She shrugged. "I suppose. I just hope I can be as good a queen as you are. I've heard all about your adventures from Alvis."

I held back a derisive snort. Me? A good queen? Hardly. Gemma needed to pick another hero. But I didn't want to hurt her feelings, so I changed the subject.

"You and Alvis seem to be good friends."

She nodded. "He and Xenia helped me escape from Seven Spire. The three of us spent weeks together traveling back to Glanzen. I was so happy when Alvis decided to stay at Glitnir and open his jewelry workshop."

Alvis had a new workshop? A smile lifted my lips. It was good to know that some things would never change.

"I'm trying to get Alvis to make me his apprentice, just like you were, but he hasn't said yes—yet." She pouted a moment, but determination gleamed in her eyes. Alvis might not realize it yet, but he was fighting a losing battle with this girl. "And I'm so glad that Xenia came with you. I haven't seen her in person since she went to her castle in Unger, although I've talked to her quite a bit since then."

"You've talked to Xenia? How?"

She shrugged again. "Alvis has a Cardea mirror in his workshop. He talks to Xenia all the time. He also talks to that other woman who came with you, the one with the blond hair and the scar on her face." Gemma shivered. "She looks like a fierce warrior."

I thought of all the long hours, days, and weeks that Serilda had spent training me. "You have no idea."

"I don't understand why my father was so upset about you coming to Glitnir," Gemma said. "I told him how you saved me during the massacre, but for some reason, he didn't want you to come here. Neither did Rhea. I think that's one of the reasons why she was so nasty to you earlier."

I kept quiet, letting her talk and analyzing her words. So Prince Dominic hadn't wanted me to journey to Glitnir. Why not? Other than blaming me for Frederich's and Hans's deaths like Rhea and the nobles did. Then again, that was reason enough.

"I was so happy that Uncle Lucas came with you too," Gemma continued. "He never visits or stays long enough. Not since Helene broke his heart and he snuck off to join that gladiator troupe a couple of years ago. It was *quite* the scandal, him slipping out of the palace in the middle of the night without telling anyone. Grandpa Heinrich was angry, but Dahlia was downright furious. She's been trying to get him to come home ever since."

I remained quiet, still absorbing her words and all their implications. So everyone at Glitnir knew that Helene had broken off her engagement to Sullivan. I could understand why he had left. I wouldn't have wanted to stick around and be reminded of my lover humiliating me either. And with him being a bastard and her eventually getting engaged to Frederich, one of the legitimate princes . . . The humiliation would have been even harder to bear then, along with everyone's pity.

"But everything will be okay now that Uncle Lucas is here, and you too." Gemma gave me a sly, knowing look. "I was up on the tower roof with Grimley just now. I saw you watching him and Helene."

I grimaced. I'd been here only a few hours, but Gemma already knew how I felt about Sullivan. I wondered who else had noticed. Most likely far more people than I wanted. I would have to be careful about how I interacted with Sullivan, although it was probably already too late. No doubt the nobles were already gossiping about what might be going on between us and whether he was fucking me or not.

"But you shouldn't worry about Helene," Gemma added.

"Why not?" I muttered. "She seems smart and accomplished, not to mention wealthy and beautiful."

More beautiful than any other woman at court, and far more beautiful than me.

All my Blair cousins had been lovely, with vast fortunes and highly skilled paint and thread masters to make the most of their natural good looks. And of course Vasilia and Madelena, the two princesses, had been quite stunning. But Helene Blume was in a league by herself, with the kind of epic, storied beauty that made everyone else seem dull in comparison, as though she were a sparkling, flawless diamond and the rest of us were misshapen lumps of coal clumped around her.

"Oh, Helene is definitely smart and clever and beautiful."

"But?"

"But she broke his heart," Gemma said in a wise, serious voice. "Uncle Lucas will never forgive her for choosing her family and her father's money over him. Besides, I've seen the way he looks at you."

"And how is that?"

She shrugged again. "The way my father used to look at my mother, before she died. And the way he and Rhea look at each other now, when they think no one is watching."

I wondered what would happen to Dominic and Rhea's yearning for each other when he was forced to marry someone else.

"My father and Rhea really should know better." Gemma shook her head. "Someone is *always* watching at court."

"Does that bother you? Your father and Rhea?"

"Of course not. My mother is gone, but she would want my father to be happy." Her nose scrunched up. "Well, as happy as anyone can be at court. But my father won't get to be happy with Rhea. My grandfather wants him to marry someone else. I heard them arguing about it the other day." She sighed. "It's just more stupid protocol that will only end up breaking everyone's hearts."

Amusement filled me. "You're awfully young to know so much about protocol and broken hearts."

Instead of smiling at my teasing, Gemma turned her head so that she was staring east, and a distant, dreamy look filled her blue eyes. "I met a boy in the mountains when we were escaping from Bellona."

"And what's so bad about that?" I asked, still teasing her.

"A Mortan boy," she whispered, as if she didn't dare say the words too loudly. "He tried to kill me, and I tried to kill him."

Oh. My mouth formed the word, but no sound escaped my lips.

"I still dream about him," Gemma whispered in that same low, rapt voice. "Sometimes, I talk to him in my dreams, and he talks back to me."

I didn't know what to say to that either, but I didn't want to pry, so I just sat there, offering her my silent support. I knew all about how dreams and memories could haunt you.

But the most curious thing was the magic that fluttered around Gemma, as light and fragile as a butterfly's wing, as though she really was seeing that Mortan boy, wherever he was. The scent was both sharp and subtle at the same time, like the hardest stone mixed with the softest lilac. I'd never smelled magic like that before, but I had an idea of what it was—of what *she* was.

After a few more seconds of silent contemplation, the magic faded, and Gemma shook her head, as if forcibly banishing the boy from her thoughts.

"So tell me. Who else looks at each other the way that Dominic and Rhea do?" I asked in a light voice, trying to distract her.

She smiled, but her expression had a hard edge to it. "You want to know all the court gossip."

Despite her seemingly happy demeanor, Gemma was still a royal, still the crown princess, which meant that she was always in the thick of court intrigue. No doubt the Glitnir nobles were just as conniving and cutthroat as the ones at Seven Spire.

I shrugged. "Gossip is information, and information is always useful, especially in my situation. In case you haven't noticed, you and Grimley are the only people at Glitnir who like me."

I didn't mention the jalapeño rage I'd sensed in the throne room, or how I had suddenly, inexplicably tripped during my fight with Rhea, or my sneaking suspicion that someone here wanted me dead. Gemma had been at the Seven Spire massacre, so she knew the perils of being a royal, especially of being queen.

Someone *always* wanted to kill the queen.

Gemma nodded, then settled herself against Grimley's side, like he was an oversize pillow. I didn't see how that could possibly be comfortable, but it didn't seem to bother her. She patted the spot beside her, and I too settled myself against the gargoyle's side. It wasn't as bad as I'd expected, although it still felt like I was leaning up against solid stone, albeit stone that just happened to be surprisingly warm and flexible.

"Now," Gemma said, grinning. "Let me tell you about life in Glitnir."

The crown princess was quite the fount of knowledge. She might only be thirteen, but her observations were sharp and insightful, and I learned more from her than I had from Serilda, Cho, and Xenia in all our weeks of preparation.

We spent the afternoon together, sitting on the balcony, sipping lemonade, and feeding Grimley grapes, crackers, and cheeses. He also gobbled down the last of the kiwi cakes.

"What about Dahlia?" I asked. "How does she fit in here? What's her story?"

"Heinrich and Dahlia grew up together at court. He was the crown prince, and she worked in the kitchen, but they still fell madly in love. But my grandfather was promised to my grandmother Sophina, who came from a wealthy family, and he married her instead of Dahlia," Gemma said. "But Dahlia still loved my grandfather, so she stayed at the palace as his mistress. My grandmother eventually had my father and Uncle Frederich, while Dahlia had Uncle Lucas."

"And they were all one big happy family?"

She snorted. "Of course not. Everyone says that my grandmother despised Dahlia and that the feeling was mutual. But my grandmother died when Frederich was young, and Dahlia stepped in and helped raise him and Dominic."

"But the king never married her," I murmured.

"Nope. Apparently, he asked her to marry him several times after my grandmother died, but Dahlia always said no. But the two of them seem happy enough, so no one really says anything about her anymore. She's like a grandmother to me, and even my father treats her like she's part of our family."

Curiouser and curiouser. I wondered why Dahlia hadn't married the king after his first wife had died. After all, that would have greatly improved both her and Lucas's standing at court.

I opened my mouth to ask Gemma another question when a knock sounded on the main chamber doors.

"My queen? May I come in?" Calandre's voice drifted inside. "It's time to get ready for dinner."

As if I had any choice in the matter since I was the one who'd been locked in here. But I called out to her. "Just a minute!"

I got to my feet, as did Gemma and Grimley. I held out my arms, and Gemma hugged me again. She stepped back, and I leaned forward and patted Grimley's head. He wagged his tail, and the sudden, strong motion knocked the clay pots off the railing and sent them crashing down to the ground.

Gemma winced. "Don't worry. I'll clean those up before the servants find them. And I'll see you at the dinner."

She smiled at me again, then climbed up onto Grimley's back like he was a pony. The gargoyle flapped his stone wings and soared up into the air. Gemma waved at me, and then the two of them dove below the balcony, out of sight.

"My queen?" Calandre knocked again, and the distinctive sound of a key turning in a lock rang out.

I sighed, then left the balcony and headed inside to get ready for dinner.

Calandre, Camille, and Cerana spent the next hour fussing over me. I once again refused to wear a gown, but the thread master did make me don a fresh tunic. I also insisted on taking my sword and dagger. Calandre didn't like it, but she could hardly argue given my earlier fight with Rhea.

Instead, she sighed and reached for some more pins on the vanity table. "Well, let's at least make sure that your crown doesn't fall off and drop into the soup bowl."

She jabbed even more pins into my scalp, making me wince, but I couldn't argue with her either. I'd already attracted enough attention without doing something as stupid as losing my crown during dinner.

Calandre slid a few more pins into my hair, then pronounced me fit for royal company. She and her sisters left the chambers, and I followed them through the open doors.

Paloma was waiting in the hallway, along with several Bellonan and Andvarian guards. All the guards had their hands on their swords and were eyeing each other with barely restrained hostile intent. Apparently, my defeating Captain Rhea had created even more tension between the two groups. Terrific. Just terrific.

Under the tense, watchful gazes of the Andvarians, Paloma

and the Bellonan guards escorted me through the hallways. We passed by the open doors that led into the throne room. The lights had been turned down low in there, but I could still make out the royal crest—that snarling gargoyle face—gleaming in the white and gray diamonds embedded in the top of the jet throne. I just hoped that tonight's dinner went better than my first meeting with the king had.

Eventually, we wound up in front of another set of double doors that were also standing wide open. I drew in a breath, then let it out and strode forward.

The king's private dining hall was much smaller and simpler than I expected. Tables lined the walls, while a larger, longer table took up the center of the room. A few bits of silver gleamed in the gargoyle faces carved into the columns, and a diamond chandelier shaped like a large crown hung over the main table, but those were the only embellishments.

More than three dozen people were gathered inside, including Serilda, Cho, Xenia, and Sullivan, and it looked as though I was the last to arrive. Of course. I was the only one who'd been locked in her room all afternoon.

Heinrich was sitting at the head of the center table, and he nodded, acknowledging my presence. I did the same. I started to go over to the king, but Xenia stepped up beside me.

"We should make a lap around the room first," she murmured. "And try to smooth things over with the nobles. I already suggested it to Sullivan, and he agreed to tell his father. You and Heinrich can talk during dinner."

I sighed, but I dutifully followed her, smiling and exchanging inane chitchat with the Andvarian nobles. They were all polite enough, but lingering anger and mistrust filled their faces, and they all smelled of vinegary tension and sour-milk reluctance. They didn't like me any more than the guards did.

Captain Rhea was also here, stationed against the wall

behind the king's chair. Every once in a while, she shot me a nasty look, but she didn't approach me. That was probably best for both of us. But I wasn't angry with her. Not anymore. Not since I had realized that Rhea's father had died during the Seven Spire massacre and that she was in love with the crown prince.

My gaze flicked over to Sullivan, who was talking to Heinrich, Dominic, and Gemma. I could understand and sympathize with a love that could never be.

Eventually, my path led me over to Dahlia, who was sipping champagne and chatting with Helene. They were the last two people I wanted to see right now, but it would have been rude to ignore them, so I plastered a smile on my face.

"Lady Sullivan, Lady Blume." I tilted my head to them. "How lovely to see you both again."

"And you as well. And I daresay the circumstances tonight will be far better than they were earlier, eh?" Dahlia smiled, her eyes crinkling with what seemed like genuine warmth. "And please, call me Dahlia. Any friend of Lucas's is a friend of mine."

"Thank you. And please call me Everleigh. And thank you for the refreshments that were waiting in my chambers. That was very thoughtful."

Dahlia toasted me with her champagne glass.

I turned to Helene. "And, Lady Blume, please call me Everleigh as well."

"Thank you, and please call me Helene. *Lady Blume* reminds me too much of my mother." She crinkled her nose, which somehow made her look even lovelier. "It's an honor to meet you, Everleigh. Gemma has been regaling us with tales of your bravery for weeks."

"The princess is too kind," I murmured.

I glanced over at the table. Gemma winked at me, and I winked back at her. She was the only child here, but she seemed more than capable of holding her own. Then again, princesses tended to grow up faster than most. They had to in order to survive all the cruel games people wanted to play with them.

"Tell me, Everleigh, what are your plans during your visit?" Dahlia asked. "I would love to host you for breakfast in the morning."

I studied her, but her request seemed sincere. Besides, I could hardly say no, since she was the king's mistress and Sullivan's mother. "That would be lovely."

Dahlia smiled at me, then turned to Helene. "And of course you'll come too, my dear."

"Of course," Helene said. "I'm quite interested to hear your stories, Everleigh, especially about life in the Black Swan troupe. Is it true that you killed another gladiator in a black-ring match?"

Thankfully, a series of bells rang out, saving me from having to answer.

Everyone took their places. The nobles were positioned at the tables along the walls, with the royal family sitting at the center table. To my surprise, Sullivan was seated on one side of the king, with Dahlia on the other. Helene was next to Sullivan, with Rhea across from her. And finally Gemma and Dominic were seated next to me, since I was at the opposite end of the table from Heinrich.

Serilda, Cho, Paloma, and Xenia were relegated to one of the tables with Alvis and the nobles.

I drew in a breath, discreetly tasting the air, but I didn't smell the hot, jalapeño rage that I'd sensed in the throne room. It didn't seem as though the person who wanted me dead had been invited to dinner. Perhaps my secret enemy was only a minor noble, servant, or guard, someone who could be more easily dealt with than the rich, powerful, and important people here. Either way, I relaxed a bit.

More bells rang, and servants carrying bowls and platters streamed into the room. And so the dinner began.

The food was excellent. Cold and hot soups brimming with spices. Light, refreshing salads with crisp lettuces, crunchy vegetables, and creamy dressings. Platters of exotic cheeses paired with sweet fruits and crunchy nuts. Baskets of hard, crusty baguettes slathered with savory dill and other herb butters.

The main course was a red-pepper-crusted steak with garlic mashed potatoes and roasted butternut squash sprinkled with cinnamon and dripping with honey butter. For dessert, there were raspberry, blackberry, and kiwi sorbets served with thin, crispy vanilla shortbread cookies. It was one of the best meals I'd ever had, and I enjoyed every single bite. Especially since nothing was poisoned.

During the meal, the conversation stayed lighthearted and innocuous. Everyone was doing their best to pretend that the throne room fight hadn't happened, and I went along with them, asking questions about the food, the weather, and all the other usual chitchat.

Every once in a while, I would look at the other end of the table to find Heinrich studying me with narrowed eyes. Beside me, Dominic did the same thing, although he seemed far more nervous than contemplative like his father did. The two of them were definitely planning something.

Eventually, the dishes were cleared away, and the nobles said their goodbyes to the king and streamed out of the hall, leaving the people at the main table—Heinrich, Sullivan, Dahlia, Helene, Rhea, Dominic, Gemma, and me.

Serilda, Cho, Xenia, Paloma, and Alvis also stayed behind, although they took up positions along the wall next to the Bellonan and Andvarian guards.

"Now that we've enjoyed a fine meal, it's time we get down

to business," Heinrich pronounced, staring at me. "If that is agreeable with you, Everleigh."

"Of course, Heinrich. We have much to discuss."

"Yes, we do." A shadow passed over his face. "But first and foremost, I would like to know exactly what happened to my son. Alvis has told me, of course, and Gemma and Lady Xenia too, but I would still like to hear it from you."

My stomach clenched. I had expected him to ask me about the massacre, and I had come prepared. But he wouldn't like what I was about to show him. None of the Andvarians would.

"Perhaps this will answer some of your questions." I reached into my pants pocket and pulled out an opal that was roughly the size of my palm.

"A memory stone?" Heinrich asked.

"Yes. Queen Cordelia wanted to record the luncheon before … everything happened."

I leaned forward and laid the memory stone on the table where everyone could see it. Then I drew in a breath and tapped on the stone three times to activate its magic.

The opal started glowing with a pure white light, and the flecks of blue, red, green, and purple in the surface rose up, sparkling like stars suspended in midair before zooming over and attaching themselves to an open space on one of the walls. The flecks of color grew larger, brighter, and sharper before finally coalescing into a single, clear image—my face.

From there, the royal massacre played out as it had that day on the Seven Spire lawn, and everyone in the dining hall saw Vasilia stab Prince Frederich and then fry Lord Hans to a crisp with her lightning. Screams, shouts, blood, death. The memory stone showed every horrible, brutal, grisly detail of the massacre right up until my hand closed over the opal, shutting off its magic.

Once the stone had finished playing, I tapped on it three

more times to preserve the memories inside for future viewings. Then I slumped back in my chair, suddenly exhausted and sick to my stomach, as if the massacre had just happened instead of nine months ago. I felt this way every time I watched the images. No doubt the refreshed memories in my own mind would stalk me in my sleep tonight and make me wake up screaming as they had so many times before.

Dominic, Gemma, Helene, Dahlia. They all had similarly horrified expressions, while the twin scents of Heinrich's ashy heartbreak for his slain son and Rhea's salty grief for her murdered father stabbed me in the gut.

Dahlia gave the king a sympathetic look, reached over, and squeezed his hand. A brief, grateful smile flickered across Heinrich's face, although it quickly vanished, swallowed up by his grief.

Dahlia gestured at a servant holding a tray that featured a silver tea set. The servant placed the tray on the table and stepped back. Dahlia poured some hot, steaming tea into a cup, dropped a single sugar cube into it, and stirred the brew. Her motions were smooth, graceful, and unhurried, as though she had performed this ritual hundreds of times, and I got the sense she did this for the king every night at dinner. Once the sugar had dissolved, she handed the cup to Heinrich, who nodded his thanks and started sipping the tea.

I studied the older woman. She really did seem to love him. Amazing. Especially since he had married someone else. True, it had been Heinrich's duty as king, but it still must have hurt Dahlia terribly.

I didn't know that I could have watched while the man I loved wed another woman, much less had children with her— legitimate children with all the wealth, power, and privileges of the Ripley royal name and heritage. But it seemed as though Dahlia's love for Heinrich, and his for her, truly was stronger than the duties and obstacles that had strived to keep them apart. Good for them.

My gaze flicked to Sullivan. Even though he had seen the images of the massacre before, he was still as upset as Heinrich, Dominic, and Gemma about Frederich's murder. I hoped that he would look at me, so I could smile or nod or give him some other small sign telling him that I understood his pain.

But he didn't—he didn't so much as glance in my direction.

Helene leaned closer to Sullivan, then threaded her fingers through his, trying to comfort him the same way that Dahlia had Heinrich. Now was definitely not the time for jealousy, not with the screams of the dead still echoing in my ears, but I couldn't help but wish that I was the one holding his hand.

"Thank you for showing me that," Heinrich said, breaking the tense, heavy silence. "Seeing what happened to Frederich, Hans, and the others makes my decisions about a great many things much clearer and easier."

I waited for him to elaborate, but he didn't, so I spoke up. "As you can see, Cordelia had absolutely nothing to do with the massacre. Neither did I. It was entirely the work of Vasilia, along with Maeven and Nox, the two Mortans."

Heinrich nodded, agreeing with me, as did everyone else at the table. Even Rhea gave me a small, reluctant nod, and she seemed far less hostile.

A bit of confidence filled me. So far, this was going as well as I could have hoped. Perhaps I wasn't as bad at being queen as I thought.

"Bellona and Andvari need to align with each other, and with Unger too," I continued, trying to close the deal I'd come here to make. "Our three kingdoms need to stand united, or the Mortan king will invade our lands, slaughter our people, and conquer us all one by one."

Heinrich nodded again. "I've been thinking about such an

alliance ever since I learned the truth about Frederich's death. Your coming here and showing me what happened to my son has only made me more certain about the course of action we should take next."

"And what action would that be?"

The king stared at me, his blue eyes as cold and hard as chips of ice. I had seen that same expression on Sullivan's face more than once, especially when he was going to be particularly difficult or stubborn about something. Whatever he wanted from me, Heinrich had already made up his mind that he was going to get it—no matter what.

My confidence vanished, replaced by a growing sense of dread, and I was once again reminded that I had been queen for only a few months, while Heinrich had been ruling for decades.

"An action that best benefits Andvari," he replied. "After all, *we* are the ones who were targeted and slaughtered, so we are the ones who must appear strong now, especially since we are the ones who are the closest to Morta."

I wanted to point out that my family had been slaughtered right alongside his and that Bellona and Unger also shared borders with Morta, but I took a more diplomatic approach.

"What are you proposing?" I asked in a wary voice.

"A simple trade," Heinrich said. "I will sign your treaty and align Andvari with Bellona and Unger . . ."

"If?"

The king gave me a cold, thin smile and gestured at his son. "If you marry Dominic."

CHAPTER THIRTEEN

My heart clenched, my stomach dropped, and shock scorched through my body like a magier's lightning bolt.

Me? Marry Dominic?

Out of all the things Heinrich could have said, out of all the things he could have proposed, out of all the things he could have demanded, my marrying Dominic had never even crossed my mind.

Perhaps I should have expected it, given what had happened with Fullman and Diante back at Seven Spire. But all the Andvarians—Heinrich included—had been so hostile that I'd barely had any hope for a treaty, much less a larger, more permanent alliance. I had certainly never thought about marrying the king's son.

At least, not *this* son.

And I was painfully aware of that *other* son, of Sullivan, sitting beside his father, the same sick shock on his face that I felt in my own heart. Even more than that, I could smell the hot, peppery anger blasting off him in waves, already mixing with minty regret and dusty resignation.

Sullivan might have been surprised by his father's proposal, but he was already bracing himself for my answer, and he
actually thought that I was going to agree to his father's ridiculous demand. He actually thought that I would say yes without
putting up a fight. And perhaps most important, he actually believed that I would be cruel and heartless enough to marry his
brother.

An arrow of hurt slammed into my gut that Sullivan thought
so little of me, but my own cold rage quickly rose up to freeze
out the pain. Rage that Heinrich had sprung this trap on me in
front of a roomful of people. Rage that he was demanding this.
Rage that he was practically *ordering* me to do it, as though I
were one of his subjects, instead of the leader of my own kingdom. Apparently, the father thought even less of me than his
son did.

As much as I wanted to give in to my shock, hurt, and rage,
surge to my feet, and storm out of the dining hall, I forced myself
to stay seated and keep my face calm and blank. Because like it or
not, I was the queen of Bellona, and I had a duty to my kingdom,
to my people, to at least listen to what Heinrich had to say—no
matter how distasteful I might find it.

So I leaned back in my chair and steepled my hands together
in my lap, pressing my fingers into each other to stop them from
curling into fists. "And what would I get out of this marriage?" I
asked, careful to keep my voice steady and even.

Heinrich shrugged. "You would marry Dominic here, in
Glitnir, before the end of your visit. Then he would return to
Bellona with you."

I looked at Dominic, who met my gaze with a neutral one
of his own. His face was as calm and blank as mine was, but he
too smelled of minty regret and dusty resignation. He didn't
like his father's idea, but he would do his duty for the good of
his kingdom.

And then there was Rhea. Her lips were pinched together in a tight, thin line, and she stared down at the table instead of looking at me, Heinrich, or especially Dominic. She too would do her duty, even as the scent of ashy heartbreak rolled off her.

I don't understand why my father was so upset about you coming to Glitnir . . . He didn't want you to come here. Neither did Rhea. Gemma's voice whispered in my mind. *But my father won't get to be happy with Rhea. My grandfather wants him to marry someone else. I heard them arguing about it the other day.*

I thought she'd just been sharing some juicy gossip. I'd never expected that gossip to involve me or so many other people in this room—or for it to hurt us all so very much.

"So I would marry Dominic before the end of my visit, and he would return to Bellona with me." I repeated the king's words to give myself a few more seconds to think. "And where would Gemma live?"

Heinrich's gaze cut to his granddaughter. "Here at Glitnir. So as not to disrupt her studies."

Gemma's face paled, and she looked from her father to her grandfather and back again. After several seconds, when she realized that Heinrich was serious, she focused on Dominic. Gemma opened her mouth, probably to plead with her father not to go, or to at least take her with him to Bellona, but Dominic shook his head in a sharp, clear warning.

The princess slumped back in her chair and dropped her head, but not before I saw the gleam of tears in her eyes. She had already lost her mother, and she didn't want to be separated from her father too. My heart twisted. I knew how horrible it was to lose your parents, how small, helpless, and adrift it made you feel. I didn't want that for her.

I didn't want *any* of this.

"It's a fair proposal," Heinrich said. "This way, we both get what we want."

I couldn't fault his logic. A royal marriage *was* one of the best ways to bind two kingdoms together. Cordelia had tried to do it with Frederich and Vasilia, and now Heinrich wanted to do it with Dominic and me.

The king fell silent, and everyone turned their attention back to me, cataloguing and analyzing every slight rise and fall of my chest, every subtle shift of my body, and especially every faint expression that flickered across my face.

A hard truth punched me in the heart—that up until now, I had just been playing at being queen. Dealing with the nobles and their petty squabbles, weeding the turncoat guards out of Seven Spire, even surviving Maeven's assassination attempt. Those trials had all just been practice for this moment, when my thoughts, words, and actions would truly shape what happened to my kingdom and to my people, perhaps for generations to come.

The crown of shards on my head had never felt heavier.

Still, I remained silent, desperately trying to think, even as my gaze moved from one person to the next, studying their reactions just as they were all still studying mine.

Stern, confident Heinrich. Sad, resigned Dominic and Gemma. Resolute Rhea. Sympathetic Dahlia. Smug, smiling Helene. Of course she would be happy about this. I couldn't have a relationship with Sullivan if I was married to Dominic.

I looked past the table at my friends standing along the wall. Serilda, Cho, and Alvis all looked as shocked as I still felt, and Paloma had her hand on her mace, as though she was ready to grab it and beat down anyone who tried to stop me from leaving.

Xenia's lips were puckered in thought, as were those of the ogre on her neck. She wasn't surprised by the proposal, and she was probably already thinking about how my saying yes or no would affect everyone here, as well as in the kingdoms beyond.

And finally, there was Sullivan, who was still sitting right next to his father. I couldn't tell exactly what he was thinking or feeling, since he was staring at the wall instead of looking at me, but a muscle *tick-tick-tick*ed in his jaw like the second hand on a clock, and his hands clenched the arms of his chair, as if he needed something solid to hold on to in order to keep from unleashing the emotional volcano bubbling up inside him.

"I've heard about your problems with the Bellonan nobles," Heinrich continued. "How they have been . . . less than pleased with your leadership. Marrying Dominic would go a long way toward earning the support of your own people."

Yes, yes, it would. Fullman, Diante, and the other nobles might not have wanted me to come to Andvari, but even they would agree that my marrying the crown prince was a shrewd, advantageous move, especially given all the wealth and prosperity Dominic would bring to Bellona in the form of new trade agreements and the like. All that money would help soothe the nobles' anger that I hadn't married one of them and allay their doubts about their continued prosperity during my reign.

"Plus, we would present a fully united front to the Mortans," Heinrich added. "Not only now, but for future generations to come."

More shock scorched through me, but it was quickly drowned out by sick understanding. Heinrich was talking about whatever children I might have with Dominic.

I forced myself to study the crown prince. Dark brown hair. Blue eyes. Strong, muscled body. Dominic was a handsome man, and many women probably would have been thrilled to bed him, but the idea left me feeling cold and nauseated. He wasn't the one I wanted.

He would *never* be the one I wanted.

Dominic managed to smile at me, but he must have sensed my disgust because the expression quickly faded away.

I turned my attention back to Heinrich. "Your proposal certainly would benefit us both."

Like it or not, every word Heinrich had said was true. Marrying Dominic would solve several of my most immediate, pressing problems. It would appease the Bellonan nobles, help me secure the throne, and unite our kingdoms against the Mortans.

But I was a Bellonan, and I knew how to play the long game. So I could see how the marriage would benefit me now—and just how much *more* it would benefit Heinrich and Andvari in the long run.

Heinrich already had two heirs—Dominic and then Gemma. He would sacrifice Dominic to me and send his only living legitimate son to Bellona, but he would keep Gemma here at Glitnir and groom her to be queen of Andvari.

On the surface, it seemed like a simple trade—until you factored in whatever children Dominic and I might have. And those children, well, they could lead to other possibilities.

Very dark and deadly possibilities.

"Well?" Heinrich asked. "What do you say, Everleigh? Shall we unite our kingdoms in marriage?"

Despite all my misgivings, I still seriously, seriously considered it. Marrying Dominic might be distasteful, but so were lots of other things I'd done lately, and many more things I would do as queen.

For the first time since I'd taken the throne, I didn't look to my friends for guidance, support, or approval. *I* was the queen, and this was *my* decision.

I was also very careful *not* to look at Sullivan again. My feelings for him couldn't be a factor. Not in the slightest. This was about what was best for Bellona, not for my heart. For the first time, I got an inkling of what it really meant to be a Winter queen, and it wasn't about magic at all. No, it was about making the hardest choices under the most difficult circumstances to achieve the greatest good.

I breathed in and out, trying to slow my pounding heart and calm my frayed nerves. The nobles' floral perfumes and spicy colognes filled my nose, along with the lingering scents from dinner, but there was another, stronger aroma that surprised me. Sour, sweaty eagerness, mixed with a large dose of rotting desperation—and it was coming from the king.

I stared at Heinrich again, and I finally noticed how pale and strained his face was, despite his stern expression. His blue eyes seemed weak and watery as well, and Dahlia kept sneaking glances at him, a concerned frown on her own face.

In that moment, I made my decision.

"No."

Everyone stiffened, shocked by my cold, flat refusal, and that tense, heavy silence dropped over the room again.

"No," I repeated in a louder, stronger voice. "I will not marry Dominic."

Heinrich blinked a few times, as if he wasn't sure he'd heard me correctly. But then my words sank in, and an angry flush swept up his neck and flooded his pale cheeks. "Perhaps you should reconsider, Everleigh. After all, you've only been queen for a short while. Perhaps you need more time to think things through and truly appreciate my generous offer."

I let out a small, bitter laugh. "Oh, I've been queen long enough to recognize a scheme. Although I will say that yours is one of the most subtle and skillful that I've heard in a long, long time. Even the Seven Spire nobles would be impressed by it, and believe me, they are not easily dazzled."

Heinrich's eyes narrowed. "I don't know what you mean."

I stabbed my finger at him. "You know *exactly* what I mean. So does anyone with even half a brain. You keep Gemma here to be your queen, while my children inherit the Bellonan throne.

But they would also be *your* grandchildren, wouldn't they? And if something *unfortunate* were to happen to me, some tragic *accident,* well, I'm sure that Grandfather Heinrich would be more than happy to step in and raise my children. That, in essence, would give you not one but two kingdoms."

"That's not what I had in mind," he protested.

"Oh, I think it's *exactly* what you had in mind," I snapped back. "Vasilia killed Frederich, and you want revenge. How could you not? Bellona took your son away from you, and now you want to take Bellona away from the Blairs, away from *me*. I don't blame you for your desire for revenge. But it won't get you what you want, and it certainly won't help you protect Andvari from the Mortans."

More anger stained Heinrich's cheeks an even darker, uglier red. "If you don't agree to marry Dominic, then there will be no alliance between Andvari and Bellona. Not so much as the smallest trade agreement."

I shrugged. "Fine. If that's how you want to play this game."

Heinrich slammed his hand down onto the table hard enough to make the tea slosh out of his cup. "This is not a fucking game!"

I let out another laugh, this one louder, harsher, and tinged with even more bitterness. "It's all a fucking *game*. I've known that ever since I was a child. If you don't realize it, then you're not as smart as I thought you were."

"And you're not as clever as you think you are," Heinrich hissed. "Because this is how deals get done. Perhaps you should ask your advisors for their opinions before you so recklessly throw away my more-than-generous offer."

More cold rage surged through me, and this time, I didn't try to hide it. I planted my elbow on the table and leaned forward, staring him down. "I don't have to consult with my advisors. *I am the queen.* Face it, Heinrich. You need me far more than I need you, and your proposal reeks of desperation."

His blue eyes glittered with rage. "I am the king of *Andvari*, the wealthiest kingdom on this continent. I don't need help from *anyone*, especially not some lowly noble with no money and no magic who only sits on the throne because all her other stronger relatives are dead."

People gasped at his insults, and his words were as sharp as a sword plunging into my heart. Heinrich had just voiced all my doubts and insecurities, and all the things that the nobles, servants, and guards had been whispering behind my back for months now at Seven Spire. That sickening uncertainty filled me again, and I ducked my head, half expecting my crown to fall off and roll away in agreement.

But my crown didn't fall off—it didn't move at all. Even more surprising, it didn't feel nearly as heavy as before. In fact, for the first time since I'd put it on, it felt *right*.

Everything that Heinrich said was true. I was only queen by chance, by accident, but I *was* queen. It didn't matter how I had gotten here, only what I did while the crown was on my head. And that would *always* be protecting Bellona and her people—and fuck Heinrich and anyone else who was stupid enough to doubt me or tried to keep me from doing my duty as queen.

More of that cold rage filled me, along with strong, hard confidence. I lifted my head and squared my shoulders, sitting up tall. Then I smiled at Heinrich, but there was no warmth in my expression.

"You might have money, thanks to your gold and diamond mines, but your kingdom is small, which means that your population is small, which means that your army is small. And we all know that the Mortan army is *not* small."

Heinrich's lips pressed together, but he couldn't deny the truth of my words any more than I'd been able to deny his.

"Now, you could use some of your glorious wealth to buy legions of mercenaries to shore up your army, but mercenaries fight only until the money runs out. The Mortan king can throw his army at you for *years* and slowly chip away at your own ranks, along with any mercenaries, until he finally bankrupts you. Once that happens, the mercenaries will flee, and Andvari will be left utterly defenseless."

I wished that Captain Auster was here. He would have been so proud of me for finally putting my military history lessons to good use.

Heinrich kept glaring at me, and his hands curled into fists on top of the table, but I wasn't done with him. Not by a long shot.

"More important, *your* kingdom is the one that Morta will invade first, the one that they will swallow up first, to get all that wealth you're so proud of. And once the other rulers see that happen, I imagine that they will all be quite happy to align with me then."

I gestured at Xenia, who was still standing along the wall. "Lady Xenia is a cousin to the Ungerian queen. Tell me, Xenia: Do you think your cousin would be more amenable to aligning with Bellona than King Heinrich is?"

Xenia stepped forward and bobbed her head, playing her part perfectly. "Of course, Your Majesty. I've already spoken with the queen about an alliance, which she is quite eager to make."

I dropped my hand and leaned back in my seat. "An alliance that won't cost me anything, especially not my hand in marriage now and my throne, life, and kingdom later. So you see, Heinrich, you might have great wealth, but in the end, that's all you have. So why don't *you* consult with *your* advisors before you so recklessly throw away *my* more-than-generous offer."

My insults and demands delivered, I surged to my feet,

threw my dinner napkin onto the table, and stormed out of the dining hall.

I strode down the hallway, cold rage still coursing through my veins.

What a blind, stubborn, stupid fool Heinrich was. Why try to force me into a marriage that neither his son nor I wanted? Why not just align with me outright? Didn't he see that I was trying to do what was best for Andvari and Bellona? Didn't he realize that Morta was the true threat to us, along with our people?

But I supposed it didn't matter anymore. Once again, I had let my temper get the best of me, and I'd probably insulted Heinrich too badly for him to consider any proposal I might make now. Instead of being a good queen, a wise queen, and helping my kingdom, I'd just mucked things up even worse. I wasn't a mere pretender—I was an epic *failure*, plain and simple.

At times like this, I desperately missed life at the Black Swan. Things at the gladiator troupe had been black and white, more or less, with only a few shades of gray. Work, train, fight in the arena. Simple, clean, brutal.

Being queen was none of those things—except brutal—and there were so many damn shades of gray that I'd forgotten what black and white, wrong and right, even fucking looked like.

I was so angry that I didn't pay attention to where I was going, and I wound up in an enormous library. Floor-to-ceiling cases filled with books covered the walls and stretched up three floors to a round, domed ceiling made of black, white, and gray glass that formed a gargoyle face. A fire crackled merrily in the fireplace in the wall, driving back some of the drafty chill, while cushioned settees and chairs were scattered throughout the rest of the library, along with tables covered with books and maps.

I should have turned around and tried to find my way back to my chambers, but I was still too angry for that, so I marched over to the far wall, which was made of glass and overlooked the Edelstein Gardens.

I wasn't sure how long I stood there, glaring out into the dark, shadowy night, but eventually, footsteps sounded behind me. I drew in a breath, and a familiar scent filled my nose— vanilla mixed with spice. I sighed with relief. Sullivan was here.

I opened my mouth and turned around to call out a greeting, but the words died on my lips. Because Sullivan wasn't standing in the library—Dominic was.

"May I come in?" he called out in a low, cautious voice.

I shrugged. "It's your library."

He strode over to me, and together, we stared through the glass. Outside, several fluorestone streetlamps burned along the cobblestone paths, tinting the trees' metallic leaves a soft, shimmering gold. But I soon grew tired of admiring the view, and I studied Dominic out of the corner of my eye.

Dominic looked eerily like Sullivan, but he was taller and thinner than his younger brother, and his scent was more warm spice than cold vanilla. But the real difference was that he didn't bring a smile to my face or make my heart trip over itself the way that Sullivan always did. And he never, ever would.

"I'm sorry about my father," Dominic said. "I haven't seen him lose his temper like that in a long time. Not since the day he realized that Sullivan had left Glitnir."

His choice of topic surprised me, but I decided to play along.

"And why would your father care so much about that?" I asked. "Sullivan's not the crown prince; he's not the heir. It's not like *you* ran off and joined a gladiator troupe."

A faint smile curved Dominic's lips. "True. But as you saw at dinner, my father is used to getting his way, and he wanted Sullivan to marry into another noble Andvarian family. We all love Sullivan, and we all felt sorry for him when Helene called off their engagement. He should have stayed here. We could have helped him through his heartache."

And that was probably another reason why Sullivan had left. The proud magier wouldn't have wanted anyone to pity him, especially not his own brother.

"But perhaps things will finally work out for Sullivan and Helene, now that he's back home," Dominic continued. "It would be nice if someone around here finally got what they wanted."

He stared out into the gardens with a calm expression, but he couldn't quite disguise the bitterness that tinged his voice.

"And what do you want, Dominic?"

"To apologize for my father," he repeated. "And to explain. My father has not been . . . well. Frederich's death, and then fearing that Gemma was dead as well—it's all taken a great toll on him."

I thought of Heinrich's pale, strained face and weak, watery eyes. For the first time, I felt a bit of sympathy for the king. Losing his son had obviously broken his heart, and he was trying to deal with his grief and protect his people from the larger Mortan threat at the same time. No wonder he wasn't well.

"Frederich was the youngest," Dominic said. "He was always the lightest, the happiest one of us, always playing peacemaker between Sullivan and me, always laughing and joking. Frederich was my father's favorite because of that. He was *everyone's* favorite because of that, and we all miss him terribly. And then seeing exactly what happened with the memory stone, how Vasilia just . . . Well, I don't think it helped my father. Not really. It certainly didn't help me."

His eyes dimmed, his face darkened, and his shoulders slumped. The scent of ashy grief gusted off him, along with a strong tang of garlic guilt. I frowned. What did he have to feel guilty about?

"But maybe the worst thing is that part of me is glad that Frederich was the one who died," Dominic said in a low, rough voice. "Better him than Gemma. Better my brother than my daughter. When I thought that she was gone, when I thought that she was *dead* . . ."

His voice trailed off, and he couldn't finish his awful thought. He scrubbed his hand over his face, but the motion didn't hide the anguish in his features.

"My father lost his son, but I got to keep my daughter. And I'm *happy* about that—happier than you could possibly imagine." He grimaced. "Does that make me a horrible person?"

"No," I replied in a soft voice. "It just makes you human. I was happy that I survived the massacre, even though everyone else died. I'm still happy that I'm alive. And guilty. And confused. And wondering why I lived. Why me, instead of someone else?"

Dominic didn't respond. Neither one of us had an answer for that.

"It wasn't my intention to cause you, your father, or Rhea any more pain by showing you all the memory stone," I said. "I'm sorry for everything that has happened to you and your family. Truly, truly sorry."

On impulse, I reached out and laid my hand on his shoulder. Dominic seemed surprised by the gesture, and he turned toward me, his gaze locking with mine.

Dark brown hair. Blue eyes. Strong, handsome features. Once again, I was reminded how eerily similar he was to Sullivan, right down to the lightning magic that I sensed coursing through his body. In some ways, Dominic was even more handsome than his younger brother. His body was taller, his shoulders were broader, his nose was straighter.

But his nearness didn't make my heart stutter, my breath catch in my throat, or my body hum with desire. And perhaps most important of all, he didn't look at me with the same fierce intensity that Sullivan always did, like he wanted to hold me close and devour me at the same time.

"You have lovely eyes," Dominic said in a low, husky voice, studying my face. "I've always heard about the Blair eyes, the tearstone eyes. They really are gray-blue, just like people say. Although yours look bluer right now, as dark as the tearstone shards in your crown."

I grimaced at the reminder that I was still wearing the crown, although I supposed I should be grateful it hadn't fallen off when I'd stormed out of the dining hall.

"Do you tell all the women you meet in libraries how pretty their eyes are?" Perhaps it was the warm, romantic glow from the fireplace, or the fact that my fingertips were still resting on his shoulder, or his resemblance to his brother, but my own voice came out a bit huskier than I expected.

A teasing grin curved his lips. "Just the ones who refuse to marry me."

I barked out a laugh, and some of the tension between us eased. I dropped my hand from his shoulder, but Dominic kept staring at me, and I did the same thing to him. Emotional confessions aside, I was a queen, and he was a prince, and we were both trying to figure each other out—

More footsteps sounded, and I turned around, expecting to find Paloma with her mace in her hand. But once again, I was wrong. Paloma wasn't here.

Sullivan was.

He was next to the fireplace. His mouth was open, as though

he was going to call out to me, but his jaw clenched shut at the sight of me standing so close to Dominic in the dark, dreamy shadows. I knew what it looked like, what Sullivan thought it was. I could see the hurt shimmering in his eyes and smell his peppery anger all the way across the room.

"I came to find you, highness," he growled. "To apologize for how my father treated you, but I see that Dominic has already beaten me to it. He looks like he's doing an admirable job of consoling you. Then again, his nickname *is* Prince Charming."

"Sully, wait . . ."

He whipped around and stormed out of the library. I sighed. I didn't blame him for that, or for jumping to conclusions. But I got another sickening surprise as Sullivan marched into the hallway.

He hadn't come here alone.

Helene was standing outside the library, along with Rhea. Judging from their expressions, the two women had seen and heard everything.

Helene studied me for a moment. Then her lips creased into a sly smile, and she headed after Sullivan.

Rhea glanced at me, then focused on Dominic. A muscle ticked in her jaw, and she too whirled around and strode away, heading in the opposite direction from Sullivan and Helene.

Dominic and I stayed silent for a few seconds, listening to the sound of their footsteps fade away.

"I don't think that could have possibly gone any worse," I muttered.

"Of course it could have gone worse," Dominic said. "Sullivan could have blasted me with his lightning, or Rhea could have stabbed me with her sword. Or both."

I snorted. "I think we both know I'm the one Rhea wants to stab."

We looked at each other. Dominic's lips twitched, and he

chuckled. Yeah, me too. Better to laugh than cry, especially given this tragic comedy of errors and misunderstandings.

"You seem to care a great deal about Lucas," Dominic said after we'd both stopped laughing.

There was no point in denying it. "Is it that obvious?"

"Only to everyone," he teased.

I rolled my eyes. If he had been anyone else, I would have punched him in the arm, but I'd already screwed up enough things tonight without assaulting the crown prince. "I could say the same thing about you and Rhea."

He sighed. "Is it that obvious?"

"Only to everyone," I teased him back.

Dominic smiled a little at that, but he didn't laugh again. He couldn't, and neither could I.

"How long?" I asked.

"I don't know exactly. I was devastated when Merilde, my wife, died, two years ago. Rhea was Merilde's best friend, and we helped each other deal with her loss. Eventually, one day, I just . . . noticed Rhea in a way I never had before. What about you and Lucas?"

I shrugged. "I broke into his house and stole his jacket, along with one of his pillows. He found me sleeping in the corner the next morning. Needless to say, he was not pleased."

"I bet he wasn't. Lucas never liked anyone going into his room or taking his things without asking, not even his toys when we were children."

Dominic smiled again at those memories, but the warm expression quickly faded from his face. "But we can't think about Lucas or Rhea."

"No, we can't," I whispered. "No, we can't."

We stood there in silence for a moment before Dominic cleared his throat, changing the subject.

"You should think about my father's proposal."

I reared back in surprise. "About marrying you?"

He nodded. "You don't know me, but the two of us want the same thing—to protect our kingdoms from Morta. Together, I think we can do that."

I drew in a breath, tasting his scent, which was filled with lime truthfulness. He really did want to protect his people—and mine—from the Mortans, and he would do whatever was necessary to make it happen. I admired his determination and his willingness to do his duty, even if he was dooming us both in the process, along with Sullivan and Rhea.

A faint grin curved his lips. "Besides, you seem pleasant, and I can be quite charming, in case you haven't heard. I think we would get on together well enough."

"Oh, yes. I had heard that about you, but *charming* only goes so far when you're talking about marriage."

He grimaced, and his grin slowly faded away. "True enough. I should get back to the dining hall and check on my father and Gemma." He hesitated. "Just . . . think about what I said. Please, Everleigh?"

"I will." I paused. "And I suppose that I should retire to my chambers before I start any more fights tonight."

He grinned at my black humor. I smiled back at him, and together, we turned to leave.

We'd taken only a few steps when a blond woman hurried into the library. For a moment, I thought she was one of the palace guards. But her head was down, hiding her face, and she was moving much more quickly than usual. But the thing that really caught my eye was the fact that her sword was clutched in her hand rather than holstered on her belt.

Several more guards followed her into the library, cutting Dominic and me off from the exit. I drew in a breath. The guards all reeked of sour, nervous sweat, along with vinegary tension and sharp tangs of magic.

I'd smelled that combination of scents before—on the turn-coat guards roaming the halls of Seven Spire the day of the royal massacre.

"Guards?" Dominic called out in a confused voice. "Is something wrong?"

He started toward the blond woman, but I grabbed his arm, stopping him.

"Those aren't your guards," I said.

The woman lifted her head, and that's when I realized that she had one familiar feature—amethyst eyes. She grinned, then twirled her sword around in her hand and advanced on us. The men surrounding her drew their weapons and did the same.

They were Mortan assassins—and they were here to kill me.

CHAPTER FOURTEEN

ominic stood there, his eyes wide, frozen in place, as if he couldn't believe that he was being attacked in his own palace. I could have told him that this wasn't about him and that Maeven had sent these assassins to kill me, since she hadn't managed to do it at Seven Spire, but I didn't get the chance.

Led by the blond woman, the assassins advanced on us, a solid line of deadly intent. At first, I wondered why they didn't charge forward, but then I realized that they were trying to pin us up against the glass wall so they could more easily hack us to pieces.

I yanked Dominic back. That snapped the prince out of his surprise, and he raised his hand, dark blue lightning flashing to life on his fingertips.

I silently applauded myself for not letting Calandre talk me into wearing a gown and pulled my sword out of the scabbard on my belt.

"You take the ones on the left," I murmured. "I'll take the ones on the right. Don't let them pin you up against anything. Always keep moving. You stop moving, and you're dead."

Dominic nodded and reached for even more of his lightning. I lifted my sword higher and focused on the assassin closest to me, all the while listening to the opening strains of the phantom music that always played in my mind whenever I was in a fight.

Then, with one thought, everyone attacked.

Three assassins converged on me, yelling and swinging their swords. I dodged the first assassin, then the second one, but the third one was a mutt with speed magic, and I barely managed to avoid his hard, fast blow. He was definitely the most dangerous of the three men, so instead of moving away, I whirled around, stepped into his body, and grabbed hold of his wrist.

And then I blasted him with my immunity.

I might not have my gladiator shield strapped to my arm, but in a way, my immunity was better than any shield, and it immediately snuffed out his speed magic. It still felt strange to actively, forcibly call up my power instead of hiding it, but something about wielding my magic as a weapon also felt extremely, satisfyingly *right*.

The assassin must have had some enhanced strength as well, because the tip of his sword plunged to the ground, as if the weapon was suddenly far too heavy to wield. He struggled to lift the blade, not understanding why his magic had suddenly vanished.

I let go of his wrist, whirled around, and sliced my sword across his chest. The assassin's blood spattered all over me, but I welcomed the wet, stinging warmth on my body and the strong, coppery stench in my nose. Those two things told me that he was dying and I wasn't.

The assassin screamed and crumpled to the floor. I stepped over his twitching body and looked for the next enemy to fight.

The first assassin yelled and charged at me again. I ducked to the side just as his weapon came whistling down. He was closer than I'd realized, and his blade sliced cleanly through the edge of my tunic sleeve, exposing the silver bracelet on my right wrist.

I grimaced. Calandre was not going to like having her fancy embroidery ruined, but I imagined—hoped—that she would like it even less if I died, so once again, I lashed out with my sword, swiping it across the assassin's stomach. He too screamed and staggered back into one of the tables, bouncing off it and falling to his knees.

That assassin was also bleeding out, so I risked a quick glance over at Dominic.

The crown prince hurled a large ball of blue lightning at one of the assassins in front of him. The assassin tried to avoid the blast, but the lightning slammed into his shoulder, making him scream and fall to the ground. His sword dropped from his charred, blackened fingers, and his whole right arm was now a melting, bubbling husk of flesh.

The stench of singed hair and fried skin filled my nose, overpowering the blood. I'd heard that Dominic was a powerful magier, but I hadn't realized that he was almost as strong as Sullivan.

Dominic growled and tossed a ball of lightning at another assassin advancing on him. That assassin avoided the blast and swung his sword at Dominic, but the prince sidestepped the blow, pivoted to the side, and punched the other man in the face, making his head snap back. Then Dominic wrenched that man's sword out of his hand, flipped it around, and stabbed the blade into the assassin's chest. That man also fell to the ground screaming.

And that was all I saw before another assassin came at me.

This man had seen what I'd done to the other two, so he didn't recklessly charge forward. Instead, his eyes narrowed, and he studied every little thing about me, just like I was doing to him.

As we circled around each other, that phantom music started playing louder and faster in my mind. The assassin moved in to attack, and I let the swelling notes sweep me away. The music played and played, and my hands and feet moved in time to the beat as I perfectly performed the moves, the steps I needed to in order to stay alive and kill my enemy.

Left, right, twirl in for a strike . . . Left, right, avoid the counter-strike . . .

And on and on it went until the assassin lifted his sword a second too late, and I slid past his defenses and buried my weapon in his stomach. The man screamed, and I twisted the blade in deeper. He screamed again, and I yanked the sword out of his stomach and shoved him away. He joined the other two assassins I'd already killed on the floor.

My head snapped left and right, searching for more enemies to fight. And I found them—all gathered around Dominic.

Four assassins were left, along with the woman who'd led them in here, and they had cornered the prince in between the fireplace and the glass wall.

With one hand, Dominic brandished his stolen sword at them. In the other, he held a ball of lightning, ready to unleash it on whoever attacked him first. The assassins were so determined to kill the prince that they didn't notice that I was still alive.

And I suddenly realized that winning this battle wasn't the only thing I needed to do—I also needed to protect the prince. Because if I survived this assassination attempt and he didn't, then I doubted I would leave Glitnir alive, queen or not.

The nobles would say that Vasilia had killed Frederich and that I had come here and killed Dominic. The people would scream for blood—my blood—and no doubt Heinrich would be happy to give it to them.

Maeven had set a clever trap. Killing Dominic and then letting the Andvarians kill me would be almost as good as murdering me herself.

I tightened my grip on my sword. That wasn't going to happen. None of it.

Dominic spotted me creeping up behind the assassins. He flicked his eyes to his right, telling me to focus on the men on that side. I nodded back, then raised my sword and rushed forward.

In front of me, the assassins attacked Dominic, who hit one of them in the face with his lightning. That man dropped to the ground, shrieking and clawing at his burning eyeballs and melting skin, but the other assassins kept coming at the prince.

The assassin in front of me snapped up his weapon, but I closed the distance between us, grabbed his shoulder, and yanked him back toward me—and the point of my sword. The weapon plunged into his side, making him scream. I twisted the blade in deeper, then yanked it out and shoved him away.

Another assassin whirled around in my direction, but I was already moving toward him, and I slashed my sword across his chest and kept going, heading toward Dominic.

The prince blasted the remaining man with his lightning, then faced the final assassin—the blond woman.

She had been hanging back during the fight, but now there was no one between her and Dominic. He yelled and raised his sword, but the woman lifted her hands, and a wave of air blasted out of her palms and slammed into the prince, throwing him back against the wall.

My eyes widened. She was no ordinary mutt assassin—she was a weather magier who had just been waiting for the right moment to unleash her magic.

Dominic's head snapped back against the wall, cracking the glass and leaving a spray of blood on it. His sword dropped from his hand, and he hit the floor alongside it.

Fear squeezed my chest, and for a moment, I thought he was dead.

Then Dominic let out a low groan of pain and slowly pushed himself up onto his hands and knees, although he was clearly dazed.

An evil smile spread across the magier's face, her eyes lit up with power, and a ball of purple lightning crackled to life in her palm. She was too close to miss, and Dominic wasn't going to be able to avoid the strike or fend her off with his own magic.

I sprinted in that direction, with my free hand stretched out in front of me, even though I knew that I would be too late to close the distance between us and that I wouldn't be able to touch the magier in time to snuff out her magic and keep her from killing Dominic.

"No!" I screamed.

The magier whipped around to me. Her eyes were the same eerie, electric purple that Libby's had been, and the caustic stench of her magic was the same as well. She was another member of the Bastard Brigade.

For a split second, I thought—*hoped*—that the magier would toss her deadly lightning at me instead of Dominic, since he was already down on the floor, and I was still upright and the greater threat. But instead, she whirled back around, determined to kill him first.

Desperate, I yanked my dagger off my belt and threw it at her, but my running stride spoiled my aim, and the blade sailed wide and *thunk*ed into a bookshelf instead of her back.

The magier didn't seem to notice my flying dagger. She reached for even more of her magic, and the lightning in her palm burned bigger and brighter.

I forced myself to run even faster and stretch my free hand out as far as it would go, hoping that I could at least get a finger on her. One little fingertip on her skin was all I needed to unleash my immunity and throttle her magic. I still wasn't close enough to touch her, but something strange happened.

Her magic vanished anyway.

Well, perhaps *vanished* wasn't the right word. The purple lightning crackling in her palm wavered, just for a moment, as though it were a candle flame being threatened by a strong gust of wind. Surprised, the magier glanced down at her hand, as if she didn't know what was wrong with her power.

I didn't know what was wrong with her power either, and I didn't care. Her one second of hesitation let me close the distance between us, and I knocked her away from Dominic and down to the floor.

The magier screeched, and her lightning flew out of her hand and slammed into my chest. I screamed in pain and surprise, and I couldn't stop my hands, arms, and legs from convulsing as the lightning sizzled through my body. Her power was so strong that it knocked my tearstone sword out of my hand, and the weapon slid across the floor out of reach.

The magier realized that she had the advantage, and she locked her hand around my right wrist and sent another wave of magic scorching through me. This time, the horrid stench of my own singed hair and fried flesh filled my nose, and I could feel my skin burning, burning, burning from her intense power.

It wasn't enough that the members of the Bastard Brigade were determined to kill me. Oh no. Every single one of them had to be a bloody magier too who wanted to incinerate me with their fucking lightning.

I was really starting to hate the Mortan royal family, bastards and all.

The magier shocked me over and over again. The rest of the

library fell away, and all I could see, hear, feel, smell was her damned purple lightning slamming into my body.

I tried to fight it, tried to push back against her magic with my own immunity, but I couldn't even catch my breath long enough to scream between the bolts of lightning, much less grab hold of my own power. Her magic was seconds away from completely overcoming my immunity and frying me to a charred crisp—

Suddenly, the magier let out an angry shriek and flew backward, away from me. For a moment, I didn't understand why, but then the scent of cold vanilla with just a hint of spice swirled through the air, overpowering everything else, and a blast of blue lightning streaked through the air above my head. My heart lifted.

Sullivan.

He strode forward, his long gray coat snapping around his legs, and put himself in between me and the magier. While the other woman scrambled to her feet, Sullivan glanced down, making sure that I was still alive. Murderous rage filled his face, and his eyes gleamed like electrified sapphires. Without a word, he focused on the Mortan magier, lifted his hands, and blasted her with his lightning again.

The weather magier was strong, but Sullivan was stronger, and he cut right through her defenses and knocked her back down to the floor, hitting her with his blue lightning. The magier screamed and convulsed just like I had.

For several seconds, all I could do was lie still and suck down breath after breath, trying to slow my racing heart and stop the twitching in my arms and legs. The whole time, Sullivan kept blasting the magier with his power, as if he never wanted to stop hurting her for how she had hurt me.

And I realized that Sullivan *wasn't* going to stop—not until he killed her.

As much as I wanted the magier to suffer for what she'd done to me, and Dominic too, her death wouldn't give me any answers about Maeven. So I forced myself to roll over onto my hands and knees and then stagger to my feet. I stumbled forward and grabbed Sullivan's arm.

"Stop!" I yelled, although my voice came out as a low, croaking rasp since my throat was a bit charred, along with the rest of me. "Sully, stop! We need her alive!"

Sullivan looked at me, dangerous blue lightning crackling in his eyes, just like it was still hissing and spitting on his fingertips. I tightened my grip on his arm.

"Please," I rasped.

His gaze traced over my face, as if he was double-checking to make sure that I was really standing next to him, and not a dead, burned husk on the floor. He shuddered out a breath, let go of his power, and dropped his hands to his sides, although pale blue smoke wafted off his fingertips, bringing his heady vanilla scent along with it. I wanted to step forward, bury my face in his neck, and just breathe in that scent—*his* scent—over and over again, until it blotted out everything that had just happened.

Down on the floor, the magier finally quit screaming, although her arms and legs kept convulsing as the last bits of Sullivan's power streaked through her muscles. She finally got her breath back, sat up, and glared at us with hate-filled eyes.

"You idiots," she sneered. "Do you really think you can stop the Bastard Brigade? Do you really think you can stop the might of Morta? You might have thwarted us tonight, but we'll keep coming and coming until all of you are dead. Do you hear me? You're already dead! All of you! You just don't know it yet—"

I stepped up and kicked the magier in the face. Her nose broke with a loud, satisfying *crunch* under the toe of my boot, her head snapped back, and she dropped down to the floor.

I loomed over her, making sure she was truly unconscious. Good. I didn't want to listen to her crow any longer.

"Highness!" Sullivan said. "Are you okay?"

I wiped the sweat off my forehead with a trembling hand. "More or less. What about Dominic?"

I looked over at the crown prince, who was still slumped up against the glass wall. His eyes looked unfocused, but he was blinking, and he drunkenly waved his hand at the sound of his name.

"You're not okay," Sullivan said. "You're hurt."

He gently took hold of what was left of my tunic sleeve and lifted my arm up where we could both see it. I immediately wished that he hadn't, since my entire right arm was a blistered mess of flesh, except for a ring of smooth, perfect skin around my bracelet. Even now, I could still feel the cold, hard power pulsing through the crown crest. I shuddered. Those seven blue tearstone shards were the only things that had kept the magier from burning me alive.

But it was still a gruesome, painful injury, and the magier's lightning kept crackling through my skin like it was never going to stop. I drew in a ragged breath, and the acrid aroma of my own fried flesh filled my nose again. Given my mutt magic, I could literally smell my skin melting, melting, melting.

My stomach roiled. I forced down the bitter bile rising in my throat, but white and gray stars started winking on and off in front of my eyes.

"Evie!" Sullivan said. "Evie!"

He hardly ever called me *Evie*, which made it even more special when he did. I started to tell him how much I loved the sound of my name on his lips, but those white and gray stars darkened to an ominous black.

Try as I might, I couldn't stop those black stars, and Sullivan's concerned face was the last thing I saw before the darkness pulled me away from him.

Hands grabbed my shoulders, pulling me away from my father's body.

I dug my feet into the floor and stretched out my hand, but I couldn't reach him. A sob rose in my throat, but it didn't matter that I couldn't reach him.

My father was dead.

The hands turned me away from that awful sight, but I was greeted by another one—my mother's panicked face.

"Stay behind me, Evie!" she yelled, although I could barely hear her over the screams and shouts filling the dining hall.

All I could do was nod. My mother tried to smile, but her features twisted with worry, and she shoved me back and up against the wall.

My position gave me a clear view of the dining hall, although I wished that it didn't, since everyone was screaming, yelling, fighting, and dying. The Mortans had chosen the perfect moment to attack, and they'd taken everyone by surprise. Our guards raised their swords and rushed forward, trying to drive back the invaders, but the Mortans just kept coming and coming, like waves crashing onto a shore, and they cut our men down one by one.

A guard actually broke through the deadly line of Mortans and rushed toward the magier in the midnight-purple cloak. The woman's hood was up, hiding much of her face, but I could see her lips. They were painted a dark, blackish purple, and they curved up with delight at all the chaos, death, and destruction.

The guard screamed, raised his sword high, and charged at the woman, who watched him come with that same amused expression. Right before the guard would have cut her down, the woman casually flicked her fingers, sending more of her sharp, deadly hailstones spinning toward him. The hailstones punched into the guard's chest, killing him where he stood, and he dropped to the floor without a sound. Another screaming sob rose in my throat, along with more bile, but I choked them both down.

The weather magier must have sensed my horrified gaze, because she looked at me. I still couldn't see her face, but her purple lips drew back into another, wider smile, exposing her white teeth, and she headed in my direction, casually flinging her cold magic at anyone who got in her way.

While the fighting raged on, my mother dropped to her knees beside my father. She cupped his face in her hands, tears streaming down her cheeks. Then she wiped away her tears, reached down, and yanked my father's sword and dagger from his belt.

She surged back up onto her feet and shoved the dagger into my hand. "Here! Take this!"

My sweaty, trembling fingers curled around the cold, hard hilt, and I slid the weapon into my dress pocket to keep from dropping it. Out of the corner of my eye, I saw one of the Mortans running toward my mother.

"Look out!" I screamed.

My mother whipped around, and a blue ball of magic erupted on her palm. She reared her hand back to throw her magic at the assassin, but he slashed out with his sword, forcing my mother to lurch to the side and spoiling her aim. The ball of magic slipped through her fingers and dropped to the floor, spraying hard bits of snow and ice everywhere.

*My mother hit the wall and bounced off, losing her
grip on my father's sword, which clattered to the ground. She
stumbled back toward the assassin. He yelled, raised his
weapon, and started to bring it down on her head—*

Clang!

A sword thrust forward, stopping the assassin's blade.

*Suddenly, Ansel was there. The assassin's eyes widened in
surprise, but Ansel coolly spun around and slashed my father's
sword across the other man's chest. With a loud, bloody gurgle,
the assassin hit the floor, landing on top of my father.*

*I had never seen my tutor so much as hold a sword before,
and I'd never dreamed that he actually knew how to use one.
But another assassin came up on my mother's left side, and
Ansel stepped forward and cut that man down as easily as he
had the first one.*

*Ansel turned back to my mother, a smile on his face. How
could he look so happy at a time like this?*

*The scent of sour, sweaty eagerness blasted off his body, but
it was quickly overpowered by the caustic stench of magic. My
head snapped to the right. The Mortan magier was drawing her
hand back to throw her power at Ansel.*

"Watch out!" I screamed again.

*I darted forward and shoved him out of the way. A dense
ball of purple hailstones exploded against the wall where he'd
been standing. A few of the hailstones clipped my shoulder,
their sharp edges slicing into my skin and making me scream.
I gritted my teeth and reached for my immunity, using it to
snuff out the worst of the stinging cold, although I couldn't do
anything about the blood running down my arm.*

"Evie!" My mother rushed over to me.

She started to grab my injured arm but then thought better of it. Instead, she took hold of my other shoulder, her gaze searching mine. "Are you okay?"

I didn't have to look at my arm to know that it was badly cut as well as frostbitten. I could still smell the stench of the magier's power, and I could feel all the damage her hailstones had done. Tears streamed down my face from the intense pain, but I gritted my teeth and forced myself to nod at my mother.

"We have to get out of here!" Ansel yelled. "This way!"

He waved his hand at my mother, who pushed me forward.

"Follow Ansel!" she yelled. "Hurry! Hurry!"

I cradled my injured arm up against my chest, then fell in step behind my tutor.

Ansel swung my father's sword in vicious arcs, cutting down every assassin who got in his way. All the while, he headed toward the corridor that led from the dining hall to the kitchen. Behind me, my mother blasted anyone who came near us with her ice magic.

"Get the Blairs!" I heard the Mortan magier yell over the continued chaos. "Don't let them escape! Or the traitor!"

Traitor? Who was a traitor?

But I didn't have time to figure it out. The stench of magic filled the air again, and I knew what was coming next.

"Watch out!" I screamed. "Get down!"

In front of me, Ansel ducked, and another ball of purple hailstones sailed over his head and slammed into one of the wall tapestries, slicing it to shreds. Ansel cursed and veered away from it.

I glanced back over my shoulder. The Mortan magier was standing in the middle of the dining hall, magic now swirling in both her palms. Even from this distance, I could feel how *strong she was. She easily had enough magic to kill all three of us at once.*

My mother must have realized that too, because she shoved me forward. "Hurry, Evie! Get into the hallway! Now!"

Ansel disappeared into the hallway. Despite the stinging pain in my arm, I forced myself to move faster and follow him into the corridor. My mother rushed in behind me. She started to push me forward again, but I slipped around her, putting myself in between her and the magier.

"Evie! What are you doing?" she screamed.

But I didn't have time to explain. Instead, I shoved my mother forward, even as I reached for my immunity, calling it up, up, up, just like she had taught me to. I imagined my immunity like a hard, strong gladiator's shield covering my body—

The magier's power hit the wall beside me and exploded with a thunderous roar. Her cold lightning blasted over me, but this time, I was ready for it, and I gritted my teeth and pushed back with my own immunity.

For a moment, I didn't know which one of us would win—if I could shatter the magier's power or if it would freeze me alive. But my plan worked, and her lightning and hailstones hit the invisible shield of my immunity, broke apart into brittle chunks, and dropped to the floor.

"Evie!" In a panic, my mother grabbed my injured arm this time. "Come on!"

I hissed with pain, but I didn't stop her from pulling me along behind her.

Together, we followed Ansel down the hallway and into the kitchen. No one was fighting in here; the area was deserted, although several pots and pans were boiling over on the stoves.

Surprise flickered through me. Why was the kitchen empty? I would have thought that some of the servants would have been hiding in here. Or perhaps they had fled as soon as the fighting had started. Either way, no one was here to help us.

"This way! This way!" Ansel hissed.

He crossed the kitchen and opened one of the side doors. My mother followed him, still dragging me along behind her.

The three of us rushed outside into the cold, snowy, moonlit night. Ansel turned right. Keeping low, he hurried along the side of the manor house. My mother pushed me forward, and I fell in step behind my tutor.

Ansel never hesitated, not for a second, and he kept plowing forward. It was like he knew exactly where to go without even looking around to see where the assassins might be. Weird.

We quickly rounded the corner of the manor house and moved over to one of the barns. Ansel led us along the length of that building as well.

He stopped at the far corner and stabbed his finger at the trees in the distance. "The assassins are still in the manor house. We can escape through the woods."

I frowned at the certainty in his voice. How did he know there were no assassins in the woods?

My mother stared at Ansel in confusion, as if she was wondering the same things I was.

For the first time, a bit of annoyance and impatience flickered across his handsome features. "Your husband is dead," *he hissed.* "And you will be too if you don't come with me."

For a moment, the scent of my mother's ashy heartbreak overpowered everything else, even the stench of my own cut and frozen skin. More tears streamed down her cheeks, and she glanced back at the manor house.

I followed her gaze. Even at this distance, I could still hear people yelling and screaming inside, and through the windows, I could still see our guards fighting and dying as the Mortans cut them down. Every once in a while, purple lightning would flash, followed by loud, crackling booms as the Mortan magier unleashed her power.

The manor house was lost, and everyone inside was going to be slaughtered.

My mother must have realized it too because she shuddered out a breath, then looked at Ansel again and nodded.

He smiled wide, and a strange light flared in his eyes, making them burn an even brighter violet. Then he grabbed my mother's hand and dragged her off toward the woods.

My mother planted her feet in the snow and reached back for me. I rushed up beside her, and she threaded her fingers through mine and pulled me toward the woods . . .

For a moment, I could still feel the warmth of my mother's fingers against mine, still see the fear and panic in her eyes, still smell her ashy heartbreak.

My hand twitched, but my palm slid over silk sheets instead of her skin. My eyes popped open, and my gaze cut left and right. It took me a moment to recognize my surroundings and realize that I was in bed in the guest chambers at Glitnir.

I shuddered out a relieved breath. For several seconds, I lay there, just breathing in and out, trying to slow my racing heart and mentally shake off my nightmarish memory—

A soft *creak* sounded. Someone was in the room.

Panic filled me, but then I breathed in, and a familiar scent filled my nose—cold vanilla mixed with a hint of spice.

Sullivan was here.

chapter fifteen

I sat up, my heart picking up speed again.

Sullivan was sitting in a chair close to the fireplace, with his legs stretched out on a low ottoman. His sword was laid across his lap, and he had arranged the chair and ottoman so that he was in between my bed and whoever might come through the closed doors.

The warm, cheery glow from the fire highlighted his dark hair and the stubble on his chin. His head was wedged into a corner of the chair, and soft snores rumbled out of his mouth. It touched me that he was guarding me, protecting me.

I glanced down. Someone had cleaned me up while I'd been unconscious, and I was now wearing blue silk pajamas. I gingerly touched my right arm, which was bandaged from the top of my shoulder all the way down to my fingertips. I moved my arm back and forth and flexed my fingers—everything worked the way it was supposed to. One of Heinrich's bone masters must have healed me.

I drew in another breath, and a light scent filled my nose, like honey mixed with lemons. I could smell and feel some sort of cool salve underneath the bandages. Probably an ointment to help further heal my gruesome burns.

I glanced around the room again. Someone—Paloma, most likely—had propped up my tearstone sword, dagger, and shield in a chair beside the bed, while someone else—Calandre, most likely—had laid my crown on the vanity table, along with my bracelet.

Sullivan must have heard me stirring because he let out a sudden, short snore, as though he had just startled himself awake with his own loudness, then opened his eyes. He glanced at the doors, as if to make sure they were still closed, then looked over at the bed.

He blinked a few times, and then his eyes widened as he realized that I was awake. Sullivan set his sword aside, got up, and hurried over to the foot of the bed. Then he reached out and grabbed one of the gargoyle bedposts, as if he didn't trust himself to come any closer to me.

"Highness! How are you feeling?"

"I'm okay. Just tired and sore." I propped up some pillows behind my back. "What's going on? Where is everyone?"

"Everyone's fine," Sullivan said, rushing to reassure me. "Serilda, Cho, Paloma, and the Bellonan guards are making sure that Calandre, her sisters, and the other servants are safe. Xenia is off doing whatever it is that she does."

"And Dominic?" I asked.

"He's fine too. He had a nasty cut on the back of his head from hitting that glass wall, but one of the bone masters healed his injuries. The last time I checked, Gemma and Rhea were still fussing over him."

Some of the tension drained out of my body. "Good."

The crown prince had survived, which was the most important thing right now, even more important than my own survival. Although I couldn't help the guilt that flooded my chest. Maeven had been trying to kill *me*. Dominic had just been unfortunate enough to get in her way, and he had almost paid the ultimate price for her vendetta against me.

"And how is Heinrich handling things?" I asked.

Sullivan grimaced. "You mean the fact that another one of his sons was almost assassinated while you were in the immediate vicinity? Not well. He was going to throw you and the others out of Glitnir as soon as you woke up, but my mother pointed out that it wasn't your fault the Mortans attacked. So he's going to let you stay—for now."

I was surprised I hadn't woken up in the dungeon—or that I'd woken up at all. "Well, I suppose that's better than Heinrich asking Rhea to bring him my head on a platter."

Sullivan grimaced again. He didn't appreciate my black humor. Not right now.

His hand tightened around the bedpost, and he shifted back and forth on his feet, as though he was suddenly uncomfortable. He let out a tense breath and lifted his gaze to mine.

"I'm sorry," he said. "For how I acted before in the library. Maybe if I had stayed, none of this would have happened."

"It's not your fault. Maeven wants me dead, and she'll do anything to make that happen, no matter who she has to work with or who she has to hurt."

I hadn't meant to, but I had just echoed what Felton had said about the Mortans. Maeven and her Bastard Brigade had already proven they could get to anyone at any time and anywhere, but I started to wonder exactly how so many of them had infiltrated Glitnir.

The obvious and most troubling answer was that they were working with someone inside the palace.

The more I turned over the idea in my mind, the more certain I became, especially given the hot, jalapeño rage that I'd sensed in the throne room earlier. Someone at Glitnir wanted me dead, and they were willing to align themselves with the Mortans to make it happen.

Why me, though? Sure, someone could want revenge for the Andvarians being slaughtered at Seven Spire, but Maeven's involvement made me think this was about something much bigger than mere revenge. But how could my death possibly benefit one of the Andvarians?

"Well, I still feel guilty," Sullivan said, interrupting my dark thoughts. "Seeing you in the library with Dominic, with the fire crackling and the moonlight streaming all over your face . . . It reminded me of . . . a similar situation."

"With Helene?" I asked in a soft voice.

He jerked back as though I had slapped him. "What do you know about Helene?"

I gestured at the glass doors. "I was out on the balcony earlier. I heard the two of you talking down below in the gardens." I paused, choosing my next words carefully. "You and Helene seem to have quite an interesting history."

Sullivan barked out a bitter laugh. "That's one way of putting it. But if you heard us talking, then you know that I was engaged to Helene."

My heart squeezed tight, but I nodded. "Yes. It sounded like it ended . . . badly."

"That's one way of putting it," he said, echoing his own harsh words.

Sullivan shoved his hands into the pockets of his long gray coat and started pacing. He made a few passes back and forth before he spoke again.

"The Blumes are one of the wealthiest and most powerful families in Andvari, so Helene grew up at court with me and my brothers. We were all a little bit in love with her at one time or another. Dominic and Frederich eventually grew out of it and moved on to other women, but I never did. I always loved her, and she loved me back." His steps slowed. "At least I thought she did."

"Until she called off your engagement."

He nodded and resumed his pacing. "The older my brothers and I got, the more obvious it became that I was the bastard son, the bastard prince, and that's all I would ever be. That my brothers would *always* be held in higher regard, that I would never have any real power or influence at court, and that the other nobles would never treat me as an equal. Marcus, Helene's father, never liked me, and he wanted more for himself and his daughter, more power, money, and influence than I would ever have."

"So he forced her to break off your engagement," I said.

"Yes. I loved Helene, and I was devastated when she said that she couldn't marry me. I told her that I didn't care about her father, or his money, or having power at court, or anything else—that I only cared about *her*."

Once again, his steps slowed, and anguish filled his face. It took him a moment to resume his pacing and his story.

"So I asked Helene to run away with me. I told her that as long as we loved each other, everything else would work itself out. But of course Helene's father got wind of it, and he threatened to disinherit her, along with her younger sisters. She told me that she couldn't leave them with nothing. I understood that, truly I did, and I probably would have done the same for my mother, if our positions had been reversed."

"But?"

He let out a tense breath. "But part of me has always thought that Helene didn't want to end up with nothing either. That her father's money meant just a little bit more to her than I did."

The raw, naked hurt in his voice made my own heart ache, but I didn't respond. Nothing I could say would take away his pain.

"After Helene refused to run away with me, I packed my things and left the palace," Sullivan said. "I didn't have a real plan or destination in mind, except to get as far away from Helene and Glitnir as possible. A few weeks later, I wound up in a town where the Black Swan troupe was performing. Cho spotted me in the crowd. He knew who I was and asked me to have a drink with him and Serilda after the show. Somehow, I ended up telling them my whole sad story. Serilda asked me to join the troupe that night, and I've been with the Black Swan ever since."

Of course Cho had recognized Sullivan and realized that his magic, fighting skills, and connections would make him a fine addition to the troupe. But I was willing to bet that Serilda's magic had also told her much more about him, that she'd gotten some hint or glimpse of how Sullivan might influence future events. After all, Serilda had known that Vasilia would one day kill Cordelia, even when Vasilia was just a girl. I wondered what Serilda had seen about Sullivan that had made her bring him into her troupe.

"Eventually, I heard that Helene was engaged to Frederich. The news didn't really surprise me, but it still hurt, much more than I expected. It was just another instance where I had been passed over for one of my brothers, for one of the legitimate princes."

Sullivan shook his head, as though he was trying to push away his bad memories. "I've been back to Glitnir several times over the years to visit my mother, but only when I knew that Helene wasn't at court. But now here I am with Helene again, while Frederich is dead."

He let out another harsh laugh. "You were wrong before at dinner, highness. Life isn't a game. It's a fucking *joke,* and only the gods are laughing."

I didn't want to cause him any more pain, but I needed an answer about something, not just for my head but for my heart too. "Did you have any idea what your father was planning? That he was going to demand that I marry Dominic?"

Sullivan jerked to a stop, and he grabbed the bedpost again, as if he once again needed something to hold on to. "No," he said in a low, strained voice. "I didn't know about his plan, but it doesn't surprise me. In some ways, my father is just as ambitious and ruthless as the Mortan king. I'm sorry he blindsided you."

"That's the way these courtly games are played. It wasn't your fault. *None* of this is your fault. It's not anyone's fault, except for Maeven and her damned Bastard Brigade."

I paused, wondering if I should ask the other questions on my mind, but I didn't want to play games with Sullivan, so I voiced my thoughts. "You and Dominic seem to be on good terms, though."

Sullivan pushed away from the bedpost, but instead of resuming his pacing, he went over to the balcony doors, leaned his arm up against one of them, and stared out through the glass into the dark night.

"I love Dominic. He's always been a good brother. He and Frederich always treated me like I was one of them, like we were all *equal,* even though we all knew we weren't. Dominic was the most important, since he was the heir. Then Frederich, since he was the spare. And then there was me, somewhere far, far below."

Sympathy filled me, but I stayed quiet. I got the feeling that if I interrupted, he would stop talking, and I wanted to know more about his life at Glitnir. I wanted to know more about *him.*

"And now it's just Dominic and me. My mother says that my father has been taking Frederich's death particularly hard. That it's made Heinrich physically ill, and that he just can't seem to get over his grief. If my father had lost Dominic tonight too . . ." Sullivan's voice trailed off, and he shook his head. "It might have killed him outright."

He fell silent, still staring out into the night, lost in his own thoughts. It was several moments before he spoke again. "Sometimes, I wish that my mother had never stayed at court. That she had lived out in the city or the countryside. Anywhere but *here*."

"Why?"

"Don't get me wrong. I loved growing up with my brothers." Sullivan softly rapped his knuckles against the glass door. "But I always felt like I was on one side of a door, staring through the glass at Dominic and Frederich. I could see them, but I could never truly be with them; I could never truly be one of *them*, no matter how hard I tried."

His face remained blank, but the scent of his ashy heartbreak filled the room. I might not be able to protect him from his memories, but I could help him deal with the pain that came with them. So I threw back the covers, got out of bed, and walked over to him.

"I'm sorry," I said. "For everything that's happened to you. But I'm especially sorry for everything that's happened to your family because of mine."

"It's not your fault, highness. None of this is your fault. We're just trapped in an impossible situation."

I reached out and squeezed his shoulder, offering him all the support and comfort I could with that one small gesture.

Sullivan turned toward me, hot hunger flaring up and melting the icy pain in his blue eyes. The same hunger coiled through me, burning through my veins even brighter and faster than the magier's lightning had scorched through my body.

My fingers curled tight around his shoulder, and I longed to touch him—to *really* touch him.

To run my fingers through his hair and rumple it even more than it already was. To trace the faint laugh lines at the corners of his eyes, skim my hand down his face, and stroke my fingertips through the stubble that darkened his jaw. To smooth my palms over the curve of his neck, along his broad, muscled shoulders, and then down his chest until I could feel his heart pounding under my fingertips.

But most of all, I longed to kiss him and to have him kiss me back. To have his lips and tongue tangled up with mine. To run my hands over every muscled plane of his body and bring him as much exquisite pleasure as I could, even as his hands did the same to me. To feel the hot, hard length of him pressing me up against the glass doors, or sinking down onto the soft bed with me, or even drawing me down to the cold stone floor.

But I didn't want to just fuck Sullivan, like Helene had said in the gardens earlier—I wanted to feel his heart too. I wanted to see the heat, the passion, in his eyes, and the care, and the concern. I wanted us to feel and fly and fall together until neither one of us could tell where the other left off and we began.

So I took a chance.

"I'm right here, Sully," I murmured in a low, husky voice. "I'm on this side of the glass—with *you*. I'll always be right here with you."

He wet his lips, and he actually swayed toward me, as though he was going to lower his head and press his lips to mine. My breath caught in my throat, and my fingers clenched even tighter around his shoulder. We stood there, frozen in place, staring into each other's eyes.

"You say that now, but we both know that it's not true," Sullivan rasped. "That it can *never* be true. Because you're a queen, and I'm a bastard, and nothing will ever change that. No matter how much we might want it to."

A shudder rippled through his body, and he stepped away from me. My hand slipped off his shoulder, and I had to clench my fingers into a tight fist to keep from reaching for him.

Sullivan turned away, putting even more distance between us, so he didn't see the embarrassed blush that scalded my cheeks. A small victory, but I'd take what I could get, especially given the hurt that stung my heart over and over again, like a morph's talons ripping me to shreds.

This was twice now that he had rejected me. What a glorious fool I was. Perhaps I was more like Maeven than I cared to admit. She kept trying to kill me, and I kept trying to get Sullivan to . . . well, I didn't know what, exactly. Love me, perhaps? Or at least bend his principles and lust after me the same way that I did him. But Maeven kept failing in her mission, and I kept failing at this . . . whatever *this* truly was.

Sullivan cleared his throat and faced me again. "I should have told you before, but all the Mortan assassins are dead, except for the weather magier."

Back to business, then. More hurt knifed through my heart, but I pushed it aside.

"Where is she?" I asked.

"In the dungeon. Rhea has been questioning her, but so far, the magier hasn't said anything. Rhea is going to try again in the morning."

I frowned, surprised that the magier hadn't killed herself, like Libby had at Seven Spire. Perhaps the magier hadn't had the chance yet. I glanced over at an emerald-crusted clock on the nightstand. Just after midnight, which meant that morning was hours away. Determination surged through me, and I hurried over to the armoire, threw open the doors, and started grabbing clothes.

"What are you doing?" Sullivan asked. "You should be resting."

"There's no time to rest. I want to talk to the magier before she tries to hurt herself. Can you take me to the dungeon?"

He nodded. "Of course, just let me summon Paloma and some of the guards."

I stabbed my finger at him. "No—no Paloma, no other

guards. We go down there right now. Just you and me. I don't want anyone else to know what we're doing."

His eyes narrowed in understanding. "You think the magier is working with someone inside the palace?"

I once again thought of that hot, jalapeño rage I'd sensed in the throne room, along with that gust of magic when I had tripped and Rhea had almost skewered me with her sword. I hadn't told anyone what I'd sensed, and I didn't tell Sullivan about it now. I wanted to keep my suspicions to myself. At least until I knew exactly who wanted me dead and why.

I shrugged, not really answering his question. "I want to know exactly how the weather magier and those fake guards got inside the palace. So can you take me down there?"

He nodded.

"Good. Then let me get dressed."

Ten minutes later, Sullivan cracked open one of the doors to my chambers. He glanced outside, then opened the door the rest of the way, revealing the empty hallway beyond. Serilda, Cho, Paloma, and the Bellonan guards must still be making sure that the servants were safe.

Sullivan and I slipped out of the chambers, hurried along the hallway, and went down a flight of stairs. From there, we crept through the palace, keeping to the shadows and moving from one corridor to the next. Eventually, we ducked into a small alcove filled with gargoyle statues to let a couple of Andvarian guards pass by out in the hallway.

"You're awfully good at avoiding the guards," I whispered.

He grinned. "It was a game my brothers and I used to play. Our rooms were in the same hallway, and the three of us would sneak out in the middle of the night. Whoever got the farthest away without getting caught by the guards was the winner. I won more often than not."

The guards marched by, and we slipped out of our hiding spot and hurried on. We wound our way down several sets of stairs until we reached the dungeon.

Two guards with spears were posted in front of an open archway. There was no way to sneak past them, so we didn't even try. Sullivan strode forward, his boots snapping against the flagstones, as if he had every right to be here. I walked along behind him, my head ducked and the hood of my midnight-blue cloak pulled up over my hair. I hadn't put on my crown, so hopefully the guards wouldn't look too closely and realize who I was.

But the guards definitely recognized Sullivan, and they bowed their heads.

"My prince," one of the men said. "How may we serve you?"

"I want to see the magier," Sullivan said in a loud, authoritative voice. "Rhea sent me to see if I can shock some answers out of her." He held up his hand, and blue lightning flashed on his fingertips.

The guards nodded, lowered their spears, and stepped aside, letting him pass. I ducked my head and followed him. I half expected the guards to stop me, but Sullivan's order was enough for them to let me through as well.

Just like at Seven Spire, the dungeon here featured several long hallways with cells embedded in the walls, although I couldn't tell if anyone was languishing inside the small rooms, given the solid metal doors that fronted them.

Sullivan stepped into another hallway and walked down to the far end, where the corridor opened into a much larger room in the very back of the dungeon.

Thick tearstone bars cordoned off part of the space, forming a single cell along one wall. A few dim fluorestones were set into the ceiling, but there was enough light to see the magier lying on a cot in a pool of shadows in the back of the cell.

Sullivan went over and touched a panel in the wall, making the fluorestones blaze to life and flooding the area with light.

"Get up," he snapped. "It's time for you to answer some questions."

But as soon as he said the words, I knew we wouldn't be getting any answers.

The weather magier was lying on the cot, her hand dangling off the side, right above a glass that was resting on the floor, as though it had slipped out of her fingers. Water had dribbled out of the glass, forming a small pool. Her purple eyes were fixed and frozen open, and black blood had trickled out of her mouth, down the side of her face, and spattered onto the floor next to the glass.

The magier was dead.

CHAPTER SIXTEEN

ullivan yelled for the guards to fetch the bone masters, but
it was too late. The magier was as dead as dead could be.

After that, the dungeon became a circus of chaos, with
people running around and everyone demanding to know how
this had happened.

Captain Rhea was among those who entered the dungeon,
and she kept shooting me suspicious glances, as if she thought
I had something to do with the magier's death, even though I'd
been unconscious in my chambers when it had happened.

While everyone else ran around, shouting and accusing
one another, I stood quietly in the corner, studying the dead
magier. Other than the cot and a wooden bucket in the corner
that stank of human waste, the only other thing in her cell was
the glass on the floor.

My nose twitched. I could smell the soft, sweet lavender,
along with a faint undercurrent of rot, in the spilled water. It
wasn't wormroot, but I was pretty sure it was the same poison
that Libby had tried to give to me in the Seven Spire throne

room, and the same poison that had been on the dagger that she'd used to kill herself.

Whether the weather magier had taken the poison herself or someone had slipped it into her water . . . Well, that was anyone's guess.

But I would put my money on someone poisoning the magier. Someone had helped her and the other assassins slip into the palace. If I had been that person, I would have come here and killed the magier the first chance I got in order to keep my association with the Mortans a secret.

According to Sullivan, all sorts of people had been in and out of the dungeon ever since the magier had been brought here. Heinrich, Rhea, the guards, my friends. They'd all had access to the magier, along with dozens of others, and no one could remember who had given her the glass of water.

Either way, this mystery wasn't going to be solved, at least not tonight, so I returned to my chambers and crawled back into bed. I fell asleep almost immediately, and I didn't wake up until a hand shook my shoulder the next morning. My fingers slipped under my pillow and wrapped about the dagger there even as I cracked open my eyes.

Paloma was leaning over me, a concerned look on her face. The ogre on her neck had the same worried expression. "Are you okay? I knocked on the door and called out, but you didn't answer."

Even though I wanted nothing more than to roll over, burrow back under the covers, and sleep for the rest of the day, I forced myself to let go of my dagger and sit up. "I'm okay. Just tired. What's wrong now?"

Paloma shrugged. "Nothing, really. At least nothing new. But if you want to have breakfast with Dahlia, then Calandre says that you need to get dressed."

I groaned. Having breakfast with Sullivan's mother was the last thing I wanted to do, but I was already in enough trouble without insulting the king's mistress. So I got out of bed and let Calandre and her sisters work their magic on me.

Thirty minutes later, with Paloma by my side, I knocked on a door not too far away from my own chambers. The two Andvarian guards stationed outside gave me suspicious glares, their hands on their swords, but Paloma dropped her own hand to her spiked mace, and the guards thought better of confronting me.

"Come in," a light, pleasant voice called out.

"I'll wait out here," Paloma muttered, still eyeing the guards.

I nodded, opened the door, and went inside.

The chambers were quite large, easily twice the size of mine. A freestanding screen made of black bamboo and studded with amethysts in the shape of flying birds divided the back half of the room from the front, with a four-poster bed peeking out from behind it. Another screen wrapped around part of an armoire, forming a dressing area. To my right, an open door led into a bathroom studded with silver fixtures.

A writing desk, a vanity table, chairs, couches. The furnishings were similar to the ones in my chambers, but swatches of gold and silver gleamed on every surface, along with sparkling gemstones. Even when compared to the rest of the palace, these objects were truly dazzling, as though someone had gone through Glitnir room by room, picked out the finest pieces, and brought them all here.

I looked over at a table covered with a light gray cloth that was perched in front of the fireplace. A gray porcelain tea set patterned with purple flowers was laid out on the table, along with platters filled with eggs, bacon, fruit, and more. The hearty breakfast aromas made my stomach rumble.

A couple of servants were standing along the walls, but I focused on the two women sitting at the table—Dahlia and Helene.

Dahlia was wearing a green silk gown, and her only jewelry was a gold, heart-shaped locket embossed with the same large, fancy cursive *D* that had been on the card she'd left in my chambers with the refreshments yesterday. Her black hair was smoothed back into a bun, and understated makeup accentuated her green eyes.

Dahlia looked as poised and regal as any queen, but Helene was absolutely stunning in a pale violet gown that brought out her long, wavy auburn hair and jade-green eyes. Delicate vines done in silver thread curled up the sleeves of her gown, before spreading across the bodice and forming a flower garden. Amethysts and emeralds winked in the center of many of the blossoms, while a silver signet ring set with emeralds flashed on her index finger.

Dahlia pushed back her chair and walked over to me. "Everleigh! Thank you so much for coming, especially after all that awfulness last night."

I wondered if she was talking about the threats and insults that Heinrich and I had hurled at each other over dinner or the assassination attempt later on. Probably both. Despite the overwhelming opulence, plenty of ugly things lurked in the shadows at Glitnir.

Dahlia smiled and patted my arm. My nose twitched, but all I could sense was her rose perfume. Normally, I would have enjoyed the pleasant aroma, but Dahlia had doused herself with the scent, making it cloyingly sweet. My nose twitched again, and I had to work to keep from sneezing in her face.

She turned and gestured at the other woman. "I hope you don't mind, but I also invited Helene."

"How nice," I murmured, matching her politeness.

Helene got to her feet, came over, and air-kissed my cheeks. I returned the gesture with far less enthusiasm, although thankfully her lavender perfume was much lighter than Dahlia's rose scent and didn't make me want to sneeze.

"Come." Dahlia gestured at the table. "Sit. Eat. Relax."

I did as she suggested. The servants stepped forward, piled several plates high with eggs, bacon, and fruit, and set them in front of me. I drew in several discreet breaths, but I didn't smell or sense any magic. The food wasn't poisoned, but I still waited for Dahlia and Helene to start eating before I put the first bite of bacon in my mouth. I also opted for kiwi juice, instead of the hibiscus tea the other women were drinking.

Dahlia and Helene engaged in the usual polite chitchat, asking me about Seven Spire, the weather, and other harmless, inane things. This was a game I had played many times before, and I slowly relaxed, although I only answered their specific questions and didn't volunteer any extra information in return. But the meal passed pleasantly enough, and the servants eventually cleared the food off the table and left the chambers.

Once they were gone, Dahlia smiled. "Now, we can speak a bit more freely."

Helene leaned forward. "Yes, I want to know everything that happened last night. Of course I saw you and Dominic in the library, but to think that assassins would be so bold as to attack the two of you in there." She shuddered, as if she simply couldn't imagine such a thing.

"Yes, it was quite unexpected," I said in a neutral voice. "As was the weather magier's death later on in her cell."

I still had no idea who had poisoned the magier, but this seemed like as good a place as any to start fishing for information.

Helene nodded. "Sullivan asked me to examine her body. Whatever poison she took was almost immediately lethal."

I frowned. Helene hadn't come into the dungeon while

I'd been there. "Why would Sullivan ask you to examine the magier's body?"

"Helene is a plant master," Dahlia explained. "So she knows all about plants, along with the poisons you can make with them."

The younger woman gave a not-so-modest shrug. "The Blumes are rather famous plant masters in Andvari. We have several large farms in the countryside where we grow fruits and vegetables, but we're most well-known for our gardens here in the city. We use the plants and flowers to make face creams, perfumes, and the like, all of which we infuse with beauty glamours and other magics. My father passed away several months ago, so I run the family business now."

Dahlia reached over and patted her hand. "Helene also helps to maintain the Edelstein Gardens. You should see her greenhouse workshop. It's almost as lovely as the gardens."

A pleased blush flooded Helene's cheeks, and she smiled at Dahlia.

So not only was Helene Blume stunningly beautiful, but she was also extremely smart and wealthy and a powerful plant master. No wonder Sullivan had loved her. Even I was impressed with her, despite myself.

But I pushed my jealousy aside and kept fishing for information. "So what did you find when you examined the magier's body? Wormroot poison?"

I knew that it hadn't been wormroot, but I wanted to see what Helene would say about the poison.

Helene drummed her fingers on the tabletop. "No, it wasn't wormroot. I'm not quite sure what it was. I've never encountered it before, but the Mortans are known for finding clever ways to kill their enemies."

Yes, they were, and Maeven was probably more motivated than most, especially since I'd now survived three of her assassination attempts. The Mortan king couldn't be happy with her continued failures to eliminate me.

"I'm going to look through some of my father's journals in my workshop and see if I can find anything useful," Helene finished, then took a dainty sip of her tea.

"Is there any way to tell if the magier took the poison herself?" I asked.

Helene blinked in surprise, while Dahlia's hands curled around her teacup.

"Well, no, not really," Helene admitted. "But legend has it that Mortan assassins are under strict orders to kill themselves rather than be captured and questioned. Rhea and the guards didn't find anything on the weather magier when they searched her, but the magier could have had that poison hidden away in a hollow button or tooth or something like that. You know how sneaky the Mortans can be."

Dahlia murmured her agreement, then poured herself and Helene some more tea, as if closing the mater.

Frustration filled me, but I let them change the subject. I didn't think that the magier had killed herself. Otherwise, she would have done it in the library the second she realized that she wasn't going to escape, not waited until after she'd been taken to the dungeon.

And once again, I couldn't help but wonder who at Glitnir was working with the Mortans and why that person wanted me dead. What did anyone here have to gain from my demise? Despite all the vicious, cutthroat games I'd seen the nobles play at Seven Spire, I couldn't figure out the answer to my question. Or maybe Maeven and her accomplice were simply that much smarter than me. Either way, I wasn't exactly brimming with confidence, especially when it came to my chances of making it back to Bellona alive.

So I sat there and silently stewed while Dahlia and Helene chatted about other things, including some noblewoman who was getting married.

Helene gave me a sly look. "Perhaps that's not the only wedding we'll have to attend."

She was obviously talking about Heinrich's insistence that I wed Dominic. I took another sip of my juice to hide my grimace and give myself a few more seconds to think of a clever reply.

"Oh, I doubt that," I drawled. "Dominic will probably never want to be in the same room with me again, given what happened in the library. Being around me is probably quite a bit more hazardous to his health than he would like."

Dahlia and Helene tittered politely at my joke. Helene opened her mouth, probably to ask some more pointed questions about Dominic, but I looked at Dahlia.

"Although you and Heinrich seem very content," I said. "Perhaps the two of you should be planning a wedding. Seeing their king happy would do a great deal to boost the morale of the Andvarian people."

Dahlia let out a hearty laugh. "Oh, my dear, I have no desire to marry Heinrich. Perhaps when I was young and starry-eyed, but not now."

"But you would be queen," Helene pointed out, with a pretty pout on her face, as if she couldn't imagine anyone ever turning down that particular opportunity.

Dahlia shrugged. "I'm quite happy with my current arrangement with Heinrich. Besides, I don't want to be queen. It's far too much work for far too little reward."

I drew in a breath, but she reeked of lime truthfulness. It was the first scent, the first emotion, I'd been able to sense over her strong rose perfume. Her answer surprised me. I would have thought that she would have demanded that Heinrich marry her after the first queen—Dominic's mother—had died. Then again,

I was hardly an expert on love and relationships. And Dahlia was right. As queen, she would have to become even more involved in the nobles' petty disputes and games. I'd been queen for only a few months, and I was already thoroughly sick of that.

Dahlia stared at me. "Everleigh knows what I mean. Being queen isn't nearly as much fun as everyone thinks it is. Am I right?"

"Well, not when you're dodging assassins right and left," I drawled, deciding to play her words off as another joke. "That does tend to tarnish one's crown."

The two women both politely chuckled again.

A knock sounded on the door, and a servant entered and said that Helene was needed to deal with some business in her workshop. She hugged Dahlia, air-kissed my cheeks again, and left.

Dahlia got to her feet. "It's such a lovely morning. Let's take a walk."

She stuck her head out into the hallway and told her guards to meet us downstairs, along with Paloma. Then she crossed her chambers and opened one of the glass doors. I followed her.

We stepped outside onto the same balcony where I had seen Dahlia yesterday. Unlike my balcony, which was now devoid of greenery, thanks to Grimley and his massive tail, potted plants and flowers of all shapes and sizes lined the railing here.

"What a stunning collection you have," I said.

"Oh, they're not mine. Not really. Helene gave them to me," Dahlia replied.

She trailed her fingers over the plants and flowers as she walked along the balcony, making the green leaves and bright blossoms bob up and down. She drew her hand back for a moment, so that it wouldn't touch the spiky needles on a small gray cactus, then ran her fingers along the rest of the greenery sitting on the railing.

"I'm not much of a gardener, and the poor things wouldn't even get watered if the servants weren't around," Dahlia confessed. "But Helene knows that I love flowers, and she often gives me cuttings from her greenhouse. She's like the daughter I never had."

Helene would have been Dahlia's daughter—or at least her daughter-in-law—if she had married Sullivan. I wondered how Dahlia could be so friendly with the woman who'd broken her son's heart. I didn't think I could have managed it.

Unlike my balcony, this one featured a set of stairs, and Dahlia and I spiraled down them. Her two guards were waiting at the bottom, along with Paloma.

Dahlia set off down one of the paths that led into the gardens. I walked beside her, with the guards and Paloma trailing along behind us. It was a warm autumn day, and nobles, servants, and guards were going about their gossip and duties. Everyone bowed their heads and murmured greetings to Dahlia, while I received more flat, suspicious stares.

But the walk was pleasant enough, and Dahlia shared little facts about the gardens, along with the people we passed, as we moved into the hedge maze.

"It seems as if you know everyone at Glitnir, from the nobles to the servants," I said, after she stopped to inquire about the newborn grandson of one of the kitchen cook masters.

Dahlia shrugged. "I suppose that I do. That's where I started out, you see. In the kitchen."

"You were a servant?"

Xenia had mentioned that, but I wanted to hear Dahlia's story.

"Oh, yes. I was sent to work in the palace kitchen at a young age, so I grew up around Heinrich and the other nobles. The thing I loved best about Heinrich is that he always treated me as an equal. I was so happy that he did the same to Lucas."

From everything I'd seen and heard, Heinrich was a good, fair, just king—except for his insistence that I marry Dominic.

"You've done quite well for yourself at court," I said. "Your chambers are lovely, and everyone seems to respect you a great deal."

Dahlia smiled, but the expression didn't quite reach her eyes. "Yes, well, no one wants to piss off the king's mistress. I imagine things are similar among the nobles at Seven Spire."

I didn't respond because things weren't similar at Seven Spire. Oh, we had our share of torrid, illicit love affairs. The hearts and initials carved into the wall on the royal lawn proved that. But I'd never seen any mistress with the amount of respect, power, and wealth that Dahlia had. She was the de facto queen of Glitnir, only without the official weight and concerns of the crown on her head. It seemed as though she'd found a way to have the best of both worlds. I envied her that.

"I'm sure you're wondering why I haven't married Heinrich, given how many years ago his wife died." Dahlia shrugged. "But official titles have never mattered very much to me."

"So what does matter to you?"

"The only thing I truly care about now is what is best for Lucas," Dahlia said in a firm voice.

I smiled. "He talks about you a lot. The two of you seem very close."

"We are. Close enough for him to have spoken to me about you as well."

My stomach clenched, but I forced myself to ask the obvious question. "And what has he said?"

She looked at me out of the corner of her eye. "My son is very . . . fond of you, Everleigh. He spoke about you quite often, even before he knew who you really were, and you became queen of Bellona."

I didn't respond, but happiness warmed my heart.

Dahlia motioned to her guards, who were still trailing along behind us. They stopped and gestured for Paloma to do the same. My friend looked at me, but I nodded, telling her that it was okay.

We had reached the center of the hedge maze—the gargoyle's nose that I had spotted from my balcony yesterday. The area was far bigger than I'd realized and a garden unto itself. Trees and flower beds ringed much of the circular space, while black, gray, and white water lilies bobbed up and down on a pond off to the side. It reminded me of Serilda's pond at the Black Swan compound, although no black swans were gliding across the water here.

The centerpiece of this garden-within-a-garden was an enormous gazebo. Glossy ebony wood formed the floor and created a pretty lattice pattern in the low wall that circled much of the structure. Gleaming white marble columns studded with silver gargoyle faces with jeweled eyes supported the round, domed roof, which was also made of marble. White and gray diamonds arranged in the shape of water lilies glimmered on the ceiling, along with jet cattails, mirroring the real flowers and pond in the distance.

Dahlia settled herself on one of the cushioned benches that jutted out from the wall and overlooked the pond. I also sat down, and we admired the picturesque scene, as well as the flashes of people moving back and forth along the paths in the distance.

"This spot is called Gargoyle's Heart," Dahlia said, breaking the companionable quiet. "It's rather infamous as a lovers' rendezvous. Heinrich and I used to sneak out of the palace and meet at the gazebo when we were young. Lucas also brought Helene here. And now, here you are. Another noblewoman, a queen, who has caught my son's eye."

My heart clenched at the thought of Sullivan and Helene, but I forced my jealousy aside. I had no claim on him—none at all.

Dahlia turned to me, her face serious. "I don't want my son's heart to get crushed again. Lucas is very . . . particular about how things are, and even more so about how people treat him. I accepted my role at Glitnir long ago, but he's never grown used to his, to being one of the king's sons but not quite equal to the others. Not in the ways that such things matter at court. He learned his mistake the hard way with Helene, and it's a mistake that I don't want him to repeat with you, Everleigh."

I opened my mouth, but Dahlia waved her hand, cutting me off. The motion made the *D* embossed on the gold heart around her neck gleam in the sunlight.

"I can see that Lucas cares about you and that you care about him," she continued. "But you are a queen, and he is a bastard prince. We both know how sadly this story is going to end. Lucas already went through that heartbreak with Helene, and I don't want him to go through it again. It would be worse with you. Because he knows that he can't ever have you. Not like he had Helene. Not like he would have had Helene, if her father hadn't interfered."

Every word she said was like a dagger twisting deeper into my heart, especially since they were all true.

"I care about Sully a great deal. He's been a good friend." I drew in a breath. "But you're right, and we both know that's all he can ever be. He knows it too, which he has made perfectly clear."

Dahlia studied me, but she must have heard the reluctant agreement in my voice and seen the painful sincerity in my eyes. "Good. I'm glad that you and Lucas are both clear about what the future holds."

"And what do you think the future holds for him?"

She reached up and toyed with her locket, sliding the heart back and forth on its gold chain. "Lucas has been touring with the gladiator troupe long enough. It's time for him to come home to Glitnir permanently." She bit her lip, as if she wasn't sure that she should confide in me. "You've probably noticed that Heinrich is not . . . well. He just hasn't been able to recover from Frederich's death. Not that any parent could ever truly recover from losing a child, but his declining health troubles me."

"What about the bone masters?" I asked. "Haven't they been able to help him?"

"Unfortunately, a broken heart is one thing that magic simply cannot heal. I worry that Heinrich will be gone sooner rather than later, and I want Lucas to spend as much time with his father as possible. Surely, you understand how important family is, Everleigh. Especially since all of yours is gone."

Her green eyes bored into mine, and her words had far more bite than I'd expected, but she was right. I knew exactly how important it was to spend time with the people you loved before they were taken away. I didn't want to stand in the way of Sullivan reconnecting with his father, especially since Heinrich was so ill.

"I understand."

Dahlia smiled, reached over, and patted my hand. To my surprise, I sensed a small but steady current of power running through her body the second her fingers touched mine. As far as I knew, Dahlia wasn't a magier or a master. Perhaps she was a mutt with a bit of enhanced strength or speed. But she removed her hand from mine before I could tell exactly what kind of magic she had.

"Thank you for understanding, Everleigh," she murmured. "Your kindness means more than you know."

I smiled back, but the expression slipped from my face the second she gazed at the pond again. She might appreciate my kindness, but I felt like my heart was one of the water lilies dancing on the surface of the pond. Only instead of currents, I had people twirling me this way and that, trying to force me to do what they wanted.

I wondered who would win in the end—or if the currents, people, and agendas that went along with them would suck me under and drown me for good.

ahlia excused herself, saying that she needed to check on something in the kitchen, but I got the sense that she'd delivered her message, warning me away from her son, and that she was giving me time to digest her words.

Dahlia's guards left with her, and Paloma stepped into the gazebo.

"That looked intense," she said.

"How much did you hear?"

She shrugged. "All of it."

I gave her a sour look.

Paloma shrugged again and pointed at the ogre face on her neck. "Morphs have excellent hearing, remember?"

I sighed. "Where are the others?"

"Serilda and Cho are trying to figure out how the Mortans snuck into the palace last night. Sullivan is having breakfast with Heinrich and Dominic, and Xenia is doing the same with some noblewomen. But I think that's just an excuse for her to gather gossip and spy on them."

"She does excel at that," I murmured. "Well, if everyone else is busy, then I finally have time to get some answers about a few things."

"I think you mean *we* have time to get some answers," Paloma said.

I arched my eyebrow. "You're not going to lock me in my room again?"

"If I thought that it would do any good. But knowing you, you'd just find some way to escape."

"Probably. I am rather incorrigible that way."

Paloma sighed. "Now I know why Auster has so much gray hair. Keeping you safe is *exhausting*. I let you storm out of the dining hall last night, and you get attacked by Mortan assassins less than an hour later. It's like you're a magnet for trouble. I shudder to think what would happen if I left you alone in your chambers all day."

I grinned. "You have no idea."

Thanks to some helpful signs, we found our way out of the hedge maze and back inside the palace. I asked a servant for directions, and ten minutes later, Paloma and I climbed a set of stairs and stopped in front of a door.

Blue, black, and silver pieces of stained glass joined together to create a lovely frosted forest scene on the door. My heart ached, and I traced my fingers over the colorful shards. This door looked just like the one that had fronted his workshop at Seven Spire before it had been destroyed during the massacre.

I knocked and waited until a muffled voice growled at me to enter. I turned the knob and stepped through to the other side, along with Paloma, who shut the door behind us.

An enormous round room took up this level of the tower. Large, arching picture windows were set into the walls, letting in plenty of the late-morning sun, and several fluorestones embedded in the ceiling also blazed with light, further brightening the area.

A long table covered with several pairs of tweezers, stacks of soft white polishing cloths, and other jeweler's tools ran down the center of the room, while glass cabinets filled with precious metals and colorful gemstones hugged the walls. The workshop was eerily similar to the one he'd had at Seven Spire, right down to the metallic tang of magic that filled the room.

My heart ached again. I'd missed this. I'd missed *him*.

Alvis was sitting on a stool at the table and peering down through a magnifying glass at a white velvet work tray. Gemma was perched on a stool beside him, a pencil and a pad of paper in her hands, taking notes.

Grimley was here too, snoozing in a sunspot next to one of the windows. Every soft snore that rumbled out of his mouth sounded like gravel crunching together, but the steady sound was oddly soothing.

"Evie! I'm so glad you're okay!" Gemma threw down her pencil and pad, hopped off her stool, ran around the table, and hugged me. "Uncle Lucas said that you were all right, but no one would let me come see you."

I hugged her back. "Of course I'm okay. It takes more than a few assassins and a little lightning to hurt me. You know that."

Gemma hugged me again, then drew back and started chewing on her lower lip. "Do you think it will happen again? The Seven Spire massacre. Do you think something like that will happen here? To my father?"

The obvious worry in her voice and the fear in her blue eyes sliced into my body like a sword, cutting me to the bone. Sometimes I forgot that I wasn't the only one who had lived through the massacre. Even though Gemma had survived, she had the same sort of scars on her heart as I did.

I put my hand on her shoulder and gave it a firm, reassuring squeeze. "Nothing bad is going to happen to you or your father. Not as long as I'm here."

"Promise?" she whispered.

I squeezed her shoulder again. "I promise. Now why don't you introduce Paloma to Grimley? I need to talk to Alvis."

Paloma stepped forward, leaned down, and stuck out her hand to Gemma. The crown princess shook Paloma's hand, staring at the ogre face on her neck. Paloma grimaced, not liking the silent scrutiny, and I could tell that she was mentally preparing herself for Gemma to say something nasty. Paloma's father had kicked her out for being a morph, so she was sensitive about how other people saw her and especially the creature lurking inside her.

"Your ogre is strong and pretty," Gemma pronounced. "Just like you are."

Paloma's grimace melted into a soft, hesitant smile. That was all the encouragement Gemma needed to grab Paloma's hand and tug her over to Grimley. The two of them sat down on the floor next to the gargoyle, who grumbled and cracked open a bright, sapphire-blue eye, as if he didn't want to wake up yet. But Gemma's happy, excited chatter soon had him yawning and rolling over so that Gemma and Paloma could rub his belly.

I sat down on the empty stool next to Alvis, then peered down through the magnifying glass so I could see what he was working on.

A pendant lay on the white velvet tray. A flat piece of silver formed the base, which was common enough, but the design was truly stunning. Alvis had arranged small pieces of black jet so that they formed a gargoyle's face, while tiny, midnight-blue shards of tearstone glittered as the creature's eyes, nose, teeth, and horns. I glanced at Grimley. Not just any gargoyle's face—his face.

"A present for Gemma," Alvis explained. "Although she doesn't realize it yet."

"She's a mind magier, isn't she?"

He blinked in surprise. "How did you know?"

"She told me that she dreams about a Mortan boy. That she can see and even talk to him sometimes. Only mind magiers can do things like that. Plus, I can smell her magic. It's not like anything I've ever sensed before." I paused. "But she's going to be very, very strong someday. I can tell that much."

Alvis let out a low, harsh laugh. "She's already strong. She's the only reason we made it out of Bellona alive."

I waited for him to explain, but he fell silent, so I focused on the gargoyle pendant again. "You used jet and tearstone, just like you did for Serilda's swan pendant."

He nodded. "The jet will help block the thoughts that Gemma hears from other people's minds, and the tearstone will help her work with and focus her own power."

"Who else knows about her magic?"

Alvis shrugged. "It only manifested when we were fleeing from Seven Spire. I don't think anyone else except Xenia and I know about it yet, and I want to keep it that way for as long as possible."

Mind magiers were very rare. Some historians claimed that only a few were born every generation, but perhaps that was for the best. Mind magiers could walk through dreams, see and talk to people over great distances, and even move objects with their minds. I was betting that Gemma would grow up to do all that and more—much, much more.

"Well, the pendant is lovely, and I'm sure it will help her." I tapped the work tray. "Although I thought that you didn't believe in giving people presents."

A rueful grin curved Alvis's lips at my teasing. "I don't—except for my apprentices."

"So Gemma is your apprentice now?" I kept teasing him.

He shrugged again. "She spends enough time in here. She might as well be useful. And she keeps asking me questions about everything. And I do mean *everything*." Another, larger grin curved his lips. "She reminds me of another little girl I knew once upon a time."

I smiled at that, but his words reminded me of the real reason I'd come here—answers.

So I pushed up my tunic sleeve and tapped my finger on my silver bracelet. "Why did you make this for me?" My hand fell to the sword and dagger strapped to my belt, and I tapped my finger on them as well. "And why did you make these weapons and give them to Serilda all those years ago?"

Alvis's bushy black eyebrows shot up. "That's an awful lot of questions for this early in the day."

"An awful lot has happened since I last saw you at Seven Spire."

He tilted his head, ceding my point.

"Did you know the massacre was going to happen?" I asked in a low voice only he could hear. "Are you some sort of time magier like Serilda? Is that why you made the bracelet and the weapons?"

"No, I'm not a time magier."

"But?"

"But I had my suspicions that Vasilia was up to something, although I never expected it to be anything as horrible as the massacre."

"So why give me the bracelet? Why that morning?"

He frowned. "For weeks before the massacre, it was like all the stones of the palace were muttering to me. The floors, the walls, even the columns. It was like they could all sense what was coming. And not just them. I got the same impression from all the metal in the palace, especially the guards' swords. I just felt this . . . *pressure* to finish the bracelet and give it to you as soon as possible. It's just some quirk of magic I can't explain."

I could believe that. Magic did all sorts of things we didn't expect. That's why it was, well, *magic*.

"And the weapons? You made those years ago, long before Vasilia started planning the massacre. Why?"

"I made the sword, the dagger, and the shield because of Serilda," Alvis replied. "Because of her visions."

This time, I frowned. "She told you that Vasilia would one day be the cause of Cordelia's death?"

"Yes. Cordelia might not have believed Serilda, but I certainly did. I didn't have to be a time magier or have visions to see that Vasilia was rotten to the core."

My eyes narrowed in thought. "So that's why you made the weapons out of tearstone. To specifically absorb and deflect Vasilia's lightning."

"Yes. As well as any other magic they might come into contact with." Alvis smiled at me again. "What I didn't realize back then was that the person who would wield them would have her own way to deal with magic. Even Serilda couldn't see that."

"Did you know about my immunity from the beginning? From the first day that Auster brought me to your workshop?"

He shook his head. "No, but I couldn't understand why the magic kept fading out of my jewelry designs, and after a few months, I realized that it happened only *after* you touched the pieces. That's when I first started to suspect, although you were very good at hiding your power."

"Apparently, I still am. The Seven Spire nobles don't realize that I'm immune to magic. They think that your bracelet and weapons are what protect me. I'm surprised no one's tried to steal them yet."

Alvis's face darkened. "They will, though."

I nodded. Whether you were rich or poor, noble or common,

royal or not, someone always coveted what you had, even if they already had more than you. That was just the way the world worked, especially in the cutthroat arena of Seven Spire.

"There's something else I want to know," I said, my voice dropping even lower. "Something that's more important than everything else. Something that Maeven said right before Vasilia blasted me off the side of the palace with her lightning."

"What?" Alvis asked, although his hands curled around the edge of the table, as if he was bracing himself for the questions he knew were coming next.

"Why does Maeven want me dead so badly?" I drew in a breath, then slowly let it out. "And what does it really mean to be a Winter queen?"

Alvis stared at me, an unreadable expression on his face. For a moment, I thought that he wasn't going to answer, but he finally spoke. "The Mortan royal family has hated the Blairs ever since Bryn Blair killed their king in one-on-one combat. I don't know what upset the Mortans more: that Bryn, a lowly gladiator, bested their king, or that she united the people against Morta and formed her own kingdom of Bellona. Either way, she humiliated them and thwarted their plans. That's when it all started. For every generation since then, the Mortans have been determined to destroy the Blairs. They see the Blairs and Bellona as the only things standing in their way of conquering the entire continent."

Frustration filled me. I already knew all of that, and I didn't need another history lesson about my own kingdom. "That's not what I'm asking, and you know it. Maeven specifically wanted to destroy the Winter line of the Blair family. Why not the Summers, who were considered to be more powerful? What does Maeven know about my family—about *my* magic— that I don't?"

Alvis opened his mouth, as though he was finally going to

give me some answers, but then a soft sigh escaped his lips, and he shook his head. "I can't tell you that. You have to discover it for yourself, Evie."

"Discover what?" I asked, a pleading note creeping into my voice. "Why won't you just *tell* me? I need to know before Maeven and her Bastard Brigade try to kill me again."

Alvis's lips pressed together, and the scent of his garlic guilt filled the air. He really did want to tell me, but something was stopping him. After several long seconds, he shook his head again. Disappointment filled me, along with more than a little anger.

Why wouldn't he just fucking *tell* me?

I drew in a breath to demand some answers, but Alvis slid off his stool and grabbed a black velvet tray off a table against the wall.

"Here." He came back over and set down the tray beside me. "Maybe this will help."

A bracelet rested on the black velvet. I blinked at the familiar design. Pieces of silver twisted together to resemble sharp thorns, all of which wrapped around and protected the design in the center—a crown made of seven shards of midnight-blue tearstone.

This wasn't just any bracelet—it was *identical* to the one I was already wearing on my right wrist, including the protective magic pulsing through the tearstone shards.

"May I?" Alvis asked in a soft voice.

I nodded, pushed up my sleeve, and held out my left arm. He picked up the bracelet, gently slid it onto my wrist, and carefully hooked the clasp together.

I stared at the new bracelet on my left wrist, then the matching one on my right wrist, and I realized that they weren't really bracelets at all.

"Gauntlets?" I asked. "For what?"

"Gemma isn't the only one who needs protecting," Alvis murmured. "Or help with her magic."

He smiled, but worry darkened his hazel eyes. Once again, I got the sense he knew something that I didn't—

The workshop door burst open, and Captain Rhea strode inside, followed by two guards.

I slid off my stool and dropped my hand to my sword. Across the room, Paloma quit petting Grimley and got to her feet, her hand falling down to her mace.

But Alvis wasn't intimidated by the captain's sudden appearance, and he crossed his arms over his chest. "How many times have I told you to knock before you come in?"

To my surprise, Rhea rolled her eyes, and a teasing grin crept over her face. "Yes, yes, I know. I ruined your concentration yet again. According to you, I excel at it."

To my even greater surprise, Alvis smiled back at her. I frowned. Were they . . . friends?

"Rhea!" Gemma called out in a happy voice, charged over, and hugged the captain around the waist, just like she'd done to me earlier.

"Hey, kid." Rhea ruffled the girl's hair. "We're still on for sword training later, right? You can't spend all your time cooped up in this dusty old workshop."

"My workshop is *not* dusty," Alvis grumbled, although they didn't pay any attention to him.

"Right!" Gemma said. "See you then!"

She skipped back over to Grimley, and Rhea watched her go with a smile. I drew in a breath. The scent of the captain's rosy love for the girl flooded the workshop. She cared about Gemma just as much as she did Dominic.

Rhea must have sensed my curious gaze, because she glanced

in my direction. The longer she looked at me, the quicker her happiness melted away. In seconds, she had transformed back into a stern, imposing captain. Still, she didn't seem nearly as angry and hostile as she had yesterday, and she tipped her head to me.

"Queen Everleigh. The king would like to see you." Even her voice was polite, if a bit cool.

"Why?"

"He didn't say," Rhea said. "He just sent me to get you."

I drew in another breath, but I didn't sense any smoky lie in her words. I glanced over at Paloma, who shook her head in warning, but I wanted to know why Heinrich had summoned me. Besides, he was the king, and this was his palace. It wasn't like I could say no.

"Very well." I walked over to the captain.

Paloma started to join me, but Rhea held out her hand, stopping her.

"The king requested that Queen Everleigh come alone," she said.

Paloma looked at me again, but I nodded, telling her that it was okay.

"Fine," she muttered, then stabbed her finger at me. "But don't you *dare* get into trouble. It's not even lunchtime yet."

I grinned and snapped off a cheeky salute. "I can make no such promises."

Paloma gave me a sour look, as did the ogre on her neck, before turning to Rhea. "And you better protect her the same way you would your own king. Because if *anything* happens to Evie, then rest assured that you are the very first person I'm going to come looking for, along with your men."

The two guards paled and sidled away, but Rhea held her ground. She looked at Paloma a moment, then at the ogre on her neck.

"Understood," the captain said. "I look forward to that meeting, should it ever occur."

The two women stared at each other for another moment before Rhea turned back to me. "Queen Everleigh, if you will come with me."

She stepped into the hallway, and I followed the captain out of the workshop.

Rhea led the way, with me walking behind her and the two guards trailing after me. Together, the four of us headed down-stairs to the first floor.

Rhea stopped and looked at her men. "You two, resume your previous posts. I will escort Queen Everleigh from here."

The men nodded and set off in the opposite direction. I was surprised she'd sent away the guards, so I drew in another breath, but she smelled only of garlic guilt instead of the smoky lie I would expect if this was a trap.

Rhea gestured at me, and I fell in step beside her.

As we walked along, I realized that the captain had been busy overnight. Many more guards were patrolling through the palace than had been here yesterday. Then again, the crown prince and a visiting queen had almost been killed last night. Of course there would be more guards today.

Rhea kept glancing at me and opening and closing her mouth, as though she wanted to say something. We rounded a corner and stepped into a hallway that was free of guards, and she finally worked up the nerve.

She stopped and held out her hand, and I faced her.

"I am truly sorry about last night," she said. "I don't know how those assassins got into the palace, but I *will* find out. And if I discover that one of my men, or anyone else here, helped them, then that person will wish that they had killed me instead of trying to kill you and Dominic."

I drew in a breath, tasting her scent, but she smelled so strongly of lime truthfulness that the citrusy aroma burned my nose. Rhea might not like me, but she hadn't had anything to do with the assassination attempt. I had doubted she would put Dominic in danger like that, given her feelings for him, but it was still nice to know that she wasn't working with the Mortans.

"I understand," I said. "And I am also truly sorry for what happened. It was never my intention to bring my troubles to Glitnir, and I never meant to put anyone in danger."

She nodded and started forward, but this time I held out my hand, stopping her.

"I am also very sorry about Lord Hans. My own father was murdered, so I know how painful it is to lose a parent that way. Your father's death haunts me, as do the deaths of Prince Frederich and everyone else who was killed at Seven Spire."

Rhea's topaz eyes searched mine. After several long seconds, she nodded again, accepting my apology, and some of the tension between us eased.

"I was wrong about you, and I apologize for that." She grimaced. "And for challenging you in the throne room. That was foolish and insulting, especially since you are the king's guest."

"It didn't seem foolish when you were about to take my head off with your sword," I drawled.

She smiled a little at my black humor. "Well, I certainly felt foolish when you were about to cut my throat."

I held my hand out to her. "How about we both agree not to do such foolish things from now on?"

Rhea seem surprised by the gesture, but she reached out and clasped my hand. "Agreed."

She dropped my hand, and we walked on, our silence far more comfortable and companionable than before.

Eventually, we stepped into a familiar-looking hallway, and I finally realized where we were going—the library where the assassination attempt had taken place.

We had almost reached the entrance when Dominic and Sullivan strode out of the open doors. The two princes stopped, clearly surprised, but they walked over to us.

Dominic looked at Rhea, while I stared at Sullivan. An awkward silence fell over the four of us, and no one seemed to know what to say.

Dominic turned toward me. "Everleigh, you're looking well this morning."

"As are you," I replied. "No ill effects from last night?"

He flashed me a smile. "None. And yourself?"

"None, thanks to your brother."

We both looked at Sullivan, who shifted on his feet.

Dominic smiled, reached out, and clapped his younger brother on the shoulder. "Lucas has always been better with his magic than me. See? This is why you need to come home more often. So you can save me from dangerous assassins."

The crown prince let out a hearty laugh, but we could all hear the tension in his voice. Dominic dropped his hand from his brother's shoulder. He smiled at me again, but his gaze didn't quite meet mine.

"My father is eager to see how you're doing. Good day, Everleigh."

"Good day," I murmured.

Still not quite looking at me, Dominic smiled again, then strode off in the opposite direction. Sullivan nodded, although he didn't quite look at me either. Then he turned and followed his brother down the hallway and around the corner, out of sight.

Rhea was still standing beside me, and the scent of her ashy heartbreak wafted over me.

"I'm sorry about Dominic too," I said.

"I know," she replied in a sad voice. "But it's not your fault. I always knew that Dominic would marry someone else. Just like Lucas knows that you'll marry someone else. Besides, if Dominic winds up with you, then at least I know that you'll protect him, and Gemma too."

"That's not much to take comfort in," I pointed out.

"It's all I have," she murmured.

Rhea shook her head, as if clearing away her morose thoughts, then let out a low, bitter laugh. "Sometimes I think that if we all just loved who we wanted to, and married who we wanted to, life would be so much easier, so much *simpler*. But I suppose they call it *duty* for a reason."

She gave me a grim, humorless smile, then stepped into the library. I followed her.

I had expected a whole legion of guards to be stationed in here, but the enormous room was empty, except for a few servants who were laying out a tea set on a low table in front of the fireplace, along with trays of fresh fruit, crackers, cheeses, and sweet cakes.

All traces of last night's assassination attempt had vanished. The blood and bodies had been removed, the scorched books, rugs, and other furniture had been replaced, and even the glass wall where Dominic had cracked his head had been repaired. It was like the attack had never even happened.

King Heinrich was sitting in a plush chair, staring into the crackling flames as if they held the answers to all his worries. He was dressed in a fine gray tunic, but the garment seemed loose and baggy on his frame, and the large chair almost looked like a black velvet gargoyle that was slowly swallowing him whole.

His blue eyes were dimmer, and his face was much paler

than it had been at dinner last night. He wasn't wearing a crown, and bits of gray glinted all over his head, as though his hair was made of shards of glass.

The marked change startled me. It was as if the king had suddenly aged a decade overnight. Then again, almost losing a second son to an assassination plot tended to weigh heavy on the heart.

Heinrich looked up at the snap of our boots on the floor. He nodded at Rhea, then waved me over to the chair next to his. Once the servants had finished laying out the refreshments, I sat down.

Rhea shooed away the servants, bowed to us both, and left. A soft *snick* sounded as she closed the doors behind her, leaving me alone in the library with the king.

Heinrich stared into the flames a moment longer before rousing himself out of his reverie. He gestured at the refreshments. "May I interest you in some tea? Or a sweet cake?" His voice was much quieter and far more civil than it had been last night.

"No, thank you. I'm still full from my breakfast with Dahlia."

A smile tugged at his lips. "Dahlia has always been kind that way, always welcoming people and showing them the best of Glitnir. That's one of the things I love most about her."

"She seems like a lovely woman."

His smile sharpened a bit. "For the king's mistress? That's what people usually mean, when they say things like that."

I shook my head. "I meant no disrespect."

He shrugged. "It is what it is, and we are who we are. At this point in our lives, I doubt there's anything I can do to change things, especially what people think of us."

He stared into the flames again, and I sat back in my seat, getting comfortable and letting him put his thoughts in order. Finally, Heinrich looked at me again.

"I asked you here so I could apologize for everything that happened yesterday. You're my guest, and you were almost killed. I regret that more than you know. But I especially regret how I behaved at dinner last night. I shouldn't have sprung my proposal on you like that, and I shouldn't have pressured you into accepting it. Not in front of everyone else."

"Then why did you?"

"Because I was—am—desperate, just like you said. The Mortan king will never be satisfied until he has conquered Andvari and enslaved my people, and I'm growing too weak to fight him much longer." Heinrich let out a long, weary sigh, as if his confession had further drained what little strength he had left.

"I'm sure you've guessed it by now, but Frederich's death has . . . hit me hard. Losing a child is every parent's worst fear, but I didn't know it was possible to hurt this *much*." His voice cracked on the last few words.

Sympathy filled me for the king and all the heartache he and his people had suffered. "You lost your son. There is no shame in grieving for him, Lord Hans, and everyone else."

Heinrich laughed, but there was no humor in the low, ugly sound. "You know as well as I do that kings and queens do not have the luxury of grief. But perhaps the worst part is that I thought that sending Frederich to Bellona would keep him safe, Gemma too, and help secure our kingdom. But instead, all I did was get my son killed." A shudder rippled through his body, and he seemed to sink even deeper into his chair.

"It's not your fault," I said. "You saw the memory stone. You saw what Vasilia did to her own mother and sister. No one could have prevented that. Vasilia was always going to slaughter the queen. Your son, ambassador, and countrymen were just unfortunate enough to be at Seven Spire when she decided to strike."

"Deep down, I know that, but I still feel like it's my fault."
Heinrich shook his head. "I'm just glad his mother isn't alive to
see this day. Losing Frederich would have killed Sophina, just
like it's slowly killing me."

He stared into the fire again, his pale skin stretched tight
over the sharp planes of his face. In that moment, he looked like
a skeleton who was just waiting for the last bits of flesh to peel off
his bones and reveal his true dead self underneath.

After about a minute of silent contemplation, Heinrich
stared at me again, his eyes a bit clearer and sharper than before. "But my offer still stands."

"What?"

"My offer still stands," he repeated in a firmer voice. "Marry
Dominic, and join our two kingdoms. That's the only way either
one of us is going to survive. That's the only way Andvari and
Bellona will survive, although I'm sure the Mortan king will
still do his best to crush us both."

He was most definitely right about that, especially since I
had almost been killed in this very room last night, along with
his son.

Heinrich speared me with a hard look. "This marriage
needs to happen, Everleigh. As soon as possible. You know that
I'm right."

"I don't know that you're right." I sighed. "But I can't say that
you're wrong either."

"Especially with the Regalia coming up," he added, pressing
his point.

Surprise jolted through me. "I didn't realize this was a Regalia year."

He nodded. "Yes, which is why it's even more important for
Andvari and Bellona to stand united."

The Regalia Games happened once every three years and

were a time when the leaders of all the kingdoms gathered to watch the best warriors, athletes, magiers, and masters from their respective lands compete for the glory of applause, money, and more. With everything that had happened over the past several months, I hadn't remembered that this was a Regalia year.

Heinrich was right. Given the upcoming Regalia, it was even more important for us to stand together, but I still wasn't ready to give in to his proposal.

"There has to be some other way for us to come to terms besides my marrying Dominic. Some trade agreement we can work out. I don't want this marriage, and neither does your son."

"Don't you think I know that? A man would have to be blind not to see how Dominic and Rhea look at each other. I don't like this any more than you do. It brings me no pleasure."

I threw up my hands. "Then why are you doing it?"

He sighed. "Because I have a court full of nobles just like you do. Several of those nobles lost their sons and daughters in the Seven Spire massacre, and they want blood in return for that suffering. And if they can't have your blood, then they at least want Andvarian blood sitting on your throne—legitimate blood."

He raised his eyebrows, clearly referring to my feelings for Sullivan. First Dahlia, now Heinrich. Did everyone know how I felt about the bastard prince? Probably.

"But I don't even know Dominic," I protested. "And he doesn't know me."

Heinrich waved his hand. "Bah! That's no excuse, and you know it. I had never even set eyes on Sophina before I married her. The two of you will get on well enough, which is more than most royals can say."

He was right about that, so I tried another tactic.

"And what about Gemma? I don't want to take a father away from his daughter."

Gemma had already survived enough horrors during the massacre. She shouldn't have to worry about losing her father too—or, worse, what might happen to Dominic at Seven Spire. Maeven and the rest of the Bastard Brigade weren't going to stop trying to murder me just because I married Dominic, and our wedding would make him even more of a target.

Heinrich waved his hand again. "The girl is thirteen. She's practically grown. Besides, she knows how these things work, and she'll come to terms with it. And it's not like she'll never see Dominic again. He will visit her every chance he gets."

"And to escape from me, the horrible Bellonan wife that his father forced him to marry," I said in a wry voice.

Heinrich shrugged. "Dominic was lucky in that his first wife, Merilde, was a love match. You know how rare that is for most people, let alone royals. Now it's time for Dominic to do his duty to his kingdom, just as I did mine by marrying his mother."

The king stared into the fire again, his eyes dark and distant with memories. I wondered if he was thinking about his first wife or Dahlia. Perhaps both. It seemed as though the two women were tangled up together, just like Dominic, Sullivan, Rhea, and I all were.

Heinrich focused on me again. "I don't want to force Dominic to marry you, but the massacre has tied my hands. I can't be seen as letting you get away with what Vasilia did. I have to extract my pound of flesh from somewhere, and this is the simplest, most bloodless solution. Surely you can understand that."

I did, more than he knew. But I couldn't afford to give up that pound of flesh to him, and I couldn't afford to appear weak either, not here, and especially not in the eyes of the Seven Spire nobles.

On an impulse, I reached over and grabbed his hand. I opened my mouth to tell him that together, we could find another way to fix our problems.

But the strangest thing happened. The second my skin touched his, I realized that I could feel magic pulsing through his body. Only it wasn't his magier power, and it wasn't anything like Dominic's or Sullivan's lightning.

No, this was something else—something dark, something sinister, something I doubted Heinrich even knew was there, given how soft and subtle it was.

Poison.

CHAPTER EIGHTEEN

I tightened my grip on Heinrich's hand and concentrated, wondering if I was only imagining the sensation, but I felt the same thing as before. A small, dark, deadly current running through his veins, right along with his magic.

Someone was poisoning the king.

Who? Why? When had they started? And when were they planning to finish the job?

Those questions and a dozen more crowded into my mind, but one thing seemed certain—the poisoner had to be someone close to the king. Or at least with access to his food and drink, since those were the easiest and most logical ways to administer poison.

"Everleigh?" Heinrich asked, cutting into my dark thoughts. "Is something wrong?"

I was still holding his hand, but instead of letting go, I placed my other hand on top of his and dropped my head, as though I was overcome with emotion and collecting my thoughts. Then I tightened my grip and let loose with my immunity, pushing the cold, hard power out of my body and into his.

I had done this same sort of thing when Paloma had been poisoned with wormroot by a jealous gladiator in the Black Swan troupe. I had used my immunity to counteract the poison in her body and save her, and I was hoping I could do the same to Heinrich, even though he wasn't seconds away from dying like Paloma had been.

Back then, I had been so desperate to save Paloma that I had blasted her with my immunity over and over again until I'd finally snuffed out the poison in her veins, but I got the sense I couldn't do that with Heinrich. He was already weak, and I might kill him outright if I used too much magic too quickly.

I also didn't know what poison Heinrich had been exposed to, but it definitely wasn't wormroot. No, this poison was much softer, with a sweet lavender note, something that acted very slowly and built up over the course of several months, something that you didn't even realize was killing you until it was too late.

I sent the smallest trickle of my power into his body, testing the poison, but its magic immediately pushed back against my own, like a coral viper rearing up to strike. I gritted my teeth. This was not going to be pleasant.

But I kept going, pushing my immunity into Heinrich's body one tiny bit at a time, and I realized that the poison wasn't a viper. It was more like a series of venomous, parasitic vines running through his veins, right alongside his blood. So I imagined that I was a plant master and that my power was a pair of gardening shears, slowly cutting through all those tangled vines.

Snip, snip, snip.

I cut through one poisonous rope after another. Every time my immunity sliced through one, the others drew together, tightening their grip on Heinrich and trying to strangle my power. Even worse, I felt the poison reaching out, as if it was trying to slither from the king's body into my own. I had no idea if it could do that, but I wasn't going to let it infect me, and I wasn't going to let it kill Heinrich either. So I gritted my teeth and reached for even more of my magic, using it to shield both myself and the king.

Heinrich shifted in his seat, clearly wondering what I was doing and wishing that I would drop his hand. I tilted my head to the side and peered up at him out of the corner of my eye.

Even though I'd only cut through a small amount of the parasitic vines, I could feel and see the change in his body. His shoulders had straightened, his face had lost some of its tight, sickly pallor, and his blue eyes were clearer and brighter. He looked much more vibrant and alive, which encouraged me to keep going.

Snip, snip, snip.

As I cut through the poison, those venomous vines grew more and more desperate, and they lashed out at me over and over again, trying to break through my immunity. But I ruthlessly cut them all down and kept going.

Snip.

Finally, I cut through the last vine. I held on to Heinrich's hand a moment longer, just to make sure I'd cleansed all the poison from his system, but I didn't detect any magic in his body now other than his own magier power. So I rubbed his hand between my own two, as though I was warming it up, then let go and sat back in my seat.

I dropped my own hands down by my sides, hiding them so he wouldn't notice my trembling fingers, and slumped back against the cushion. I'd never used so much of my immunity in such a small, controlled way before, and I was utterly exhausted.

Heinrich regarded me with open curiosity, but he didn't say anything. Perhaps he didn't know what to make of me. That was nothing new. Sometimes I didn't know what to make of myself. Either way, I didn't say anything to him. How did you tell a king that someone had poisoned him? I didn't know, and I wasn't going to try to explain it, much less my immunity. I had no idea whether he would believe me, and it was a risk I wasn't willing to take.

"Are you okay, Everleigh?" he asked. "You look pale. Here, have some tea."

He leaned forward and poured some hot, steaming tea. I managed to stop my fingers from trembling long enough to take the cup from him. I sniffed the contents, but the peppermint tea was free of the cloying, floral poison that had infected him, so I took a few sips to be polite.

The awkwardness between us passed, and Heinrich leaned back in his seat, sipping his own tea.

"Mmm. This was just what I needed," he said. "Isn't it amazing how much better a cup of hot tea can make you feel?"

"Actually, in Bellona, we prefer our tea to be iced," I murmured, making inane chitchat. "We feel that the ice deepens and intensifies the flavors."

He grinned, looking even more vibrant than before. "You Bellonans are rather barbaric that way."

He must have been feeling better if he was making jokes about tea, and I forced myself to return his grin with one of my own.

"So I've been told," I murmured.

Heinrich drained the rest of his tea, then set down the cup. This time, instead of glancing into the fire, his gaze moved over to the spot along the glass wall where Dominic had been attacked. The rug there was pristine, as was the glass, but I could still smell the faint stench of the prince's blood in the air.

"I can't believe that I almost lost another son last night," Heinrich said. "Here. In my own palace. Those Mortan bastards. They won't be happy until they've killed us all, will they?"

He was talking about his family, the Ripley family, and

perhaps me too, but something occurred to me about the assassination attempt. When the Mortans had rushed into the library, they had attacked both Dominic and me.

But *more* of them had attacked the prince.

I thought back. Most of the Mortans had bypassed me and headed straight for the prince, including the weather magier. I frowned. Maeven wanted me dead, so why hadn't the majority of the assassins targeted me first? Or at least the weather magier, since she had been the most powerful? And why hadn't they attacked while I was alone in the library? Why had they waited until after Dominic had showed up?

Unless . . . I hadn't been their true target.

As soon as the thought slammed into my mind, I knew that I was right. The Mortans hadn't been here to kill me. At least, not only me.

Dominic had been their main target.

Someone had poisoned Heinrich, and someone had wanted Dominic to die last night. Who? Why? Was some noble making a play for the throne? With both Heinrich and Dominic dead, Gemma would be the heir, but she was only thirteen, and it would be easy enough to influence her—or kill her later on.

Perhaps Maeven wanted to put a puppet on the Andvarian throne, the same way she had wanted to put Vasilia on the Bellonan throne. Or perhaps this was about something else entirely. Perhaps someone wanted revenge against Heinrich and Dominic. Maybe one of the nobles who'd lost a loved one in the Seven Spire massacre wanted to take away the king's family before they finally killed Heinrich himself.

Those possibilities and a dozen others filled my mind, but there were just too many variables and unknowns to narrow down the possibilities and come up with a culprit. The only thing I knew for certain was that someone wanted the Ripleys dead—and me too.

"What are you thinking about?" Heinrich said. "I can almost see the wheels turning in your mind."

"I—" I started to tell him my suspicions, but at the last second, I held my tongue.

Heinrich had already lost one son. He wouldn't like the news that there was a traitor in his ranks, especially since that traitor had to be someone close to him, someone with access to him on a daily basis. Captain Rhea, Helene, even Dahlia. They were all potential suspects, along with dozens of guards, servants, and nobles.

Since I had no idea who might be plotting against the king, I decided not to tell him about it. After all, I had no real proof, just my own instincts and experiences with Maeven, and Heinrich didn't strike me as someone who would believe a stranger over his own people. Besides, the king and I were on somewhat friendly terms now, and I didn't want to ruin our tenuous truce.

"Everleigh?" Heinrich asked again. "What are you thinking about?"

"Your proposal," I said, an idea popping into my mind. "I'm thinking about your proposal."

His eyebrows drew together in confusion. I turned over my hasty idea in my mind, but the more I thought about it, the more I believed that it would work. And right now, it seemed like the only way—*the only way*—I could figure out who was trying to kill us all.

"I agree."

Heinrich frowned. "What?"

"I agree to your terms. I will marry Dominic."

He stared at me in disbelief, clearly wondering why I had suddenly changed my mind, but I kept my gaze steady on his.

"You're serious?" he asked.

"Absolutely."

He kept staring at me, but pure, genuine happiness quickly

replaced his confusion. He leaned forward and clapped his hands together loud enough to make me jump in my seat and almost slosh tea all over my tunic.

"Excellent! We'll announce the news at court later this afternoon, and we'll have a royal ball to formally mark the occasion," he said. "Of course, a ball was already planned as part of your visit, but now, we will really go all out with it. I'll get the servants to start working on the food, the guest list, and the invitations immediately. I want everyone to see this grand celebration and realize that both Andvari and Bellona are strong allies once again . . ."

He kept talking, going on and on about all the things that needed to be done between now and the ball. I let his happy, excited words wash over me as I drank some more of my cooling tea. Heinrich didn't realize it, but I had just discovered another piece of what it meant to truly be a Winter queen.

Lying.

Despite what I'd told Heinrich, I had no intention of ever marrying the crown prince. Rhea was right. We should all just love and marry whomever we wanted, duty and politics and money and power be damned. But that was a debate I would have another day with the Seven Spire nobles—provided that I survived my own scheme, of course.

I wasn't going to marry Dominic, but pretending to do so just might help me flush out the traitor. Someone wanted Heinrich and Dominic dead, and I was willing to bet that they would happily add me to their list once my engagement was announced.

Bellonans were very good at playing the long game, and I couldn't think of a better game to play than this one. Heinrich had said that his nobles wanted blood. Well, they weren't getting mine—or my throne.

But I would be more than happy to give them a traitor's blood.

PART THREE

The Third Assassination Attempt

CHAPTER NINETEEN

Heinrich summoned his secretary and informed the other man about his plans to turn the upcoming ball into an engagement celebration.

The secretary's eyes almost popped out of his head, and the man was practically salivating at the thought of sharing the juicy gossip. No doubt word of my engagement to Dominic would spread like wildfire through the palace. Good. Hopefully, the news would upset the traitor's plans, whatever they might be, and force that person to tip their hand. Although the downside was that I would have to be on guard until the traitor was caught—or I was dead.

Heinrich and his secretary were deep into their planning when I left the library. I looked for Rhea, hoping to break the news to her before she found out from someone else, but she wasn't standing outside.

I started to head back to my chambers when a thought occurred to me, so I asked a servant for directions and went to a different part of the palace. Ten minutes later, I knocked on a door. A muffled voice told me to come in, so I turned the knob and stepped through to the other side.

These chambers were similar to mine, although not as large and grand, but I focused on the woman sitting in a chair next to the fireplace. Her silver ogre cane was propped up against the table beside her, which boasted a decanter of Ungerian apple brandy and some glasses.

Xenia was sewing what looked like a small blanket, and she didn't look up from her work as I shut the door behind me, walked over, and dropped into the chair beside hers. A tea set was laid out on the low table in front of our chairs, along with trays littered with cake crumbs.

"Did your entertaining go well?" I asked.

Xenia shrugged, still focused on her sewing. "So-so. I learned a few new things, but nothing particularly noteworthy."

"Nothing to pass along to your cousin, the Ungerian queen?"

She shrugged again. "Nothing special, no."

"Well, perhaps a royal engagement will interest her."

Xenia's head snapped up, her attention suddenly squarely focused on me. "Whose engagement?" she asked in a sharp voice.

I grimaced. "Mine. To Dominic."

I filled her in on my conversation with the king. I also told her about Heinrich being poisoned and my suspicion that the weather magier and other Mortan assassins had really been trying to kill Dominic instead of me.

Her sewing forgotten, Xenia leaned back in her chair and studied me with narrowed eyes, as did the ogre on her neck. "You're hoping that your engagement will force the traitor to do something reckless."

"Yes. And I want you to help me catch them when they do."

"How?"

"We need backup," I said. "People none of the Andvarians have seen and who have no obvious connection to us. So tell me—where are Halvar and Bjarni?"

Halvar was Xenia's nephew, Bjarni was his lifelong friend, and both were powerful ogre morphs. They had helped me take back Seven Spire from Vasilia's turncoat guards, and I was hoping they would help me protect the prince as well.

"They're still at Castle Asmund," Xenia said. "I sent them there a few weeks ago to check on things."

The words slipped off her tongue with ease, and not a flicker of deceit marred her face or that of the ogre on her neck. Xenia was one of the most skilled liars I had ever seen, which was part of what made her such an excellent spy.

But I could still sense her smoky deception in the air, and I tapped my finger on my nose. "You do realize that I can smell when you're lying, right?"

Her lips puckered. She didn't like getting caught.

"But even more than that, I know *you*, Xenia. I've been to Castle Asmund, and it runs like a clock, just like Glitnir and Seven Spire do. You didn't send Halvar and Bjarni there to check on things. You didn't need to. No, you sent them *ahead*, to Glanzen, as soon as you realized that I was going through with this trip. So are they staying in the city, or have you managed to sneak them into the palace already?"

Xenia stared at me a moment longer, then threw back her head and laughed. Her throaty chuckles rang through the chambers, and the ogre on her neck silently chuckled along with her.

"Well done, Evie," she murmured. "Very well done. I was wondering if you would notice my little sleight of hand with Halvar and Bjarni."

I smiled, baring my teeth. "I'm a fast learner."

"Well, you're right. I did send them ahead, and they've already been here at the palace for a week, posing as Ungerian businessmen looking to buy Andvarian goods. Their chambers are right down the hall."

"Excellent. Then they've already been skulking around and picking up gossip. I want them to do more of that, especially once news of the engagement breaks. And, as a powerful and influential noblewoman, it shouldn't be too hard for you to secure them invitations to the royal ball." I gestured at the tea set and empty trays. "It looks like you've already made some new friends with your entertaining. Surely, one of them will be happy to do you a favor."

Xenia grinned. "Oh, I'm sure I can arrange that. What exactly do you want Halvar and Bjarni to do during the ball?"

"Watch Dominic and make sure that no one assassinates him."

She raised her eyebrows. "You really think that Maeven and her Bastard Brigade will be so bold as to try to murder Dominic during his own engagement party?"

I shrugged. "That's what I would do. If you're going to kill the crown prince, you might as well do so in the most public and visible manner. Besides, if Dominic dies during the ball, the Andvarians will assume that I had something to do with it, and they'll be screaming for my blood. Maeven loves death and chaos, and that would be a perfect storm of problems for Heinrich and me."

Xenia nodded. "I'll start securing the invitations. But the ball isn't for a few days. What will you do in the meantime?"

"I'll try to find the traitor on my own. I have an idea where to start."

And I did have a suspect, one who had occurred to me the moment I'd realized just how much the poison in Heinrich's body resembled venomous vines.

Xenia nodded again, studying me. "And have you told Lucas about your plan?"

My heart clenched, but I shook my head. "No. And I'm not going to."

"Good. For a moment, I thought you were going to be foolish enough to tell him."

"Why would that be foolish?"

"Because if you tell him the truth, then his reaction won't be genuine," Xenia pointed out. "And you *need* his reaction to be genuine. You need him to think that you're really going through with it, that you're determined to marry Dominic. Lucas's anger will sell your whole scheme to the traitor. He'll do all the work for you. All you will have to do is hang on to Dominic's arm and smile."

My stomach twisted with dread. That's what I was afraid of.

Xenia leaned forward and tapped her finger to the corner of her eye. "I can see when you're upset, Evie, and I can almost hear the nausea roiling around in your stomach," she said, mocking me with my own gesture and words.

"And why would I be nauseous about marrying a prince?" I drawled, trying to hide my feelings. "Why, I thought that was every little girl's dream."

She snorted. "Because you know as well as I do how much this will wound Lucas. He'll think that you're casting him aside for his brother, his *legitimate* brother, just like everyone else has his entire life. And he'll be even more wounded when he realizes that you didn't tell him the truth. He might grow to hate you. At the very least, he'll probably never trust you again."

It made me sick—absolutely, positively *sick*—to think about the pain that my deception would cause Sullivan, but everyone seemed to know how I felt about him, and I had to assume that the traitor knew as well. So as much as it pained me, I had to let Sullivan believe the worst of me. Xenia was right—his hurt and anger would do more to sell my fake engagement than any flowery speeches I could make or any mooning I could do at Dominic.

Apparently, being a queen was about more than just lying—it also involved hurting the people you cared about. Sure, the pain I was about to cause was in service of a greater good, but that didn't make doing it any easier. Then again, perhaps being a Winter queen wasn't supposed to be *easy*.

"Are you sure you want to go through with this?" Xenia asked, her tone more sympathetic.

I sighed. "I'm sure. As much as I care about Sully, I am still the queen of Bellona, and I have to do what's best for my kingdom. And for Andvari too, whether anyone realizes it or not. This traitor needs to be caught *now*, before they do any more damage. Otherwise, they'll go right back to poisoning Heinrich and targeting Dominic the second I leave Glitnir. I can't let Maeven slaughter another family like she did mine. I *won't* let that happen, not even if I have to hurt Sully. I would rather have him hate me than Heinrich and Dominic be dead."

"And what about the hurt to yourself?" Xenia asked.

"Heinrich told me that kings and queens do not have the luxury of grief." I sighed again. "This is me, not having that luxury."

She studied me for several long seconds. "Are you going to tell the others?"

"Yes. Paloma will realize that I'm lying. So will Serilda, with her magic. I have to tell them, and Cho too."

"But not Lucas. You're sure about that?"

"Yes. It has to be this way." My mouth twisted. "I might not have the luxury of grief, but I *do* have the luxury of telling others what to do. Paloma, Serilda, and Cho will agree with me. They know what's at stake, and they'll keep quiet. I just have to hope that Sully doesn't figure out what I'm really up to before we catch the traitor."

Xenia nodded, then reached over, grabbed the crystal decanter, and poured us both a glass of brandy. "Lucas isn't the only one who will be furious. So will Heinrich, when he realizes that you've lied to him."

"Hopefully, he'll be more grateful that he didn't lose another son."

She shrugged. "Perhaps. But grief and anger make people do all sorts of strange things, especially when it comes to their children."

"I'm sure you can sympathize with Heinrich." I paused. "Since you also lost a child."

Xenia's hand jerked, and brandy sloshed out of the decanter and splattered onto the table. She stared at the liquid, as if trying to gather her thoughts, then slowly set down the decanter. It took her a few more seconds to lift her gaze to mine.

"How did you know that?" she whispered.

"There was this tone in your voice yesterday in my chambers when we were talking about Heinrich grieving for his son." I tapped my nose again, but there was no mockery in the gesture this time. "And I could smell your grief then, just like I can now."

"Well, you and your damn nose are entirely too perceptive."

Xenia glared at me, and I wondered if I'd made a mistake in trying to learn more about her. But her glare slowly melted away, and she sagged back in her chair, as though all the strength had suddenly left her body, much like Heinrich had done in the library earlier.

"Yes," she finally said in a low, strained voice. "I did lose a child. Years ago. Not to assassins but to my own foolishness."

"Do you want to talk about it?"

She shook her head, and the ogre face on her neck shut its eyes, although not before a couple of tears escaped from the corners of its eyes and slid down Xenia's neck. "No."

"If you ever do . . ."

She nodded. We sat there in silence for the better part of a minute before Xenia cleared her throat, reached out, and picked up the brandy glasses. Just like that, she morphed back into her usual cool, calm self. Perhaps spies didn't have the luxury of grief either.

"Well, then," she said, passing one of the drinks over to me. "Back to the business at hand. Let us toast to your engagement, Queen Everleigh."

She held out her glass, and I reluctantly *clink*ed mine against hers. Then I put the glass up to my lips and threw back the contents. The Ungerian apple brandy slid down my throat before pooling in my stomach, although the slow, sweet cinnamon burn wasn't enough to drown out my growing dread and nausea.

Xenia took a sip of her own brandy, then settled back in her chair. "I'll say this for you, Evie. So far, your reign has not been a boring one."

I hashed out a few more details with Xenia, then returned to my own chambers. Paloma was waiting there, along with Serilda and Cho. I filled them in on my plan, along with my decision not to tell Sullivan about it.

"Are you sure that's a good idea?" Paloma frowned, as did the ogre on her neck. "He could help us search for the traitor."

"I realize that, but he also knows everyone at Glitnir. He's too close to this. I can't risk him saying the wrong thing to the wrong person."

Paloma shook her head. "It's your funeral."

Serilda and Cho shook their heads as well, agreeing with her. They might not like it, but they would keep my secret.

A sharp knock sounded, but before I could tell the person to enter, the doors burst inward, and Sullivan stormed inside. Given his clenched jaw, he'd already heard about my engagement to Dominic. I hadn't expected him to be happy about it, but seeing the raw, naked hurt on his face and smelling his ashy heartbreak almost changed my mind about my plan. Almost.

But queens didn't have the luxury of backtracking or indulging their feelings, and I had to be strong right now, not only for Bellona but for him too, whether he realized it or not.

"Hello, Sully. Come on in."

He looked at me a moment, then focused on Paloma, Serilda, and Cho. His hot, angry gaze flicked to all of them in turn. Their features were as tense as his were, and Sullivan realized that we had all been talking about him.

"So it's true. You've accepted my father's offer. You're engaged to Dominic." He spat out the last few words as though they left a foul taste in his mouth.

"Yes. I was just telling everyone of my decision."

"Telling everyone but me."

"I was going to tell you. In private. But you didn't give me the chance."

He let out a bitter laugh. "No, I suppose I didn't."

I looked at the others. "Will you excuse us? I'd like to speak to Sully alone."

Paloma, Serilda, and Cho gave Sullivan sympathetic looks and left the chambers. Cho shut the doors behind them, leaving me alone with the bastard prince.

Sullivan stared at me again. "So it's true," he repeated, his voice much duller and softer than before.

I didn't want to do this. I didn't want to lie, and I especially didn't want to hurt him. But I couldn't be Evie right now. No, right now, I had to be a queen, and my heart had to be as cold and hard as the tearstone crown on my head.

"I have to do what's best for Bellona," I said, trying to explain without actually telling him what was going on.

Sullivan's hurt and anger slowly melted into stunned disbelief and then twisted into outright disgust. He scrubbed his hand through his hair. "I knew that you would eventually marry someone. I just didn't think it would happen so quickly—or that it would be *Dominic*."

I didn't respond, and he let out another low, bitter laugh.

"Getting passed over for one of my legitimate brothers. I should have expected this. Sometimes, I think it's *all* I should ever expect. At least then, I would never be disappointed," he growled. "I really should have learned this lesson by now. Especially since it already happened to me once before."

I stiffened at the obvious insult. "I am nothing like Helene."

"At this moment, I think that you are *exactly* like her." A sad, resigned expression filled his face, although it too quickly slipped away, replaced by more anger. "Or maybe not. At least she had the decency to wait until *after* I'd left Glitnir to get engaged to my brother."

This time, I couldn't stop myself from flinching at his words. "It's not like that. Besides, you know this isn't my idea."

"No, it's my father's. I don't know if that makes it better or worse. But you didn't have to say yes to him, or to marrying my brother."

His eyes darkened, a muscle ticked in his jaw, and his hands clenched into fists again. I didn't know who he was angry at now—his father or me. Probably both of us. At the very least, he thought that I'd betrayed him, even though we had never made any promises to each other. But I would have felt the same, if our positions had been reversed.

"It doesn't really matter whose idea it was," I said. "Only that I believe this is for the best. Just give it a chance; just give *me* a chance."

I'd wanted to reassure him, maybe even give him some small hint that things were not what they seemed, but my words made him even more disgusted. A bit of lightning flashed in his eyes, his mouth flattened into a hard, unforgiving line, and the hot, peppery scent of his anger stung my nose and brought tears to my eyes. At least, that's what I told myself, instead of admitting that the tears were the product of my own turbulent emotions.

"I shouldn't have given you any chances, *highness*." He spat out the nickname as if he never wanted to say it again. "Not the first bloody one. Not after I found out who you really were, and especially not after you took the throne. I always knew there was something different about you, but by the time I realized what it was, what you were, it was too late for me."

"Then why did you give me a chance?" I asked.

"Because you were always making me smile and laugh, even when you were doing something as ridiculous as commandeering my jacket or stealing my pillow. You were *always* there. Always fighting. Always challenging me and yourself in the gladiator ring and out of it. Even after you found out that I was a bastard prince, you never treated me any differently. Not for one second. And that was so unexpected, so refreshing, so amazing to me." Sullivan shook his head, as though he was deeply disappointed in himself. "I couldn't help but be caught up by all of that, be caught up by *you*."

I didn't think that it was possible, but my heart somehow sped up and stopped, soared and plummeted, swelled with happiness and cracked apart with grief, all at the same time. He really did care about me. And I had just ruined all that care, concern, and warmth with my lies.

"And now I've chosen something else, someone else. I've disappointed you, hurt you, let you down just like Helene did." I didn't want to compare myself to the other woman, but I couldn't deny the similarities.

Sullivan gave me a thin smile, but the expression was utterly devoid of warmth. "You have to care about someone in order for them to hurt and disappoint you. And I think it's past time that I cared about you at all, *Queen Everleigh*."

This was the first time he had ever called me by my full name and rank, but those two simple words cut me to the bone, as though he had buried his sword in my chest.

Sullivan pressed his fist to his heart in the traditional Andvarian style and dropped into a deep, mocking bow before snapping back upright. "I hope that you enjoy the upcoming royal ball, Queen Everleigh, along with your marriage to my brother. I wish the two of you nothing but happiness, and I hope that you both get *exactly* what you deserve."

Sullivan gave me another cold, angry glare, then marched over to the doors. He yanked one of them open, then stormed through to the other side and slammed it shut behind him.

The resulting *bang* was hard enough to rattle the wall tapestries and more than sharp enough to completely shatter what was left of my heart.

CHAPTER TWENTY

That evening, I had dinner in the dining hall with the king, just like the night before.

Well, it wasn't just like the night before. In fact, it was just about the weirdest reversal of fortune and the furthest it could get from the previous meal. For one thing, Heinrich was in a boisterous, jovial mood. I didn't know whether it was because I'd cleansed the mysterious poison out of his system or if he was simply happy that I'd agreed to marry Dominic, but he made toast after toast to my health, Dominic's health, and everything in between.

I watched the king closely, as well as everyone he came into contact with, but Heinrich had no lingering effects from the poison, and no one seemed upset that he suddenly appeared so much healthier. The traitor had to be someone close to the king, but if they realized that I'd derailed their poisonous scheme, they hid it extremely well.

I was seated to Heinrich's left, with Dominic across from me. Dahlia was seated next to me, with Gemma across from her. Alvis and Helene were also at the table. Paloma, Serilda, and Cho were at another table, while Captain Rhea was standing along the wall with the Andvarian guards. Xenia was off doing whatever it was she did, which should include filling in Halvar and Bjarni on my plan and securing them invitations to the royal ball.

More than once, I tried to catch Rhea's eye, but she didn't look at me. Couldn't blame her for that. Dominic kept staring at her, but she didn't so much as glance at him either. Well, at least I wasn't the only one she was shunning.

Sullivan's seat was empty.

Of course Sullivan's absence didn't go unnoticed, but the big news was still my engagement to Dominic, and everyone watched us, wondering how we would react now that the deal had been struck.

For his part, Dominic was kind, witty, and gracious, asking me about Bellona, my childhood, and more. He played the part of the doting fiancé to perfection, and I couldn't have asked him to be more attentive. No wonder they called him *Prince Charming*.

I smiled, talked, and laughed, playing my role to the hilt as well. I even batted my eyes, reached across the table, and squeezed his hand on occasion, as though I was already besotted with him—or at least with the thought of marrying him and shoring up my own throne.

Oh, yes. I gave everyone in the dining hall a grand performance, perhaps the best of my life. No doubt the traitor had already heard about the engagement, but I wanted the news of exactly how bloody *ecstatic* I was to spread through every nook, cranny, and corner of the palace. The more gossip I caused and the more people I convinced, the more likely it was that the traitor would make another move, either against Heinrich, Dominic, or me.

After dinner, Dominic and I took a leisurely stroll through the palace to further sell the illusion of how deeply committed we suddenly were to each other. He led me from room to room, showing me swords, jewelry, and other treasures, as well as introducing me to the richer and more important nobles. The Andvarians might still be angry because of the Seven Spire massacre, but they were all exceedingly eager to use my marriage to their prince to further their own fortunes in Bellona.

By the time Dominic left me outside my chambers, with a chaste kiss to my hand, my cheeks ached from smiling so long and hard. But my night's work was just beginning.

Calandre and her sisters helped me undress and drew me a hot bath. They hovered around for almost an hour before I finally managed to shoo them away, claiming that I was exhausted and going to bed.

The second they left, I stripped off my night clothes and changed into a tunic, leggings, and boots. My sword and dagger were hooked to my belt like usual, and I also grabbed a blue cloak from the armoire and drew the hood over my head, casting my face in shadow.

A knock sounded on the door, and Paloma stepped inside. "Are you ready?"

I nodded. "Let's go."

Paloma was wearing a forest-green cloak, and she too had pulled up her hood to hide her braided blond hair and face. She had sent the guards away on some nonsense errand, so no one saw us leave my chambers.

We slipped through the hallways much like Sullivan and I had done last night, and our destination was the same—the dungeon.

To my surprise, no guards were posted outside the dungeon entrance, but I supposed there was no reason for them to be here, since they no longer had a prisoner to guard. We headed inside and went to the weather magier's cell.

Sullivan had locked the cell door with his lighting, but I wrapped my hands around the bars and killed his power with my immunity. A few seconds later, the last blue sparks of his magic fizzled out, and the door creaked open.

"I still don't see why you wanted to come here," Paloma grumbled. "What are you hoping to find?"

"I don't know. Some sort of clue. Something that will at least tell me whether the weather magier poisoned herself or if someone did it to her instead."

"What difference does it make?" Paloma asked. "You already think someone poisoned the magier. It's the basis of your whole traitor theory. Besides, she's dead, so it's not like she can tell us who she was working with."

"I know, but I wanted to see her cell again."

Paloma shrugged, still not seeing my point, but she kept watch while I stepped into the cell.

The area looked the same as it had last night. A cot pushed up against the back wall with a wooden bucket for a chamber pot in the corner. The bucket was thankfully empty, and the blankets, sheets, and mattress had been removed from the cot, leaving only the metal frame. The magier's body had been removed as well, although the coppery tang of her blood lingered in the air, along with the faint hint of the poison that had killed her.

Now *that* might be a clue.

I crouched down in the spot where the magier had died, since that's where the stench of the poison was the strongest. I drew in several deep breaths, drawing in the air over my tongue and tasting all the scents in it. I also spread my fingers out wide on the flagstone where the poisoned water had dribbled out of the glass, then reached out with my immunity.

The aroma was faint, as were the traces of magic, but I still recognized them as the same soft, lavender scent and parasitic, venomous vines of power that I had sensed in Heinrich.

I drew in several more breaths and reached out with even

more of my magic, but the aroma and the sensation stayed the same, confirming my suspicions. So I let go of my magic and sat back on my heels.

"Did you find something?" Paloma asked.

I nodded. "The magier definitely didn't poison herself."

"How do you know?"

I got to my feet and dusted off my hands. "Because whoever killed her also used the same poison on the king."

Paloma frowned. "That doesn't prove anything. The magier still could have killed herself."

I shook my head. "I don't think so. This poison isn't like wormroot. It's not designed to kill you right away using only a few drops. It smells too soft and subtle for that."

"So?"

"So the weather magier would have had to take a massive dose to kill herself, more poison than could be packed into a hollow button or tooth or some other small hiding space."

I spotted an empty pitcher and a glass on the table in the corner outside the cell. Everyone already knew that the magier had drunk the poison, but I still went over, picked up the objects, and smelled them. The pitcher was clean, but the glass still reeked of poison, and the floral scent was much stronger on it than on anything else.

My nose crinkled. "But a glass of water filled with poison would have been more than enough to kill her."

"But you still can't prove that the magier didn't poison herself," Paloma pointed out.

I set the glass on the table. "I know, but this magier wasn't some scared young girl like Libby was. This magier was older, stronger, tougher, more experienced. Even when she was defeated in the library, she kept spewing threats at Sullivan and me. The magier wouldn't just give up and poison herself. At least, not without trying to escape first. No, I think our mysterious traitor poisoned the magier's water, and the magier drank it without even realizing what it was."

I glanced around again, but there was nothing else of interest. I knew the how and why of the magier's death. Now I just needed to know who.

"Who was in the dungeon last night? Who was here when the magier was brought in?"

Paloma's face scrunched up, as did the one of the ogre on her neck. "Heinrich, Sullivan, Serilda, Cho, Xenia, Rhea, Alvis, Helene, Dahlia, me. Pretty much everyone who was at dinner, along with several guards. Everyone was shouting, yelling, and running around."

"So there's no way to tell who poisoned the magier. Anyone could have slipped it into her water glass during the confusion."

Paloma shook her head. "I don't think so. Sorry, Evie."

I hadn't thought that examining the magier's cell would give me a lot of information, but it had told me a few important things. Namely, that the traitor had access to both the king *and* the dungeon. That was still dozens of people, but out of all the names Paloma had mentioned, only one person had the obvious magic and skills to subtly poison Heinrich while giving the magier one large, lethal dose.

"We're done here," I said. "Let's go."

"Where to?" Paloma asked.

I grimaced. "Just about the last place that I want to go."

Twenty minutes later, I wrapped my hand around a doorknob, once again using my immunity to snuff out all the magic on the lock.

Paloma shifted on her feet and glanced up and down the

hallway. "Visiting the dungeon was one thing, but are you sure about this? Because if we get caught here . . ."

"Then bad things will happen to us. Believe me, I know." I gripped the knob a little tighter and sent even more of my immunity blasting into the lock. "I'm going as fast as I can—"

The last of the magic fizzled out in a shower of bright green sparks, but this person was cautious and had smartly locked the actual door itself instead of relying only on their power. So I reached up, plucked a pin out of my hair, and slid it into the lock. It took me only a few seconds to jimmy it open.

"Where did you learn how to do that?" Paloma asked.

I slid the pin back into my hair. "When I was a kid, I spent hours exploring Seven Spire. The most interesting books and swords and treasures were always behind locked doors or stuffed away in display cases. It was always easier and quicker to open them myself, rather than asking someone for a key. Now come on."

We slipped through to the other side, and I shut and locked the door behind us.

It was almost midnight, and most of the lights in the hallways had been turned down low for the night. But not in here. Fluorestones blazed in the ceiling, and the area was as brightly lit as Alvis's jewelry workshop. Not only did the fluorestones provide illumination, but many of them let off heat as well, all the better to nurture the area's silent inhabitants.

Plants.

Paloma and I stood in an enormous greenhouse. Flowers, trees, and vines of all shapes and sizes were nestled in brightly colored clay pots on tables that marched down the center of the room. More tables covered with glass tubes, beakers, and jars were pushed up against one wall, while still more tables boasted gloves, shears, and other gardening equipment. A writing desk bristling with pens, papers, and books took up one corner.

The ceiling was made of glass, as was the far wall, and I spotted a small beehive on the balcony outside. And just like all the other rooms at Glitnir, gold, silver, and bronze embellished many of the furnishings, along with gleaming gemstones.

Paloma let out a low, appreciative whistle. "I knew Helene Blume was rich, but I didn't know she was *this* rich. Are you sure that she's the traitor?"

That was my growing suspicion. After all, Helene was one of the wealthiest and most influential nobles, so she could get an audience with Heinrich any time she wanted. Plus, she was friends with Dahlia, which gave her even more access to the king, and she had also been in the dungeon when the weather magier had been brought in. And most important of all, Helene was a powerful plant magier. Poisoning the king and the magier would be child's play for someone with her skills, smarts, and magic.

"That's what we're here to find out," I said.

I moved over to one of the tables covered with glass tubes and beakers, which were filled with creams, lotions, and liquids. Everything was neatly labeled and stacked in wooden racks and on small shelves.

Paloma followed me. "What is all this stuff?"

"Helene and her family are known for their beauty products. The Blumes make their money selling beauty creams, glamours, and more, both here in Andvari and abroad."

Paloma picked up an open jar filled with a thick pale yellow cream and sniffed it. "Well, at least it smells good."

She handed the jar to me, and I also sniffed it. The familiar scent of honey mixed with lemons tickled my nose. I read the jar label—*Honey Burn Cream*.

This was the same scent and cream that I had sensed on my arm after the weather magier had burned me. Guilt flooded my stomach, but I pushed it away. Just because Helene had helped heal me then didn't mean that she still wasn't the traitor. I set down the jar and moved on.

Stacks of small, square papers were lined up on the table, and I flipped through them. Honey, lemons, water. They were recipe cards for Helene's creams, lotions, and more. But the ingredients were all ordinary things, so I set the cards back down where I had found them.

There was nothing unusual on the rest of the tables along the wall, so I went over to the plants that took up the center of the greenhouse.

Many of them were common flowers—roses, lilies, mums, and the like—along with more exotic blooms, like ice violets and snow pansies. Paloma dawdled along behind me, staring at first one flower, then another.

I moved into the next section, which featured dill weed, mint, and a few other herbs I recognized from cooking with Isobel in the Seven Spire kitchen. The thought of the cook master brought a smile to my face, but I wasn't here to reminisce, so I hurried on to the third and final section in the back.

This was where things finally got interesting. These plants, flowers, trees, and vines were all strange shapes, with unusual blooms in odd patterns, sizes, and colors. I didn't recognize any of them. If anything in here was poisonous, then I was betting it was one of these plants.

All the pots were neatly labeled, but the names told me nothing, so I did the only thing I could—I bent down and buried my nose in first one plant, then another, sniffing all the blossoms to see what aromas, if any, they had.

"What are you doing?" Paloma asked.

"Searching for clues."

She rolled her eyes, as did the ogre on her neck, and went back over to the tables of creams and lotions. Paloma picked up a vial of peony perfume and dabbed a drop onto her wrist.

I kept sniffing plants, both hoping and dreading that I would find something that was similar to the soft, floral poison I'd sensed in the dungeon—

There—right *there*.

I stopped and stared down at a small gray cactus about the size of my hand. The cactus had two spiky arms adorned with a few tiny flowers that looked like puffy, purple snowballs. It was quite lovely and didn't look the least bit harmful, but thanks to Vasilia, I knew how deceiving looks could be, and how the prettiest exterior could hide the coldest, blackest heart.

So I drew in another breath, really tasting the air, and I got another whiff of the flowers' soft, lavender aroma—the same lavender aroma as the poison that had killed the weather magier. My eyes narrowed, and I carefully touched my fingertip to one of the purple blossoms. To my surprise, the petals were as sharp as needles, and I could feel the magic flowing through them—the same venomous power as the poison that had been in Heinrich's body.

This was definitely the right plant, and it was quite deadly, despite its small, innocent appearance. I shivered and dropped my hand from the blossom, then read the label on the pot.

Amethyst Eye Cactus. Native to the permafrost plains of Morta.

I snorted. Of course it was from Morta. As soon as I read the words, I realized that the center of the purple blossoms *did* look like an eye, one that was glaring at me. I shivered again, straightened up, and stepped away from the cactus.

Paloma came over to me. "Did you find something?"

"Unfortunately." I pointed out the cactus. "Have you ever seen or heard of this?"

She too bent down and read the label. "Some weird little cactus from the ass end of Morta? Of course I've never heard of it. Is this what was used to poison Heinrich and the weather magier?"

My nose twitched. "Definitely. Although I'm not quite sure how. The cactus itself doesn't seem to be poisonous, only the flowers. I wonder how Helene used the flowers, if she crushed the petals or did something else to them. We know that she put the poison in the weather magier's water glass, but how did she administer it to Heinrich?"

"Does it really matter how?" Paloma asked.

"No, I suppose not."

I took another step back from the cactus, not wanting to be near it a second longer than necessary. A ray of light slipped past my body and hit the cactus, along with its purple pot. The container's rich, jewel-toned shade caught my eye, and I took a closer look at it.

It was an ordinary clay pot, and the only thing remarkable about it was its vibrant amethyst color. I had seen similar pots lining the balcony railing outside my chambers, as well as Dahlia's chambers. Dahlia had told me that Helene was always gifting her with flowers. But I had also seen this same kind of pot somewhere else—in Maeven's chambers the night that I'd spoken to her through the Cardea mirror at Seven Spire.

"What is it?" Paloma asked. "What's wrong?"

I started to tell her about the pots when a glimmer of silver caught my eye, much shinier and brighter than the metal that adorned the walls. Instead of answering her, I went over to the writing desk in the corner. Pens, pads, and books covered the surface, so it took me a few seconds to find the source of the silver gleam.

A signet ring.

A sick, sick feeling filled my stomach, and I grabbed the ring and held it up to the light. A fancy cursive *H* was embossed in the silver and circled by tiny emeralds, while curling vines were etched into the band. This signet ring was eerily similar to the one I'd found hidden in Maeven's jewelry box at Seven Spire.

"What's that?" Paloma asked, coming over to me. "And why do you look like it's a coral viper that's about to bite you?"

In a dull voice, I told her about finding the ring in Maeven's room, as well as seeing the pots in the magier's chamber when I had spoken to her.

"Let's forget for a moment that you spoke to your mortal enemy through a magic mirror and conveniently forgot to tell *me* about it." Paloma glared at me, as did the ogre on her neck. "We'll address that later. But for right now, you should be happy. You finally have proof that Helene is the traitor and that she's working with the Mortans."

But I wasn't happy. Not really. Because this would break Sullivan's heart all over again.

"Why do you look so sad?" Paloma asked. "You got your proof."

I shook my head. "I don't have proof. Not really. All I have are a cactus, a pot, and a ring. That's not enough to go to Heinrich."

Maeven was nothing if not clever, and so far, her accomplices had been just as devious. But Helene had left all these incriminating things lying around in plain sight in her workshop. Finding the cactus, the pot, and especially the ring seemed far too . . . *easy*, and I couldn't ignore my sneaking suspicion that they had been left here for me to find. But why? Was Helene really that foolish? Was she daring me to catch her? Or was someone else framing her?

I couldn't confirm my theories one way or another, so I set down the ring where I had found it, then looked over the greenhouse, making sure that everything was the same as when we'd first entered. "We need to leave before Helene or someone else comes in here."

I had barely finished speaking when I heard a key slide into the lock. Paloma heard it too, and we both froze.

"Come in." Helene's voice floated through the door. "I'll give you a tour."

My head snapped back and forth as I searched for another way out of the greenhouse. I spotted a door in the glass wall. I pointed it out to Paloma, and we hurried in that direction.

Luckily for us, this door wasn't locked with magic or anything else, and we slipped through it and stepped out onto the balcony. I darted to my right and pressed myself up against the cold stone wall of the palace, although I could still see inside through the glass. Paloma did the same thing beside me, literally breathing down my neck.

Too late, I realized that I'd left the balcony door open, and I pushed on it with my hand. It swung toward the wall, but it didn't quite shut, leaving a crack of space between the glass and the frame. I grimaced, but I didn't dare step forward and try to close it the rest of the way.

"Strange." Helene's voice drifted out through the cracked door. "I thought I locked the greenhouse with my magic, but I must have forgotten."

The plant magier strode into view, still wearing the green ball gown she'd had on at dinner. She unwound a black silk wrap from around her shoulders, revealing her muscled arms, and laid the cloth on a table. Then she turned around, a smile on her beautiful face.

My stomach clenched with dread. I'd seen her look at only one person like that.

A second later, my worst fear was confirmed, and Sullivan stepped into the greenhouse and shut the door behind him.

I hadn't seen him since he'd stormed out of my chambers earlier, but he looked much calmer now, as if he'd made a decision about something important, like exactly how much he despised me. My heart squeezed tight, but I'd brought his contempt upon myself, and there was nothing I could do about it now. Maybe not ever.

Helene strode over to a table covered with liquor bottles and glasses. She poured two snifters of what looked like Ungerian apple brandy and handed one to Sullivan. He nodded his thanks, then wandered around, staring at the plants, flowers, papers, beakers, and creams.

"You weren't kidding when you said that you had expanded your operation." Sullivan took a sip of his brandy. "I remember when you only had one little table of plants in here."

Helene beamed with pride. "Ever since my father's death, I've become much more involved in the family business. Now that I'm running things, I can finally offer some new products, just like I've always wanted to. Not just beauty creams for wealthy nobles but products that anyone can afford, like this burn cream." She pointed out the same jar that Paloma and I had examined earlier. "Things that can really help people."

"I always admired that about you," Sullivan said. "That you wanted to sell your products to everyone, even though your father only cared about pleasing the other nobles."

She shrugged. "It's just good business sense. More customers means more money. Besides, you know how much I've always enjoyed growing new plants and experimenting with new ingredients and formulas."

I wondered if those new plants, experiments, and formulas included poisoning King Heinrich and the weather magier, but of course I couldn't knock on the glass wall and ask her.

Helene eyed Sullivan over the rim of her snifter, then took a dainty sip of her brandy and set it aside. "But chitchatting about my family's business isn't why you asked me to give you a tour."

His fingers curled around his glass, but he didn't respond to her obvious opening, so Helene smiled again and walked forward, stopping right in front of him.

"I truly am sorry about Everleigh and Dominic," she said. "I can see how much you care about her."

Sullivan drained the rest of his brandy, then set the glass aside. "It doesn't matter. Not now."

Helene smiled again. "I was hoping you would say that."

She reached up and wrapped her arms around his neck. Sullivan stared down at her, an unreadable expression on his face. Helene swayed even closer to him, then stood on her tiptoes and pressed her lips to his.

For a moment, Sullivan just stood there, with her lips on his, but then his hands settled on her waist, his eyes drifted shut, and he leaned into the kiss.

My heart shattered at the sight, each cold, sharp shard twisting itself deeper and deeper into my chest. Every second they kissed made me want to scream. I longed to charge through the door, tear him away from her, and confess my lies, but I stood there in stoic silence. I had no right to be angry with Sullivan. I was the one who had hurt him and driven him away, and now I was seeing the horrible consequences of my actions.

Paloma placed a hand on my shoulder. I nodded back, grateful for her support. It wasn't her fault I wanted the one person I couldn't have.

Sullivan's kiss with Helene went on . . . and on . . . and on . . .

Suddenly, he dropped his arms from her waist and drew back. "I'm sorry." He scrubbed his hand through his hair and then down his face. "I can't do this."

"Really?" A mocking note crept into Helene's voice. "We both know that the real reason you asked me here was so that you could fuck me and get your revenge on Everleigh. And now you can't go through with it?"

Sullivan let out a tense, ragged breath and shook his head. "No, I can't."

Her eyes narrowed in understanding. "You really do care about her."

He let out another breath. "I'm sorry, Helene. I shouldn't have tried to use you like this."

She let out a light, pealing laugh. "Use me? I was the one using *you*, dear, sweet Lucas. You always were a fantastic fuck, and I was going to wring every drop of pleasure I could out of you tonight. But then you had to go and ruin it with your *feelings*."

She rolled her eyes and shook her head, as though she was deeply disappointed in him. Then she walked over, grabbed her silk wrap from the table, and draped it around her shoulders.

"What are you doing?" Sullivan asked, his face creasing with confusion.

"Isn't it obvious?" Helene said. "I'm leaving you to your anger and self-pity. Because those things, my dear, definitely do not lead to a good time for me."

Sullivan winced. "And what about fucking me for your own pleasure?"

"It's obvious that you care far more about Everleigh than you ever did about me." Her face hardened. "And I am no one's second choice."

He winced again.

Helene finished draping her wrap around her shoulders, then walked back over to him. She studied him with far less anger and hostility than before. "Do you know why things didn't work out between us?"

Sullivan blinked, as though the question surprised him, but he answered her. "Your father forced you to break off our engagement."

"That was part of it, but I also handled things badly, which I deeply regret," Helene said. "But the truth is that you always loved your precious pride and principles more than you did me, Lucas."

His eyebrows drew together in confusion. "What? That's not true."

"Oh, yes, it is," Helene said in a matter-of-fact tone. "I could have eventually found some way to be with you, with or without my father's approval. But you didn't give me a chance to do that or anything else to make things right between us. You were so caught up in everyone treating you *exactly* the same as Dominic and Frederich that you just couldn't be happy with anything different, with anything less."

"Why should I have been happy with *less*?" Sullivan growled.

"Because life can be a cruel, heartless bitch," Helene snapped. "Because we should hold on to the happiness we have and not worry about what other people think of it, or especially of us. Because caring about someone occasionally means compromising something about yourself for *their* benefit and not your own. That's what real love is, Lucas."

"You didn't compromise anything," he growled again.

She gave him a sad look. "Oh, yes, I did. I gave you up so that my sisters would have a good, secure future. So that they could marry for love, even if I couldn't."

"So what you're really saying is that you loved your sisters more than you did me." Hurt rasped through Sullivan's voice.

Helene shook her head. "It wasn't about loving them more or you less. It was about protecting *all* the people I loved the best way I could."

"And you decided to sacrifice me, *us*, for the sake of your family?"

"Yes," she replied without hesitation. "Because my sisters were young and couldn't take care of themselves, and all it would cost you was a broken heart and some wounded pride."

In that moment, my respect for Helene grew a hundredfold. Whether she was the traitor or not, she'd made the hard choice to give up Lucas for the greater good of her family. It was too bad she didn't have any Blair blood. Helene would have made a magnificent queen.

Sullivan frowned, as though he had never considered things from her point of view before, but I understood Helene's reasoning all too well, and I admired her for making such a tough choice. Sometimes, the only thing you could do was decide who you could hurt the least.

"I wonder, though . . ." Helene's voice trailed off.

"What?" he asked.

She studied him. "I wonder if Everleigh is more important to you than even your pride and principles are."

I held my breath, wondering what he would say. A muscle ticked in Sullivan's jaw, but he remained silent.

"Either way, we can't change the past, only the future. I guess we'll see how much you care about Everleigh." Helene's face softened. "I really did love you, Lucas, and I am truly sorry for all the pain I caused you. I never wanted you to feel like less with me. I just wanted you to be happy being yourself."

She stared at him a moment longer, then stepped forward and pressed a soft kiss to his cheek. Sullivan stood absolutely still, not moving a muscle. Helene dropped her head, turned around, and left the greenhouse.

Sullivan stayed where he was, staring at the open door that she had gone through. My heart ached for him, and for Helene too. She'd been in an impossible situation, and she'd made the best choices she could, even if they had hurt Sullivan and her too.

Paloma squeezed my shoulder, drawing my attention, and pointed to a set of stone steps on the far side of the balcony. I nodded, and she headed in that direction.

I glanced in through the glass again, but Sullivan had vanished, and the main greenhouse door was now shut. He had left, and it was time for me to do the same, so I closed the glass door, crossed the balcony, and hurried down the steps after Paloma.

chapter twenty-one

I never realized that being engaged could be so bloody *exhausting.*

The rest of the week passed by in a blur of breakfasts, luncheons, dinners, and more. Now that I was engaged to Dominic, every single noble at Glitnir wanted to offer their enthusiastic congratulations and slyly propose this deal or that deal over tea and kiwi cakes. The crown prince and I attended event after tedious event, and I smiled so long and hard that I was afraid my face would become permanently fixed in the fake expression.

The only good thing about our whirlwind schedule was that it kept Dominic close to me. I watched everyone he came into contact with, just in case Helene might be working with someone else, but no one tried to hurt Dominic.

Helene was at many of the events, but she never did or said anything suspicious. If I hadn't found the poisonous cactus in her greenhouse, I never would have seriously suspected her of being the traitor.

I watched her closely, especially whenever she was near

Heinrich, but she always seemed calm and cheerful, as though nothing was bothering her. I had no idea what she thought about his recovery. She had to have realized that the amethyst-eye poison was gone from his system, but Helene didn't try to sicken the king again. It seemed as though she was biding her time, waiting for the right opportunity to strike, so I did the same. This was one long game that I was determined to win.

Still, the more days that passed, the more I started to wonder if I was wrong about Helene. Sure, she had the cactus, but anyone could have slipped into her workshop and snipped a flower or two to brew the poison. The cactus's pot might look similar to ones that Maeven had, but in the end, it was just a pot. And lots of people had signet rings.

The items weren't enough to either exonerate or convict the plant magier. But if Helene wasn't the traitor, then who was? I didn't have any other real suspects, which only added to my worry.

Sullivan also attended many of the events, since he too was part of the royal family, and I often caught him staring at me, sometimes with anger, sometimes with disgust, and sometimes with longing so intense it took my breath away. But he didn't approach me, and I didn't seek him out. I didn't dare, for fear of spilling my guts about my whole convoluted plan.

But the days quickly ticked away, and all too soon it was the night of the royal ball.

I stood in front of a full-length mirror in my chambers, staring at my reflection. Calandre had crafted a simple but exquisite gown of midnight-blue velvet with a sweetheart neckline, three-quarter sleeves, and a full, floor-length skirt. Silver thread scrolled up the sleeves and down my neckline before spreading out into a large crown-of-shards crest on my chest. More silver thread scrolled down the skirt before lining the hem. My only jewelry was the two silver bracelets—gauntlets—that Alvis had made me. The midnight-blue tearstone shards in the bracelets' crown crests matched the color of my gown.

Given that this was a royal ball, I had expected Calandre to insist on my wearing heels, but she had surprised me by giving me a pair of flat, blue velvet sandals with thick straps that wound up past my ankles. They reminded me of the sturdy sandals I had worn in the gladiator arena, although they too featured my crown-of-shards crest in silver thread on the closed toes.

Camille had taken extra care with my makeup, putting smoky shadow and silver liner on my eyes and staining my lips with berry balm. Cerana had curled my hair into loose waves, but I'd refused to wear my crown.

I expected Helene—or whoever the traitor really was—to orchestrate some sort of attack tonight, against either Dominic, Heinrich, or me, or perhaps all three of us. I wanted to be able to fight, if it came down to that, and not worry about losing my crown. Keeping my head attached to my body was much more important.

"Calandre, you and your sisters have truly outdone yourselves," I murmured. "I've never looked better."

She beamed at me, as did her sisters.

I patted the sides of the dress. "And I especially like the pockets."

"I thought you might like to take your dagger to the ball, and I couldn't let you wear it on that awful black leather belt. It would have completely ruined the look of the dress." Calandre shuddered at the thought. "So pockets seemed like the perfect compromise and hiding place."

She was absolutely right, and my tearstone dagger was snugly tucked away in my right pocket. I just wished the dress was large enough to hide my sword too.

I grinned. "You know me too well."

Calandre grinned back at me.

A knock sounded, and Paloma stepped into the room. She wasn't wearing a gown, but Calandre had still made her something special. Small ogre faces done in gold thread glinted on the sleeves of her dark green tunic, and more gold thread ran in jagged, teethlike lines down her black leggings.

Camille and Cerana had given Paloma dark, dramatic eyes and red lips and had sleeked her blond hair back into an elaborate, crownlike braid that arched across her head. The ogre on her neck had taken notice, and the blond hair that curled around the morph mark was now braided in the same pretty style.

Paloma had grumbled about having her hair and makeup done, but she had kept sneaking glances at herself in the mirror, and I thought that deep down she—and her inner ogre—secretly loved the attention.

Paloma studied me. "You look nice."

"Is that supposed to be a compliment?"

She shrugged. "Nice is nice, isn't it?"

I sighed. Sometimes, I thought my friend was a little too matter-of-fact.

Paloma grinned, as did the ogre on her neck, but the expression slowly evaporated from both their faces. "Are you ready for this?"

She was talking about far more than the ball. Hopefully, tonight we would catch Helene in the act of conspiring against the Ripleys and end the threat to Heinrich and Dominic.

"I thought you were going to stop asking me that," I teased, trying to lighten the mood.

She arched an eyebrow. "Maybe I will, when you finally quit doing such new, grand, and important things."

I rolled my eyes, but I was grinning too.

I thanked Calandre and her sisters again and headed out

into the hallway, where several Bellonan guards were waiting. Paloma stepped up beside me, and we strolled through the palace, with Calandre and her sisters trailing us, along with the guards. It didn't take us long to reach the hallway that led to the throne room.

The doors were wide open, and scores of nobles were already inside, talking, laughing, eating, and drinking, while servants moved all around them. The royal ball was already well under way.

I sent Calandre and her sisters on ahead, along with the guards, and told them all to have a good time. Then I walked over to a small alcove where Cho, Serilda, and Xenia were waiting.

Calandre and her sisters had also worked their magic on my other friends. Cho was wearing his usual red jacket and ruffled white shirt, although these were made of fine material, and his jacket featured gold buttons stamped with dragon heads.

Serilda looked beautiful in a white ball gown patterned with her swan crest. Each small swan was done in black thread, with tiny blue tearstones for its eye and beak, just like the pendant hanging from her neck. A black velvet belt studded with thin silver knives was cinched around her waist. I wasn't the only one who'd wanted to have a weapon handy tonight.

Xenia also looked lovely in a dark green gown trimmed with silver thread. She was clutching her silver ogre cane like usual, which was the only weapon she needed.

"Is everything ready?" I asked.

Xenia nodded. "Halvar and Bjarni are already inside. Halvar will shadow Dominic, while Bjarni will do the same to Heinrich. If anyone tries to harm the prince or the king, then Halvar and Bjarni will stop them."

"Paloma and I will watch Helene," Cho added. "And see who she talks to."

"And I'll watch Evie's back," Serilda chimed in.

I nodded. "Good luck."

Cho, Xenia, and Paloma headed toward the ballroom, but Serilda stayed behind in the alcove.

She looked me up and down. "I had my doubts about Calandre being your thread master, but she did an outstanding job. You look beautiful, Evie."

I gestured at her gown. "As do you. It seems as though we're both black swans tonight."

Serilda smiled at my joke, then stared into the throne room. Her blue gaze grew soft and dreamy, as though she was looking at something very far away, and the hard, sharp scent of her magic, like coldiron mixed with blood, filled the air.

"What possibilities are you seeing?" I asked. "Will we catch the traitor tonight?"

Serilda shook her head. "It's too early to tell. My magic isn't . . . exact. Every choice a person makes ends a dozen possibilities and opens up a dozen more. I'm sorry, Evie. I know that's not what you wanted to hear."

No, it wasn't, but I nodded in understanding. Serilda squeezed my hand, then headed into the ball.

That left me standing alone in the alcove. I drew in a breath, then slowly let it out, pushing away my fear, worry, and dread along with it. Then, when I was ready, I walked down the hall and through the open doors.

On a normal day, the throne room was impressive enough, but Heinrich had really had the servants go all out for the ball. The floor and walls had been polished to such a high gloss that they seemed as smooth as glass, while the gray and white diamonds in the jet chandeliers cast out radiant sprays of light.

Strings of tiny gray and white fluorestones had been wrapped around the columns, along with the second-floor balcony railing. The fluorestones' soft, muted glows high-lighted the snarling gargoyles embedded in the stone columns and made their silver faces and jeweled eyes flicker and flash like fire. The gargoyles seemed as lifelike as the gladiators in the tearstone columns at Seven Spire, and I half expected one of the creatures to swipe out at me with its paw.

Nobles wearing formal jackets and ball gowns were clustered in groups, still talking, laughing, eating, and drinking. Servants carrying trays of food and drinks moved from the refreshment tables along the walls, through the crowd, and back again. Guards also lined the walls, making sure that everything was proceeding as planned. Over in the back corner, close to the raised dais, more than a dozen musicians played various instruments. Soft trills of music floated through the air, although no one was dancing yet.

But perhaps the most eye-catching things were the two enormous banners hanging on the wall on either side of the throne. One of the banners boasted the Ripley snarling-gargoyle crest done in glittering silver thread on a black background, while the other banner featured my crown-of-shards crest, also done in silver thread, but on a midnight-blue background.

The banners reminded me yet again that tonight would probably determine not only my and Dominic's fates but the fates of our kingdoms as well. My stomach twisted at the thought, but I fixed my usual bland, benign smile on my face.

I dropped my gaze to the dais. Heinrich was sitting on his throne, wearing a formal, short gray jacket that featured the Ripley gargoyle crest done in black thread over his heart. Dahlia was seated next to him in a small, plain chair. She looked beautiful in a dark green gown trimmed with gold thread. Her black hair was smoothed back into a high, elegant bun, and her gold locket gleamed around her neck like usual.

Dominic was standing beside the king, and the prince looked exceptionally handsome in his gray jacket. Gemma was wearing a dark gray gown that matched her grandfather's and father's jackets. The princess was sitting on the dais steps and talking to Alvis, who was sporting a fine black cloak over his clothes.

Rhea was standing a few feet away, speaking with Helene. The captain was wearing her usual uniform and weapons, although her black hair had been pulled back into a pretty braid, and berry balm stained her lips a dark red. And Helene was stunning as always in a pale gray gown patterned with green vines and purple flowers studded with amethysts. She smiled and gestured at something Rhea said, making her silver signet ring flash on her finger.

I didn't see Sullivan anywhere, and I had to force myself to stop looking for him.

Heinrich had wanted me to make an entrance, so I held my position in the open space in front of the doors, and people slowly started to notice me. Murmurs rippled through the crowd, although I couldn't tell if they were approving or not. The nobles, servants, and guards all turned toward me, and a hush fell over the room.

Heinrich signaled the orchestra, and their light, lilting music trailed off, replaced by a low, rolling drumbeat. The fluorestones dimmed, although a bright, glaring spotlight fell on me. It was all a bit dramatic for my tastes, but I was the guest, so I couldn't complain, although the spotlight made me feel like I was back in the gladiator arena at the Black Swan, about to step out into the ring and fight to the death.

In a way, that's exactly what I was doing.

"And now," Cho's voice boomed out like thunder, "announcing Her Royal Majesty, Queen Everleigh Saffira Winter Blair of Bellona!"

The spotlight burned a little brighter and hotter, but I smiled into the harsh glare and strode forward.

Showtime.

Unlike the last time I'd been in here, Heinrich and Dominic didn't wait for me to walk across the room. The two men came down off the dais and met me in the middle.

Dominic offered me his arm, which I took, favoring him with the most dazzling smile I could muster. Dahlia also came down off the dais, and Gemma and Alvis stepped forward as well, along with Rhea and Helene.

The plant magier sidled up to Heinrich, hovering by his elbow. I tensed, thinking she might attack him, but Helene only clasped her hands together, ready to listen to the king's speech.

I looked past her into the crowd of nobles. Two men were lurking a few feet behind Helene and Dahlia. One was a tall man with coppery hair, hazel eyes, and a fearsome ogre face on his neck, while the other was shorter and stockier with black hair, dark brown eyes, onyx skin, and a long, bushy beard. An ogre face adorned his neck as well.

Halvar, Xenia's nephew, and Bjarni, his friend, noticed me staring at them. Halvar nodded, while Bjarni winked. They were watching Dominic and Heinrich as planned. Some of the tension eased out of my body.

Murmurs rippled through the nobles, but Heinrich held up his hands, asking for silence.

"We are gathered here to celebrate Queen Everleigh's visit, along with her engagement to Prince Dominic." The king's voice boomed out almost as loudly as Cho's had. "This marriage will cement Andvari and Bellona as allies from this day forward and also bring greater opportunity and prosperity to both our kingdoms . . ."

Heinrich launched into his speech, droning on and on about what a glorious night this was, how Andvari and Bellona would be allies forevermore after I wed Dominic, and all the other usual pleasantries.

I kept my smile fixed on my face, but I tuned out his words. They didn't matter tonight. Only people's actions did.

While Heinrich talked, servants handed out champagne. Helene took two glasses off a tray and gave one to Heinrich. I watched her closely, but she didn't slip anything into his drink. I drew in a breath, tasting the air, but I didn't sense any poison in Heinrich's champagne. Perhaps Helene was going to wait until later before she sprang her trap, whatever it was.

"To Dominic and Everleigh!" Heinrich called out, finishing his speech. "May they have a long and prosperous partnership. To love!"

"To love!" Everyone echoed the words back and took a long drink of their champagne.

After that, the nobles surged forward, each one wanting to congratulate Heinrich on his shrewd new alliance and Dominic and me on our upcoming marriage. As I smiled and nodded and shook hands, I watched everyone who approached the king and the prince, but no one said or did anything suspicious, and Helene kept her distance from them, talking to Dahlia instead.

Finally, all the nobles had been placated, and Heinrich signaled for the musicians to start playing again.

Dominic bowed to me, then held out his hand. "May I have this dance?"

I placed my hand in his, as was expected. "Of course."

The nobles fell back, and Dominic whirled me around the

center of the room. Only the two of us were dancing, and I felt more on display than ever before. Thankfully, that first dance was a short one. Heinrich held out his hand to Dahlia, and the two of them started dancing, along with the nobles.

Dominic smiled. "I should have said this before, but you look absolutely stunning, Everleigh."

"And you look very handsome yourself."

He stared at me as we swayed from side to side. "You seem a bit distracted. What are you thinking about?"

I couldn't tell him that I'd been scanning the crowd for Mortan assassins, so I shrugged. "Nothing in particular."

The corner of his lips curved up into a small, crooked grin that was so much like Sullivan's that it made my chest ache. "Ah, you just broke my heart. I was hoping you were thinking about me and how well we move together."

"Of course," I murmured. "You are a lovely dancer."

That wry smile curved his lips again. "Just not the man you want to be dancing with."

I didn't see the point in lying. "No."

Dominic nodded. "I can't say that I've ever been truly jealous of Lucas before, but I feel a faint twinge of it when it comes to you."

I raised my eyebrows. "Only a faint twinge?"

He shrugged. "There's no use being jealous when you know that something is forever beyond your reach, and you are definitely beyond my reach, thanks to Lucas."

His voice was light and flirty, but his gaze flicked to the right and locked onto Rhea, who was talking with a handsome nobleman.

"Just like Rhea is forever beyond your reach?" I asked.

He shrugged again, but I could smell his ashy heartbreak.

"It doesn't have to be that way. You are the crown prince of

Andvari. You should marry whomever you want. And if the nobles don't like it, then tell them to fuck off and go haunt someone else's court." I paused. "As long as it's not mine."

He chuckled, thinking that I was joking. "My current fiancée might take a bit of umbrage at that."

"I'm not going to marry you, Dominic. I was *never* going to marry you."

Surprise flashed in his eyes, and he finally realized that I was serious. His steps slowed, and he stopped dancing, right there in the middle of the floor.

"What do you mean, you were never going to marry me?" Dominic asked, his voice growing sharper and more suspicious with every word. "What game are you playing, Everleigh?"

I hadn't meant to say so much, but I couldn't take my words back. Even more than that, I didn't *want* to take them back. I was tired of lying to everyone, especially Sullivan. Besides, if Helene and the Mortans didn't strike during the ball, then I would have to confess my scheme. Dominic deserved to hear the truth from me, especially since he and Rhea were also suffering because of my lies.

I opened my mouth to tell him everything when a familiar voice cut me off.

"May I have this dance?"

Sullivan stepped up beside his brother. Like Heinrich and Dominic, Sullivan was dressed in a short, formal gray jacket, but he was easily the most handsome of the three men. His dark brown hair gleamed under the lights, and his eyes were as bright and blue as I'd ever seen them. But even more than that, there was an intensity to him, a fierceness that whispered that he wouldn't be denied what he wanted tonight, and I couldn't help the hope that flooded my heart that he still wanted me.

Our gazes met and held, and Sullivan studied me from head to toe, heat sparking in his eyes.

"You look exquisite tonight, highness." His low, husky voice slid across my skin and made something hot and hard coil deep inside me.

"So do you, Sully," I murmured. "So do you."

All around us, people kept dancing, although whispers rippled through the crowd. Sullivan asking his brother for a dance with me, his newly announced fiancée, had already set the nobles' tongues wagging.

Dominic glanced back and forth between the two of us, then leaned down and kissed my cheek. "Like I said before, there's no use being jealous when you've already lost," he murmured in my ear.

I looked at him. "Then you should go get the woman you truly want."

Dominic stared at me a moment longer. Then he winked, drew back, and bowed to his brother. "She's all yours, Lucas."

Dominic winked at me again, then headed straight for Rhea. He didn't notice Halvar trailing along behind him. Since Dominic was safe for now, I turned back to Sullivan and held out my hand.

"Shall we?" I asked in a low voice.

He stepped forward and curled one hand around my waist, even as he took my hand in his. The heat from his fingers scorched my own. "Yes, we shall."

The music ramped up to a fast, lively reel, and we fell into the steps. We didn't speak during the dance. I didn't want to talk to Sullivan. No, right now, I simply wanted to soak up every little thing about him and pretend like this was our engagement party and that we could really be together, instead of the fact that I'd probably torn us apart forever with my lies.

The bright, sharp glitter of his blue eyes. The strong, warm feel of his hand in mine. The bunch and flex of his shoulder under my fingertips. His cold vanilla scent sinking deep down into my lungs. I concentrated on all that and more, so much more, until my heart was hammering in my chest even faster than the music was playing.

Eventually, the reel slowed down into a more traditional waltz, and Sullivan and I stepped even closer together, staring into each other's eyes. The rest of the throne room fell away, and all I could see, hear, feel, and smell was him holding me close.

"I've been thinking about that night at Castle Asmund," Sullivan said, his voice once again a low, husky whisper. "Do you remember that night, highness?"

"I could never forget it."

That was the night when I'd first admitted to myself that I had feelings for him, that was the night when I'd confessed those feelings to him—and that was the night when he had first rejected me.

"I made a terrible mistake then, the worst mistake of my life," Sullivan murmured, still staring at me. "And it's a mistake that I'd like to correct. If you'll still have me."

My breath caught in my throat, but I forced myself to be cautious. "But what about—"

"I don't care about Dominic or your engagement or what my father or anyone else thinks," he growled.

I shook my head. Maybe it was wrong, but those things had never even occurred to me. I had been going to ask about how much I had hurt him, but he didn't give me the chance.

Sullivan pulled me even closer, his blue gaze burning into mine. "I've wanted you for months now, highness, and I think it's finally time to do something about it. What do you say? Do you still want me too?"

"Of course I do," I whispered, my heart still hammering in my chest.

"Wait a few minutes, then slip out one of the side doors and meet me at the hedge-maze entrance," he murmured.

The music stopped, and the dance ended. Sullivan and I stood there, frozen in place. Then he pressed a chaste kiss to my hand, turned, and walked away.

He vanished into the crowd of nobles, all of whom stared at me, whispering about our heated dance. My cheeks flushed at the sudden, sharp attention, but I plastered my benign smile on my face again. Then I turned and walked in the opposite direction from Sullivan.

I did a lap around the room, nodding and smiling at everyone. While I skirted around the nobles, I also looked for my friends.

Bjarni was a few feet away from Heinrich, who was speaking with some nobles, while Halvar was lurking near Dominic, who was talking with Rhea in the corner close to the musicians. Cho, Paloma, and Xenia were all moving around as well, keeping an eye on everyone.

My gaze locked with Serilda's, and she pointed at a door in the wall. She had obviously seen my dance with Sullivan and was telling me that she and the others had everything under control and that I should go after him. I flashed her a grateful smile.

I did another lap around the room, but it didn't seem like the Mortans were going to strike anytime soon. Maybe I had been wrong, and nothing bad would happen tonight. I still had my doubts, but Sullivan was waiting for me.

So on my third lap, I walked over to the door Serilda had pointed out, twisted the knob, and stepped through to the other side. A few nobles were milling around on the terrace outside, but I quickly moved past them. The second I was alone, I picked up my skirt and started running.

Even though it was only a short distance away, it seemed to take me forever to reach the gardens. With every quick step and swish of my gown, my heart hammered a little faster in my chest. By the time I made it to my destination, my body was thrumming with anticipation.

Sullivan whirled around at the rustle of my skirt. I slowed down and stopped in front of him. His blue gaze raked over me just as it had before in the ballroom, and heat sparked in his eyes—the same heat that was running through my own body.

He held out his hand, and I took it.

Still staring at me, Sullivan pulled me into the gardens. He led me down a path and into the hedge maze. It was darker in here, but he knew exactly where he was going, and he guided me through the twists and turns. Eventually, the rows of evergreen bushes fell away, revealing the trees and flowers that flanked the gazebo in the heart of the maze.

Just like the throne room, the gazebo had been decked out in strings of gray and white fluorestones that wrapped around the railing before climbing up the columns and spreading out across the roof. It was a beautiful, dreamy scene, and I couldn't have asked for a more romantic spot.

Sullivan pulled me into the center of the gazebo, then dropped my hand. We stood there, facing each other, both of us breathing hard. My heart kept hammering in my chest, even as more and more anticipation surged through my body, but I didn't move toward him.

Our last few months together had been building up to this one moment, the one I had dreamed about, and the one I had prepared for by taking all the appropriate herbs and precautions. And now that it was finally here, I wanted to make it last as long as possible.

Sullivan stared back at me, drinking me in the same way that I was him. Then slowly, very, very slowly, he stepped toward me. My breath caught in my throat, and I fisted my hands in the folds of my gown, still trying to make the moment last as long as possible.

He lifted his hand and gently cupped my cheek, his fingers splaying over my face as though he wanted to feel as much of my skin as possible at one time. I sucked in a breath at the warmth of his skin against mine.

He took another step toward me and curled his other hand around my waist. This time, my breath caught in my throat.

He took a third and final step toward me, and I swayed closer to him.

Sullivan stared at me a heartbeat longer, then lowered his head and crushed his lips to mine.

CHAPTER TWENTY-TWO

The kiss was everything I had ever imagined.

Everything I had ever dreamed about when I was lying in bed late at night, picturing him beside me.

Everything I had ever wished and hoped and thought it would be.

And then some.

Sullivan's lips crashed into mine, and he growled and pulled me even closer so that our bodies were flush together from lips to chests to thighs. I tangled my fingers in his hair and kissed him back just as feverishly. Our lips and tongues dueled together the same way we had in the gladiator training ring, each one of us fighting for dominance, although the pleasure we brought each other made us both the victors.

Even as I kissed and kissed him, my hands trailed along his neck, then across his broad shoulders and down his muscled chest. I splayed my fingers over his heart the same way he had touched my face. Perhaps it was my imagination, but I could hear and feel the frantic beating of his heart. Or perhaps that was my own heart picking up speed with each passing second.

That first touch of our lips together ignited every single nerve ending in my body, and hot, electric desire crackled through my veins, stronger than any magier's lightning. I wanted him more than I had ever wanted anything, and I was finally going to have him.

In between kisses, I grabbed Sullivan's jacket and tugged him backward with me. I was heading for one of the cushioned benches that lined the gazebo, but Sullivan had other ideas, and he pinned me up against one of the columns and tore his mouth away from mine. I dug my hands into his hair, feeling the silky locks slide through my fingers even as his lips scorched a path down my neck and chest.

Sullivan reached the sweetheart neckline of my dress, and he pushed the fabric aside, exposing one of my breasts. My nipple hardened in the cool night air.

His bright, fierce gaze locked with mine. "You're even more beautiful than I imagined," he rasped.

He dipped his head and swirled his tongue around my nipple before catching it in his teeth and nibbling it gently. I gasped with pleasure, and he sucked on it hard. I gasped again, louder this time, and more of that hot, electric desire sizzled through me.

"I love it when you make that sound," he growled.

I dug my fingers into his hair again, urging him on. Sullivan lavished attention on that breast, then exposed the other one and did the same thing to it, making more and more pleasure spike through me.

He lifted his head, and I cupped his face in my hands and crushed my lips to his. Our tongues dueled together again, but it wasn't enough. I wanted to touch him the same way that he had touched me, so I broke off the kiss and went to work on the buttons on his jacket. The second that the last one slid free, Sullivan stripped off the jacket and tossed it aside. I yanked on his tunic, and he lifted his arms so that I could pull it all the way up and over his head and off.

I tossed the shirt aside, then stared at his bare chest, which was all hard, glorious muscle, dotted here and there with white lines and a few other small, puckered scars. I ran my finger down one of the marks that cut close to his heart.

"The hazards of working for a gladiator troupe," he explained.

"Well, then, let me kiss them and make them better."

I leaned forward and softly kissed that scar, along with his other ones. Sullivan stood rock-still, but every touch of my lips and slide of my tongue made him tremble.

"Amazing," I murmured. "Even your skin tastes like vanilla and spice."

I started to kiss his scars again, but Sullivan put his finger under my chin, lifting my head. Then he dropped his hand and stepped away from me.

"Are you sure you want this?" he asked in a hoarse voice. "Are you sure you want . . . me?"

The faint tremor in his voice made my heart ache. He wasn't just asking about the sex. He wanted me to want *him*, bastard prince and all. And I did—more than he would ever know.

I stepped forward, cupped his face in my hands, and stared into his eyes. "I've never been more certain about anything, Sully."

All sorts of emotions flashed in his eyes. Relief. Satisfaction. And something that was much hotter and far deeper than mere desire, something that was so intense and electric that it took my breath away.

He stared at me a moment longer, then reached down and grabbed the bottom of my dress, lifting my skirt up and out of the way. I hissed as his warm hands skimmed my bare thighs, then slid higher. He hooked his thumbs into the sides of my silky undergarments, then drew them down. I stepped out of them, and he tossed them aside. They landed in a pile with his jacket and tunic.

He dropped to his knees in front of me, grabbed one of my legs, and slowly, carefully hooked it up and over his shoulder. His gaze on mine, he reached out and stroked my soft, dark curls. I tensed with anticipation.

Sullivan gave me a wicked grin. "Let's see how you taste, highness."

He leaned forward, licking, nibbling, and sucking on my core just like he'd done to my breasts. Jolt after jolt of pleasure spiked through me, my entire body trembled, and I had to wrap my hands around the column behind me for support.

He stopped and looked up at me. "I love how you taste," he growled.

He leaned forward and went to work with his mouth again, swirling his tongue around, even as he stroked me with his fingers. The pressure in my body built and built until it suddenly exploded in a fiery wave of pleasure. I groaned as the orgasm ripped through me, and my body went limp and languid.

Sullivan carefully slid my leg off his shoulder and got to his feet. He leaned forward to kiss me again, but I reached out, grabbed his shoulders, spun him around, and pinned him up against the column.

"My turn," I rasped.

"I always do as my queen commands," he murmured.

I ran my hands over his bare chest again, slowly trailing my fingers down, down, down . . . I cupped his hard, thick cock through his leggings, making him hiss with pleasure. Then I grabbed the laces on his leggings, slowly undoing them. It didn't take me long, and I slid my hand inside his pants, stroking him the same way that he had me.

Sullivan groaned. "I didn't realize you were such an expert in torture, highness."

"Oh, Sully. I haven't begun to torture you yet."

I gave him another wicked smile, then dropped to my knees and ran my tongue over him, licking, nibbling, and sucking, just as he had done to me. Sullivan groaned again, and his body jerked and twitched as he fought for control.

Finally, he let out another growl, reached down, and eased me away from him. Then he dropped down to his knees as well. We stared at each other for a moment, both of us breathing hard, knowing what was coming next.

Then, with one thought, we came together.

I wrapped my arms around his neck, kissing him even more feverishly. I thrust my tongue into his mouth over and over, and he matched me move for move. Sullivan kneaded my breasts again, then grabbed me around the waist, pulling me even closer. The next thing I knew, he was falling back against the gazebo floor and carrying me along with him.

Sullivan grabbed my skirt again, pulling it up and out of the way, even as I yanked the laces of his pants aside. I leaned forward, looming over him, and he reached up and gently caressed my cheek. Still staring at him, I moved forward, then slid down on top of his cock, taking him deep inside me.

We both groaned at how fantastic it felt.

I pulled back a little, then slid forward again. And then again. And then again.

Sullivan put his hands on my hips, urging me on, even as he pumped his hips up to meet mine. Our breaths came in ragged gasps, even as our movements became quicker, harder, faster. Even though he was all that I could feel, hear, taste, smell, it wasn't enough, and I still needed—*wanted*—more.

Sullivan drew me down on top of him, then rolled me over onto my back. Our gazes met and held for a long, intense moment. Then I locked my legs around his waist, and he thrust even deeper into me. And he didn't stop.

Over and over, we rocked together, that exquisite pressure building and building, until it finally coursed through us both in one bright, hot, electric explosion.

Afterward, we lay on the gazebo floor, our arms wrapped around each other.

I sighed with happiness. "I wish the world would stop and I could stay here forever."

Sullivan's arms tightened around me. "Me too, highness. Me too."

I nuzzled my face into his neck, drinking in his clean vanilla scent. I let myself inhale it over and over again, imprinting it and this one perfect moment into my mind. Then, when I was sure that I would always remember it, that I would always remember him and how he'd made me feel, I slowly disentangled my body from his and sat up.

"What are you doing?" he asked.

"Unfortunately, duty calls, and I have to go back to the ball."

I pulled my neckline up where it belonged, then got to my feet and retrieved my undergarments from where they had landed. I slid those on and smoothed down my skirt. My hair was a tangled mess, so I ran my fingers through the locks, trying to straighten them out.

Sullivan sat up as well. "What do you mean you have to go back to the ball?"

"I need to check on Dominic."

I was worrying about Helene and how she still might target the crown prince, so I said the words without really thinking about them.

"I see," Sullivan said in a cold, flat voice. "Going to make sure you're still engaged to my brother even after you just spent the last half hour fucking me?"

I grimaced. Too late, I realized that it was exactly the wrong thing to say, especially to Sullivan, and especially given what had just happened between us.

"That's not what I meant. You don't understand."

"Oh, I understand perfectly," he snapped. "We had a nice little rendezvous, but it's over now. You care about me, just not enough to choose me over Dominic, and I'm getting passed over for my brother yet again. I truly am the biggest fool, never learning that lesson."

Sullivan surged to his feet, stalked over, and grabbed his clothes. He yanked on his tunic with sharp, angry motions.

I opened my mouth to tell him everything. How I had never intended to marry Dominic, how I thought that Helene had poisoned Heinrich, how our friends were watching to make sure Mortan assassins didn't hurt his father or brother during the ball. I was going to confess it all and ask for his understanding and forgiveness.

But then a gust of wind blew through the gazebo, bringing a familiar scent along with it—the hot, caustic stench of magic.

I froze, wondering if I'd only imagined the aroma. My nose twitched, and I drew in a breath, tasting the air. The scent came again, stronger than before.

My stomach dropped. The last time I had smelled this particular stench of magic had been on the royal lawn at Seven Spire the night I had killed Vasilia. The scent now meant the same thing as it had then.

Once again, someone wanted to kill me.

I drew in another breath, this time to warn Sullivan, but more and more magic flooded the air, far too much magic for just one person. My stomach clenched again. Unless I was gravely mistaken, my would-be murderer had brought several magiers here.

My gaze snapped back and forth, searching the area beyond the gazebo, but all I saw were the trees, flowers, pond, and hedge maze. I wondered how long the magiers had been out there. The thought that they had seen and heard my passion with Sullivan disgusted me, but I forced the emotion aside.

Instead, another thought rose up in my mind—why were they holding their positions, instead of surging forward and attacking us? They should strike now, while Sullivan was distracted and the two of us were isolated. But I didn't get the sense that the magiers were creeping any closer. So what were they waiting for?

Sullivan shrugged into his jacket, and a bit of blue lightning sizzled out of his fingertips and sparked against the silver buttons as he fastened them. And I suddenly realized why the magiers were holding their positions.

They were waiting for Sullivan to leave before they killed me.

After all, they would have a far easier time murdering me if he wasn't around. And the assassins probably wanted to keep things quiet as they killed me so they could escape afterward. Battling Sullivan and his lightning would definitely not be easy or quiet.

Sullivan didn't have my mutt magic, so he didn't sense the other magiers. Instead, he finished buttoning up his jacket, then turned toward me, an angry expression on his face.

"Well, highness?" he snapped. "What don't I understand?"

In that moment, I knew what I had to do. The magiers were waiting for Sullivan to leave, and I was going to give them exactly what they wanted. There were too many magiers for Sullivan and me to fight off, and I wasn't going to let him die because of me.

I had to protect the prince one last time, even if that meant hurting him yet again with my words.

I shrugged. "Apparently, you don't understand how the world really works, Sully. Helene tried to explain it to you the other night in her greenhouse, but I see that it just didn't sink in."

His jaw clenched. "You were spying on Helene and me? Why?"

I shrugged again. "I was roaming the halls, looking for you, hoping to apologize, when I saw you enter her workshop. So I crept up and cracked open the door. I heard everything the two of you said."

It wasn't exactly the truth, but what was one more lie at this point?

"And what did Helene say then that you find so relevant now?" Sullivan growled.

"That sometimes people have to do things they don't like for the greater good." I squared my shoulders and lifted my chin. "I am the queen of Bellona, and I have to make sacrifices for my people, for my kingdom, whether I want to or not."

"Like marrying Dominic?"

"Exactly like that."

"So what was *this*?" he asked, throwing his hands out wide. "Why did you come with me, if you're still so dead set on marrying my brother?"

I braced myself for what I had to say next. "It's no secret that I've wanted you for months, Sully. And the feeling was mutual. Tonight, we both finally got what we wanted."

His eyebrows shot up. "And now what? You're done with me? Just like that?"

"Just like that." I kept my face cold as I stared at him. "What did you think was going to happen? That I would break off my engagement with Dominic just because we fucked? You should have known better. You said it yourself that queens don't consort with bastard princes."

He jerked back as though I had slapped him. Hurt flickered in his eyes, and the twin scents of his dusty resignation and ashy heartbreak burned my nose. But I still hadn't made him angry enough to storm off to safety, so I decided to twist my verbal daggers in even deeper.

"Why did you dance with me in the ballroom?" I asked. "Why did you bring me here?"

He frowned. "What do you mean?"

"I mean that what happened between us was more about Dominic than it ever was about me." I tilted my head to the side, studying him. "After all, what better way to finally beat your brother than by stealing me away from our engagement party and fucking me?"

Sullivan flinched again. "That's not why I brought you here. I wanted to show you how I feel about you. This doesn't have anything to do with Dominic."

"Maybe, maybe not. But it's a nice bonus, isn't it? Showing Dominic, Heinrich, and the nobles that I care about you more than I ever will about him. Rubbing your brother's face in the fact that I left the ballroom with *you* instead of *him*."

"Dominic loves Rhea," Sullivan snapped. "He doesn't care about you. Not like I do."

My heart squeezed tight at his words, but I forced myself to keep spewing lies and venom. "You told me once that you would never be satisfied with just one night with me. What do you think this is, Sully?"

A muscle ticked in his jaw. "I don't know, but I want to find out. Together."

He stepped forward and held out his hand. That one simple gesture almost broke me, but I hardened my heart. Nothing mattered except making sure that he left the gardens, that he left me behind—forever.

"I am the queen of Bellona, and you are a bastard prince," I repeated, making my voice as cold as possible. "We had our one night, and now it's over."

More hurt flashed in his eyes, but it was quickly drowned out by anger—so much *anger*. My heart squeezed tight again, but I made myself stay cold and impassive, as if I didn't care about him at all.

"I truly thought that you were different," Sullivan said in a harsh, accusing voice. "I truly thought that titles and power and what other people think didn't matter to you."

"And now?" I asked the inevitable question, knowing his answer would crush my heart.

He let out a low, bitter laugh. "And now I realize that *I'm* the one who doesn't matter to you. Not in the slightest." His face hardened, and his eyes glittered like ice. "I hope that you enjoy your marriage to Dominic, Your Majesty."

He pressed his fist to his heart and gave me a low, mocking bow. Then he straightened up, whirled around, and stalked away. I watched him leave the gazebo, cross the grass, and disappear into the hedge maze. The sharp *snap-snap-snap-snap* of his boots against the flagstones felt like knives ripping into my heart, slicing it to shreds.

I waited until the sound of his footsteps had faded away and I was sure he wasn't coming back before I spoke again.

"You can come out now."

For several seconds, nothing happened, but then a figure wearing a midnight-purple cloak stepped out of a pool of shadows close to the hedge maze.

And she wasn't alone.

Several more figures, also wearing dark cloaks, slipped out of the shadows as well. The figures surrounded the gazebo, then drew back their hoods. I didn't recognize their faces, but they all had the same purplish eyes.

They were all members of the Bastard Brigade.

The woman in the purple cloak glided forward and stepped into the gazebo. She waited a moment, making sure that I wasn't going to attack her, then reached up and flicked back her hood, revealing her face.

Blond hair sleeked back into a high, elegant bun, dark, amethyst eyes, a smug smile creasing her beautiful features. She looked the same as when I had seen her through the Cardea mirror at Seven Spire.

"Hello, Maeven. I was wondering when you were going to show yourself."

"Hello, Everleigh. You're looking particularly lovely tonight." Her gaze pointedly flicked over my still-tangled hair and rumpled gown. "Illicit affairs suit you."

My hands clenched into fists, but I forced myself to stand still and not rise to her obvious bait. "I see you brought some more of your charming relatives with you."

Maeven gave a not-so-modest shrug, then waved her hand. "Take her."

The assassins rushed forward and converged on me. I braced myself, thinking they were going to blast me with their magic, but they swarmed me instead.

I fought back, of course, punching, hitting, and kicking with all my might. But there was nothing that I could do. Not against so many of them.

I landed a few blows, but multiple sets of hands quickly latched onto my arms, holding me still. A fist zoomed forward and snapped into my face. Pain exploded in my jaw, and the world went black.

CHAPTER TWENTY-THREE

Ansel dragged my mother into the woods, and my mother dragged me along behind her. Together, the three of us formed a human chain, running away from Winterwind.

Yells rang out from the manor house in the distance, and I looked back over my shoulder. Through the trees, I spotted men armed with swords and torches pouring out of the kitchen door that we had come through a minute ago.

"Where is the Blair bitch?"

"We have to find her!"

"No one escapes!"

Their shouts tore through the air, and it was only a matter of time before they found our footprints in the snow and chased after us.

But once again, Ansel didn't appear to be concerned. Even more curious was the fact that my tutor seemed to know exactly where he was going, even though I'd never seen him so much as walk out here before. We moved deeper and deeper into the woods, and the shouts of the Mortan assassins quickly faded away.

Five minutes later, we ran into a small clearing. To my surprise, two horses laden down with saddlebags were tied to a tree. My heart lifted. We were going to escape after all.

But then I noticed that these weren't two random horses. One was a black stallion that belonged to Ansel, while the gray mare was my mother's mount. I frowned. How had they gotten out of the barn and all the way back here?

My mother sucked in a surprised breath, and she stopped and let go of Ansel's hand, along with mine. My tutor hurried over to his horse and stuck my father's sword into a saddlebag, then turned back around to us.

"What's wrong? We have to leave," Ansel hissed. "Now! Before they find us!"

"Why are these horses waiting here?" my mother whispered, voicing my thought.

Ansel opened his mouth, but my mother snapped up her hand. He bit back whatever he'd been about to say, but I could smell his garlic guilt. He reeked of it.

My mother stared at him with wide, horrified eyes. "You planned this," she accused. "You knew that the Mortans were going to attack Winterwind. That's why you had the horses waiting. So you could escape."

Ansel stalked over and grabbed her hands, squeezing them tight in his. "So we could escape, Leighton. I did it for you."

"But . . . why?" my mother asked in confusion.

Ansel stared at her, a strange, bright, almost fanatical light flashing in his eyes. This time, instead of garlic guilt, the stench of his cherry lust filled the clearing. The scent made me want to vomit.

"Because I love you," he declared. "And I know that you love me too."

My mother's eyes widened again, and she tore her hands out of his. "I love Jarl, my husband! Not you! Why would you ever think that?"

"Because you were always smiling at me, and talking to me, and laughing at my jokes," Ansel said. "I knew that you loved me, even if you couldn't show it whenever your idiot husband was around."

My mother sucked in a ragged breath and swayed on her feet. "You . . . you handed Jarl that glass of wine. You poisoned him. You killed him."

"I did it for us!" Ansel yelled, his voice rising to a near scream. "So we could finally be together!"

His voice boomed through the woods loud enough to make the owls nestled in the snowy trees squawk and take flight. My heart pounded, even as my stomach twisted itself into hard knots.

Ansel had murdered my father so he could . . . what? Be with my mother? Or whatever sick, twisted fantasy he'd invented in his head? Part of me didn't want to know the answer.

Anger burned in my mother's gray-blue eyes, and her lips curled up in disgust. She glared at him, then dropped her gaze, as if she couldn't stand to look at him anymore. She froze, as if something had caught her eye. Then she surged forward, reached out, and tore the bronze pocket watch off his vest.

She looked at the fancy cursive M engraved in the metal. The symbol must have meant something to her, because she held the watch out to him.

*"You're one of them," she said, spitting out the last word.
"You're a fucking Mortan."*

*Ansel grimaced, but he didn't deny it. My mother gave him
another disgusted look, then threw the watch at him. It bounced
off his chest and dropped into the snow.*

*"You have to come with me, Leighton," Ansel said, pleading
with her. "I'm trying to save you."*

*She shook her head and stepped away from him. "You
murdered my husband," she hissed. "I'm not going anywhere
with you!"*

*Then her eyes narrowed, and she actually smiled, as if
something about this whole horrible situation pleased her. "Your
relatives won't be happy you've betrayed them. They'll come for
you, and they'll give you all the horrors you deserve."*

*"No, we certainly are not happy about that," another
voice murmured. "And you're right. Ansel is going to regret
betraying us."*

*The three of us whirled around. The magier in the
midnight-purple cloak was standing in the clearing. Her hood
was down, revealing her blond hair and bright, eerie purple
eyes, and a ball of cold lightning crackled in her palm.*

*My mother lurched forward, putting herself in between the
magier and me.*

*Ansel wet his lips, held his hands out in front of him in
supplication, and tiptoed forward. "Marisse, wait, let me
explain—"*

*Marisse snapped up her hand and blasted him with her
magic. Purple hailstones mixed with cold lightning streaked
through the clearing and slammed into Ansel's chest, cutting
into and then freezing him where he stood. He screamed and
screamed, but there was nothing he could do. A few seconds*

later, he dropped to the ground, with several hailstones sticking out of his chest like knives and his eyes bulging like glassy marbles in his frozen face.

Marisse stared down at Ansel, then shook her head. "Ansel always was weak and foolish. I can't believe he thought that he could save you, or that you would willingly go with him after he murdered your husband." She shrugged. "But love makes us do stupid things, doesn't it?"

My mother didn't answer, but I could smell her lemony worry. My nose twitched. I could also smell the cold, crisp scent of my mother's magic as she reached for it, gathering it up and up inside her. I did the same with my immunity.

"And now, Winter queen," Marisse hissed, "it's time for you to die, along with your precious daughter—"

Blue light flashed to life in my mother's palm, and she snapped up her hand and threw her magic at the other woman. The light split apart and sharpened into long, jagged needles of ice. Hope filled my chest. All we needed was one needle to skewer the magier, and we could escape.

But Marisse unleashed her own magic. Her purple hailstones blasted apart my mother's blue needles, and all the pieces of ice crashed together and shattered in midair.

"Run, Evie!" my mother screamed, even as she raised her hand for another attack. "Run!"

But I never got the chance. Marisse was faster than my mother, and she snapped up her hands, unleashing more of her sharp, deadly hailstones, along with bolts of cold lightning. My mother pushed back with her own power, but one of the hailstones slipped past her defenses and slammed into her chest, spinning her around.

Her hot, sticky blood spattered onto my face.

I hissed, jerked back, and slapped my hand to my cheek before pulling it away. I stared down in horror at the scarlet specks staining my fingertips, at the awful sight of my mother's blood on my own skin. Then, determination filled me, overcoming my fear and panic. I'd already lost my father to these Mortan bastards. I wasn't losing my mother too, even though I had no idea how I could save her or myself.

But it was already too late.

My mother staggered forward, and I realized that Marisse's hailstone had plunged into her heart like an amethyst dagger. Blood gushed out of the wound, staining the purple ice an ugly, mottled brown.

Marisse laughed and lifted her hand for another strike. My mother must have seen my eyes widen because she wrapped her arms around me, still determined to protect me.

"Mama!" I screamed. "Mama!"

My mother tightened her grip on me. "Use . . . your magic . . ." she mumbled. "Save . . . yourself . . . Evie . . ."

More sharp hailstones punched into my mother's back, making her scream again. She pitched forward, and we both tumbled to the ground. My mother fell on top of me, still trying to protect me, and her warm blood oozed over my neck and chest, even as my body sank deep into the wet snow.

A bolt of cold purple lightning slammed into my mother's back, making her scream again. Marisse wasn't finished with us.

Wave after wave of power blasted into my mother. My right hand was trapped in between our bodies, but I wrapped my left arm around my mother's back, even though the lightning froze my skin. For several seconds, I screamed along with my mother, but then I forced myself to grit my teeth and grab hold of my immunity.

Somehow, I managed to push back against the magier's icy lightning. Oh, my hand and arm were still frostbitten, horribly so, but the magier's lightning didn't freeze the rest of my body, like it was doing to my mother.

Desperate, I squeezed my mother even tighter, trying to share my immunity with her, trying to shield both of us with my magic. But she was already more dead than alive, thanks to that gruesome wound in her chest, and I could feel the magic freezing what little life she had left.

My mother drew back, and her gray-blue eyes filled my vision. Blair eyes, tearstone eyes, just like mine. She opened her mouth to say something, but all that escaped was a soft sigh, and she pitched forward, her head dropping down to my shoulder.

That's when I knew she was dead.

Tears streamed down and froze on my face, and a sob rose in my throat, but I choked it down and focused on my immunity. I didn't know how long I laid in the snow, clutching my dead mother and fighting back against the magier's cold power.

Eventually, the purple lightning dissolved into a shower of ice pellets. By this point, I was half buried in the snow, with my mother's frozen body on top of me, her arms still wrapped around me, even though they were cold and as stiff as boards. My own hand and arm were somehow frostbitten and burning at the same time, and this horrible, throbbing pain pulsed through my body with every breath.

As much as I wanted to unwrap my arm from around my mother, I forced myself to lie absolutely still. Footsteps crunched through the snow. The magier was coming to make sure we were dead.

I hadn't realized it until now, but I'd shut my eyes during the attack, and I forced myself to crack them open.

My mother's cold, frozen face loomed up in front of mine.

Thankfully, her eyes were closed, but her skin had turned a horrible blackish-purple, and she reeked of frosted death.

Somehow, I choked down a shrieking sob. My gaze flicked left and right, but I was buried so deep that all I could see was the snow rising up on either side of me, with the sickening sight of my mother's frozen face in the middle. I kept lying still and quiet, scarcely daring to breathe—

Lightning zinged through the air, blasting my mother's body off mine. I yelped and reached out, but she was gone, tossed across the clearing. I scrambled up and onto my feet and whirled around.

Marisse was standing right in front of me, an amused smile on her face. "Don't you know? Playing dead has never worked for anyone."

Rage surged through me at her mocking words, and my hands fisted in the folds of my dress. To my surprise, I felt something hard through the fabric, and I realized that the dagger my mother had given me in the dining hall was still in my pocket. My breath caught in my throat, but I started worming my right hand into the opening.

Marisse looked me up and down, taking in my wild, disheveled hair, my blood- and snow-crusted dress, and the bluish-purple tint to my left arm and fingers. Her eyes narrowed in thought. "What kind of magic let you survive mine?"

Instead of answering, I shifted on my feet, using the motion to hide my hand darting inside my pocket. My fingers fumbled through the fabric, but they finally closed around the dagger. I clenched the hilt.

Marisse shrugged. "I suppose it doesn't matter, since you're still going to die."

She lifted her hand, and more of those damned purple hailstones started swirling around her fingertips. "Any last words, little girl—"

I didn't wait for her to finish speaking or, worse, throw her magic at me. Instead, I yanked the dagger out of my pocket, lunged forward, and stabbed it into her heart.

Marisse's eyes bulged, and she screamed in surprise. Her hailstones slipped through her fingers and splattered onto the ground. She staggered back, but I followed her. I yanked the dagger out of her chest, then stabbed her with it again.

And I didn't stop.

I stabbed the magier over and over again, cutting into every part of her I could reach. She screamed and screamed and tried to throw her magic at me, but my attack was too brutal, frenzied, and vicious, and she couldn't summon up so much as a single spark of power.

It seemed to take forever, although it couldn't have been more than ten seconds before her eyes rolled up in the back of her head, and she dropped to the ground. I loomed over her, the dagger still clutched in my hand, but the magier's eyes were fixed and frozen.

I don't know how long I stood there, breathing hard, her blood dripping off my hand, my entire body shaking with rage and grief and fear. But slowly, I realized that the magier was dead, and that I wasn't, and that I couldn't just stand here lost in the fog of my feelings.

So I shoved the bloody dagger back into my dress pocket and glanced around, still trying to steady myself. My gaze zoomed over to my mother's body. My heart squeezed tight, *but I turned away from her crumpled form. I didn't look at my mother again.*

I couldn't.

Instead, I surveyed the rest of the clearing. The horses were long gone, having fled as soon as the magier killed Ansel, but something metallic glimmered in the snow, close to his body, and I shuffled over to it.

Ansel's pocket watch.

The sight filled me with disgust, since it was another reminder of all the horrors he had brought down upon my family. I started to leave the watch here, but for some reason, I crouched down and scooped it up. The fancy engraved M on the bronze cover gleamed at me like a sly, mocking eye, as if it were happy to be watching my suffering.

My hand fisted around the watch. I was tempted to hurl it as deep into the woods as I could, but I didn't. The watch was the only thing of value I had, and I might need to trade it for food.

Plus, a small part of me didn't want to let it go. No, I wanted to keep the watch as a memento—and a promise to myself.

I would never forget this day and what the Mortans had done to my family. I didn't know how or when, but someday, I would have my revenge on them.

But first, I had to escape. Shouts sounded in the distance, and I didn't want to be here when the Mortans found their dead magier. So I shoved Ansel's watch into my pocket next to my bloody dagger, got to my feet, and staggered deeper into the woods . . .

My eyes fluttered open, and I spotted several dark, shadowy trees in the distance. For a moment, I thought I was still in the snowy woods that awful night so long ago, but then I realized that I was in the gazebo in the Edelstein Gardens. Someone had propped me up against one of the cushioned benches.

I blinked a few times, focusing on my surroundings, even though the small effort made fresh pain bloom in my jaw. I touched my chin. My face had already puffed up and bruised from where one of the assassins had hit me. Still, I was lucky I had woken up at all.

"Are you sure the guards are gone?" a familiar voice hissed.

Maeven was crouching in the shadows at the front of the gazebo, peering out into the gardens. The other assassins were also crouched down and hiding in the shadows inside the structure.

"They're gone," one of the assassins murmured.

"Why were they out here?" Maeven asked.

The assassin shrugged. "They're looking for the Ripley brat. Apparently she got bored and snuck out of the ball."

Maeven and the assassins kept staring out into the gardens. They didn't realize that I was awake, so I moved my hand onto my lap, patting my side. Where was it? Where *was* it?

My fingers touched a hard lump tucked away in the folds of my gown, and I sighed with relief. The assassins must not have searched me, because my tearstone dagger was still hidden in my pocket. I didn't know how much good one small weapon would do me, but at least I had a chance to fight back.

Maeven looked over her shoulder at me. She got to her feet and snapped her fingers at the assassins. They too stood and faced me, and I was once again surrounded.

I sighed, reached out, and slowly pulled myself up into a seated position on the bench cushion, as though I didn't have the strength to stand. My face throbbed again, the sensation spreading out through my skull, but I pushed away the pain.

Still, it was best to appear as weak as possible, so I let out a soft groan and gingerly touched my bruised chin again. While Maeven and the assassins stared at my face, I dropped my right hand down to my side, discreetly wiggled it into the folds of my dress, and wrapped my fingers around the dagger in my pocket.

Thank you for the pocket, Calandre. I just hoped the weapon would be enough to save me.

When I had a good, firm grip on my dagger, I dropped my other hand from my face, straightened up, and glanced around. I was sitting on one of the cushions in the back of the gazebo, with Maeven standing in front of me and the other magier assassins spaced around me in a loose semicircle. I drew in breath after breath, tasting the air.

The assassins reeked of magic, and their eyes burned a bright, eerie purple. I didn't know if they all had lightning magic like Maeven, or fire, or ice, or something else, but it didn't really matter. They were all ready, willing, and eager to blast me with their power the second I did anything they didn't like. Maeven wasn't taking any chances on my escaping her trap. Not this time.

"Ah, Everleigh," Maeven purred. "I'm so happy you're awake."

"Why am I awake? Why haven't you killed me yet?"

"You have a couple of wandering Andvarian guards to thank for your stay of execution. But don't worry. Your reprieve is going to be extremely short-lived. I just have to set the scene first. My cousin insisted on it."

For a moment, it was almost like she was speaking a foreign language I didn't understand. But then her words sank into my mind, along with their horrible implications.

"Cousin? You have a *cousin* at Glitnir? Another member of your Bastard Brigade?"

Throughout the gazebo, the other Mortans stood up tall, seemingly proud of that name and all the awful things that went along with it. Fools.

"Oh, yes," Maeven said in a smug voice. "We have relatives in every kingdom on this continent and the ones beyond. But I'm particularly proud of this cousin. She's done such a good job of keeping an eye on the Ripleys and feeding us intelligence over the years."

So the traitor was someone close to the king, just like I'd feared. I opened my mouth to ask more questions when another scent drifted over to me—a strong, rosy perfume.

My heart clenched, and my stomach twisted. I'd smelled that perfume before, and I knew exactly who it belonged to. But the implications of sensing it here and now were downright sickening.

"You captured her without getting Lucas involved. Excellent." A voice floated out of the darkness, confirming my terrible suspicions.

Footsteps sounded, and a woman stepped into the gazebo and walked up next to Maeven. Like the magier, this woman was also wearing a midnight-purple cloak, and she reached up and lowered the hood so I could see her face.

Part of me was still desperately hoping Helene was hiding under there, but of course it wasn't her. It was so much worse than that.

It was Dahlia.

CHAPTER TWENTY-FOUR

Even though I had suspected that she was here, shock still jolted through my body, burning through me even more intensely than a magier's lightning.

"*You're* the traitor?" I whispered. "You're a *Mortan*? A member of the Bastard Brigade?"

A thin smile curved Dahlia's lips. "One of the longest-serving members, as a matter of fact."

With her black hair and green eyes, Dahlia didn't look anything like Maeven or the other assassins, the majority of whom had blond hair and purple eyes. My gaze dropped to the gold locket around her neck, the heart embossed with a large, fancy cursive *D*. I cursed my own foolishness. Dahlia had been wearing a Mortan symbol this whole time. I had just been too blind and suspicious of Helene to see it.

I drew in a breath, and the overpowering scent of Dahlia's rose perfume washed over me again. The aroma was another clue that I'd missed. No one wore that much perfume by accident. Sullivan must have mentioned my magic to her at some point, and Dahlia had deliberately doused herself with the cloying rose scent to keep me from smelling her emotions—and her evil intentions. Smart of her, and stupid of me not to realize it before now.

"I was sent to Glitnir as a child with instructions to climb as high as possible," Dahlia continued. "And I've done quite well for myself, just like you said, Everleigh."

"So all this time, all these years, you've been the king's mistress because you were *ordered* to?" I asked. "So you could spy on him and report back to the Mortan king?"

"Something like that," Dahlia said.

My mind whirled around, trying to make sense of the depths of Dahlia's deception and everything she'd done, all the secrets she must have shared with Maeven and the Mortans that had led to us all ending up here.

"So you would have known the second Heinrich decided to marry Frederich to Vasilia. You would have known about the Andvarians' trip to Seven Spire weeks, if not months, in advance. That's how Maeven was able to assassinate Frederich, the rest of the Andvarians, and the Blairs at the luncheon."

Another thin smile curved Dahlia's lips. "Oh, yes. I was able to help with that and a great many other things."

I stared at her, horror filling every single part of my body. But then another, even more terrible thought occurred to me.

"And Sully?" I whispered. "Does he know who you really are? *What* you really are? Is he . . . one of *you*?"

My heart squeezed tight. I thought that I'd been protecting Sullivan, but if he knew about his mother, if he was part of her deception, if he'd brought me out here, fucked me, and then left me for the Mortans . . .

I didn't know how I would *ever* recover from that.

Dahlia let out an amused laugh. "Of course not. I've thought many times about telling him, but he's far more like his father than I anticipated." She frowned. "Lucas actually loves Andvari and wants to do what's best for its people and creatures."

Relief slammed into me, even as guilt knifed through my stomach. Of course Sullivan didn't know who and what his mother really was. He was a good man, and I was ashamed of myself for doubting him, even for a second. But I shoved my guilt away, still trying to make sense of Dahlia's schemes.

"So you're the one who's been poisoning Heinrich. How?"

Then I remembered that first dinner in the dining hall, when Dahlia had taken such great care in fixing the king a cup of tea.

"The sugar cube," I said. "The one you dropped in Heinrich's tea and so thoughtfully stirred around so that it would melt. That's how you've been poisoning the king. One sugar cube at a time."

"Well, aren't you clever," Dahlia said. "But yes. Heinrich is a creature of habit, and I've been poisoning his after-dinner tea for months, ever since Frederich died. I had to be careful not to give him too much at once, to make his decline seem like it was born of a broken heart, rather than my slowly killing him. I initially wanted to give Heinrich one large, fatal dose, but Maeven said that it would be so much more satisfying to watch him suffer. She was right."

Dahlia smiled at her cousin, then looked at me again. "I saw him right after your meeting in the library. I was most upset when I realized that you had cured him and destroyed all my hard work." Her eyes narrowed. "How *did* you do that, Everleigh? How did you cure Heinrich?"

"I told you that she's a Winter queen," Maeven cut in. "Ruining our plans is what they do best."

Dahlia frowned, not liking her cryptic answer. I didn't like it either. Once again, I felt like Maeven knew something about my magic that I didn't.

"But how could you have made the poison?" Then I remembered the faint spark of magic I'd sensed when I'd touched her hand in the gazebo earlier this week. "You're a plant magier, just like Helene is."

Dahlia nodded. "Yes. I don't have Helene's raw, obvious strength, but it doesn't take much magic to grow an Amethyst Eye cactus and harvest the poison from the flowers. Helene was nice enough to give me the plant, never knowing what it could be used for. And then, when I realized that you'd discovered Heinrich was being poisoned, it was easy enough for me to slip my cactus into her greenhouse so you would suspect her."

I'd thought the cactus had looked familiar when I'd found it in the greenhouse, and now I remembered seeing the plant on the balcony railing outside Dahlia's chambers. So she had put her own plant in the greenhouse to convince me that Helene was poisoning the king, and I'd fallen for her simple trick. What an idiot I was.

My mind kept spinning, and I thought back to that jalapeño rage I'd sensed in the throne room. "You wanted me dead from the start. You used your magic to trip me when I was fighting Rhea."

Dahlia shrugged. "The carpet wasn't a plant, so I couldn't do much more than twist it around your foot, but it almost worked."

"You sent Frederich and Gemma off to die at Seven Spire, you've been poisoning Heinrich, and you helped that weather magier slip into the palace so that she and those other assassins could try to kill Dominic in the library." I ticked off her crimes. "But *why*? You're not married to Heinrich, so you won't be queen when he dies."

Dahlia let out another amused laugh, although this one had a bit more bite to it. "I told you before, Everleigh: I *never* wanted to be queen."

Once again, she reeked of lime truthfulness, just as she had when she'd said those same words to me before.

"But with Henrich, Dominic, and Gemma dead, the only other member of the royal family would be . . . Sullivan." My eyes widened in understanding. "You're telling the truth. You don't want to be queen. But you would be quite happy being the *mother* of the king. That's what this has all been about—putting *Sullivan* on the throne."

The implications spun through my mind. With all the legitimate heirs dead, Dahlia would present Sullivan as the perfect solution. The other nobles might kick up a fuss, but that's when Helene's wealth, power, and influence would come in handy.

Helene might not know about Dahlia's true scheme, but she still cared deeply about Sullivan. Helene would help Dahlia put him on the throne, although I doubted that Dahlia would let her live long afterward. And Sullivan would feel duty-bound to take on the responsibility, never realizing that it was exactly what his mother wanted, what she'd been planning for years.

"Of course this has all been about putting Lucas on the throne," Dahlia sneered. "My son is a powerful magier. He's always been stronger than his brothers, and he'll be an excellent king. Under my guidance, of course. With you dead, it won't be too difficult for me to find some way to dispatch Heinrich, Dominic, and Gemma. And, after an appropriate mourning period has passed for the Ripleys, Lucas will marry a woman of my choosing, someone of good Mortan stock, although he won't know that."

A sick, sick feeling filled my stomach. "And then when their children are on the throne, Andvari will belong to Morta."

I'd thought that Bellonans were good at playing the long game, but Dahlia put us to shame. She'd been playing a long game ever since she was a child, and now, she was going to force Sullivan to play it too, whether he realized it or not.

"This will break Sully's heart when he finds out," I said.

Dahlia shrugged again. "He'll never know that I was involved. Besides, he'll be too busy being king to wonder how he got the throne."

She was probably right about that, but I didn't tell her so.

"Did you ever care about Heinrich? Even a little? Or was he just a mission?"

For the first time, a bit of hurt flickered in Dahlia's eyes, overcoming her smugness. "I *did* care about Heinrich," she admitted. "Until he married another woman over me. That was the beginning of the end for us, even if he was too blind and stupid to realize it."

"But that was his duty as king," I pointed out.

"Oh, fuck Heinrich and his damned duty." Dahlia spat out the words. "He certainly wasn't thinking about his *duty* every time he came to my bed. No, if he truly cared about me, if he truly loved me, then he would have married *me*, despite the fact that I was a poor kitchen servant. But no, Heinrich wanted to appease his father and the nobles, so he married that wretched Sophina instead. As far as I'm concerned, Heinrich is getting *exactly* what he deserves."

As much as I hated to admit it, she had a point. And I could see how her hurt had slowly grown and festered over the years. Heinrich wasn't the only one who'd been poisoned. Whether she realized it or not, Dahlia had also done it to herself.

"And Sully?" I asked. "Do you love him at all? Or is he just another game piece for you to move around and manipulate?"

"Of course I love my son," Dahlia snapped. "Just as Maeven loves her children."

More shock blasted through me. Maeven had *children*? How many? Who were their fathers? Were they legitimate nobles? Or bastards like her?

My gaze zoomed over to the magier, but her face had gone ice-cold. She didn't like Dahlia revealing that information.

"I have *always* loved my son, from the moment he was born," Dahlia continued, not noticing Maeven's chilly stare. "That's why I'm doing this—so he can have the future he *deserves*. So he can finally be king and look down his nose at everyone who's ever done that to him."

Once again, she had a point, although I didn't tell her so.

Maeven laid her hand on Dahlia's shoulder. "It's time to put the next part of our plan into action."

The hot, peppery scent of Dahlia's anger filled my nose. She was still pissed I'd dared to suggest that she didn't love her son, but she nodded at Maeven.

"Excellent! Now I finally get to do something that I've been wanting to do for quite a while now," Maeven purred again.

I tensed, expecting her to blast me with her lightning, but Maeven had something else in mind. She reached into her cloak and pulled out a glass vial filled with a dark purple liquid. Even though the vial was tightly stoppered, I could smell the soft, lavender scent of the liquid inside. More amethyst-eye poison—a large, single, fatal dose.

"Going to kill me like you did the weather magier in the dungeon?" I asked.

"I couldn't free Lola from the dungeon, and Rhea was going to question her," Dahlia said. "I couldn't risk Lola slipping up and revealing my true identity."

"So you slipped poison into her water, and she drank it without realizing what you were doing. You killed Lola, the weather magier, your own cousin." I let out a bitter laugh. "There's not much loyalty between members of the Bastard Brigade, is there?"

"It's not about loyalty—it's about getting the job done no

matter what, no matter who we have to sacrifice." Maeven lifted her chin with pride. "That's what true soldiers do."

Dahlia nodded, as did the other assassins. I gave them all a disgusted look.

"You are not *soldiers.*" I spat out the word. "Soldiers fight for their kingdom, for their people, for a leader and a cause they believe in."

"And that perfectly describes me and my many cousins," Maeven crowed.

The other assassins stood up even taller with pride. They really did believe that their cause was noble and just and that they were serving the greater good. They didn't see how their king so casually used and sent them to their deaths, just as all the other legitimate heirs had done before him. For a moment, I almost felt sorry for the members of the Bastard Brigade. Almost.

More disgust rolled through me, drowning that sympathy. Still, their blind, foolish pride sparked an idea. I might die here, but I was still going to do as much as possible to further my own long game with Maeven, the one she didn't even realize we were playing yet. So I slowly stood up and turned to the side, hiding the fact that my hand was still curled around the dagger in my pocket.

"There's one big difference between soldiers and the lot of you."

Maeven arched an eyebrow. "And what would that be?"

I looked her in the eyes. "Soldiers get to come home after the battle is won and the war is over. And when they do, they are celebrated for their bravery, for their sacrifices, for protecting their own people despite the terrible cost to themselves. Tell me, Maeven, has your brother ever celebrated you? Or your accomplishments? Has he ever warmly welcomed you home after a job well done?"

For the first time, a bit of hurt sparked in her eyes, and I could tell that the answer to my questions was a resounding *no*. So I kept going, trying to plant as many seeds of doubt as I could.

"He's never done any of those things, has he? Your brother, the king, has never once thanked you for serving him. I bet that when you go home to Morta that you barely have time to sleep in your own bed before he sends you on another mission in some far-flung kingdom."

Agreement flashed across her face before she could hide it.

I gestured at Dahlia. "She's the perfect example. Taken from her home when she was a child and forced to come here. Forced to slink around and spy. And when she caught the king's eye, forced to fuck him so that she could rise even higher. Tell me, Maeven. Has your king ever ordered you to fuck someone?"

More agreement flashed across her face, along with a good bit of anger, and her fingers tightened around the vial in her hand as though she wanted to smash the glass into my face. Not to poison and kill me, but just to make me stop talking and revealing all these ugly truths.

"You and your precious Bastard Brigade career from battle to battle until you make a mistake, and someone kills you," I said, my voice as cold as ice. "Face it, Maeven. You're not a soldier. You're *expendable,* just like Libby, Lola, and all your other cousins."

Maeven stiffened, as though I'd just slapped her across the face, and the scent of her jalapeño rage exploded in the air, making my nose burn with its sudden, sharp intensity. Her jaw clenched, and her fingers fluttered, as though she was an instant away from blasting me with her lightning. Murderous hate darkened her eyes, making them seem more black than purple, but something else glittered in the depths of her gaze—begrudging agreement.

Oh, yes, I might die here, and Maeven might keep serving

her king, but I'd told her what she really was to her brother, what she'd known she truly was all along, and she couldn't ignore it anymore. I wondered what she would do with that information, and all the rage and hurt that came with it. Too bad I wouldn't be alive to see it.

"Enough talk," Dahlia said, a sharp note creeping into her voice. "The ball is almost over, and her friends will start looking for her soon."

And there went my faint, desperate hope that I could stall the Mortans long enough for someone to realize they were here and sound the alarm.

Maeven snapped her fingers. Two of the other Mortans stepped up beside her, and the three of them slowly approached me. I was still trapped against the bench, but I tightened my hand around the dagger still hidden in my pocket. I had killed a Mortan magier with a dagger before, and I was taking some of these bastards with me before they finished me off.

Maeven stopped about five feet away and held up the vial where I could see it. Sparks of silver shimmered inside the dark purple liquid.

"Amethyst-eye poison, mixed with wormroot and a few others," Maeven purred. "Just to make doubly sure you die. Not even those pretty tearstone bracelets on your wrists will deflect enough magic to save you from this."

For a moment, I didn't understand what she was talking about, but then I realized that she still didn't know about my own natural immunity. She still didn't realize that I could destroy magic. I didn't know if I had enough power to counteract her foul poison, and I couldn't let her force me to drink it. No, I had to make a stand and attack her now, before the other magiers surged forward and pried my mouth open and Maeven poured that poison down my throat.

I tightened my grip on my hidden dagger, getting ready to

yank it out of my pocket, whip it up, and drive it into Maeven's chest. I drew in a breath to steady myself, when a new scent filled my nose—magic mixed with crushed gravel.

New hope sprang to life in my heart, and I scanned the shadows behind Maeven. In the distance, I spotted a faint burn of blue, like two matches had just flared to life in the darkness. A smile spread across my face.

"Why are you smiling?" Maeven hissed. "I'm about to kill you, you idiot."

My smile widened, and I pointed my finger to the right. Maeven's eyes narrowed. She thought it was some kind of trick, but she couldn't help but look in that direction, as did Dahlia and the other Mortans.

"What are you pointing at?" Maeven muttered. "I don't see anything—"

With a loud, grumbling roar, a gargoyle erupted out of the hedge maze.

Grimley bounded out of the shadows, loped across the grass, and slammed into the Mortans standing at the front of the gazebo, knocking them down.

With another loud, grumbling roar, the gargoyle reared back on his hind legs like a stallion, then slammed his stone paws on top of the assassins, driving them into the gazebo floor and crushing their bones. Then he bounded from side to side, swiping out with his talons and raking them across the assassins.

The Mortans never had a chance, and their pain-filled shrieks and screams soon died down to choked, bloody gurgles as the gargoyle stomped and slashed them to death.

Grimley's appearance distracted the two assassins in front of me, and I whipped my dagger out of my pocket, surged forward, and sliced the blade across the first man's throat. He too died with a bloody gurgle.

The second man lifted his hand to blast me with his magic, but I lunged forward and buried my dagger in his chest. I twisted the blade in deeper, then ripped it out.

That man screamed and clutched at his chest, and I shoved him away. He stumbled backward straight into Dahlia, and she shrieked in surprise as he knocked her down.

Maeven turned toward Grimley and reared her hand back to throw her lightning, but the gargoyle lowered his head and charged. She tried to dart out of the way, but his wing clipped her side, making her yelp and stumble to the ground. She lost her concentration, and her lightning fizzled out in a burst of hot sparks.

"Evie!" a voice yelled. "Evie!"

I whirled around to find Gemma running toward me from the other side of the gazebo, with a dagger clutched in her hand. Perhaps it was the soft light, but her dagger gleamed the same dull silver as mine, as if it was also made of tearstone.

"Gemma!" I yelled, rushing over to her. "What are you doing here?"

"I got bored, so I snuck out of the ball and went up on the roof with Grimley," she said in a high, breathless voice. "I saw Maeven and the Mortans creeping through the gardens, so I followed them. I couldn't let them hurt you or anyone else. You saved me at Seven Spire, and now, I saved you."

My heart swelled with pride, and I reached out and hugged her tight with one arm. "Yes, you did," I said in a fierce voice. "Yes, you did."

More yells and screams rang out as Grimley continued to smash and slash his way through the Mortans.

Some of the magiers tried to summon up their lightning, fire, and ice, but the gargoyle kept bounding from one side of the gazebo to the other and back again, knocking the magiers to the ground. A few of them managed to stay upright long enough to hit him with their magic, but his stone skin was a thick, natural barrier against their power, and the lightning, fire, and ice didn't so much as scorch his body.

"Here," Gemma said, holding out the dagger in her hand. "I brought you this. Alvis made it for me, but I don't know how to use it yet. Not like you do."

I took the dagger from her. It *was* made of tearstone, and the hilt featured the same gargoyle crest as the pendant around Gemma's neck.

"Thank you for this. Now you and Grimley need to get out of here."

"What? No!" Gemma said. "I want to stay. I want to help you fight the Mortans."

I shook my head. "No, you need to get to safety. You and Grimley need to go to the throne room and tell everyone what's happening. I'll watch your back, and I'll be right behind you. Okay?"

Gemma didn't like the thought of leaving me, but she nodded. "Okay."

I hugged her close again for a moment. "You and Grimley run back to the throne room as fast as you can. One . . . two . . . three . . . go!"

"Grimley!" Gemma yelled. "Let's go!"

She waved her hand at the gargoyle, then turned and sprinted out of the gazebo, heading away from me and the Mortans. Grimley let out another loud, grumbling roar and charged through the middle of the structure. He plowed through the Mortans again, making them scream and tumble to the ground. I grinned. I was really starting to like that gargoyle.

Gemma vanished into the hedge maze, and Grimley loped along behind her, also disappearing from sight.

Two assassins staggered to their feet and headed after Gemma and Grimley. I sprinted forward and slashed out with my daggers, slicing the blades across the assassins' backs. The two women screamed and tumbled back down to the ground.

I started to run out of the gazebo and follow my friends into the hedge maze when the hot, caustic stench of magic filled the air. On instinct, I ducked down and spun to my right. A ball of purple lightning exploded against the stone column where my head had been. I whirled around.

Maeven was standing in front of me, another ball of purple lightning already sparking to life on her fingertips. The magier had gotten back up onto her feet, along with Dahlia. About a dozen assassins were also still alive. Some of them were clutching swords in their hands, while others were cradling balls of lightning, fire, and ice in their palms.

"Seems your little scheme has gone sideways," I sneered at Maeven and Dahlia. "As soon as Gemma reaches the throne room, it's all over for you two."

"And I can still kill you right here and now," Maeven hissed back. "Die, Winter queen!"

She drew back her hand and tossed her lightning at me, but once again, I ducked out of the way. The magic hit another column and exploded, sending sparks and smoke boiling up into the air.

Maeven screamed in frustration and tossed more lightning at me, but I dodged it as well. Then, before she could summon up any more magic, I tightened my grip on the daggers in my hands and ran toward her, just as determined to kill her as she was to murder me.

She waved her hand at the other magiers. "Get her, you idiots!"

Three assassins with swords charged at me. I let out a loud yell and stepped up to meet them.

I dodged the first assassin, then the second one, but the third one came at me head-on, and I snapped up one of my daggers to block his attack. Our weapons *clang*ed together, and that one loud, harsh note unlocked that phantom music in my head. Suddenly, Serilda's voice was whispering in my mind, and Xenia's cane was beating out the rhythm of the deadly dance.

The assassin pressed his advantage, trying to shove his sword into my chest, but I snapped up my other hand and stabbed him in the throat with my second dagger. I ripped the blade free, cutting off his choking scream, then sliced my dagger across his stomach, spilling his blood and guts all over the gazebo floor.

Then I whirled around to do the same thing to the second man, then the third.

Their screams tore through the air, punctuating the music in my mind, and blood spattered everywhere, as though I were dancing in the rain. Only this rain was death, and I was the one pouring it down on everyone.

I finished with those three assassins, but there were still several more left, and they reached for even more of their magic. Lightning, fire, and ice sizzled, crackled, and frosted their hands, even as the same magic burned in their eyes.

I was standing in the middle of the gazebo, surrounded by the magiers. Their magic surrounded me as well, and I wasn't strong enough to overcome all of it at once. Maeven had been right before. Not even the tearstone daggers in my hands and the bracelets on my wrists would save me from this much magic.

Despite knowing how badly this was going to end, I gripped my daggers even tighter, and I reached for my immunity, pulling it up, up, up and pretending that it was a strong, malleable shield coating my skin.

I was going to die fighting, just like a true gladiator would.

"And now, Winter queen," Maeven snarled, moving to stand in front of me, "you will finally feel the full might of Morta."

She lifted her hand, and another ball of purple lightning popped to life in her palm, stronger than all the other magiers' power combined, and far stronger than any other magic I had ever felt before, much less tried to extinguish with my own immunity. I ground my teeth, bracing myself for what was coming next—and just how much it was going to hurt.

Maeven reared back her hand. Magic streaked through the air, but it didn't hit me.

It hit *her.*

Blue lightning slammed into Maeven, throwing her out of the gazebo and onto the grass beyond. My heart lifted.

Sullivan was here.

More blue lightning streaked through the air, narrowly missing the magier closest to me, and I saw Sullivan running toward the gazebo, more magic crackling on his hands.

"Evie!" he yelled.

"Over here!" I screamed.

The Mortan magiers froze, not sure which one of us to attack. Then half of the magiers turned toward me, and the others turned toward Sullivan. Dahlia might have told the Mortans not to hurt her son when Sullivan had stormed away from the gazebo earlier, but that wasn't an option anymore.

Fighting—*killing*—was the only choice any of us had now.

I snapped up my daggers and charged at the assassins closest to me, plunging into the pack of them. The magiers yelled and screamed and unleashed their lightning, fire, and ice, slamming their power into my body, but I held on to my immunity and used my own cold, hard power to extinguish every spark of magic that touched my skin.

I didn't care what happened to me. No, the only thought in my mind was getting to Sullivan, and I would cut down every single person—every single fucking *thing*—who got in my way. That sharp, painful need to reach him blotted out everything else.

"Evie!" he yelled again.

I would have yelled back, but I didn't want to waste precious energy doing anything that wasn't bringing me closer to him. The stench of magic filled my nose, so much of it that I couldn't tell where it ended and I began. But I reached for even more of my immunity, and I ruthlessly snuffed out every single bit of lightning, fire, and ice that stopped me from getting closer to Sullivan.

Something strange happened. The longer and harder I used my immunity, the more I could sense all the magic around me. And not only could I sense the magic, but it almost felt like I could *touch* it, as though the magiers' lightning, fire, and ice were tangible, physical *things* that I could hold in my hands the same way I was holding my daggers.

Then another ball of lightning blasted against my body. I shook off the odd thoughts, used my immunity to extinguish the magic, and kept going.

Sullivan sent bolt after bolt of lightning zinging out at the magiers he was battling, as well as ducking their blasts of power in return. But one of the Mortan magiers managed to clip Sullivan's shoulder with his fire, making Sullivan stumble to the ground. The magier reared back his hand, getting ready to unleash more of his fire. I opened my mouth to scream a warning at Sullivan, but I didn't have to save him.

Dahlia did it for me.

She darted forward, sank her fingers into the magier's hair, pulled back his head, and cut his throat. Then she shoved him away, and the dying man *thump*ed to the ground in between her and Sullivan.

His head snapped up, and he stared at her in confusion. "Mother? What are you doing here?"

Dahlia stared at him, that bloody dagger still clutched in her hand. I ran in that direction, yelling at Sullivan to get away from her, although he didn't hear me over the shrieks and screams. But I didn't have to save Sullivan from his mother either.

Once again, she did it for me.

Dahlia looked at me, and I could smell her dusty resignation even above the stench of all the blood and magic in the air. She lifted her hand, showing me the vial of amethyst-eye poison. She must have picked it up from wherever Maeven had dropped it. Dahlia used her thumb to pop the stopper off the top of the glass.

She gave me a hard, grim smile, then tilted up the vial and drained the contents.

Sullivan scrambled back to his feet. "Mother! What are you doing?"

Dahlia shook her head and staggered away from him. She hit one of the cushioned benches and slid off, crumpling to the ground. Sullivan hurried over to her.

"Mother?" he yelled. "Mother!"

Out of the corner of my eye, I saw another ball of purple lightning flare to life, and I whirled around in that direction.

Maeven had finally gotten back up onto her feet, but she wasn't targeting me anymore. No, this time, she was going after Sullivan. She gave me an evil smile, then reached for even more of her lightning, far more lightning than what she had been going to use on me.

She was going to kill Sullivan.

CHAPTER TWENTY-FIVE

ully!" I screamed.

I raced toward him, cutting down any assassin stupid enough to get in my way. Even though I was moving as fast as possible, I wasn't going to reach him in time.

One of the magiers plowed into me and knocked the dagger out of my right hand. I tried to keep going and run past him, but he caught me around the waist, holding me in place.

"Sully!" I screamed again. "Sully, look out!"

His head snapped up, and he finally realized that Maeven was targeting him. His eyes widened, and he lifted his hand to summon up his own magic to block her attack, but he was too late. Maeven snapped her hand forward, throwing every last bit of her power at him.

For a moment, I felt like I was underwater, and everything was happening in long, slow waves of motion.

I churned and churned my legs, dragging the magier along with me. I also stretched my empty hand out in front of me, wishing that I could somehow reach Sullivan in time, wishing that I could do something, *anything,* to keep Maeven's lightning from killing him. Wishing that I had the power to throttle her magic without even touching it or her.

Even as that last desperate thought filled my mind, I felt a wave of . . . of . . . *something* pulse out of me. It felt like my immunity, like that cold, hard power that was buried deep down inside my body, only this power wasn't inside me anymore.

It was *outside.*

For the last several months, I had thought of my immunity like a gladiator shield, this invisible, malleable barrier that I could wrap around my own body to protect myself. Sometimes, I also thought of my power as a large, hard fist that I could use to crush other people's magic.

But for the first time, I realized that I could actually *feel* my power in my hand, just like I could feel the actual dagger clutched in my other fingers. Maybe my immunity could be more than just a shield or a fist.

Maybe it could be a sword—one that I could wield just like I would a gladiator blade.

That strange, slow sensation of being underwater vanished, and everything snapped back to its normal speed.

Even though that magier was still holding on to me, I reached for my immunity and let that cold, hard power fill the palm of my hand. And then I flung that power outward as though it were a sword that I was hurtling at Maeven's damned purple lighting.

I held my breath, wondering if I had just been imagining the whole thing and had just doomed Sullivan to death.

But it *worked.*

That invisible sword of my power slammed into Maeven's lightning, shattering it into a shower of sparks an instant before it would have hit Sullivan.

For a moment, everyone froze. Me, Sullivan, the remaining magiers. Even the man holding me around the waist loosened his grip and staggered away. Everyone looked at me, wondering what had just happened.

Maeven's eyes widened with shock. "No!" she whispered. "No, it can't be!"

This time, she reared her hand back and threw her lightning at me. I didn't even really think about what I was doing. I just lifted my hand and swatted her magic aside, as if it were a fly that was annoying me.

And I realized that I had done the same thing to Libby's magic when she had tried to kill me in the Seven Spire throne room. Only then, I'd been holding my sword, and I'd thought that the tearstone weapon had deflected most of her power, instead of my own immunity.

Maeven's eyes widened again, and she did something completely unexpected—she backed away from me.

"Kill her!" she screamed. "Kill her now!"

The magiers whipped back around to me. With a loud, collective roar, they charged forward and threw everything they had at me. Lightning, fire, ice, even their physical swords and daggers in some cases.

And one by one, I overcame them all.

All the lightning, the fire, the ice, the swords and daggers. I snuffed out the magic with my own immunity, dodged the weapons, and used my dagger to cut down my enemies.

I killed one assassin after another, wading through them all to get to Sullivan, who was doing the same thing on the opposite side of the gazebo. We finally met in the middle when there were no more Mortans left to kill.

"Evie! Are you okay?" Sullivan asked, his voice raspy from screaming.

Blood, bruises, and burns covered him from head to toe, but he was alive, which was all that mattered.

"I'm okay. You?" My voice was just as raspy as his was.

He lifted his hand as if to cup my cheek, or maybe even pull me close and kiss me, but at the last second, he thought better of it and dropped his arm back down to his side. I wanted to reach for him too, but this tense, awkward silence fell over us. Now that the danger had passed, I didn't know what to do, not given all the ugly things we'd said to each other in this very spot less than an hour ago.

Sullivan glanced around. "Wait. Where's Maeven?"

I looked out over the bodies that littered the gazebo, but hers wasn't among them. "She's not here."

I held back a vicious curse. Of course she wasn't here. Maeven was like a coral viper who always managed to slither away after she'd bitten you.

A low groan sounded. Sullivan and I both turned around, and I realized that there was one person who hadn't escaped.

Dahlia.

She was lying where she had fallen beside one of the benches, still clutching that empty vial.

"Mother!" Sullivan yelled.

We both hurried over and dropped to our knees beside her. I could smell the amethyst-eye poison on her breath, sweet lavender that was turning to rot with each passing second.

"What was she doing out here?" Sullivan asked. "And why did she take that poison?"

I opened my mouth, but then I thought better of it.

Dahlia lolled her head to the side and looked up at me with pain-filled eyes. "He'll figure it out sooner or later. You might as well tell him."

"Tell me what?" he asked.

I quickly told him everything Dahlia had said about sending

Frederich and Gemma to die at the Seven Spire massacre, poisoning Heinrich, and trying to kill Dominic.

The more I talked, the more anguish filled Sullivan's face. When I finished, he stared at his mother in horror, as if she were some monster he'd never seen before.

"She did all those things just to try to put me on the throne?" Sullivan asked, his voice a dull, ragged whisper.

"Yes." I didn't want to cause him any more pain, but I couldn't deny what Dahlia had done.

I leaned over and placed my hand on top of Sullivan's. He jerked, but for once he didn't pull away, and he curled his fingers into mine.

"She's not gone yet," I said in a low voice. "I can still use my immunity. I can still try to save her."

"No," Dahlia rasped. "No. I made my choice. Let me die."

Sullivan shook his head, telling me that he would honor her last wish. Then he leaned forward, so that he could stare into her face.

"Was it all a lie?" he asked in a low, anguished tone. "Did you ever care about me? Did you ever really love me?"

"Of course I love you," Dahlia rasped.

She reached up and tenderly cupped Sullivan's cheek. He flinched, as though her touch burned, but he didn't pull away from her.

"I know you think I'm a horrible person. Maybe I am. But I always loved you," she said. "Remember that, if you will."

Tears filled his eyes, and a muscle ticked in his jaw, but he nodded. "I'll remember," he said in a sad, resigned voice.

"Good boy . . . You always were such a . . . good boy." She smiled at him a moment, then her face turned serious. "Don't make the same mistakes that I did . . . Don't let your anger and duty rule you . . . Otherwise, you'll end up like me . . . bitter and alone . . ."

Dahlia drew in another breath, as if she was going to say something else, but her voice escaped in a soft exhale. A bit of black blood bubbled up out of her lips and trickled down her chin, and her hand slipped from Sullivan's face.

He caught her hand and slowly lowered it to the ground. Still clutching her fingers in his, he bowed his head, tears sliding down his face for the mother he'd never truly known.

Serilda, Cho, Paloma, and Xenia found us in the gazebo, still huddled around Dahlia's body. Gemma followed them, along with Grimley, Alvis, Heinrich, Dominic, and Rhea. Halvar and Bjarni also appeared, but they kept to the edge of the gardens.

Once my friends realized that Sullivan and I were okay, they wanted to know what had happened. Sullivan drew Heinrich, Dominic, Gemma, Alvis, and Rhea aside and told them about Dahlia, while I did the same to Serilda, Cho, Paloma, and Xenia.

Everyone was stunned by the news, except for Serilda, who stared at Dahlia's body with a thoughtful look. I wondered if this was one of the possible outcomes she'd seen with her magic, but I didn't ask.

I had expected Heinrich to be so furiously angry about Dahlia's betrayal that he would immediately disown Sullivan and order him thrown out of the palace. But instead of raging and lashing out, the king stared down sadly at Dahlia's body, as if he couldn't believe that she had wanted him dead.

Sullivan cleared his throat. "You'll want me to leave now and never return," he said in a soft, resigned tone, voicing my thoughts.

Everyone looked back and forth between him and the king.

Heinrich stared down at Dahlia's body a moment longer, then focused on Sullivan.

His face hardened. "You are my *son*," he declared in a loud voice. "You will *always* be my son. I could never love you less. I can only love you *more*."

Then he stalked over, wrapped his arms around his son, and hugged him tight, like he never wanted to let him go. Sullivan reached up and hugged his father back just as tightly, and the two of them stayed like that for a long, long time. Eventually, Sullivan turned and hugged Dominic, as well as Gemma.

I had some questions of my own, which Gemma answered. She had run into Sullivan on the outskirts of the gardens and had told him that I was under attack. He'd told her to find Dominic and the others, as well as summon the palace gargoyles to the throne room to protect Heinrich. Then Sullivan had rushed to my aid. He had saved me, but he'd lost his mother in the process.

Guilt twisted in my gut at the hurt I'd caused him yet again, but there was nothing I could do to take away his pain. And I couldn't help but feel sorry for Dahlia. She had been trapped between two worlds, Morta and Andvari, and she had never truly belonged to either. And now she was dead, and Sullivan had to pick up the pieces of his broken heart over his mother's secret agenda.

Rhea summoned the guards. Together, with my friends, they did a thorough sweep of the gardens, along with the rest of the palace, in hopes of finding Maeven, but I knew that she was long gone. Sure enough, Rhea reported back that there was no sign of Maeven anywhere, although the guards had discovered several strixes hidden in a barn on the palace grounds. The Mortans had apparently used the giant, hawklike birds to fly over the walls and avoid the gargoyles, as well as the guards posted at the gates. Maeven must have used one of the creatures to escape the same way.

Eventually, I wound up sitting by myself on one of the cushioned benches, watching Sullivan stare down at his mother's body yet again.

A rough tongue licked my hand, startling me out of my guilty reverie, and Grimley plopped down beside me. He licked my hand again, then leaned forward and sniffed my fingers, just like he'd done on the balcony outside my chambers a few days ago.

"Magic killer," he rumbled in his deep, gravelly voice. "Magic master."

The gargoyle had said the same thing to me that day on the balcony. I hadn't understood what he'd meant back then, but I did now. I also knew why Alvis had said that I'd have to discover for myself what it truly meant to be a Winter queen. He was right. I wouldn't have believed him if he'd told me what he thought I could do with my immunity, but now I did.

More importantly, I believed in myself—and my magic.

I scratched Grimley's head. Well, as much as I could scratch living, breathing stone, but the gargoyle seemed to enjoy it, and his tail *thump*ed with happiness. At least someone was happy tonight.

My gaze drifted back over to Sullivan. His whole world and everything he thought he'd known had just been shattered. I could understand that, especially since I was feeling that way myself, at least when it came to my magic.

My heart ached for him, and I longed to go over, wrap my arms around him, and tell him that it was all right, that everything was going to be okay. But I couldn't do that because it would have been a lie, and I was finished lying to him. My lies had brought him nothing but pain, misery, and heartbreak, and I doubted he would ever forgive me for my deceptions.

Especially since I didn't know how I could forgive myself.

So while our friends ran around, dealing with the blood,

bodies, and crises, I sat there and watched him grieve for the mother who had betrayed him, his family, his kingdom, and everything that he believed in.

I wished that I could take back everything that had happened over the past few days, that I had never come to Glitnir, and especially that I had never destroyed Sullivan's family.

CHAPTER TWENTY-SIX

That was just the start of a long, long night that bled into a long, long day.

Besides my friends and I, the only other people who knew the truth about Dahlia being a traitor were Heinrich, Dominic, Gemma, Alvis, and Rhea, and we all agreed to keep it that way. Rhea told the guards that Dahlia had heard the commotion in the gardens and had died defending Sullivan, while Heinrich did the same to the nobles, who were still talking, laughing, eating, drinking, and dancing in the throne room.

The news of the Mortan attack put an end to the royal ball. The nobles left, and Heinrich ordered the servants and guards to leave as well, saying they could clean things up in the morning. Rhea and my friends were still busy dealing with the bodies in the gardens.

The last of the servants scurried out of the room, leaving me alone with Heinrich. The king let out a weary sigh and sat down on the dais steps. I walked over and sat down beside him. I had returned Gemma's dagger, but I was still carrying mine, and I laid the bloody weapon on the stone step beside me.

A glimmer of silver caught my eye. The decorations were still up, including the two giant banners that featured my crown-of-shards crest and the Ripley gargoyle crest. The symbols in both banners winked at me, almost in sympathy. I grimaced and dropped my gaze from them.

Heinrich and I sat there in silence for several minutes before he finally spoke.

"I really did love Dahlia," he said in a soft voice. "I *always* loved her. From the very first moment I saw her working in the kitchen when she was a child. And I thought she loved me too. But now, to realize that it was all a lie . . ."

"She did love you," I said, trying to comfort him. "And she loved Sullivan too."

"Just not as much as she loved Morta," he rasped. "I don't know what to make of it. I don't know how to *feel* about it."

He ran a hand through his hair. At least, he tried to, but his fingers hit the silver crown on his head. Heinrich yanked off the crown and gave it an angry glare, as if it were the source of all his problems. I knew exactly how he felt.

His fingers curled around the wide band, as though he was considering throwing it across the room. But in the end, he sighed again and laid it down on the step beside him, just as I'd done with my bloody dagger.

"So where do we go from here, Everleigh?" Heinrich asked in a weary voice.

"I'm not marrying Dominic. I only agreed to your proposal to try to find the traitor and protect you and your family. I just never dreamed that it was Dahlia."

"I knew that you weren't going to marry Dominic," Heinrich said. "I knew it from the first time you looked at Sullivan. But I had to prove to the nobles that I was still a strong king, and getting you to marry Dominic seemed like the best way to do that. You came here in friendship and to apologize for something that wasn't even your fault, and I treated you badly. I'm sorry for that."

I nodded, accepting his apology.

Heinrich turned toward me, his face serious. "You will have your treaty, Everleigh, and it will be exactly the way you want it. Andvari will stand with Bellona against the Mortans. You have my word on it, and you have more than earned it."

He held out his hand, and we shook on it.

"Yes," I said in a grim voice, "I did earn my treaty. I just wish that it hadn't cost so many people so much suffering, especially Sullivan."

Heinrich gave me a sad, resigned smile, but he didn't say anything else, and we sat there in silence, drawing what quiet solace we could from each other.

Eventually, I left Heinrich in the throne room and went back to my own chambers. Calandre and her sisters sucked in horrified breaths at the sight of all the blood, rips, and tears in my ball gown.

I winced. "I'm sorry. So sorry. I didn't mean to ruin your hard work."

Calandre stared at the ruined gown a moment longer, then gave me a bright smile. "It's nothing, my queen. Just a dress. I can always make you another one."

"You're a terrible liar, but I appreciate the effort."

This time, Calandre's smile was far more genuine. "Let's get you out of that horrid garment. Things will seem much better after you've had a nice, hot bath."

To my surprise, she was right. Calandre and her sisters fussed over me for more than an hour before they tucked me into bed. I fell asleep even before they had closed the doors to my chambers. Thankfully, my dreams were free of any nightmarish memories of my past. Or perhaps that was because I had lived through another nightmare tonight.

Either way, I woke up late the next morning feeling . . . not quite refreshed, but at least strong enough to face a new day of trouble. I had breakfast in my chambers with Paloma, Serilda, Cho, and Xenia, who updated me on what was happening. Captain Rhea was drastically increasing security, but they all agreed that Maeven was gone and that Glitnir was free of the Mortan threat—for now.

Serilda told me that Sullivan was having breakfast with Heinrich, Dominic, and Gemma. Good. As much as I wanted to make sure that he was okay, I was glad that he was with his family. Hopefully, they could help him come to terms with the truth about Dahlia.

Eventually, my friends left to check in with Rhea again, as well as to start the preparations for our journey back to Bellona. Now that Heinrich had agreed to my treaty, I didn't want to stay in Glitnir any longer than necessary, especially given all the awful things that had happened while I'd been here.

It was time to go home to my own problems.

I was scheduled to meet with Heinrich to hammer out the details of our treaty over lunch, but instead of going to the king's dining hall, I took a detour and climbed the steps to Alvis's tower workshop. I knocked on the door and waited for him to tell me to enter.

Gemma and Grimley were here, and the princess ran over and hugged me. "Evie! I'm so glad you're okay!"

"Of course I'm okay, thanks to you and Grimley."

I hugged her back, then went over and petted Grimley, who was lying in his sunspot. I left the two of them to play together and walked over to Alvis, who was perched on his stool, working on his latest design.

A long, jagged block of light gray tearstone was laid out on the table. It hadn't been cut yet, but Alvis was holding a piece of white chalk, and he'd already sketched out a design on the block.

"A tearstone sword?" I raised my eyebrows. "How come I'm not surprised?"

He shrugged. "I already made the girl a dagger. I might as well make her a sword too."

"And a shield?" I teased.

He grinned a little. "And a shield, eventually. Maybe even another dagger. Or a spear. Or a bow and a set of arrows. Whatever weapons she likes."

I nodded. He leaned forward, peered through his magnifying glass, and made some more marks on the tearstone. I watched him work in silence for several minutes, while Gemma fed Grimley small shards of opals that were left over from one of Alvis's jewelry designs.

"I was going to ask you to come back to Seven Spire. I was going to offer you your old space in the dungeon and all the gold and gems you could ever desire to work with."

He looked up and arched an eyebrow at me. "And now you're not? How disappointing."

"You should stay here with Gemma. She needs you more than I do." A wry smile curved my lips. "Besides, you need a new apprentice, and I'm far too busy as queen to fetch your tools."

"You are a wonderful queen, Evie," Alvis said in a serious voice. "Bellona couldn't be in better hands."

"Why? Because I'm a Winter queen?" I asked, my tone a bit snide.

He shook his head. "No. Not because of your magic, but because of *you*, because of the strong, caring person you are. Your magic is part of you, but it's not the most important part. Remember that."

"I will. And I want you to know that I finally figured out what it really means to be a Winter queen."

"And what's that?" he asked in a guarded tone.

"My whole life, everyone always told me that I was a mutt, and I always thought of myself that way too. That I had an enhanced sense of smell and my immunity and that was it." I waggled my fingers. "These small, random magical skills that everyone overlooked or mocked or dismissed as weak, unimportant, insignificant. They were right, and they were wrong. I am a mutt. But that's not *all* that I am."

"So what else are you?"

I straightened up. "I'm a master."

"And your element?"

"Magic." I waggled my fingers again. "I can control magic."

Satisfaction gleamed in Alvis's hazel eyes. "Yes, yes, you can."

"I always thought that I had to actually touch something in order to snuff out its magic, but in the gardens, when I was trying to save Sullivan, I pushed my power outside myself, just like a regular magier would," I said. "And I realized that I can still kill magic, still destroy it, but that I can *control* it as well. That I can wield my immunity like a sword, and maybe even other people's magic along with it."

"A master has complete control of their element," Alvis said. "You can do anything to magic that I can do to metal and stone. You just have to practice and work and figure out how, just like I had to figure out my power for myself."

He hesitated, as if he wanted to say something else. Finally, he did. "But realizing that you're a master isn't what it means to be a Winter queen. Not really."

I let out a breath. "I know. Being a Winter queen doesn't have anything to do with my magic, powers, or abilities. It's about being hard enough, strong enough, to do what's right for Bellona, and for all the people who are counting on me, no matter what the personal cost is to myself. That's what being a Winter queen really means. Serilda told me that once. I didn't think she was telling me the truth then, but I do now, after everything that's happened."

Alvis nodded, then reached over and took my hand. "And you are a fine Winter queen, Evie. A very fine Winter queen."

I smiled and threaded my fingers through his. "That's because I had good teachers like you along the way."

He smiled back at me. And just like with Heinrich, the two of us sat there in silence, watching Gemma and Grimley play and soaking up the quiet strength of each other's company.

Three days later, I was right back where I started—in the Glitnir throne room.

Given everything that had happened, I never wanted to set foot in this room again, but this was a happy occasion . . . more or less.

"Today, I am pleased and honored to announce a new treaty with Queen Everleigh," Heinrich said, his voice booming through the room. "One where we will be united in friendship, a strong, long-lasting friendship that will stand the test of time."

The two of us were standing at the bottom of the dais, with the nobles gathered around us. Heinrich beamed at me, and I returned his smile.

"Thank you, King Heinrich," I replied, clinking my champagne glass against his. "To friendship. And new beginnings."

"To friendship!" he roared.

Everyone echoed the words, and we toasted to the new treaty. The nobles smiled and nodded at me, but I could almost see the wheels spinning in their minds as they wondered exactly how I'd gotten out of my engagement to Dominic and had still gotten my treaty to boot. From what Xenia had told me, rumors were flying through the palace, and each one was more outlandish than the last. Everything from my thwarting an assassination attempt on the king's life, to saving Dominic from certain death, to battling a whole platoon of Mortan assassins mounted on strixes.

Well, perhaps the rumors weren't so outlandish after all.

I heard the murmurs among the crowd, but I kept my benign smile fixed in place. I didn't care what they thought of me, and I would let Heinrich explain the treaty to them however he liked. They were his nobles, not mine, and I had plenty of my own to deal with at Seven Spire.

Once all the pleasantries were said, all the hands were shaken, and all the champagne was drunk, I returned to my chambers, where Calandre and her sisters were packing up my clothes. I didn't want to be in their way, so I left them to their work. Besides, there were some people I needed to see before we left.

I didn't have to go far to find the first pair. Dominic and Rhea were ensconced in the same shadowy alcove that Sullivan and I had hidden in the other night. The two of them had kept their distance from each other the past few days, but now that they were alone, they were making the most of their time together.

I waited until they had stopped kissing before I cleared my throat. Dominic and Rhea broke apart, but when they realized that it was just me, they curled their arms around each other's waists again.

"I'd better get an invitation to the wedding," I drawled. "Especially since it involves my ex-fiancé."

Dominic laughed, then stepped forward and grabbed my hands. "Not only did you tell me to go get the woman I love, but you also saved my family from a Mortan plot. Forget a mere invitation. I should make you a groomsman."

I grinned. "You're right. You should make me a groomsman."

Dominic laughed again and squeezed my hands. "Thank
you, Everleigh. For everything. But I'm afraid that I must leave
you two lovely ladies behind. Duty calls, as it always does."

He winked at me, kissed Rhea's cheek, and set off down the
hallway.

"He really is charming," I murmured.

Rhea grinned. "You have no idea."

"I'm so happy for the two of you, and I'm sorry for any pain
that I caused."

She waved away my apology. "You were trying to do what was
best for everyone. I understand that. I'm just grateful that you
saved Dominic and his family from the Mortans."

I held out my hand. "Until we meet again?"

She nodded and shook it. "Until we meet again."

Rhea went back to her duties, while I moved on to the next
person that I wanted to speak with.

A few minutes later, I knocked on a door. A voice told me to
come in, so I twisted the knob and stepped into the greenhouse.
Helene was sitting at the writing desk, staring at the Amethyst
Eye cactus perched on the corner.

She swiveled around in her chair. Surprise flickered across
her face, but she pushed herself to her feet and crossed her arms
over her chest. "Everleigh. To what do I owe this visit?"

I drew in a breath, then let it out. "I wanted to apologize."

She arched an eyebrow. "For thinking that I was a Mortan
assassin who was poisoning the king and plotting to put my ex-
lover on the throne?"

I grimaced. "Among other things."

I didn't know exactly what Sullivan or anyone else had told
her, but Helene was smart, so I wasn't surprised that she knew

what had really happened. I walked over to her, and we both stared down at the cactus. Her silver signet ring was sitting next to the plant.

She reached out and tapped her finger on the ring. "Dahlia gave me this ring the day before you arrived. She said it was similar to one her mother had worn. I was so thrilled. I never realized that it was a Mortan design and that she was plotting to make me her scapegoat."

She fell silent, staring at both the ring and the cactus. After several seconds, she faced me again.

"I understand why you suspected me," Helene said. "The cactus and the ring were in my workshop, and I had the necessary skills and magic to make the poison. It was the most logical conclusion."

"Perhaps. But part of me also wanted it to be you. Because of Sullivan, and everything the two of you shared. Petty, I know."

She shrugged. "Perhaps. But I probably would have done the same." She gave me a small smile. "Jealousy makes fools of us all."

"As does love," I added in a soft voice.

We both stared at the cactus again, but our silence was companionable.

"Is it wrong that I actually admire Dahlia's ingenuity?" Helene asked. "I always thought that I was one of the smartest, strongest plant magiers in Andvari, but she outwitted me with a bloody *cactus*. And not even a very big one."

She puckered her lips in an exaggerated pout. I barked out a laugh, and she did the same.

"Enough about Dahlia and her schemes," I said. "Let's talk about something more pleasant—and far more useful."

Helene frowned. "Like what?"

I strode over to another table and picked up a jar. "Like this burn cream you used to heal my arm. It's amazing. I want to order some and invite you to Seven Spire to discuss it and your other formulas with Aisha, the head of my bone masters."

Helene's jaw clenched. "You don't have to buy my forgiveness."

I shook my head. "I respect you far too much for that. Your cream is wonderful, and I want to be the first one to buy it. This is business." I paused. "Although I would like to get to know you better, perhaps even become friends, if you are willing."

Helene studied me a moment, but she must have realized that I was being serious because a sly, satisfied smile spread across her face, and she stepped forward and threaded her arm through mine. "Oh, Everleigh. Mixing business and pleasure is one of my favorite things. You and I are going to get along fabulously."

Helene was right. We did get along fabulously. She was smart and clever and funny, and I enjoyed her company far more than I expected. I made arrangements with her to ship a case of burn cream to Seven Spire, then left her workshop.

I didn't want to go back to my room, and I didn't want to see anyone else right now, so I slipped outside, walked through the hedge maze, and ended up at the gazebo.

The blood and bodies had been removed, and the structure was once again pristine. Memories of the battle with Maeven and the magiers floated through my mind, along with my time with Sullivan.

If I closed my eyes and concentrated, I could still feel his lips on mine, still feel his hands sliding across my skin, still feel him moving with me. I would never forget that one perfect moment we'd shared, even if everything else between us had been burned away to poisoned, ruinous ash.

I sat down on one of the cushioned benches and stared out over the pond, watching the water lilies twirl to and fro. I hadn't been here long, maybe five minutes, when familiar footsteps sounded. I drew in a breath, enjoying his cold, vanilla scent, although the sharp tangs of his minty regret and ashy heart-break made my own heart squeeze in response.

Sullivan stepped into the gazebo and slowly approached me. "May I sit?"

I waved my hand. "Of course."

He walked over and sat on the bench beside me. I had been trying to give him some time and space to come to terms with everything, so I hadn't seen much of him over the past few days. His face was pale and haggard, despite the stubble that darkened his chin. His eyes were dim, his shoulders were slumped, and his entire body seemed brittle and thin.

Dahlia's funeral had been held yesterday, and she had been buried as a hero instead of the traitor she was. Of course I had wanted to talk to Sullivan after the funeral, had wanted to comfort him, but he'd left the moment the service was finished, as if he couldn't stomach all the nice things people were saying about his mother. I wouldn't have wanted to hear the lies either.

"You should be proud," Sullivan said in a low, strained voice. "You finally got your treaty. My father told me that he gave you everything you wanted and then some."

"Yes, he did."

But I didn't want to talk about the treaty. I wanted to talk about him, about *us*, or if there even was an us anymore. So I drew in a breath, then let it out and said the words I had been wanting to for days now.

"I'm sorry," I said. "For lying to you. For letting you think that I was going to marry Dominic. I shouldn't have done that, especially when Paloma and the others knew the truth."

"I understand," he said in that low, strained voice again.

"You were trying to figure out who was poisoning my father and trying to hurt my family. I would have done the same, if I'd been in your position."

"Thank you for that. Even though I don't deserve your forgiveness."

Sullivan let out a harsh, bitter laugh. "My mother is the one who doesn't deserve my forgiveness. And do you know what the worst part is?" He paused a moment, then answered his own question. "I keep thinking that it's *my* fault. That I said or did something that convinced her to go through with her scheme. That I'm the reason she did all those awful things. That I'm the reason Frederich, Hans, and all those other people are dead."

He stared at me, anguish burning in his eyes, and I grabbed his hand.

"It is *not* your fault. *None* of this is your fault, Sully. Your mother made her own choices, her own decisions."

"But I keep thinking that I should have known more about who she really was. That I should have asked more questions about where she came from and why she stayed at the palace all these years." He shook his head. "I was always so caught up in how people treated me compared to Dominic and Frederich that I never wondered what *she* thought about being treated the same way. I never realized how much it hurt her too, or how much she hated my father."

He fell silent, then raised his anguished gaze to mine again. "Do you think what she said was true? That she . . . loved me?"

I grabbed his other hand and squeezed it too. "Absolutely. She saved you from that assassin, from another member of the Bastard Brigade. She saved your life. In the end, she chose *you* over her mission, Sully. Never forget that."

He nodded, and we fell silent. He seemed a little calmer now, although just as sad as before.

"What are you going to do now?" I asked.

He shrugged. "I don't know. My father and Dominic have asked me to stay at Glitnir, to help them prepare for war against Morta, if it comes to that."

"And what do you want to do?"

"I just want to run away again and join another gladiator troupe. Go to some far-flung place where nobody knows who I am, or especially what my mother was."

"You know, I ran away to a gladiator troupe once," I said. "It worked out okay for me."

My joke finally coaxed a small smile out of him.

"Maybe you should do that," I said, my voice turning serious. "Maybe you should go away for a while. Maybe you should take some time to figure out who you are and who you want to be."

"Maybe I should."

"Well, wherever you go, you'll always have a place at Seven Spire." I paused. "With me."

The words hung in the air between us, and I wondered if I'd said too much. No, I decided. One of the reasons we were in this mess was because I hadn't said *enough*. I might never see Sullivan again, and I wasn't going to leave without telling him how I felt.

"And what kind of place would that be, highness?" he asked in a soft voice.

"Whatever you want it to be."

I meant every word. I didn't care that Sullivan was a bastard prince. I never had, but now it seemed like the most trivial thing, after all that we had been through. I didn't care what Sullivan's title was, or if he even had a title, and I certainly didn't care what the Seven Spire nobles or anyone else thought about us. Not anymore. All that mattered was how I felt about him, and him about me.

Surprise sparked in his eyes. For a moment, I thought that he might say yes, but then his surprise vanished, swallowed up by regret.

"I'm sorry," he rasped, "but I can't. Not right now. Maybe not ever. I'm sorry, highness. I wish things were different. I wish that *I* were different."

"It's okay," I whispered back. "I understand."

I leaned forward and pressed my lips to his. Unlike the last time we'd been in the gazebo, this was a gentle kiss, just the briefest, softest touch of my lips against his. Still, I breathed in deeply, drawing the scent of him deep down into my lungs and locking it away in my heart. Then I sat back.

"Good luck, Sully," I whispered. "I want nothing but the best for you."

"And I want the same for you, highness," he whispered back.

I got to my feet. I trailed my fingers down his cheek, then turned and hurried away before he saw the tears streak down my face.

chapter twenty-seven

The next morning, my friends and I left Glitnir. We took the train back to Svalin, and we arrived at Seven Spire a few days later.

Captain Auster had managed to hang on to the palace, although a dozen new crises had arisen while I'd been gone. So I busied myself with those, as well as the demanding nobles.

Dealing with these fresh problems helped keep my mind off Sullivan, although I found myself thinking about him every time I had a moment alone. I wondered if he was still at Glitnir or if he had left and gone somewhere else, somewhere he could figure out who he was and what he wanted to do with his life.

As a going-away present, Alvis had given me a Cardea mirror so that I could talk to him, Gemma, and Grimley in his workshop. We spoke every few days, but Alvis and Gemma never mentioned Sullivan, and I didn't inquire about him.

Part of me didn't want to know where he was. Because if I did know, then I would have been tempted to go to him, ask him to come to Seven Spire, and stay with me. But I'd seen how disastrously that had turned out for Heinrich and Dahlia, and I wasn't going to ask Sullivan to repeat his mother's mistakes or abandon his principles for me. At this point, they were just about the only things he had left.

One night, after a particularly long and boring court session, I escaped to my room. Three weeks had passed since I had returned to Seven Spire, although after dealing with the ever-demanding nobles today, it felt like three years.

Calandre and her sisters drew me a bath and did their usual ministrations. Then, once they had left me alone and I was sure that no one else would check on me, I did the same thing that I'd been doing every single night since I'd returned to Seven Spire—I used the secret passageway behind the bookcase to sneak out of my chambers and go to Maeven's room.

I had ordered her chambers to be sealed off again, and I was the only one who had a key to the door. I had finally told Paloma, Serilda, Cho, Auster, and Xenia about my previous conversation with Maeven before we had left for Glitnir, but I hadn't told them that I'd been coming here every night, hoping that she would appear in the mirror again. She hadn't yet, but her room was quiet, peaceful, and the absolute last place anyone would look for me. So I sat down to get some work done while I waited to see if Maeven would appear.

I laid a stack of papers on the writing desk, right next to two other items already sitting there—Maeven's signet ring and Ansel's pocket watch.

Thanks to my dreams, my memories, of the Winterwind attack, I'd been thinking about my tutor a lot, and when we'd returned to Seven Spire, I had fished his watch out of its hiding place in one of my vanity table drawers.

I traced my index finger over the large, fancy cursive *M* embossed on the bronze watch cover. The initial was the same as the *M* on Maeven's silver signet ring, and the stylized *M* was also part of the Mortan royal crest—the only part it seemed like the members of the Bastard Brigade were allowed to wear.

Including Dahlia. Her gold heart locket with its distinctive *D* had been buried with her. Heinrich had told me that her locket had contained a painted portrait of Sullivan, along with an *M* engraved on the inside. I supposed it was fitting, since Sullivan and Morta were the only two things that Dahlia had ever truly loved.

I wasn't quite sure why I had kept Ansel's watch all these years, or why I had dragged it back out now, along with Maeven's ring. Maybe I wanted to remind myself that the people we loved the most could have the darkest secrets—and to be extra careful who I put my trust in.

I scooted the watch and the ring off to the side and got to work, still waiting for Maeven to appear.

And she finally did.

I'd been reviewing some new trade agreements with Unger for about an hour when a bright silver light flared, and the surface of the Cardea mirror began to ripple. I put down my pen, walked over, and stood in front of the mirror.

A few seconds later, Maeven came into focus on the other side. Blond bun, amethyst eyes, elegant gown. She looked the same as always, but there was one noticeable addition to her features—a deep, jagged wound surrounded by an ugly, purple bruise on her left cheekbone.

I recognized the mark for what it was—someone had backhanded her, and his ring had left behind a large, lasting impression. Most likely her brother the king, unhappy with her latest failure to kill me.

"Hello, Maeven. I've been expecting you."

She seemed surprised by that. "Have you been waiting up for me every single night since you returned to Seven Spire? Why, Everleigh, how sweet. I didn't know you cared so much."

I shrugged.

"So why are you here?" she asked.

"I wanted to know whether or not you were still alive." I pointed to her cheek. "Looks like your brother the king gave you a little souvenir. I'm guessing he wasn't very happy that your entire scheme turned out to be a massive failure. You lost all those magiers and strixes, your secret weapon in Dahlia, and any shot you had at the Andvarian throne, all at once. It was a truly glorious defeat."

Maeven's hand drifted up to her cheek. She realized what she'd just done, grimaced, and dropped her hand back down to her side. "My relationship with my brother is none of your concern."

I shrugged again. "I suppose not. Tell me, though. Are you going to keep that nasty little wound he gave you? It would be a terrible shame to ruin your beautiful face with it. Did you know that Serilda has a similar scar near her eye from where Cordelia backhanded her years ago? I think that keeping such an ugly mark on her face reminded Serilda of what she was fighting for. Will your scar do the same for you?"

I paused, but she didn't answer, so I kept talking, trying to cut her to pieces with my words.

"Or will your king even give you a choice in the matter? Probably not. After all, he doesn't give you a choice in anything else, does he? You and your Bastard Brigade are just good little soldiers, fighting, fucking, betraying, and killing for him from the day you're born until the day you die. No matter what the cost is to any of *you*."

Maeven's lips pressed together in a tight, thin line, but the motion must have made her wound ache because she grimaced and forced herself to visibly relax her features. She still didn't respond to my harsh words, though.

I tilted my head to the side, studying her. "So why are *you* here, Maeven? Why did you appear in the mirror tonight?"

"Perhaps I wanted to see how you were doing," she murmured.

"Why? So you can start plotting how to kill me again?" I
shook my head. "There is another option, you know."

"What's that?"

"You could just give up."

Maeven threw back her head and laughed. And laughed and
laughed and laughed some more. Anger spiked through me, but
I forced myself to listen to her loud, mocking chuckles.

She finally stopped laughing, wiped the tears out of the
corners of her eyes, and looked at me again. "Oh, Everleigh. You
are nothing if not entertaining. Part of me will almost regret
killing you."

This time, I was the one who threw back my head and
laughed. "Please. We both know that you're not going to kill me—
that you *can't* kill me. Not with your magic, anyway."

Maeven's eyes narrowed. "And why is that?"

I held up my hand and waggled my fingers at her. "Because
I'm a Winter queen, and I have a power that makes you very,
very afraid. Because I can destroy your magic, and the king's
magic, and all of Morta along with it. That's why you really
want me dead, isn't it? That's why you wanted all the Blairs
dead at the massacre, but especially the Winter line. You didn't
want to take a chance that any of the Blairs were magic masters
like me."

Her lips puckered, and she didn't respond, but I kept going.

"When you tried to kill Sullivan with your lightning, I
snuffed out your power with a wave of my hand. You saw me do it.
That's when you knew for sure what I truly was."

"So what?" she snapped.

"So I saw how fucking *scared* it made you," I snapped back.
"How very scared *I* made you. No magier ever wants to lose their
power. It's the thing they secretly fear the most. I promise you

this—if you come at me again, I will shatter your magic just like I did in the gardens. And then again, and again, until I've completely destroyed your magic. Until I've completely destroyed *you*."

I leaned in even closer to the mirror. "Tell me, Maeven. What will your precious brother the king do when he realizes that you've lost your magic and that you're of no further use? I don't think he'll be very pleased. And I don't imagine that Bastard Brigade members get to quietly live out the remainder of their lives in some quaint little cottage."

She didn't respond, but agreement flashed in her eyes, along with the faintest flicker of fear.

"Face it," I said. "You have two choices. You can keep trying to kill me and risk my destroying you and your magic in return."

For a moment, I thought that she wasn't going to ask me the obvious question, but she finally did. "Or?"

"Or you can *stop*. Just stop and get away from your brother, from Morta, from this whole twisted life you've been forced into."

"No one has ever *forced* me into anything," Maeven snarled. "*I* make my own choices, and *I* decide my own fate. Not you or my brother or anyone else."

"It doesn't seem that way to me."

"You know *nothing* about me or my brother or anything else," she hissed, her hands clenching into fists. "But there is one thing that you will know, far sooner than you think. And that's death, Everleigh. *Your* death, along with the death of your precious Bellona and everything you love."

I leaned forward even more. "Well, then, at least I'll die for something I love, for something I truly *believe* in, and not because some tyrant sent me on a fool's errand because he was too much of a coward to come and face me himself."

Maeven's lips pressed together, but she couldn't deny the

truth of my words. She glared at me a final time, then gave a sharp wave of her hand. The surface of the mirror rippled again, and that bright silver light flared. I had to shut my eyes against the intense glare, and when I opened them again, she had vanished, and the mirror was just a mirror again.

A thin, satisfied smile curved my lips. Despite our mutual threats, I considered our conversation a great success. I had told Maeven that she had only two options—die trying to kill me or leave the king and Morta behind forever—but the truth was that she had a third option.

I wondered if she realized that yet and exactly what that option was. If not, she soon would, given the seeds of doubt and fear I'd planted in her mind. I just wondered whether she would decide to make that third option a reality.

But I'd done all that I could, and only time would tell if my long game with Maeven ended the way I wanted it to—not in her death, but in something far, far worse.

I returned to my chambers. For once, I slept well, and I woke up the next morning feeling refreshed. Plotting against my enemies invigorated me.

But my light, happy feeling quickly evaporated as the day wore on, and it was completely gone by lunchtime.

I sighed and shifted on my seat, trying not to show how utterly bored I was. It was mid-afternoon, and I was once again in the throne room, listening to Lord Fullman, Lady Diante, and the other nobles drop not-so-subtle hints about which one of their sons, nephews, and grandsons I should marry. Despite returning home with the new Andvarian treaty, the nobles were still determined to wed me off.

I opened my mouth to tell Fullman, Diante, and everyone

else in no uncertain terms to quit trying to foist their male relatives off on me when a faint ringing sound caught my ear. For a moment, I thought that I'd just imagined the noise, but the sound came again and again, each note a bit louder than the one before. I frowned.

Was that . . . a bell?

Fullman, Diante, and the other nobles glanced around, also wondering what that sound was.

I glanced over at Paloma, who was standing at the bottom of the dais. She was smiling, as was the ogre face on her neck, as if she knew exactly who and what was making that noise. I looked at Captain Auster, who was standing on the other side of the dais. He too was smiling. Next, I peered up at the second-floor balcony, where Serilda, Cho, and Xenia were sitting, along with Theroux, Aisha, and several other members of the Black Swan troupe. They too were grinning, as were Calandre and her sisters.

"What's going on?" I asked.

Paloma's grin widened. "Why don't you go out to the royal lawn and see for yourself?"

What could possibly be happening on the lawn? I eyed my friend, but she didn't say anything else.

By this point, I was getting annoyed, so I got to my feet and walked down the dais steps. The nobles moved aside, and I marched past them, heading for the closed double doors at the far end of the throne room.

"My queen?" Fullman called out. "Where are you going?"

"To see what the bloody noise is," I snapped back.

Two guards opened the doors at my approach. I glanced over my shoulder. Paloma and Auster had fallen in step behind me, as had all the nobles. Everyone wanted to see what was going on.

I quickly made my way through the hallways, pushed through the glass doors that led out to the royal lawn, and stepped outside. I looked around, but the lawn was empty, except for a few servants going about their chores. Still, the sound was much louder here than it had been inside, and I realized that it wasn't coming from the royal lawn—it was echoing up to it from somewhere down below.

I looked over my shoulder. Paloma and Captain Auster were still behind me, and Serilda, Cho, and Xenia had joined them, along with the nobles and everyone else who'd been in the throne room. The nobles were as confused as I was, but my friends looked at me expectantly, as if I should know exactly what was happening.

Finally, Paloma rolled her eyes and pointed at the wall that cordoned off the lawn. "Maybe you should check out the view, Evie."

I frowned at her again, but I walked over to the wall and peered down, still trying to find the sound of that loud ringing noise. Everyone followed me, lined up along the wall, and stared down at the river and bridges below.

"Look!" Cho said, his voice booming out. "Down there! At the end of the Pureheart Bridge!"

I peered in that direction. A man was standing at the far end of the Pureheart Bridge, right beside the Heartsong Bell—and he was ringing it.

Over and over again, the man pulled on the long rope, making the clapper bang against the inside of the bell and emit a loud, pealing noise. I lifted my hand to shade my eyes from the sun and squinted, trying to make out his features. The man moved around to the front of the bell where I could see him, and my breath caught in my throat.

Sullivan.

He was the one yanking on the rope, and he was the one making the bell chime. He'd already attracted quite a crowd on that side of the river, and more and more people hurried in that direction, eager to see what was going on.

Behind me, a soft, resigned sigh sounded. "Damn," Diante murmured. "I wish I'd thought of that."

I kept staring at Sullivan, still not quite believing that he was here. "What is he doing?"

Paloma elbowed me in the side. "What does it look like he's doing? He's going to climb up here to get you. Isn't that the grand Bellonan love tradition?"

"That idiot!" I hissed, even as my heart soared. "He's going to fall and break his fool neck!"

But she was right, and that was exactly what Sullivan was doing. He rang the bell again, then looked up. He must have spotted me because he let go of the rope. Everyone on the lawn fell silent, as did the crowd gathered along the river. Sullivan waited until the last cheery echoes of the bell had faded away before he cupped his hands around his mouth.

"Queen Everleigh Saffira Winter Blair!" he yelled. "I'm here to profess my love to you and to prove it, in true Bellonan style! What do you say?"

I cupped my hands around my mouth and yelled back at him. "That you're a fool and that you're going to fall to your foolish death! Come up to the palace, and we can talk about this like normal people!"

Sullivan grinned, his eyes flashing like sapphires in the sunlight. "But we're not normal people, highness. I may be a fool, but I'm a fool in love!"

Several people in the crowd down below *aah*ed at his words, as did some of the nobles up here on the lawn. Even Captain Auster dabbed at the corner of his eye, as if he was suddenly overcome with emotion.

Sullivan turned to the crowd gathered around him and held his arms out wide just like I'd seen Cho do dozens of times during a gladiator show at the Black Swan arena. "Good people of

Svalin! What do you say? Shall I take up this Bellonan challenge to prove my true love? Shall I put on a good show for you, along with my lady, my queen, up there high in her grand palace?"

The crowd roared in response, as did everyone on the lawn. How could they not?

Sullivan grinned up at me, then strode forward across the bridge.

"He's actually serious," I whispered. "He's actually going to do it."

"Of course he's serious," Paloma said. "He wouldn't be here otherwise."

I whirled around to my friend. "Did you know about this?"

Her smug grin, along with the one on the ogre on her neck, was all the confirmation I needed.

"But when— How—" I sputtered.

Paloma put her hands on my shoulders. "The when and the how don't matter. Not right now. All that does is that he's here."

Her amber eyes gleamed with sincerity. She was right. Sullivan was here, and that was all that mattered.

A wide, crazy, happy grin spread across my face, and I turned back to the wall and looked down, as did everyone else on the lawn.

Sullivan was on this side of the bridge now, staring up at Seven Spire's jagged cliff face and trying to figure out where to begin climbing. Finally, he picked a spot, stretched up a hand, and reached for the nearest rock.

I swear that I felt his fingers close around that first rock as though he was reaching inside my chest and was somehow touching my heart at the same time. I stood there, holding my breath, my hands clenched into fists on top of the wall, while he stretched out another hand and reached for a rock a little higher up than the one before.

He did this over and over again, slowly but steadily scaling up the cliffs. Ten feet, twenty, fifty, a hundred. He was doing it, and he was actually going to make it all the way up to me.

Until he slipped.

Sullivan grabbed a rock, but it cracked off the cliff, sending him sliding down. My heart stopped, and my breath caught in my throat. For a moment, I thought he was going to lose his grip completely, bounce off the jagged rocks below, and fall to his death, but he managed to catch himself at the last instant.

With only one hand on the rocks, he hung there in midair for several seconds before he finally found a crack in the cliff face that he could shove his boots into and regain his balance.

He let out a low, angry snarl, then shrugged out of his long gray coat and tossed it aside, as if it was weighing him down. A gust of wind caught the coat and sent it spinning out across the river. It hit the rippling surface, and the water quickly drowned it.

Sullivan looked up at me. A bloody gash slashed across his forehead, cuts and bruises dotted his hands and arms, and his black tunic and pants hung in tatters where the rocks had shredded them during his fall. But his eyes were as bright as ever, and his mouth was set in a determined line. He took a few seconds to get his breath back, then reached for another rock above his head.

And suddenly, I knew what I had to do.

"I'm not waiting around up here. I'm going down to him."

I swung my legs up and over the wall so that I was standing on the other side and staring down at the cliffs below.

"Queen Everleigh!" Fullman protested. "You can't do this! Tradition clearly dictates that he must climb all the way up here by himself! With no assistance whatsoever!"

"And I am the *queen*," I snapped back at him. "I love him, and I'm going to help him. I don't care what you or anyone else says, and I'm going to make my own tradition starting right now. And if you don't like it, then too damn bad."

Fullman opened his mouth to protest again, but I stared him down, and he swallowed his words. I looked at the other nobles, and they all slowly wilted and bowed their heads under my cold glare.

Diante was the only one who met my gaze. After a moment, she shrugged and gave me a wry smile, as if she knew that she had lost and that there was no stopping me. Even more surprising, she actually curtsied. "As you wish, my queen."

I nodded back at her, then turned around and stared down at the cliffs. I drew in a deep breath and let it out before leaning down and grabbing hold of the first rock.

"What are you doing?" Sullivan called out. "I'm supposed to come to you."

"And I don't want you to break your fool neck!" I yelled back. "Just stay where you are."

He ignored me, of course, and started climbing even faster. I did the same thing, picking my way down the side of the cliff and trying to get to him before he slipped again.

I couldn't bear to lose him again.

Somehow, we met in the middle, on a small outcropping of rock that was just big and strong enough to hold the two of us. We were both breathing hard, and it took us a moment to find our words. My heart was beating so hard and painfully that I thought it might explode, but it was worth it to see Sullivan again, to see the love shining in his eyes, the love I knew was reflected in my own gaze.

"I thought you were staying in Glitnir with your family," I said in a breathless voice. "Or running away to join a gladiator troupe."

"I thought about doing both of those things. But there's nothing for me at Glitnir, and the only troupe I want to be in is the Black Swan—with you."

He reached up and brushed a bit of hair back from my face,

smearing blood from his cut fingers onto my skin, but I didn't care. I didn't care about anything but the fact that he was standing here with me.

"But what about your mother?" I asked. "And everything that happened?"

He grimaced. "I'm still dealing with that. I'll probably *always* be dealing with that." He paused for a moment, then looked at me again. "But my mother was right about one thing. She told me not to make the same mistake she did, not to let my anger rule me. And Helene was right too. I was so wrapped up in how other people saw me that I let it ruin some of the good things in my life."

His grimace melted away, and determination filled his face. "But I'm not going to do that anymore. I'm not going to worry about what other people think of me, and I'm not going to throw things away just because they aren't exactly how I want them to be. Instead, I'm going to fight like the fiercest gladiator for what I love, and what I love is you, Evie."

My heart soared, but I forced myself to think things through like a true Winter queen would. "But what about your father? And Andvari? What about your people, your kingdom?"

Sullivan gave me a fierce look. "*You* are my kingdom. You always have been, ever since that first morning I found you sleeping in the corner of my house. You're all I've ever wanted, highness, and you're all that I need, Evie."

"You're my kingdom too," I whispered.

I cupped his face in my hands, then stood on my tiptoes and crushed my lips to his. Sullivan growled and pulled me closer.

All around us, I could hear cheering. From the people on the bridge and lining the river below, from my friends above on the royal lawn, even from the nobles. But their cheers were nothing compared to the feel of Sullivan's lips on mine, his skin against mine, his heart beating under my fingertips, hammering just as hard as mine was.

We would have kept right on kissing, but something slapped my shoulder. Sullivan and I broke apart. I looked up and realized that Paloma had dropped down a rope to the two of us.

"How about you two lovebirds do the smart thing and climb up here before you both plunge to your deaths?" Paloma said in her usual matter-of-fact tone.

I ignored her, turned back to Sullivan, and wrapped my arms around his neck. "Do we have to? I want to stay here for just a little while longer."

He grinned back at me. "I was thinking the same thing, highness."

He reached up and grabbed the rope, yanking it out of Paloma's hands. Then he tossed it aside, and it floated down to the river below to be swept away, just like his jacket had been.

All around us, the crowd roared again, but I only had eyes for Sullivan, and he for me. He grinned at me again, and I pulled his head back down to mine.

And as I kissed him, I made a vow to myself—that I would spend the rest of my life protecting my prince.

Turn the page for a sneak peek at the next book in
Jennifer Estep's Crown of Shards series

CRUSH THE
KING

Coming in 2020

enia had some other business to take care of, so Paloma and I left her finishing school.

It was almost six o'clock, and the sun was slowly sinking behind the Spire Mountains that ringed the city. The December air was already quite chilly, but it would turn even colder once the last golden rays vanished behind the high, rugged peaks and took their meager warmth along with them. My nose twitched. A faint, metallic scent hung in the air, indicating that it would snow before the night was through.

Only a few people were walking on the side streets that flanked Xenia's finishing school. Most had their heads down and their arms crossed over their chests, trying to stay as warm as possible in their scarves, coats, and gloves, and no one gave Paloma and me a second look as we made our way over to one of the many enormous square plazas that could be found throughout Svalin.

We stood in the shadows in a narrow alley that ran between two bakeries and looked out over the plaza. Brightly painted wooden carts manned by bakers, butchers, farmers, tailors, and other merchants lined all four sides of the area, while a large gray stone fountain of two girls holding hands bubbled merrily in the center.

People of all shapes, sizes, stations, and ages moved across the gray cobblestones, going from one cart and merchant to the next and shopping for breads, meats, cheeses, vegetables, clothes, and more. Still more people cut directly through the

plaza, bypassing the colorful carts and loud, squawking merchants, skirting around the gurgling fountain, and steadfastly
trudging home after a long, hard day at work. Miners, mostly,
wearing thick, dark blue coveralls, boots, and hard, ridged hel-
mets, all of which were coated with light gray fluorestone dust.

I opened my mouth and drew in breath after breath, letting
the air roll in over my tongue and using my mutt magic to taste
all the scents swirling through the plaza. Fresh, warm bread and
almond-sugar cookies from the bakeries next to the alley. The
coppery stench of blood from the meat on the butchers' carts. The
sharp, tangy cheeses. The bits of dirt on the farmers' potatoes and
other produce. The fine layers of crushed, chalky stone clinging
to the miners.

I sensed all that and more, but the one thing I didn't smell
was magic.

Normally, I would have welcomed its absence. More often
than not, I sensed the hot, caustic stench of magic only when
someone was trying to kill me. But this evening, I found the lack
of power disappointing.

"I don't like this," Paloma muttered, her hand on her mace.
"You shouldn't be here. What if this rumor about another Blair
is just a trick to get you out of the palace and into the city where
you're more vulnerable? And leaving Xenia's finishing school
without any guards is just asking for trouble."

In addition to being my best friend, Paloma was also my
personal guard, a job she took very seriously.

"Coming here without any guards is part of the plan. We're
trying to blend in, remember?" I arched an eyebrow at her. "Besides, didn't you once tell me that a gladiator and an ogre morph
like yourself is worth twenty regular soldiers?"

"That was Halvar." Paloma's chin lifted with pride. "But he
was right. I *am* worth twenty soldiers."

422   JENNIFER ESTEP

Halvar was Xenia's nephew and a powerful ogre morph, just like Paloma was. He and Paloma were good friends, along with Bjarni, another ogre morph.

I rolled my eyes. "Well, then you should be happy that we left the finishing school. Xenia is just as skeptical about this rumor as you are. If the two of you are right, then we're probably going to run into trouble."

Paloma's eyes gleamed with anticipation, and the ogre on her neck grinned, showing off its jagged teeth. "It has been a while since I've gotten to fight anyone." She plucked her mace off her belt and gave it an experimental swing, making the spikes whistle through the air. "It'll be good to get in some practice before the Regalia and knock the dust off Peony."

It took me a moment to realize who—or rather what—she was referring to. "You named your mace *Peony*?"

She gave me an incredulous look, as if my question were utter gibberish. "Of course. Years ago. Haven't you named your sword yet?"

"No."

"Well, you should. And your dagger and shield too."

My hand dropped to the sword belted to my waist, and my fingers traced over the crown-of-shards crest in the hilt. The sharp points of the shards digging into my skin always comforted me. Perhaps because the sensation reminded me of all the other Bellonan queens—especially the Winter queens—who had come before me.

Hmm. Maybe I should take Paloma's advice and name my sword . . . *Winter*. Nah, that was too obvious, too on the nose, too cliché. I'd have to think of something more original.

Paloma kept swinging her mace, as if she were warming up for a gladiator bout.

"Why Peony?" I asked.

She froze mid-swing and slowly lowered the weapon to her

side, her knuckles going white around the handle. "My mother always wore peony perfume," she said in a low, raspy voice.

Sympathy filled me, and I reached over and squeezed her arm. Paloma gave me a small, sad smile, then turned her attention back to the plaza.

"I still don't like this," she repeated. "You're far too exposed and vulnerable, and that cloak is barely a disguise. At least put your hood up so people can't see your face so clearly."

I opened my mouth to point out that half the people in the plaza were wearing cloaks and that her swinging that giant mace made her far more noticeable than me, but Paloma and her inner ogre both gave me a fierce glare. So I bit back my words and pulled up my hood, hiding my black hair and casting my face in shadow.

"I don't know why you're so worried," I murmured. "It's not like we came here alone."

I waved my hand at the fountain in the center of the plaza. A forty-something woman with slicked-back blond hair and a scar at the corner of one of her dark blue eyes was tossing pennies into the fountain, as though she were making wishes. She was wearing a black cloak, although I could still see her white tunic with its distinctive black-swan crest peeking out from beneath the flowing fabric. She also had a tearstone sword and dagger belted to her waist, just like I did.

Serilda Swanson, the leader of the Black Swan gladiator troupe and one of my advisors, nodded at me, then discreetly pointed her finger to her right.

I looked in that direction and focused on a forty-something man with glossy black hair, black eyes, golden skin, and a lean, muscled body on the far side of the plaza. He too was wearing a black cloak over a red jacket and a ruffled white tunic. A sword and a dagger hung off his belt as well, and a morph mark was visible on his neck—a dragon face with ruby-red scales and gleaming black eyes.

Cho Yamato, the Black Swan ringmaster, was leaning up against a bakery cart, nibbling on a giant raspberry-peach cookie. Cho had a serious sweet tooth, as did his inner dragon. He noticed my gaze and winked at me, then gestured up at the roof of a building across the plaza.

A man was standing next to a silver spire that decorated one corner of the roof. He was tall and handsome, with dark brown hair, intense blue eyes, and a bit of stubble that clung to his strong jaw. A midnight-blue cloak was draped over his shoulders, and his black tunic was perfectly tailored to his muscled body. He too was wearing a sword and a dagger, although he kept flexing his fingers, ready to unleash his lightning magic at the first sign of trouble.

I drew in a deep breath. Even among all the floral perfumes and musky colognes swirling through the plaza, I could still pick out his unique scent—clean, cold vanilla with just a hint of warm spice.

Thanks to my mutt magic, scents and memories were often tangled up together in my mind, and his rich, heady aroma made my heart quicken, my stomach clench, and hot, liquid desire scorch through my veins. All sorts of images and sensations washed over me. My lips on his, our tongues dueling back and forth, my fingers sliding through his thick, silky hair, my palms skimming down his bare, muscled chest, then going lower and lower, even as his hands slid across my skin . . .

Lucas Sullivan, the magier enforcer of the Black Swan troupe and my unofficial consort, grinned, as if he knew exactly what I was thinking and couldn't wait to return to the palace to make it a reality.

I grinned back at him. That made two of us.

"Oh, quit mooning at Lucas," Paloma grumbled. "That will get you killed quicker than anything else tonight."

I grinned at him a moment longer, then turned my attention

back to the plaza. "See? The others are in position, and I am perfectly safe. Now, we just have to wait and see if anyone shows up."

In addition to hearing whispers that another Blair might still be alive, Xenia and her many sources had started spreading their own rumor in return—that *any* Blair who came to this plaza tonight would be taken in and guaranteed safety at Seven Spire palace.

Xenia and her network had been spreading the rumor for about two weeks, and my friends and I had ventured here tonight to see if anyone would take the bait.

Paloma eyed the people moving through the plaza. "Even if this woman, this supposed Blair, does show up, how are we going to pick her out of the crowd? There are hundreds of people here. We might not even see her."

"I don't have to see her." I tapped my nose. "My magic will let me sense hers."

"But you don't even know what she is," Paloma pointed out. "She could be a magier or a master or a morph. Or she might just be a mutt like you are. It might not even be a woman. Maybe it's a man."

I shrugged. "Magic is magic. I can always smell it, no matter what kind or who it belongs to. Besides, if there's even the smallest bit of truth to the rumor . . ."

My voice trailed off, and a hard knot of emotion suddenly clogged my throat. That damn hope was rising up in me again, trying to trap me with its warm, honeyed sweetness, but I pushed it back down.

"Then that means at least one of the Blairs, one of your cousins, is still alive." Paloma gave me a sympathetic look, then shook her head, dismissing the promising thought just like I had. "But you still need to be careful. It wouldn't surprise me if Maeven started this rumor to lure you out of the palace so she and the rest of the Bastard Brigade can try to kill you again."

Maeven was the bastard sister of the Mortan king and the one who had orchestrated the Seven Spire massacre. She was also the leader of the Bastard Brigade, a group of bastard relatives of the king and the other legitimate Mortan royals. Over the past several months, Maeven and her Bastard Brigade had tried to kill me numerous times, although I had managed to thwart most of their schemes and stay alive—so far.

"You might be right," I admitted. "Maeven is certainly clever and devious enough to float a rumor about another Blair to get me here, but I have to learn for myself whether it's true. And if it is a plot on her part, then we'll kill her assassins, just like we have before."

"And if it's not another Mortan plot?" Paloma asked.

"Then we'll find out exactly who this person is, where they've been, and how they've managed to stay alive. And especially why they didn't come to Seven Spire after I took the throne and decreed that Blair survivors should return to the palace."

Part of me was happy that one of my cousins had potentially survived the slaughter, but part of me was also dreading the family reunion. I was only queen because all the other Blairs were dead. What if this mysterious cousin had been higher in line for the throne? What if they had a better claim on the crown? What if they had more magic than I did?

And if any of that were true, then came the biggest question of all—should I step aside?

That was what protocol and tradition would dictate I do. But what was best for Bellona? Because I couldn't imagine anyone out there—Blair or otherwise—who wanted to protect my kingdom and her people more than I did.

I hadn't wanted to be queen, but now that I had finally secured my position, I didn't want to give it up just because someone else had had the good fortune to survive the massacre. If I was being brutally honest, I also didn't want to give up all the power and privileges that came with being the queen of Bellona. It was heady and thrilling to be respected and even feared, especially since I had spent all those long years being the royal stand-in, the royal puppet, at Seven Spire. Perhaps that made me petty and selfish, just like Vasilia had been.

But most of all, I didn't want to give up the throne because of how it would impact my chances of finally taking my revenge on Maeven and the Mortan king. I wanted to make them suffer for what they'd done to the Blairs, to my family, to *me*, and I had a far better chance of getting that revenge as queen, rather than going back to just being Lady Everleigh.

"Well, I hope this person shows up soon," Paloma grumbled, breaking into my turbulent thoughts. "I don't want to stand around in the cold all night."

She stamped her feet and pulled her forest-green cloak a little tighter around her body. Autumn had already come and gone, and winter was quickly taking hold in the Spire Mountains. In addition to the impending snow tonight, the wind had a bitter chill that promised that even colder, harsher weather was on its way.

"Don't worry. Xenia and her spies said to meet at this fountain at six o'clock, and it's that time now. Someone should show up soon."

Paloma sighed and stamped her feet again, but the two of us held our position in the alley, and Serilda, Cho, and Sullivan remained vigilant in their spots around and above the plaza.

The sun might be setting, but fluorestones were flaring to life inside the surrounding buildings, as well as the streetlamps that dotted the walkways lining the plaza. The soft, golden lights must have made the goods look even more attractive because the merchants were still doing a brisk business, and it was hard to pick out anyone suspicious, much less a familiar face.

Ever since Xenia had told me that one of my cousins might

be alive, I had been racking my mind, trying to figure out who it could be, but I hadn't come up with any possibilities. So I stared out into the plaza, peering at everyone who walked by.

I was so busy studying the faces of the adults that I almost missed the girl.

She was young, sixteen or so, and dressed in several layers of thin, grubby rags. Her clothes might have been dark blue at one time but were now almost black with grime. Her face wasn't much better. Dirt streaked across her cheeks, and her nose was red from the cold. A pale gray winter hat covered her head, although her dark brown hair stuck up at crazy angles through the gaping holes in the knit fabric.

The girl stopped about twenty feet away from us, standing in the shadows next to a bakery cart. Her head snapped back and forth, as though she was looking for someone, although she seemed to be focusing on the area around the fountain. She tapped her hand on her thigh in a nervous rhythm, even as she shifted back and forth on her feet, like she was ready to run away at any moment. A few red-hot sparks flashed on her fingertips, flickering in time to her uneasy motions, although she quickly curled her hand into a fist, snuffing out the telltale signs of magic.

I drew in a breath, letting the air roll in over my tongue and tasting all the scents in it again. The breads, the cookies, the bloody cuts of meat, the fluorestone dust. I pushed aside all those scents and concentrated on the girl. My nose twitched, and I finally got a whiff of her scent—the hot, caustic stench of magic mixed with a sweet, rosy note.

"There," I whispered, discreetly pointing the girl out to Paloma. "I think it might be her."

Paloma peered in that direction. "Who is she? Do you recognize her?"

I shook my head. "No. I've never seen that girl before, but I can smell her magic. She's definitely a fire magier, and a fairly strong one at that." I hesitated, trying to push down my treacherous hope yet again. "She could be a Summer queen. Lots of them had fire magic."

"Then what is she waiting for?" Paloma asked. "Serilda is still throwing pennies into the fountain. That's the signal."

It had been Xenia's idea to say that any Blair seeking asylum at Seven Spire should approach the blond woman tossing pennies into the fountain. The girl had come to the right plaza at the right time, so she must have heard the information, but she still didn't approach Serilda.

Instead, she stared at Serilda a moment longer, then turned around and ran away.

For a moment, I stood there, stunned. My friends and I had been plotting this for days, and everything had been going according to plan. But now, instead of talking to Serilda like she was supposed to, the girl was heading deeper into the crowd and getting farther away with each passing second.

Desperation rushed through me, propelling me forward, and I charged out of the alley.

"Evie!" Paloma hissed. "Evie, wait for me!"

But I couldn't wait, not without losing sight of the girl. So I plunged into the crowd and chased after her.

The girl must have had some practice picking her way through crowds because she slipped through the throngs of people as easily as one of the Black Swan acrobats could tumble across the arena floor.

Several times, I lost sight of her, only to push past someone and see her gray hat bobbing along in the distance. I felt like a fisherman trying to reel in a particularly difficult catch. Every time I almost got close enough to latch onto her shoulder, she sped up and put three more people in between us. She never looked back, but I wasn't exactly being subtle with all my shoving and pushing, and she must have realized that someone was following her, given the annoyed shouts that sprang up in my wake.

"Evie!" Paloma hissed again from somewhere behind me. "Slow down! You're going to get your fool self killed!"

She was probably right, but I couldn't slow down. Not until I knew whether this girl was actually a Blair. The burning need to know—and the rising hope that I wasn't the only one left—drove me onward.

The girl broke free of the plaza and darted onto one of the side streets. I glanced back over my shoulder. Paloma was still pushing through the crowd behind me, but Serilda, Cho, and Sullivan were nowhere in sight. Not surprising, given how much farther across the plaza they'd been. Well, my friends would just have to catch up. I wasn't losing the girl. Not now.

I rushed down the side street, racing around the people ambling along and window-shopping. My boots clattered on the cobblestones, my hood slipped off my head, and my cloak streamed out behind me like a dark blue ribbon, but I hurried on.

I reached the end of the street. Just when I thought I'd lost her completely, I spotted her gray hat disappearing into an alley. I hurried up to the entrance and stopped, peering down the dark corridor.

The alley ran for about thirty feet before opening up into another, much smaller plaza, but no carts and merchants were set up here, and no pretty stone fountain bubbled in the center. Instead, cracked wooden boards, broken bottles, busted bricks, and other trash littered this area.

Buildings ringed the plaza, with another alley leading out the far side, and debris was piled in heaps along the walls, as though the people living and working in the rooms above simply opened their windows and tossed their garbage outside, not caring where it landed below. The stench of sour milk, rotten meat, and other spoiled food almost knocked me down, and I had to pinch the bridge of my nose to hold back a sneeze.

In just a few streets, I had gone from one of the most affluent parts of Svalin to the beginning of the slums. Sadness filled me, the way it always did at the thought that people—*my* people— lived like this, but I shoved the emotion aside. I could be sad later, after I'd found the girl.

I held my position at the alley entrance, looking and listening, but I didn't see the girl running out the far side, and I didn't hear any footsteps. She must still be in the plaza somewhere. Maybe she thought I was a threat. Maybe she was hiding until I left. Or maybe this was her home.

I peered at the piles of debris lining the walls, but there didn't seem to be a pattern to them, and I didn't see any makeshift shacks made of scraps of wood, metal, and stone. Still, as nimbly as the girl had slipped through the crowd, she could easily slither behind a stack of boards or hunker down behind one of the overflowing trash bins.

I glanced back over my shoulder, but I didn't see Paloma. Despite her dire warning that I was going to get myself killed, I wasn't a complete reckless idiot, and I realized that this would be the perfect place for assassins to ambush me. But I also couldn't afford to lose the girl, so I drew my sword and cautiously crept down the alley, peering into the shadows. I also tasted the air again, trying to pick up the scent of the girl's magic, although all the rotting garbage made it difficult.

Something rustled behind a trash bin, and I froze, tightening my grip on my sword.

A black rat roughly the size of a small dog ambled out from behind the bin. It paused in the middle of the alley for a moment, staring at me with its bright black eyes before scurrying away and disappearing into a pile of trash on the opposite side.

I let out a tense breath and crept forward again. I stopped in the open space in the center of the plaza and slowly turned around, studying the piles of debris.

The sun had finally set, and the murky gray twilight was quickly being swallowed up by the oncoming night. A few lights burned in the buildings that ringed the plaza, but they did little to drive back the encroaching darkness. If the girl was hiding here, I couldn't see her, so I drew in breath after breath, tasting all the scents in the air again. It took me a few seconds to push past the garbage, but I finally got a whiff of hot, caustic magic.

For a moment, I thought it was the girl's magic, and my heart lifted with fresh hope. Then I drew in another breath, and I realized that this magic had much more of an electric sizzle than the girl's fire power—and that it was far too strong to be just one person's magic.

As soon as the realization filled my mind, the shadows around me started moving, shifting, and rising, as people slithered out of piles of trash all around the plaza and climbed to their feet.

One second, I was alone. The next, I was surrounded by roughly a dozen magiers. Paloma had been right.

It was a trap.

aBOUT THE aUTHOr

Andre Teague

Jennifer Estep is a *New York Times, USA Today,* and internationally bestselling author who prowls the streets of her imagination in search of her next fantasy idea.

In addition to her **Crown of Shards** series, Jennifer is also the author of the **Elemental Assassin, Mythos Academy, Bigtime,** and **Black Blade** series. She has written more than thirty books, along with numerous novellas and stories.

In her spare time, Jennifer enjoys hanging out with friends and family, doing yoga, and reading fantasy and romance books. She also watches way too much TV and loves all things related to superheroes.

For more information on Jennifer and her books, visit her website at www.jenniferestep.com or follow her online on Facebook, Goodreads, BookBub, and Twitter—@Jennifer_Estep. You can also sign up for her newsletter at www.jenniferestep .com/contact-jennifer/newsletter.

BOOKS BY
NEW YORK TIMES AND *USA TODAY* BESTSELLING AUTHOR
JENNIFER ESTEP
CROWN OF SHARDS SERIES

PROTECT THE PRINCE
A NOVEL

Everleigh Blair might be the new gladiator queen of Bellona, but her problems are far from over.

From a court full of arrogant nobles to an assassination attempt in her own throne room, Evie knows dark forces are at work, making her wonder if she is truly strong enough to be a Winter Queen…

KILL THE QUEEN
A NOVEL

"*Kill the Queen* is the definition of epic fantasy: exciting, original, and filled with characters who jump off the page. Jennifer Estep enters the arena and takes no prisoners. Long live the Winter Queen."

—Ilona Andrews
#1 *New York Times* bestselling author

Gladiator meets *Game of Thrones*: a royal woman becomes a skilled warrior to destroy her murderous cousin, avenge her family, and save her kingdom in this first entry in a dazzling fantasy epic from the *New York Times* and *USA Today* bestselling author of the Elemental Assassin series—an enthralling tale that combines magic, murder, intrigue, adventure, and a hint of romance.

HarperCollins*Publishers*